MW00717226

The
Denton Experience

Family and Friends – Faces and Places

By

David Morris Denton

PublishAmerica
Baltimore

© 2004 by David Morris Denton.

All rights reserved. No part of this book may be reproduced, stored in a retrieval system or transmitted in any form or by any means without the prior written permission of the publishers, except by a reviewer who may quote brief passages in a review to be printed in a newspaper, magazine or journal.

First printing

ISBN: 1-4137-3872-9
PUBLISHED BY PUBLISHAMERICA, LLLP
www.publishamerica.com
Baltimore

Printed in the United States of America

Acknowledgments

The telling of *The Denton Experience* did not start out as a book; it just sort of happened over time. The core of experiences reflected here represents the life forces of a household of eight persons, including the parents and six siblings. Probably at no time in American history was the significance of *family* greater than during the years of the great depression and World War II. Perhaps at no place in America was the role of family more central than in the mountains of the south. At that *time* and in that *place* it was as if the Denton household was born in the nineteenth century and thrust into the late twentieth century all in the span of time associated with a single generation.

Of that household of eight, one remains. The family, however, is as vibrant as it ever was and the Denton Experience is being lived out in other households waiting for another telling in another time. Although many of the family members and friends named in these stories are gone, the themes and the sentiments felt and expressed in these rememberings are undying. To those familiar faces, to those lovely and lonely places to my family and friends this book is dedicated.

Note: The cover picture of Santeetlah Lake and the photo of Stecoah Gap appear courtesy of White Dove Images and with the permission of Marilyn Strickland.

Introduction

This publication represents a sampling of memories, thoughts, attitudes and beliefs gathered over a lifetime. They are the products of membership in a family of the southern mountains. The reader will find elements of history, genealogy, politics and philosophy. Personalities are described as well as the life experiences, which helped shape and define them. Rather than attempt to describe characteristics of the Denton family in terms of physical features shared in common, or some other specific identifier, this family is thought of in terms of a particular inclination of the mind and soul, an attitude, not easily described, but immediately recognized when encountered. Thus, the titling of this collection of tales as...*The Denton Experience.*

Table of Contents

The Denton Experience

At the extreme southern tip of the state of Maryland, there's a place called Point Lookout...a desolate piece of real estate, part marshland, part sand, covered with scrub pine trees and sea grass. One can stand on Point Lookout and look across the mouth of the Potomac River and see the hazy outline of the landscape of Tidewater, Virginia in the distance. By shifting one's eyes a bit to the east, there's nothing but a vast expanse of water, and somewhere out there the Chesapeake Bay merges with and becomes one with the Atlantic Ocean. This area is now a state park and near the center of the park stands a stone monument, a memorial to the Confederate soldiers who died in one of the most miserable and gruesome of the federal prisons. The people who made the decision to locate a federal prison at Point Lookout did their job well, knowing in advance that the chances of escape were few. It is rumored that some Confederate prisoners who tried to escape by water were simply shot like fish in a barrel. Those who attempted to flee through the swamps and marshes fared little better. Those marshes are mosquito infested and Confederate prisoners died like flies from malaria, typhoid, dysentery, and malnutrition.

A few years ago I stood at the base of this stone memorial which, ironically, is the only monument ever erected by the United States, I believe, to the memory of an enemy. It is strange that such a thing would happen, but also appropriate. Anyway, while searching the endless lists of names of southern soldiers who died there, I came across the name Denton. Something deep in my being responded and I felt a kinship with this faceless name from out of the past. He was one of us and he had died there, and that mattered. In due time this man's military records were tracked down and I learned that he enlisted with the 61st Tennessee Volunteers in 1861 near Cleveland, Tennessee, just a few miles and a few days from the place and time at which Grandaddy John enlisted. This Denton was captured at the Battle of Petersburg, Virginia and died at Point Lookout, a prisoner of war. There are some puzzling entries in his military records. Consecutive entries in his military papers suggest: (1) that he was transferred to the prison at Elmyra, New York; (2) that he had died; and (3) that he was transferred for exchange to Point Lookout, Maryland. Was he among those prisoners who died on the train because of inhumane treatment and horrible overcrowding? Did he run afoul of his captors and come to an untimely end? Was he trying to escape, or had he simply not survived the abuse and neglect that took literally thousands of his brothers on that godforsaken point of land jutting out between the mouth of the Potomac River and the Chesapeake Bay?

Several days ago someone gave me a reprint from the magazine entitled *Military Images,* which included a picture and a brief vignette of a Sgt. Andrew Denton with the 43rd Tennessee, CSA. This Denton was born at Strawberry Plains, Jefferson County, Tennessee. He enlisted at Knoxville and the members of his regiment originally were armed with "common hunting rifles bored out to carry a Minie ball 20 to the pound." On June 22, 1863, forty-seven men of the 43rd Tennessee were ordered to overrun an entrenched Yankee outpost. The assault was successful, but 27 of the attackers were killed including Sgt. Denton. A search for his resting place has proved unsuccessful, and it is assumed that he rests today somewhere in an unknown, unmarked grave. We, of course, don't know this man, but he was family and we care.

To each of us there are small pieces of our lives which take on increasing importance as time passes. One of those small pieces of my own existence, which continues to increase in personal meaning, is the annual Denton Family Reunion. Family reunions are a part of our heritage…they are a part of who we are and what we stand for. Family reunions can take on deep and profound symbolic meaning for the members involved. Numbers change, faces change, families grow, members disperse, some leave the fold for awhile, old folks pass on, some who are not so old pass on, and still the cycle continues. To walk among the members of a gathering like this, to commune for awhile, and to break bread together is to strengthen the timeless concept of family. Within the framework of our sacred familial bonds, the handshakes, the embraces, the kisses are ways of re-establishing and maintaining contact with each other, with our own, and with ourselves.

The concept of family has always seemed to be an important one for the Dentons. It couldn't be said that our family relationships have always been the most sweet and harmonious, but no one from within or without the family has ever suggested that we don't care about each other. Traditionally, Dentons are demanding people…in some cases perhaps a shade less tolerant of ourselves and our own than we would be of those outside the family. Down through the generations our people have been people who held fiercely to their own principles and who were never particularly afraid to give voice to their beliefs and their stands on particular issues.

(Let me pause at this moment to say that the statements being made are personal perceptions and reflections. Your own perceptions of family characteristics may well be quite different, and that's as it should be because these differing perceptions, as they become translated into thought and behavior on the part of each of us, provide that wonderfully, happy, mosaic of interwoven, interlocking, multi-colored family relationships. Living some distance away from most members of the Denton family may have heightened the intensity of the meaning of family for me…possibly even it could have sharpened my sense of objectivity. Time and distance do change the way things are seen and understood, and sometimes time and distance do much to enlarge one's appreciation of things like family. At any rate, family is very important to me…being a Denton has immeasurable meaning to me and the reflections collected here reveal, at least in part I hope, the strength and the depth of these feelings. My purpose is simply to share in this way what I hope is already obvious to you in other ways.)

Life is made up of passages…there are stages and phases to our existence as individuals, and the same can be said of families. With each generation, as the young members grow up, there's the pulling away from the restrictions and control represented by family...there's the cyclical search for independence, the need on the part of each generation to establish its own identity, the need to be free and to deal with the world on its own terms. With each generation, too, there's always the time for "coming home..."a time to rediscover the importance of family and the central need in life to be among, and a part of, one's own. There are few things in our culture as precious as name...family tradition...family history.

Every summer now we gather somewhere on Little Snowbird Creek. It's a wonderful time and a wonderful place, so fitting and appropriate. Little Snowbird Creek is so much a part of our lives...it seems so natural that we would congregate here. Some come early, many stay late...there are new babies to be admired and bragged on...accomplishments to be recognized...pride to be shared, enough to go around. There are new members to the family to be introduced as well as potential new members. Entire generations fade away and are gone...Grandaddy Charlie, Aunts Melissa and Mollie, Uncles Forrest, Arthur, Grover, and "Cub" are no more...but the power of their lingering spirits is heavy upon this place. We treasure their memories and we measure the impact of the footprints they left behind. The current generation of family patriarchs and matriarchs has already passed its zenith and is looking toward the inevitable sunset. The inexorable decline of one generation is balanced by the emergence of another. As we experience the passing of time, we are sometimes rudely reminded that it tends to accelerate with each passing summer. We are faced then with a compulsion to drink deeply of this sweet experience, and our appreciation for those little things which set us apart from all other families is increased. Before dinner, people tend to gather in small clusters representing the units and the subunits of the family...representing the geographical distribution of family members...and representing, too, a complex network of interpersonal relationships. By the time the feast is spread, the mild tension, the uncertainty, the nervousness, and anxiety, which are common emotional responses to such an experience, have subsided, the small clusters of people have dispersed and the group has become family. But there's something more than food and fellowship…there's something more subtle than the exchange of greetings…these things are important…yes…they are all a part of the ritual…but in a gathering like this, one senses something of more substance…that something is the quality we call family. If we look at the faces of the people gathered here, we see and sense characteristics which are uniquely associated with the Dentons of western North Carolina, and these characteristics span several generations. If we look at the way people present themselves…the way they walk…the mannerisms of speech…we know immediately there is something special here. The bone structure of the head and face, the set of the nose, the substantial forehead with the typically receding hairline (the good Lord was abundantly kind to the Dentons…He knew that to put an adequate brain in a head, there had to be space enough to accommodate it. Bold statements like this are permitted within the sanctity and privacy of a family gathering), the ruddy complexion which bears evidence of our ancestry and, most particularly, clear blue eyes, softened ever so slightly by a mistiness which reveals many things but which conceals possibly more…these are some of the trademarks of the Dentons. A few years ago while in Robbinsville for a short visit, I happened to run into a member of the Hall family from the Tallulah community. He said, "I know you're a Denton, but I don't know which one." I told him my name and then he responded, "Why you Dentons look enough alike that you could be registered." That characteristic of mistiness which I mentioned a moment ago concerning the eyes of Dentons, whether they are brown, blue, or green, I remember most vividly in the expressions of my Grandaddy Charlie Denton. That quality was also there in the eyes of Dad, Aunt Melissa, Uncle Arthur, dozens of cousins and my brothers and sisters.

There are other characteristics which we share, which provide an uncommonly strong bond among our members. One of these is our deep symbolic tie to this place. Little Snowbird has a strange and powerful influence on us, and I suppose that this influence has a thousand different shades of meaning. I have never fully understood the attraction of this place…the beauty of this hidden valley is obvious but there's something more. At certain times of the year I feel somehow drawn toward this place. In the springtime when the Serviceberry trees are in bloom, wherever I see them, I am reminded of this place, or in October when the ridges are aflame with color, or in the dead of winter when the Hemlock trees are dark against these gray hills, I am pulled, but most of all in the wet heat of mid summer when the gnats are thick and hungry and when the mist and haze settles into the valleys and coves, I am at one with the spirit of this place. The spirit, the mood, the being of Little Snowbird both attracts and repels…it is a place that is both enticing and foreboding. John Queen, who shared family membership in every way, except by blood, knew and understood and loved Little Snowbird, and he, too, was confused and made helpless by its power and contradictory moods. Some of my earliest recollections of the haunting feeling that grows in one's breast in this place were formed by experiences shared with John Queen when he was living on Little Snowbird. I was a boy at the time and my Snowbird experiences were times of complete release. The mental pictures and the emotions are still there…Uncle Forrest complaining "by the lands…"one of Oleta's boys had misplaced one of his tools…Aunt Mollie stirring a huge iron skillet full of Hickory King corn…my brothers and the Elliott boys robbing a wasp nest for fish bait, or simply swimming naked in some dark pool at a bend in the creek. John Queen stood outside Coleman's cabin (this is before it burned down), he was facing toward Staggerweed…it was late in the day and the shadows were long…he stood for a moment, dropped his head, and slowly turned around, and as he walked back toward the cabin he remarked in the manner of understatement common to John Queen and his breed, "Sure is lonesome out here." As he walked into the cabin I lingered for a moment and became aware of the oppressive weight of this lonesome feeling that he talked about. Loneliness is no stranger to any of us who grew up in the hills. Often, that lonesome feeling has boxed me in upon returning to these hills, especially after having been away for awhile. Perhaps some of you, or maybe all of you, have experienced this and have responded in your own way to the feeling that these ridges were closing in on each other and upon you as well. I remember, in a childish way, that look of melancholy on Aunt Melissa's face, at least in my own perception, that expression showed up in photographs, too. Could it be that the weight of lonesomeness was an unduly heavy burden for this dear, sweet woman? The lonesome nature of these mountains is not limited to Little Snowbird. I guess it is all a part of the blue mood of these southern Appalachians. My mom knows about lonesome because she's told me what it is like. Maybe we are just assigning human qualities to these inanimate hills when all the time what we are really talking about is a part of our own nature. Cousin Vic understands this kind of nature and carved out for himself a little piece of Snowbird to which he could retreat on an hour's notice. For some of the rest of us, we have to carry our piece of Little Snowbird around in our heart or soul, or somewhere deep down inside our being. But as surely as tomorrow comes, we always return. This place lifts our spirits and we face life from an elevated plane, but we are trapped too in the deep, dark folds and wrinkles of these ancient mountains. These contradictions are perhaps measures of our humanity, and they remind us that the capacity to experience beauty and to sense absolute freedom must be balanced by the capacity to feel pain and to know the profound loneliness and isolation that can engulf us in a place like Little Snowbird.

It is my personal belief that the Denton family is growing closer together. The reunions over the last several years have been remarkably happy times for me, and I believe for others who are involved. Aside from the formal part of the reunion each year, there has been something else happening, which is really special. On the night before the reunion, or the night following, many family members have been getting together under the hemlock trees and on the logs around the campfire to tell stories and to sing. These gatherings have been more personal and intimate, and they have allowed for and encouraged a different kind of expression. Music soothes the spirit and allows for communion to take place at a different level. Speaking only for me, but hoping and believing that these sentiments are yours too, at no time in my existence do I feel a more complete sense of belonging than I do when we sit around that campfire, our voices blending in song, and our minds and emotions interwoven and forming a grand tapestry of feelings and pictures and experiences spanning two or three generations, and drawing us all together within the bounds of that timeless and precious institution we call family.

Cousin Vincent has been steadfast in his efforts to bring family together down through the years, and I feel compelled to mention him in particular because of that special presence he has and because of that contagious spirit of his personality which infects all of those around him. Last summer he sprang a pleasant surprise on us by singing, in its entirety, an original song which he had composed aboard ship somewhere in the South Pacific during World War II. Most of us had no idea that he had written this song, and many of us were not even aware that he enjoyed singing. By sharing these experiences together we learned something wonderful about each other and about ourselves. I suppose I shall always find a safe and warm place in my memory to keep those pictures and sounds and feelings of our gathering around the fire last year. I can hear those voices of Aunt Maggie and my mother, profoundly pure and gentle, echoing the themes of another time and another generation. I can hear too those vibrant and younger voices of Eric and Bill Williams and Jimmy Denton…the mellow alto of my wife Peggy…and that brassy tenor voice of Vincent. In the background I can hear perhaps a dozen other voices blending in a soft and sustaining harmony. I can see the glow of the wood fire reflecting on the faces of our people, and under the spreading limbs of the hemlock, I feel caught up in the common spirit of this shared experience. The fullness of the moment is captured singularly in the incomparably gentle expression on the face of my brother as he sits among, and communes with, family members.

The Denton experience affects individual family members in profoundly different ways. Some settle quickly and easily into identifiable roles within the family…these roles and places are quite comfortable for them and for other members of the family as well…it just seems easy and natural. For other members of our group, who feel as deeply and care as much, the Denton experience can be puzzling and unsettling. Some feel their way tentatively around the periphery of the group, hungering for that feeling of complete unity and searching for that special place in which their sense of full family identity can be realized. This searching, and not quite finding…this wanting, and not quite having, has been felt at times, I believe, by my sisters. Living the Denton experience has not always been easy for the women in this family. As these sentiments are being put to paper, I am thinking of Aunt Mollie and my great grandmother…celebrating the Denton experience for them was perhaps not filled so much with the wonderful symbolism which we enjoy today as it was filled with that sense of endless separation from other people and the dullness of hard work never finished. The cumulative influence of the experiences of our ancestors touches our lives today in a very real sense. We can't change history, but we are changing the present and the future through this purposeful focus on the deeper meaning of family.

Out of this experience comes change and growth — and new appreciation for ourselves and for each other. We learn to be a little freer to express a tender sentiment…a little freer to yield to the magic of unharnessed laughter. We grow in understanding of ourselves from what we see reflected back to us in the faces of those whom we love and who love us. We change because the dimensions of living the Denton experience have been enlarged. We are family and we belong!

David M. Denton
Summer of 1985

The family on Santeetlah before 1900
Seated: L-R John, Albertine, Melissa, Grover,
Standing: Arthur, Mae, Mollie, and Baxter Cook

The Dentons of Little Snowbird and Santeetlah

Among the descendants of John Hamilton Chastain Denton there has been, and continues to be, strong interest in the history of the Denton family. Very little information before the time of John Hamilton Chastain Denton has been available. Most of what the present generations of Dentons know about their ancestors is by word of mouth. This is, indeed, unfortunate because the sense of family identity and the pride held by members in the Denton name is acutely strong. Until recently, we had more information on the early history of the Denton surname than we had on our actual forebearers in America. It has been established through earlier work that the Denton surname came into being in northern England centuries ago. The name Denton was originally a place name and is common throughout northern England. It literally means "the village in the valley" or "the homestead in the valley." The places in northern England bearing the name Denton typically are found in a wooded valley with a stream. Surname research done in England suggests that the first family taking Denton as a permanent surname lived in Yorkshire on the river Wharfe near the town of Ilkley in the 1200s.

For the past few years an effort has been made to gather information on the Dentons in America and to trace, insofar as possible, our ancestry back to England. Over the past five years I have been able to gather hundreds of pages of information on the Dentons and most of this has been provided by one of our relatives living in California. Her name is Mrs. W. Lorena Pristas, and her mother was a Denton from Cherokee County. Mrs. Pristas is a direct descendant of Jonas Denton, a brother to Samuel Denton who was the father of John Hamilton Chastain Denton. Mrs. Pristas has been gathering data on the Denton family for years and her search has included court records, deeds, Bibles, land transactions, genealogical studies, micro-film, war records from the Revolutionary War, the War of 1812, the Civil War, publications of all kinds, and numerous other sources.

Another major source of information has been one of our relatives named William Derel Denton, a family historian living in Elizabethtown, New York. Through correspondence with these two sources, I have amassed hundreds of pages of information weighing approximately six pounds. As one can imagine, this information is extremely difficult to organize because it comes from a myriad of sources covering a huge span of time and in its recording and re-recording down through the generations has been subjected to a multitude of human errors. Nevertheless, we are fairly close to being able to establish our ancestry all the way back to England. In the paragraphs ahead I shall attempt to identify very briefly the line of descent from the Reverend Richard Denton who came to this country from England in 1630 right down to the present generations. My search and the searches of others, which have been much more extensive than mine, leave little doubt that the Dentons of Little Snowbird and Santeetlah descended from this good man, the Reverend Richard Denton.

GENERATION I

From the New England Genealogical Register 11/241: Reverend Richard Denton came to America between 1630 and 1635 from the Parish of Owram, North England, on the ship *James*. According to the book by E. Whitley and some of the descendants of the Reverend Richard Denton, he was a preacher at Halifax, England. "He was among the first settlers of Wethersfield, Connecticut and occasionally exercises his profession while in that place. He removed with a part of the Church to Rippowoms (Stamford) in 1641 and was the first of that place. After remaining at Stamford a few years, Mr. Denton, with some of the principal men of the plantation, again removed, went to Long Island, and began the town of Hempstead. He continued the minister of that place until his death which occurred in 1663." In his publication, *Magnalia*, Dr. Cotton Mather, the well-known American writer and spiritual leader, speaks of Mr. Denton, "First at Wethersfield, then at Stamford, his doctrine drops as the rain, his speech distilled as the dew as the small rain upon the tender Herb, and as the showers upon the grass." The Reverend Richard Denton was a Presbyterian and founded the Christ's First Presbyterian Church at Hempstead, Long Island, New York, in 1644. It is said to be the oldest Presbyterian Church in America. The following statement appeared on a bulletin board in front of the Presbyterian Church at Hempstead in 1921: "This Church was established in 1644. It is the oldest Presbyterian organization in the U.S. founded by the Reverend Richard Denton from Halifax, England, who came to America to obtain religious liberty. The first building erected in 1648 was sometimes used as a stockade as a protection from Indians." From a brochure of the 250th Anniversary of Christ's First Presbyterian Church of Hempstead 1894, we quote: "Among those who left their churches in England and came to this country on account of opposition to dissenters was a non-conformist minister of the Presbyterian type, by the name of Richard Denton. He was born in Yorkshire, England in 1586 of a good and reputable family, and received his education at the University of Cambridge from which institution he graduated in 1623. For a period of seven years after his graduation he was the settled minister of Coley Chapel, Halifax, Yorkshire, England but the Book of Sports and many other accounts on the part of the King and Bishop were of such a character that this young divine could not accept them and rest conscientiously by their conclusions; so in 1630 he gave up his work and with many of his followers, set sail for America."

It is particularly interesting to those of us alive today to have been given a description of this particular ancestor by someone like Cotton Mather. In addition to the statement included in an earlier paragraph, Cotton Mather, in describing Richard Denton, said: "Though he were a little man, yet he had a great soul; his well accomplished mind in his lesser body was an Iliad in a nutshell. I think he was blind of an eye yet he was not least among seers of Israel; he saw a very considerable portion of those things which eye have not seen. He was far from cloudy in his conceptions and principles of divinity, whereof he wrote a system entitled, "Soliliquia Sacra," so accurately considering the fourfold statement of man in his created purity, contracted deformity, restored beauty, and celestial glory."

The Reverend Richard Denton had six children. These children were: Timothy Denton born July 23, 1627, Nathaniel Denton born March 9, 1628, Samuel Denton born May 29, 1631, Daniel Denton born July 10, 1632, Phebe Denton born September 20, 1634, and John Denton born 1636.

GENERATION 2

Samuel Denton was the 3rd son of the Reverend Richard Denton and was born in 1631. He was married to Mary Smith and died March 15, 1712/13. The Hempstead, Long Island, New York, town records show Samuel Denton and others taking up land, fifty acres each, on the same terms as the first proprietors. Samuel Denton and his wife, Mary, raised a large family totaling thirteen children. The order of birth of children is not certain, but this is probably the order and approximate dates of birth: Jane 1659, Dinah 1661, Benjamin 1663, Samuel, Jr. 1663 also, Mary 1668, James 1670, Hannah 1673, Abraham 1675, John/Jonas 1677, Phebe 1679, Martha 1681, and Elizabeth 1684.

GENERATION 3

John/Jonas (son of Samuel Denton, son of Reverend Richard Denton). John/Jonas was born about 1677 in Hempstead, Long Island, New York, and died 1756 in Frederick County, Virginia. He married Jane Seaman in about 1700. He moved his family to the North Branch of the Shenandoah River in Shenandoah County, Virginia. John/Jonas and his family were some of the very first settlers in this region of Virginia and their names appear on the earliest records. His children were: Samuel born 1698, Sr. Capt. John Denton born 1700, Joseph 1702, Mary 1704, Benjamin 1705, Robert 1706, Jonathan 1707, and Hannah 1711.

GENERATION 4

Sr. Capt. John Denton was born 1700 in Hempstead, Long Island, New York, and died in 1765 in Frederick County, Virginia. He married Sarah O'Dell who was born 1727 in Rye, Westchester, New York and died in Washington County, Tennessee in 1796. Their children were: Jonah/Jonas, Samuel Denton was born between 1745 and 1750 and died 1911 Pendleton District, South Carolina. Thomas was born about 1741, Abraham died 1774 in Augusta County, Virginia.

GENERATION 5

Samuel Denton I (son of Capt. John/Jonas, son of Samuel Denton, son of Reverend Richard Denton).

Again our line of descent is traced to Samuel, son of Capt. John Denton. Samuel is identified here as Samuel Denton I for simple purposes of identification. Without question, the most commonly used name in all the Denton generations is the name Samuel. In the material that has been researched, there seems to be more confusion and more errors associated with this Samuel Denton than any of the other members in our direct line of succession. It will probably take years before all of the questions have been answered through documentation, but there seems little, if any, question that Samuel Denton I is ours.

He was one of the sons of Capt. John Denton. and was born about 1745–50. Samuel was a Revolutionary War patriot and was given 529 acres of land in Washington County, North Carolina (Tennessee). Part of this land was sold when Samuel Denton I moved to Pendleton District, South Carolina (Pickens County). The 1790 census shows this Samuel Denton living in Pendleton District, South Carolina . He married Jemima (last name unknown). They had the following children: Jemima 1770 (married John Chastain), Jonathan born 1773 (married Susannah Conlee), Samuel II born 1775, died after July 23, 1818, probably in Haywood County, North Carolina. John 1778 (married Cloe Chastain). Rebecca born August 28, 1779 and died 1850, Gilmer County, Georgia (married Benjamin Chastain) Martha, born 1785 Pendleton District, South Carolina died in Fannin County, Georgia.

GENERATION 6

Samuel Denton II (son of Samuel Denton I, son of Capt. John, son of John/Jonas, son of Samuel Denton, son of Reverend Richard Denton).

Samuel II moved from South Carolina to Haywood County, North Carolina. At that time new lands were being opened up throughout the mountainous area including Tennessee, North Carolina, South Carolina, and Georgia. Samuel II appears in Haywood County census in 1810 and 1820. As mentioned earlier, he married Elizabeth Chastain. The War of 1812 records show this Samuel and Elizabeth having two sons. Another son, Samuel III* was born about 1810. Based on court, jury, road, and census records, this is the only Denton family in Haywood County, North Carolina between 1808 and 1834. Records show a family of eight children. It is thought that some of the names listed could be sisters of Samuel II rather than daughters. It is unclear exactly when this Samuel died, but it was sometime before 1850. He could have died in North Carolina, or more probably Georgia since his wife was in Union County, Georgia in 1850.

GENERATION 7

Samuel Denton III (son of Samuel Denton II, son of Samuel Denton I, son of Capt. John, son of John/Jonas Denton, Sr., son of Samuel Denton, son of Reverend Richard Denton).

Samuel III who was born about 1810, probably in Haywood County, North Carolina. He lived in North Carolina, Georgia, and principally Polk County, Tennessee. He was shown to be a farmer and a school commissioner in Polk County, Tennessee. The 1860 census shows Samuel III of Polk County, Tennessee to be about 52 years old. The 1850 census shows the following children: Jefferson H 1836(?) Georgia; Elizabeth 1839, Georgia; John Hamilton Chastain 1840, Georgia *; William T. 1844, Georgia; Sarah E.1845, Georgia; Mary C. 1846, Georgia; Martha J. 1847, Tennessee; and Charity 1848, Tennessee. The 1870 census shows three additional children. These were possibly the sons and daughters of a brother or sister: Manda, Hulda, and Samuel.

GENERATION 8

John Hamilton Chastain Denton (son of Samuel Denton III, son of Samuel Denton II, son of Samuel Denton I, son of Capt. John, son of John/Jonas, son of Samuel Denton, son of Reverend Richard Denton).

All of us representing this strain of the Denton family are direct descendants of John Hamilton Chastain Denton who was born in Georgia, 1840, and served with the Third Tenn-Mounted Infantry in the Civil War. John Hamilton Chastain married Albertine Turner and they produced nine children: Charles Zachary 1868, Chalmers Forrest, John Llewellyn, Maggie, Melissa, Grover, Arthur, May, and Mollie. John Hamilton Chastain Denton moved with his family to Little Santeetlah Creek in 1879. As many of the Dentons before him, and as is true of many of his descendants, he was constantly searching for a place that provided beauty, tranquility, and just a bit of shoulder room. The more things change, the more they stay the same.

Anyone reading this material must understand that there remains the strong possibility of error. Research, of course, will continue and it is hoped and expected that in the years ahead documented proof will be available to establish forever the line of descendency from the very beginnings of the Denton family in England right down to the present generations. We are, however, at this time closer than at any time in the past to a clear understanding of who our ancestors were in each succeeding generation. This paper really is nothing more than a sketchy summary of work accomplished by other people who share that deep desire to establish without doubt the origins and the history of our family. The major contributor to this effort has been our cousin, W. Lorena Pristas, of Chula Vista, California. Credit should also be given to her friend, Evylene A. Canup, who finished the work. This summary statement was written and is being distributed for a single purpose, that being to enhance that special feeling of family spirit and unity shared by all of us through whose veins flow Denton blood.

David M. Denton
July 4, 1982

Denton – A Search for the Family Name

Even though this may be one of the few written accounts of the Denton family's search for its beginnings, the search itself is probably much older than any of us, or all of us for that matter…at least in the intellectual or psychological sense we can be fairly certain that our people for generations have experienced the need to establish a tie with their progenitors at some distant point in time and space. This concern with one's origin or "roots" seems uniquely American for reasons, which are rather obvious. We, as a nation of people, are essentially transplants from other places, other peoples, and other cultures. This fascination with the past, on the part of Americans, seems to have special significance because so many American families lack a direct genealogical link with their ancestors abroad. This is true, at least in part, because many of the early immigrants to the new world were unable to preserve and maintain genealogical records on paper. Thus, complete family histories were reduced to the questionable memory of a very few people. Further, it could also be assumed that in some cases, persons coming to our country from abroad were quick to erase any and all ties with the past for reasons best left to the imagination. This obsession with beginnings is unquestionably increased by the growing depersonalization of our society. The stirrings down inside one's breast can be very strong and in this case are being yielded to without undue resistance.

The attached paper is not to be considered a genealogical work but more precisely a history of the Denton surname. It is based heavily upon surname research accomplished by a friend, who lives outside the city of Huddersfield in county Yorkshire, Northern England, Dr.

George Redmonds. Dr. Redmonds was referred to me by a mutual friend from Oxford. After months of correspondence with Dr. Redmonds, he was commissioned to complete a limited search of the Denton surname. During the last trip to England, I visited in his home and talked at length with him and we had an opportunity to discuss my interest in the family name in some detail. He is a fascinating man and lives in a small stone "clothiers" cottage, which has been used for generation upon generation by families who made their livelihood weaving cloth from wool. His home is located in the same part of Northern England where Charlotte and Emily Bronte lived. His home is almost in the shadow of the remains of an ancient castle, and looking out his window is like looking back into history.

There is probably no more beautiful place in the world than the Yorkshire Dales. The Dales are a series of parallel valleys running generally in a southeasterly direction in the West Riding section of county Yorkshire, Northern England. Flowing through each of the Dales is a crystal clear river, or stream, surrounded by gently rolling countryside not unlike that found in Frederick County, Maryland. The countryside in the Dales has a somewhat softer characteristic because there are fewer trees and because the grazing land appears almost carpeted. The Yorkshire Dales from north to south are: Swaledale, Wensleydale, Nidderdale, Wharfedale, and Airedale. In each of these Dales, or valleys, are to be found hamlets or villages, and towns, which are both lovely and quite ancient. The Dales are separated by higher elevations referred to locally as "moors." The moors are treeless and constantly subjected to the ravages of wind and rain. Even though strikingly beautiful, the moors are fit for little other than grazing but have the power to engender feelings of unbelievable littleness and loneliness.

Available research indicates that the first people ever to take the place-name Denton as a surname lived on the north side of the River Wharfe between the hamlets of Ilkley and Otley at a place called Denton Hall. These people assumed the Denton surname at approximately 1164. Denton Hall, however, had existed for 200 years or more when this occurred. The present manor house, which is about 300 years old, is built upon the site of the original Denton Hall, the history of which goes all the way back to 972. Even admitting a certain degree of bias, it would have to be said that few places I have seen can compare with Denton Hall in its natural beauty and appeal to man's aesthetic senses. The English oaks surrounding the manor house are ancient and no less than magnificent. The valley is perhaps a mile wide and the landscape is "soft" in its character. The River Wharfe is crystal clear and trout and salmon are abundant. The manor house faces across the valley with a backdrop for the distant view provided by the moors. I was there in mid afternoon and the constant shifting and changing of the shadows created a constant shifting and changing of moods as the sun retreated. Keep in mind that England is as far north as the Hudson Bay and consequently the autumn sun at any time of day is always rather low in the sky.

From the manor house the land slopes gently toward the river and throughout the pastureland are scattered huge oaks with a mixture of evergreens. As we drove through the gates into the courtyard, we startled two cock pheasants, which had been fighting. They simply disappeared into the garden without flying. A week before we arrived, Denton Hall had been used for the filming of the movie *Water Babies* starring James Mason. It is understandable why this place was selected…it would be hard to find a place anywhere in England more representative of the Georgian period. While there, we talked to some men who were rebuilding wire fences. All of the wire fences had been removed for the filming simply because there were no such things as wire fences during that period. It is interesting to realize that the wire fences were the only thing on the landscape to suggest the Twentieth Century.

In the following pages, the work of Dr. Redmonds has been edited and expanded to fit the purposes of this document, which are viewed as being twofold. First, there is the honest and legitimate attempt to identify the beginnings of the Denton family and second, there is the need to satisfy the nonscientific nature within us all…the need to identify ourselves as a part of something quite permanent and ongoing. This paper provides room for considerable speculation and inquiry, but is also intended to provide happiness.

David Morris Denton
December, 1976

DENTON

Although Denton is not common throughout England, it is numerous in a number of different regions, and particularly prolific in the Pennine valleys of Lancashire and Yorkshire. This distribution reflects the early history of the surname which has a number of quite distinct family origins. The reason for this is quite straightforward. Denton means simply 'valley farm' and several places were given this name during the period of Anglo-Saxon settlement. The Dentons of Norfolk

Richard MacKinley in his analysis of the 16th century Norfolk documents established that a family called Denton was living in the county in 1524. They took their name from the nearby place-name and the earliest reference so far located is to a Hugh de Denton who was living in Norwich in 1289.

The Dentons of Lancashire

There are two places called Denton in Lancashire. The first lies near Salford (Manchester) and gave its name to a family nearly 700 years ago. The following early references established the link between the family and the manor of Denton:

1304 Adam de Denton gave lands in Salford to Elias de Botham.

1309 Roger de Denton of Salford (gentleman).

1320 Alexander de Denton, mentioned in connection with the clearing of wasteland.

1341 Richard, the son of Alexander de Denton, claimed a fourth part of the manor of Denton by inheritance. The second place-name occurs near Widnes and once again it is clear that the family adopted their surname because of their land interests in the parish:

1272 John Tyrel confirmed an acre in Denton, Widnes, to the monks of Stanlaw. His uncle, Richard de Denton held it for life from the Abbot. In the same year Henry, the son of Thomas de Denton quit claimed all right in this land according to deeds in the chartulary of Whalley Abbey.

1337 John, the son of Randle de Denton of Widnes, was mentioned in a Lancashire Assize Roll.

1377 Robert de Travers granted land near Prescot to Richard de Denton and William, his son. Richard was a clerk but in minor Holy Orders, which explains his family.

1437-8 Agnes, the daughter and heiress of Emmot de Denton, granted her hereditary lands in Widnes to a man called Gilbert Bold. The family remained Catholics and Royalists and eventually had their property sequestered in the aftermath of the Civil War (i.e. 1644).

The Yorkshire Dentons

The parish of Weston, consisting of three townships or villages, lies on the north bank of the River Wharfe. Denton is one of the townships and was first mentioned in Yorkshire records just over one thousand years ago. In 972 it was spelled 'dentun.'
From 1164 at least a family deriving their name from this village held land in Wharfedale:

1164 Walter de Denton witnessed a grant of land at Kearby (near Wetherby), Gargrave and Settle. According to an early charter, this man lived at Burley in Wharfedale, the next parish, and was the owner or tenant of land in Denton. Moreover, even at this early date, the name was certainly hereditary.

1175 William de Denton, son of Walter de Denctun (sic).

1176 Walter de Denton confirmed the grant of land in Weston parish to Sawley Abbey. His daughter Agnes married Mauger le Vavasour, a member of the family who had enormous land holdings in Wharfedale, and an Alan de Denton who may have been his son, witnessed a deed for the neighbouring village of Askwith. Walter also gave 16 acres in Askwith to Richard de Otterington.

1184-9 The Dentons acquired land much further to the east in Tadcaster (Oxton), probably as a result of the Vavasour marriage. Despite this they seem to have maintained their interests in Denton. An unpublished collection of deeds for Weston, all relating to nearby property, contains, as witnesses, the names of several Dentons, e.g.

1200 Alan de Denton and Reginald his brother (Askwith).

1240 Hugh de Denton (Askwith). The same name is on an Ilkley deed for 1246.

1257-8 William, son of Walter de Denton and John, son of Adam de Denton (Askwith). (Yorkshire Deeds)

1260 Adam, son of Hugh de Denton (Askwith)

Although the deeds continue through the next two centuries there is only one other reference to the surname in 1354.

1276-7 An Inquisition into the estates held by the Vavasours \ shows lands in Tadcaster, Askwith, Sharlston near Wakefield,

Draughton and the manor of Denton. Two of those on the jury \ were John and Walter de Denton, sons of Thurston. At this point in the history of the surname the separation between the Dentons and their holdings in Denton seems to have taken place, although members of the family were still living in Wharfedale. It is interesting, therefore, to examine the references for the next hundred years to establish whether the ramification of the surname falls into any pattern.

Wakefield Manor
    1274 Gamel and William de Denton (Holme)
    1275 Alan de Denton (Holme)
    1285 "Emma, the daughter of William de Denton, gives 2 shillings for license to take a bovate of land with buildings."
    "Robert, the son of William de Denton, gives 2 shillings to take 7 acres of land with a barn from his father."
    In some ways it would be easy to think of these Dentons as migrants from East Lancashire, but this type of move was not usual and if we remember that the Dentons had already acquired interests in Wakefield Manor (Sharlston) it is easier to think of them as having moved from Wharfedale.
    Moreover, both Alan and William were names found in the Wharfedale Dentons in this century.

    1291 Adam de Denton, merchant. (In 1316 he held the office of chamberlain) (c.f. Weston Deeds c. 1260)
    1327 William de Denton (Subsidy Roll)
    1363 John de Denton, mercer.
    1373 Thomas de Denton, tailor.
    1379 Robert de Denton, tailor.
    York was the second greatest city in England in the Middle Ages and   attracted migrants from all corners of England as well as from most European counties. Clearly the Dentons listed above could have come from any of the families already mentioned.

North Riding
    1301 Roger and William de Denton (Lartington) (S.R.)
    1327 William de Denton (Lartington) (S.R.)

Hugh de Denton (Scargill) (S.R.)

From this period the surname is regularly recorded in the rural North Riding. Although the family's origin was probably in Wharfedale there is no confirmation in surviving sources. However, the main landholding families in Wharfedale in the 14th century, i.e. the Vavasours and the de Leathleys, had interests over a large area of Yorkshire, particularly the West Riding, and marriages involving the Dentons helped to spread the name, e.g. 1340 Edmond Boyville relinquished to Adam de Copley all right in the manor of Sutton in Airedale, and in Cowling which Adam had of the gift of Sir Richard de Denton (whose daughter Margaret had married Adam).

The distribution of Denton in the West Riding in 1379 at the time of the Poll Tax.

The most curious feature of this tax return/census is that every male Denton recorded had the christian name John. It is true that men often named their first-born son after themselves and a good deal of repetition might be expected. In this case, however, the evidence might be used to suggest that distinct families were involved, or that the different branches of the family were not closely related. My own view is that the second of these is substantially true. After all the name had been hereditary for over 200 years and had doubtless ramified numerically and geographically. More convincing is the fact that the distribution is on the whole concentrated in areas where the Wharfedale family of Dentons undoubtedly had land interests.

Wakefield Manor area 1379 John de Denton, cattle-dealer and Matilda his wife (Wakefield) paid 12d

John de Denton and Agnes, North Crosland	paid 4d
John de Denton and Alice, South Crosland	paid 4d
John de Denton and Alice, Quarmby	paid 4d

Wharfedale

1379 Matilda de Denton, Adel (close to Denton itself)   paid 4d
John de Denton, Bickerton (close to Tadcaster)   paid 4d
John de Denton, tailor, and wife, Bolton Percy (close to Tadcaster)
paid 6d
Ripon
1379 John de Denton, spicer   paid 6d

The Dentons who were tailors in York (see above) were probably members of the family living at nearby Bolton Percy. The usual tax at this time was 4 pence and it is significant, I think, that three branches of the Dentons were involved in trades in the three major cities of York, Ripon and Wakefield - all of them better off than their contemporaries. Continuity 1379 – 1600...

Inevitably after this period some families ramified more successfully than others. The pattern generally in Yorkshire was for families in the Halifax and Huddersfield areas to produce large numbers of descendants and for families in the remainder of rural Yorkshire, and in the large towns to be much less 'successful'. The Denton history seems, therefore, to be true to type. In York, for example, wills survive for Dentons in 1484 and 1491 and the list of York Traders takes the surname right through the century, for example:

1397 William de Denton, weaver. 1417 John Denton, carver. 1442 David Denton, son of John Denton, carver. 1461 Margery, daughter of John Denton, huckster. 1501 William Denton, butcher.

However, the surname is missing from the very full subsidy roll of 1524 and this family, if not extinct, played very little part in the subsequent ramification of Denton. This appears to be true in the Ripon area also, which apart from an isolated will (1540 Giles Denton of Swinton) is hardly ever associated with the family name. In the western valleys, however, there was quite remarkable continuity, particularly in Scammonden and the adjacent townships of Stainland, Sowood, Barkisland, etc. This was a subdivision of Wakefield manor (a 'graveship') and the manorial office of 'grave' was held on no fewer than 45 occasions by Dentons between 1375 and 1600. The first to hold the office was the John de Denton taxed at Quarmby in 1379. He was 'grave' in 1376 and followed by his son William. The following list shows the continuity. 1376 John de Denton. (Taxed at Quarmby 1379) 1384 William de) Denton. 1400-1450 William Denton. 1458 Robert Denton. 1462 Thomas Denton. 1465 William Denton. 1468 Robert Denton 1470 William Denton. 1471 Thomas Denton. 1475 William Denton. 1478 Robert Denton.

1480 William Denton
1481 Geoffrey Denton
1485 William Denton
1488 Thomas Denton
1490 William Denton
1491 Geoffrey Denton
1495 William Denton
1498 Thomas Denton
1500 William Denton
1510-1540 Robert Denton. (Taxed at Quarmby 1524 for 40x. goods)

1542 Barnard Denton. (Taxed at Stainland 1545) 1549-1570 William Denton. (Taxed at Quarmby - a wealthy man-1545) 1579-80 Edward Denton. (Land Deed, see below) 1590-91 Thomas Denton. It is, of course, possible to locate references to some of these men in other documentary sources and where possible this is indicated above. Other more detailed pieces of information are: 1515 The will of William Illingworth of Halifax. "I beqweth to Xpofer (Christopher) Denton 33s. 4d." 1521 Will of John Denton. "I give and bequeath to the vicar, my best beast as custom is."

1529 John Denton of Sowood, a tanner. (Whitley Beaumont Deeds) 1552 Grant in tail by Edward Denton of Holywell Green (Stainland) senior, to Leonard Denton, his son, of his messuages in Stainland and Elland in the occupation of Edward Denton, junior. There is also mention of another brother Richard. 1590-91 Release of property by

Grace Woodhead, "bought of Richard Denton, son and heir of Richard Denton."

Conclusion

The circumstantial evidence favours the view that most Yorkshire Dentons have their ancestry in the Wakefield, Elland, Huddersfield area and that these branches were related at an early date. There is much also to suggest that the original home was Denton in Wharfedale and that a migration c. 1275 took the name southwards. The migration seems to owe a great deal to the Leathley and Vavasour families and it is most noticeable that Leathleys in particular were in many early documents alongside Dentons, for example:

1379 Henry de Leathley (Quarmby) (Poll Tax of Yorkshire) Richard de Leathley (Huddersfield)

In the family papers of the Beaumonts, who held half of Huddersfield in the Middle Ages, there were significantly references to Dentons at Tadcaster (1560, 1574), Wakefield (1471, 1536) and Quarmby (1529, 1594). Unfortunately, the migration and dispersal took place so early that much vital evidence is now lost. The key may well lie in a close examination of the medieval land holdings of the Leathleys and Vavasours.

Denton – The Village in the Valley

To those persons who are involved directly, or peripherally, with the family, the name DENTON is of considerable interest. Unfortunately, not much has been known about the origin of the name until fairly recently. The name was generally held to be English, but no specific information was available to verify this assumption. The recent trip to England and Scotland, therefore, provided a much appreciated opportunity to do some very limited and sketchy research on the Denton name. The information below was pulled together from a variety of sources…bits of information compiled for me by friends in England and Scotland, material that I gathered on my own from old books, particularly in the York Library, and the book, Denton Hall, a history of the ancient manor house in the township of Denton near Newcastle, Halberts, a firm in Ohio, which does genealogical research, some old references on heraldry from the Frederick, Maryland Library and from Dr. George Redmonds of Surname Research, Huddersfield, England. In several instances information available from one source was corroborated by information from other sources.

Without question, the name Denton, is a very old and fairly commonplace name in England. It appears to be less common in Scotland, but some sources believe it to be associated with the old Barony of Denton in Dumfriesshire (Scotland). There was an Alan de Denton whose name appeared as a juror at an inquest at Girvan in 1260. Girvan is in the County of Ayr, which is adjacent to the County of Dumfries in Southern Scotland. In 1329 there was an Elizabet de Denton who received a legacy from the Queen, presumably of Scotland. Almost all of the other references used in this summary relate to England, primarily Northern England. The name, Denton, literally means village in the valley, particularly a wooded valley with a stream. Quoting from the book entitled, Denton Hall, "Denton in Northumberland, which for several centuries has been divided into East and West Denton, dates from the time of the Anglian invasion of Northumbria during the sixth and seventh centuries. It was a stockaded enclosure, or clearing, adjoining the Dene a picturesque little gorge in the north slope of the Tyne village, the sides of which are still clothed with vigorous wildwood. The name is descriptive of this situation." A footnote in the book relating to the above paragraph was as follows: "Denton is a very common place name in England. We find parishes, townships, or hamlets, bearing this name in Cumberland, Durham, Hampshire, Kent, Lancashire, Lincolnshire, Norfolk, Northhamptonshire, Oxfordshire, Sussex, and Yorkshire as well as in Northumberland." It has not been possible to establish whether or not all Dentons share a common ancestor or owe their name to a single original Denton family. Dr. George Redmonds suggests that in the north of England, the townships of Denton in Lancashire and in Yorkshire gave early surnames. His evidence takes these families back to 1274. His evidence further suggests that most Yorkshire Dentons go back to a family located near Huddersfield. They were there 600 years ago and their descendants still live locally. As yet, it is not possible to say which place name was responsible for the surname. Quoting now from the book, *Denton Hall*, we are reminded again of the fact that the Denton family name is truly ancient. "A family of considerable local influence, which we first met with in the time of Edward II, took its name from Denton and had property there. Denton Chare probably formed part of its positions from Newcastle, and Denton Tower it is supposed was built by some member of the Denton family.

In 1316 a John de Denton appears as the master of the hospital of St. Edmunds in Gateshead. A few years later we find another John de Denton, a Burgess of Newcastle and probably son of the master of St. Edmunds Hospital, occupying the highest positions which the town could confer upon him. In 1329 in conjunction with Robert de Tighale, he was Collector of Customs for the Port of Newcastle; from 1329 to

1332 and again in 1343 he was Bailiff of the town; for the years 1333-34, 1336-37, 1337-38, 1341-42 Mayor; and for 1331, 1332, 1334, and 1340 Member of Parliament for the town.

In 1335 the King, in recognition of the services which John de Denton had rendered in the Scottish Wars, granted to him the reversion of the manor of Woodhorn and in 1336 the vill of Newbiggin, after the death of Maria St. Paul, Countess of Pembroke on payment of an annual rent of 10 pounds, 6 shillings. The recipient of so many civic honors and royal favors came to a shameful end. In 1334 certain charges were made against him – (1) that he had received from the hands of Alan Noble, a Scot, a sum of money on condition that he, with other traitors, should hand over the town of Newcastle to the Scots on the vigil of the King's birthday in the 16th year of his reign (1342); (2) that he had undertaken to open the West Gate for three consecutive nights that the Scots might enter therein; and (3) that at the time when David the Bruce lay at Hedwyn – Laws with his army, he had supplied him and other Scots with victuals through one Adam Palfreyman, his servant. To the charges, Denton made no reply but remained mute. He was cast into prison, and there in an irregular manner put to death.

This powerful but not irreproachable man for the last ten years of his life had a considerable interest in Denton." So much for family heroes.

King Edward VI granted the manor of Hillesdon, in the County of Buckingham, to Thomas Denton, Esquire, the descendent of a very ancient family, and from him it passed in direct succession to Sir Edmond Denton who was created a Baronet in 1699. Prior to this time the manor house, during one of the Civil Wars, was made a garrison for the King, being then the seat of Sir Alexander Denton. Quoting from one of the references we read that he (Sir Alexander Denton) ..."suffered severely for his devoted attachment to his royal master. The garrison was surrendered in 1643, the house plundered and Sir Alexander committed to prison where he died broken-hearted."

The book entitled, *The General Armory*, found in the York Library in the City of York, England, identified ten famous Dentons and provided a paragraph about each. Most of the information included in this reference had to do with lineage, royal appointments, estate holdings and the arms and crest for the family name. Using the heraldic terms as found in the old reference, the Denton Arms and Crest are described as follows: "Argent 2 bars gules in chief 3 cinquefoils sable; Crest – an eagle sable." A rough translation would read that the arms has a silver background with 2 red bars with 3 black cinquefoils shown across the top of the shield. The crest consists of a black eagle. Six of the remaining Dentons listed in *The General Armory* had the same coat of arms. Three of the six remaining also had the same crest. Where there were differences, the variations were only slight; for example, in three cases the crest was shown to be a lion reclining rather than an eagle. Another variation had a Martlet on the crest instead of an eagle and one variation included Martlets across the top of the shield rather than cinquefoils. Martlets have been used in heraldry to show family succession and indicate the fourth son. Of significant interest, is the fact that Halberts, the firm in Ohio which does genealogical research, in their documentation of the Denton Coat of Arms, which they credit to the book, *Rilestap Armorial General*, show the same coat of arms as the material which I found in England. On their coat of arms they used the variation of the reclining lion on the crest.

As a matter of interest, my son, David, is preparing Denton Arms and Crest for display in the homeplace in Robbinsville and he plans to mail it to Dad.

There is a good possibility that Peggy and I will be going back to England within the next several months. Our plans aren't confirmed but we are hoping. If this trip materializes, it is hoped that considerably more research can be done. In the meantime, Dr. George Redmonds, of Surname Research, in Huddersfield, will be gathering additional information for us.

The material seems to suggest that the early bearers of the Denton surname probably lived in Northern England or Southern Scotland. Keep in mind that it is only a distance of approximately 80 miles from Newcastle in Northern England across to the County of Dumfriesshire in Scotland. The City of Carlisle, England, which also includes a township called Denton, is maybe 70 miles from Newcastle and just across the border from Dumfriesshire, Scotland. Yorkshire is but 80 miles, thereabouts, south of Newcastle; the point being that the area where most of the ancient Dentons lived was a relatively small area, geographically. The Denton Hall in Newcastle, which we visited, seems to be the earliest manor house bearing that name, and could reasonably be thought of as the ancestral home.

Denton Hall Manor House is an ancient and imposing structure surrounded by gardens, a cluster of appropriate outbuildings and nestled in the midst of a grove of massive English oaks, each one being several feet in diameter. It is made of a type of stone indigenous to Northern England. It has undergone a number of modifications through the centuries, the most recent involving the windows. Somehow the present windows don't seem to fit and detract from the overall elegance of the structure. There is a curved driveway in the front of the house and one can almost visualize elegantly appointed carriages pulled by fine horses coming and going in the course of a typical day. Not too far from the front of the house in a northeasterly direction is a strong but crudely constructed bomb shelter, lingering like a scar as a reminder of the horror of World War II to the people of the United Kingdom. As was mentioned in an earlier letter, Denton Hall is only a stone's throw from the ancient Roman Wall which transverses Northern England. In fact, one of the "mile castles" of Hadrian's Wall appropriately called Denton Hall Turret is clearly visible from the Manor House. Hadrian's Wall, when it was constructed by the Romans, or more appropriately by their slaves, marked the outer edge of the civilized world and all the land beyond was wilderness. In a way it seems appropriate that Dentons would live in such a place being able to look north toward the shadow of the Cheviot Hills in the Border Country separating England and Scotland.

Finally, an observation about the physical characteristics of the Dentons; the stature and facial features as well as the complexion of the Dentons is very much like the people of Northern England and Scotland. Generally speaking, the Scots are taller, more angular, and robust looking than the English.

This has been a fascinating exercise for me and I hope it will be of some interest to those of you who read it. So far the pieces seem to fit together, and in 1976 when most important human data has been reduced to a computerized set of digits, it is comforting and reassuring to be able to establish a link with the past, even though it might be tenuous and fragile.

David M. Denton
July 6, 1976

Talking Like a Southerner (Mountains Are Taller Than Men)

For a good part of the morning we played in the Wilkie Field. Graham was 16 that summer, just a skinny boy, barefoot and shirtless, caught up in the joy, the wonder and the uncertainty of that awkward moment somewhere between childhood and manhood. In just six short months, he would be an American patriot serving with the U.S. Navy with written consent from his dad and mom, which was required of all 17-year-old defenders of our country's freedom and honor. Wilkie Field was a wonderful place to be in mid summer. The blackberries were ripe, and they seemed especially sweet that summer. We grabbed handfuls of those wonderful fruits because by now it was early afternoon and we hadn't had a bite since Aunt Molly fed us side meat with brown gravy poured over drop biscuits and sent us on our way up Little Snowbird with cane poles and a pork and beans can full of red worms for fish bait. As the mental pictures flash through my memory like so many slides on a carousel projector, I can press the button and stop them still-frame for a moment and see the faces of John and Swann Elliott and my brother Graham, innocent faces, purple around the mouth with blackberry juice. For a long time we had played in the old field, which was now grown up with young hickories. Hickories are fun to bend and one or two slender ones we were able to tie in knots, and then we laughed and talked about what it would be like someday when we were men and would come back to Little Snowbird and point out these full grown hickory trees that had been tied in knots to our friends or to our children.

For a while that morning we had searched the ground in the old Wilkie Field, looking for a hunting knife that had been lost two summers before by brother Charles. Charles was off at war and we thought about him not only as a brother and a friend but as a hero too. We never did find the hunting knife...perhaps it's still there, and maybe if we could just find one of those tall hickory trees that had been tied in a knot 40-some years ago, we could search around on the ground and maybe find a piece of rusty metal. As we moved lazily through the broom sedge, the blackberry briars and the small bushes, we could hear the soft buzzing, of a thousand grasshoppers. We chased and caught a few because, as you know, grasshoppers make good trout bait. As the day wore on, we drifted easily back down the valley, fishing and playing, falling in the creek and using that as an excuse to swim for a while. By the time the shadows were getting long, we were sitting around under the apple trees at Uncle Forrest's waiting for Molly to call us to supper. We had fried horse apples, green beans – well seasoned with pork fat, new potatoes and some of that Hickory King corn cut off the cob, scraped and then fried up in a large black skillet. It's hard to find Hickory King corn anymore, and even harder to find someone who knows how to cook it the way Molly did. Mrs. Elliott knew how to fix Hickory King corn, but she's gone too. After supper we sat around for a while, us boys, talking to Uncle Forrest and Uncle Arthur, but mostly listening, trying to be grown up. Graham was always more grown up for his years, it seemed. He had a kind of serious look in his deep-set eyes. Arthur lit a fire because even in mid summer it could get a little chilly up in the evening, and we sat around, boys and old men, sharing a single world. About the only difference between us really was the distance in years that a couple of generations can make. Other than that we spoke a common tongue and understood each other.

"As the sun is best seen at his rising and setting, so men's native dispositions are clearest seen when they are children and when they are dying." (Kobert Boyle, 1626 – 91)

Maybe those native dispositions that we carry with us out of our childhood remain more permanently fixed in our character when our lives are spent in the shadow of these towering mountains. The experience of walking in a deep mountain valley helps in developing and maintaining a balanced view of man's relative importance. It has always been a part of the southern tradition that people define themselves in terms of places where they and their families live and have lived in generations past. The southern spirit seeks to live in harmony with the raw nature of the universe and not so much to conquer it. Southern people tend to be courteous and self-effacing. Perhaps those native dispositions of courtesy and modesty remain with them throughout their years because their characters have been shaped, in part, by the power of the natural forces around them. Southern people learn to yield to the forces of the natural world and to become shaped by them. Thus, the character of our people here in the mountains is molded and cast not only by family, but by place. Even while we are being propelled into the uncertainty and startling change of the twenty-first century, we can come back here for a day and find that there are small pieces of the world that are yet the same, and that experience keeps us in touch with who we are. Regardless of the countless changes that occur in our lives, great or small...regardless of the distance between this place and the places where we spend our lives...the southern character seems to change less in the course of a lifetime than the character of any other group of Americans.

Let me share a personal experience which illustrates this point. Several days ago the Maryland School for the Deaf hosted a conference for all employees of the school on its two campuses...roughly 350 people. During the course of this conference, several of us were reflecting upon some of the wonderful things that had happened in education of the deaf in the last several years and were discussing, in particular, the influence that the Maryland School for the Deaf has had on education of the deaf internationally. At one point I commented to this small circle of professional friends that I did not feel the great changes our school had been able to make would have been possible had it not been for the fact that I was so generously accepted and supported by my colleagues during those early years of revolutionary change. One of those present, a highly respected educator of the deaf who is now retired, smiled and said to me, "You talk like a southerner." Later, in response to my own sense of curiosity, I asked her what she had meant by the statement that I was talking like a southerner. She thought for a moment and replied that only a southerner would be that keenly aware of the feeling of being accepted or not accepted…only a southerner would enter into some activity with the feeling that he was coming in from the outside…only a southerner would be so permanently bound by that perception of self, shaped by those early influences of family and place and culture. (Not her words.) Admittedly, I was stunned at first by the meaning of what she had said. As I thought about it, I understood that there was more than a seed of truth in her observation. In looking back, I realized that during those early years of rapid change and dramatic upheaval and progress in the education of the deaf, which was being led by our school, I had never taken for granted that automatic acceptance and trust would be extended because of my position or because of any of the things that I was doing. I had assumed, as I still do, that acceptance and trust and that process of belonging are never freely granted but always earned. Could it be that we do grow up feeling always that we are somehow on the outside…that we have to run to catch up? Do we carry with us always that permanent identification with the cause of the underdog? I suppose there is such a thing as talking like a southerner and I would wager a bet that if I am talking like a southerner, I am very much at home with this group. What we say is, of course, an expression of how we feel, and talking like a southerner has a lot to do with those common attitudes and values and emotions that we share with each other, and which add a very unique quality of existence to those of us who are a part of the American South, particularly the Southern Appalachian Mountains.

I suppose such matters as population density in the metropolitan centers of our country, and such matters as growing up and living in an artificial world made up of condos and high rises make it easier for people to shed those early influences that remain for generations a part of the character of our people. Those transitory experiences, which are so much a part of life in contemporary America…the changing faces of the growing crowds of people who are constantly coming and going…the always changing artificial environment of asphalt and concrete and steel and glass, give little nourishment to the inner yearnings and longings of people. Life under such conditions, it would

49

seem to me, would cause a deadening of the spirit and a loss of that sense of personal identity related to things that are permanent and unchanging. Maybe our heritage...those of us here in this family reunion...is not a heritage of wealth and position but, instead, a heritage which is composed of a cluster of memories and attitudes and emotions...a collection of experiences shared by our kind through several generations...and most of all a definition of self in terms of a place...a natural environment created by God, scarred and defaced by man, but comparatively unchanged from the time of early settlement until today.

Just a few yards from the crumbled remains of the stone chimney at the John Denton cabin in the heart of the Joyce Kilmer Memorial Forest, is a frail lilac bush searching for sunlight under the canopy of the larger trees. This small flowering shrub, as it struggles to survive, is a living symbol of the gentler nature and tender soul of Great Granddaddy John, the folk hero of these hills, that giant of a man, Fighting John Denton. My Granddaddy Charlie carried this love of beauty in his breast, and I used to walk with him on a Sunday afternoon as he showed off the glories of his dahlia garden and his unparalleled rock garden of North Carolina wild flowers to the visiting ladies who were guests of the house. When Jimmy Denton grinds corn on what's left of the old grist mill, he's living and perpetuating a dream of his daddy. Nobody loved Little Snowbird more than Coleman Denton. And today, when Jimmy brings his family "home" for the weekend they're answering the ancestral call of John Llewellyn "Cub" Denton...four generations, but a single, perpetual dream. In her poignant poem about Alta, Leota was also describing the generous and warm nature of Melissa and Molly. She was also expressing those native instincts inherited from her daddy Vic. Because there are certain things about our place of origin which have permanence and stability, we who share these experiences have a fuller appreciation that life is a process and it's multi-generational. The grandchildren of Horace and George echo a youthful reflection of their ancestors. Despite the volumes of history that have been written describing the events taking place since the time of our ancestors who first came here, so alike are we in spirit that it is as if they came just yesterday.

If we searched the shadows carefully, we could probably sense the presence of Uncle Arthur with his fiddle under his chin and with a faint smile on his lips and a twinkle in his eyes as we sit around under the hemlocks picking and singing the old songs. If we let our imagination drift back 400 years to Yorkshire, England, the year 1586, we could witness the birth of Richard Denton, the first of our line to come to this country, a man who left his footprint on the pathways of this developing nation. We can imagine that there was a feast celebrating the birth of this baby, and if we listen carefully, we could probably hear the sounds of the bagpipes and the violins and the guitars. We should not be surprised if one or two of the tunes that we hear became traditional favorites in these hills. Richard Denton came to America about 1630 settling first in Wethersfield, Connecticut. He was a preacher from Halifax, England, and he occasionally exercised his profession in Connecticut. The Reverend Richard Denton, with some of his key followers, relocated to Long Island, New York, in 1642 and established the town of Hempstead. He was a Presbyterian and the church that he founded in Hempstead, Long Island, in 1644 was known as, and is still known as, Christ's First Presbyterian Church – the oldest Presbyterian church in the United States. About a month ago I visited that Church and read from a plaque on the wall inside the building these words: "This Church was established in 1644. It is the oldest Presbyterian organization in the U.S. founded by the Reverend Richard Denton from Halifax, England, who came to America to obtain religious liberty. The first building erected in 1648, was sometimes used as a stockade for protection from Indians." From a brochure of the 250th Anniversary of Christ's First Presbyterian Church of Hempstead 1894, we read: "Among those who left their churches in England and came to this country on account of opposition to dissenters was a non-conformist minister of the Presbyterian type, by the name of Richard Denton. He was born in Yorkshire, England, in 1586 of a good and reputable family, and received his education at the University of Cambridge, from which institution he graduated in 1623. For a period of seven years after his graduation he was the settled minister of Coley Chapel, Halifax, Yorkshire, England. But the "Book of Sports" and many other activities on the part of the king and bishop were of such a character that this young divine could not accept them and rest conscientiously by their conclusions; so in 1630 he gave up his work and with many of his followers set sail for America."

In the middle of the town of Hempstead, Long Island, New York, is an open area, the equivalent of a full city block in size. Facing the street is a marker identifying this site as Denton Green. Several yards back from the sidewalk is a tall, obelisk-shaped monument erected to the honor of the Reverend Richard Denton. Along the northern boundary of Denton Green is the current Christ's First Presbyterian Church, the church originally founded by the Reverend Richard Denton. As I stood on the ground upon which our ancestor had stood, I thought about the words of the famous Puritan leader, Cotton Mather, when he wrote about the first American ancestor carrying the Denton name: "First at Wethersfield then at Stamford, his doctrine drops as the rain, his speech distilled as the dew... as the small rain upon the tender herb and as the shower upon the grass." Do you think if we listen with our hearts we could feel his presence among us today? It's a long way from Hempstead, Long Island, to Little Snowbird, and it's a long time from 1644 to 1986, but I'll bet if he walked among us today we would recognize him not by the way he looked, not by way he dressed, but by that attitude of mind and heart which would give us that certain hint that here was a man who talked like a aoutherner!

David Morris Denton
June, 1986

Yorkshire to Sweetwater

For many generations one of the favorite spots in all of Yorkshire has been the lovely town of Harrogate. People from all over the kingdom gather there on holiday or for special conferences. The countryside is pure Yorkshire and the accommodations are superb. Following an international meeting on education of the deaf held in Harrogate, I remained over another day and traveled a few miles to the tiny village of Wakefield to meet with a son of Yorkshire named George Redmonds – a surname researcher. Mr. Redmonds lived in an ancient weavers cottage made primarily of stone. This little home sat on a hillside overlooking the green fields, stone fences and flocks of sheep common to this part of the world. The entire first floor of this cottage was given over to the looms and other paraphernalia of the weavers' trade. Some looms still held partly completed bolts of lovely wool fabric and the place gave off the aroma of wool.

A short distance away in Wharfedale near the hamlet of Ilkley is Denton Hall the manor where the place name "Denton" was first taken as a surname by our progenitors. In his tracing of the dispersal of the Dentons over a period covering two to three centuries, George Redmonds learned that the descendants of that early family had dispersed a distance somewhat less than from Robbinsville to Asheville, North Carolina. Mr. Redmonds learned too that by the time Rev. Richard Denton left Halifax, Yorkshire, and sailed to America, about 1635, the family bearing that name was not large. Today, in America, one will find only a few Dentons listed in telephone books from coast to coast. Many of today's Dentons, like us, can trace their ancestry back to the Yorkshire Dales.

Since Denton was a place name, meaning "village or homestead in the valley" it occurs over much of Northern England. For perspective we must keep in mind that the whole of Northern England consists of the counties of Cumbria, Northumberland, and Yorkshire. Hadrian's Wall or the old Roman Wall marking the outer limits to the Roman Empire crosses the width of Northern England, from the Irish Sea on the west to the city of Newcastle on the North Sea – a distance of a hundred miles or so.

Not far north of Hadrian's Wall is the border separating England and Scotland. This "Border Country" has for ages been an area of dispute and conflict. The Scots were forever staging raids across the border and beating up on the hated British. The British were also committing equally dreadful deeds against the Scots. All across Northern England one can still find fortified towers on farm buildings used to repel Scottish attacks. North of Carlisle and over the border in Scotland is a deep valley closed on three sides where the Scots would corral stolen cattle and sheep and then ambush the Brits from the hillsides as they attempted to recover their stock. This place took the name of Butter Tubs.

In the days before surnames, people living in the border country tended to identify themselves by their given names and a geographic or political addendum. For example, two men meeting on some ancient roadway in the border country might introduce themselves as follows: "Halloo, I'm John de Denton," literally "John of Denton," while the other might say, "I'm Robert – Scot," and forthwith they would attack each other. The surnames Scott and England developed just in this manner as well as the surname English. This is a small matter, but not altogether without significance to some of us – Mom's people bearing the politically identifying surname English came from Northern England, too.

The Yorkshire man with the Bible under his arm who sailed from Halifax about 1635 landed first of all in Wethersfield, Connecticut. Wethersfield is now part of the greater Hartford metro area. However, by 1642 he moved across Long Island Sound and established a church and fortress (against Indian raids) in old Hemstead, Long Island, New

York. That church, Christ's First Presbyterian Church, still serves today and is considered probably the First Presbyterian Church in America. The "Village Green" upon which the original and subsequent church buildings were erected is named "Denton Green," and is marked by a small obelisk-shaped monument dedicated to the memory of Rev. Richard Denton.

It was there in Hemstead that Richard Denton produced and reared a family. In this wild new country the adventurous spirit of contemporary Dentons first had the chance to breathe on its own. When the war of Independence broke out a sizable community of Dentons lived in the upper end of the Shenandoah Valley, Virginia in a lovely place called Powell's Fort Valley, not far from Harrisonburg. By the year 1800 our people had already dispersed as far as Washington County, North Carolina (now Jonesboro, Tennessee). The seed from which we sprang along with his brother had been given land (more than 500 acres) in what was part of the North Carolina frontier at that time. This land was given by the U.S. government in payment for service to the Colonial Army. The Dentons were already associated with the Chastains going back to the days in the Shenandoah Valley. The Chastains were French Huguenots who had fled Europe for religious reasons. The Chastains had landed at Norfolk, Virginia and made their way westward to the great valley where they hooked up with the Dentons. Great Granddaddy John carried the name Chastain as one of his middle names, and this bit of history explains it.

The meaning of freedom in human experience if a relative thing. It is probably not possible for us to grasp and internalize, in a comparative sense, the liberties that we exercise without conscious thought vis a vis the constraints endured by our predecessors in Europe. One hint may lie in the dramatic differences in geographic movement, which occurred in England and that which occurred here. From what we know, the dispersal among early Dentons in England from the time they claimed the place-name as their own until the Rev. Richard sailed to America, they has scattered scarcely more than the distance from Robbinsville to Sylva. We have been shaped by our history, the things that happened to us, those constraints upon our movement, those constraints upon our impulses and emotions, both internal and external, those liberties we enjoyed and those liberties for which we would fight or die. As a people we tended to become like the things we treasured and sought. Surely, we are becoming who we think and believe we are. As a clan we have evolved and claimed certain inclinations of mind and heart, which give us individuality, and as well, a particular and peculiar group identity.

As we look back over several hundred years, the significance of specific events, connections, relationships, stand out as markers tracing the chapters and the principal characters in the story of a family, the generations of which experience, live out, and discover for themselves, that it was a story shaped by providence.

We come as close as we can to an understanding of the forces which propelled John H.C. Denton in the fall of 1879 by reaching deep into our own consciousness to find that part of him still alive in us and examine it in the light of all that we have learned and felt in the years since. When he left Benton, Tennessee, with his family, he came to a wilderness perhaps fifty miles (as the crow flies) away in a region so rugged and remote as to have remained unsettled and even unexplored, except by the Cherokee. It is said that there had been a fight at a dance somewhere in Polk County, and that Mr. Denton had worsted several of the locals in the encounter and was leaving under duress. Maybe there were deeper reasons. For one thing he had survived the whole of the Civil War and returned to the town where he had enlisted with the 3 Mounted Infantry of Tennessee in June of 1861. Yes, he knew something about fighting and surviving. After weeks of being dug into the banks of the Mississippi, he was captured when Vicksburg finally fell in July 1863. Following repatriation, he finished out the war with his outfit and in 1865, when it was all over, he found his way home to east Tennessee.

After the war east Tennessee was not the same as before. These were bitter times what with reconstruction and the hellish punishment being visited upon the south in the late 1860s and for years to come. For some, I suppose, it was as if the war had never ended. Loyalties were and had been divided in these parts before and after the war, and for years to come the Confederates who were able to return home had to live like fugitives with a wary eye cast backward over the shoulder. But John and his wife, Albertine Turner, were trying to make a life for their children. Charles, the oldest, was born in 1868, just three years after Appomattox. He was a boy barely eleven when they yoked the oxen, hitched them to a wagon or cart and left Polk County. Charlie's grandma was visiting her folks in Ohio when John, Albertine, and the children set out for the high country over the mountains. John Denton's mother-in-law was named Jane Meroney, and she was a cousin of Jefferson Davis. Upon returning to Benton, she discovered the family was gone and made her way alone and on foot to Graham County, North Carolina. Several days after John and his family had reached the ridge top that would be the site of their new home, Grandma sensed that she had found them and called like a bob white partridge from the banks of Little Santeetlah Creek. Granddaddy John recognized the family signal and led her to the open arms of her daughter and grandchildren.

"We shall not cease from exploration and the end of all our exploring will be to arrive where we started and know the place for the first time"
T.S. Eliot, an American-born English poet from 1888 – 1965

Whatever the forces, the feelings, the needs, the hopes that pulled at the souls of John Denton and his brood as they reached the backbone of those awesome ridges defining the boundary between Tennessee and North Carolina, they must have felt that they were surveying the garden of Eden from the dome of some magnificent cathedral towering almost 6,000 feet into the clouds. Could it have been fear or dread that drove them to this new place? Or was it war's perversity and the bleakness that it had left on the Lower Country that brought them to rest in the shade and protection of Joyce Kilmer's trees. As they rested with their backs against the trunk of a massive chestnut that had fallen near the point of that lovely ridge, now at the end of all their exploring, they surely recognized that they were home and knew the place for the first time. Here, among these giant hemlocks, red oak, poplars, and chestnuts, they must have felt that they were now within some holy sanctuary with the trees as large and lovely as marble columns surrounding them and giving them shelter.

The details of their journey to Graham County still float and drift with the ethereal mist that seems always to blanket parts of this temperate rain forest. We do not know if the family traveled eastward from Benton crossing over into Cherokee County, then following Valley River towards Andrews, and crossing the Snowbird Mountains thus following one of the leads to what is now the Joyce Kilmer Slick Rock Wilderness. They could have followed Hanging Dog Creek once they were in Cherokee County and made their way into Graham across Sassafras. It is also possible that they traveled northeastward from Benton into Monroe County, Tennessee, and then crossed the Unicoi Mountains to the Carolina side, making their way down Santeetlah Creek until they reached the place they were searching for. Even though these travels took place in 1879, it must have been more of an odyssey than a journey, since their footsteps took them into the most remote, isolated, rugged and unpopulated place in all of eastern America. This could have been occurring a century or two centuries earlier in view of the mode of travel and the difficulties faced by the travelers.

It is fairly well accepted as fact within the family that Great Granddaddy John fashioned a lean-to against that huge chestnut log providing shelter for the family that first winter. Many of the largest chestnut trees were hollow by the time they finally fell, and in all probability that was true in this case. My dad, my granddad, cousin Oleta, and others have told me that John literally hewed a room out of that monstrous hollow log big enough for him to stand upright in. John was six feet three inches tall. A lean-to is a structure made of trees or poles forming a single-sloped roof, its upper edge abutting against an object, in this case a hollow log. In due time John built a substantial cabin of hand-hewn logs on a stone foundation with a large stone fireplace and chimney. This home was so well constructed that in 1944 the United States Forest Service, having jurisdiction over the property since the establishment of Joyce Kilmer Memorial Forest, dismantled the Denton home place with dynamite. The logs were hand fitted, dovetailed, bored, and pegged with hardwood pegs, so the Forest Service workers, failing to dismantle Granddaddy John's handiwork with ordinary tools, resorted to high explosives. The John Denton family represents the only people of European ancestry ever to live in the Joyce Kilmer Wilderness. It is a tragedy that this happened, but in light of the times, Forest Service personnel were afraid that hunters or moonshiners or some other undesirables might accidentally set the woods on fire. Whether or not it will ever be possible to accomplish even a limited restoration is problematical. The same uncertainty exists regarding some minimal archeological exploration on the site. While these possibilities are being pursued, there is immediate need for printed information suitable for public consumption capturing briefly the essential truths of this human-interest story.

It is interesting to try to imagine what it was like for this family, finding themselves in the center of a magnificent, old-growth forest, faced with the challenge of creating a farmstead and a home with nothing more than what God had provided plus a few simple tools and a gun. After locating a suitable spring and a source of building stones within a reasonable distance from the spot selected for their cabin, they immediately set about the endless task of clearing fields for crops and fruit trees. First of all, however, someone had to have captured and constructed mentally a vision of the place as it was to become. The oldest son was just eleven that first winter in the Santeetlah wilderness. His only company consisted of his parents, his younger siblings, and some Cherokee neighbors a few miles away. There were no schools or churches, and the town of Robbinsville was a day's ride by horseback and even further away if one was on foot. Graham County had only been cut off from Cherokee County seven years earlier in 1872. Who could have known that for the next century and more Graham County would remain the most isolated, neglected, and forgotten county in the state of North Carolina. The people who settled this land, like John Denton and his brood, depended upon their own wits and the resources at hand to build a life and generate a livelihood. Granddad Charles, in addition to his home schooling, attended Hiawassee Academy, a boarding school over the mountains in North Georgia. As progress was made in the settlement and development of Graham County, the younger brothers and sisters enjoyed increased contact with the outside world. The biggest changes in County history in the last century began to take place with the rapid growth of the lumber industry starting in the 1880s. Railroad spurs were constructed up narrow mountain valleys, and logging camps sprang up over night. It is worthy of note that once the giant lumber companies had reaped their profits and denuded the mountainsides of most suitable timber, they ripped up their railroad tracks and returned to the large industrial centers from which they came. In many respects Graham County has never fully recovered. After the timber was gone, the people had to scrape a difficult existence from the small farms up and down the narrow mountain valleys, more isolated than before. Four of Granddad Charles brothers and sisters lived out their lives in these mountains without marrying. Melissa, Mollie, Forrest, and Arthur, people of substance, character, and wit, remained unmarried due to the absence of opportunity: opportunity to meet and interact with others denied by a state of isolation difficult to imagine today.

The confluence of Santeetlah Creek and the Cheoah River is now covered with the waters of lake Santeetlah. That spot was not too far from the Denton cabin in those days. Trails and roadways through the mountains tended to follow streambeds following the course of least resistance. Today U.S. 129 follows the Cheoah River Valley to Robbinsville and continues toward Topton, following the valley of Tallulah Creek. Near Robbinsville Sweetwater Creek flows into the Cheoah River near what is referred to as the head of the lake. Up Sweetwater Creek about 3 ½ miles another family had settled several years earlier. This was the family of P. P. Harwood, a miller, farmer, and landowner of some considerable means. Phidelia Harwood's land extended from the top of the mountains on the east, all the way across the valley, to the top of the mountain on the west. This property included some very good bottomland and an excellent site for a mill.

The Harwood mill, which produced flour, cornmeal, lumber, and furniture, was powered by water. In fact, a dam of stone and earth yet remains near the old mill site, now covered with trees and underbrush. The dam formed a lake of considerable size and a millrace extending perhaps ½ mile up stream, which carried water to the turbines. That part of the creek bed was washed out by flood some many years ago. Right after World War II, my brother Noell and I tore down the old mill, and Dad used the material to construct the large barn still standing near what was the Phidelia Harwood homestead a century ago.

Granddaddy Harwood's first home on Sweetwater stood where my sister Gwen's new log house now stands. That house was also the home of Mom, Dad and their six children. All of the brothers and sisters except Charles and Mary were born there. Great Granddaddy Phidelia Harwood had a daughter named Vienna, a tall and charming young woman, who through providence would catch the eye and capture the devotion of Charles Denton, the oldest son of that untamed mountain man from Tennessee, John H.C. Denton now resident of Joyce Kilmer Forest. Those two families thrown together by destiny, aided by geography, could not have been more different. Who could have guessed that the chance meeting of Vienna Harwood, daughter of P.P. Harwood, miller, landholder, farmer, and leading citizen of this newest county of Carolina, and Charles Denton, son and heir of the quintessential mountain man John Denton, would result in matrimony, but more than that the procreation of new generations bearing evidence of the better parts of both bloodlines? With characteristic directness, Charles Denton told Vienna Harwood at the time of their introduction that he reckoned that she would make a fine spouse, and he would come a calling when she became of age. It is told that Vienna smiled haughtily at Mr. Denton's presumptiveness, but it is suspected that she set about putting together a hope chest. Charles was as good as his word, and there are a number of folks around whose presence bears testimony to that fact.

The story of the Harwood family and its journey to Graham County is worthy of a separate telling, and that will come in due time. For this tale, however, there are a couple of essentials that are included. It was said from time to time that the Harwoods came to the mountains from Davie County from the area around Mocksville, North Carolina not far from the Yadkin River. Memories linger of statements about a place referred to as "Mock's Old Field" which became Mocksville. These matters need to be searched out and established. It is of interest that the first piano in Graham County belonged to Phidelia Harwood. That piano was loaned to the Peabody Institute, an early school in Robbinsville housed for a while in the first courthouse. It is significant that music was recognized for its importance in the development of children culturally in those early times, and it is significant to those family members who treasure music to be able to identify where those influences may have originated. Finally, it might be worth noting that in Yorkshire, Northern England, there is a manor house called Denton Hall. Denton Hall is situated alongside a clean and sparkling stream in one of Yorkshire's loveliest dales called Wharfedale not far from the lonely Ilkley Moor. From the best information available, the first family taking the place-name Denton as a surname lived here. This place seems to be the place of origin of the Denton family in North Carolina. The Reverend Richard Denton, who is considered progenitor of the Denton family from which we trace our descent, was a Yorkshire man from Halifax who came to this country about 1635, settling first in Wethersfield, Connecticut, and then locating to Hemstead, Long Island, where he founded Christ's First Presbyterian Church in 1642.

Just outside the twin cities of Bradford and Leeds in Yorkshire is another manor whose beauty is worth a trip across the Atlantic. This is the estate of Harewood and it is about the distance from Denton Hall as Sweetwater is from Santeetlah. The people of west Yorkshire pronounce the name Harewood exactly as we do its American derivative – Harwood. The name Harwood probably means Harewood. Possibly there is more than accident in these mysterious connections between the Dentons and the Harwoods, connections occurring over vast expanses of time and distance. We have learned that salmon, before they die, return often against immeasurable odds to the place where they were spawned and, as a final act of commitment to future generations, leave their seed. Even in cases where the course of the brooding stream has been altered by flood, these salmon still recognize when they are home. When our great grandparents, Denton and Harwood, "came to the end of all their exploring, they arrived where they started and knew the place for the first time." We call it Sweetwater.

"Thought engenders thought. Place one idea upon paper, another will follow it and still another, until you have written a page. You cannot fathom your mind. If you neglect to think yourself, and use other people's thoughts giving them utterance only, you will never know what you are capable of."

George A. Sala 1828-95
English Journalist

Benton, Tennessee is the county seat of Polk County and is the southeastern most county in the state adjoining Monroe County, Tennessee, on the north, Fannin County, Georgia, on the south, and Cherokee County, North Carolina, on the east. This is fairly open country with gently rolling hills, which diminish as you look westward across the valley of the Tennessee River; however, as you look eastwards this gentle landscape is stopped abruptly by the very backbone of the southern Appalachians. These rugged and forbidding mountains rise quickly to the height of a mile or more creating an almost insurmountable barrier between this lovely valley and the land beyond and to the east. So imposing are these rugged mountains that Polk County, Tennessee, is the only county in the United States with two court houses: the one is in Benton and the other is in Ducktown in the great copper basin over the hills to the east. At the time that John H.C. Denton served as jailer in Benton and lived with his family in the jail, the people who lived in the eastern part of Polk County were unable to reach the court house in Benton for matters of law and politics so another courthouse was built in Ducktown. Geography has not changed so this situation still exists.

As one travels northward from Benton up the valley of the Tennessee toward Knoxville, it is obvious that there are few passages through the mountains. One such passage, as difficult as it was, involved the steep and narrow gorge cut through these mountains by waters of the Little Tennessee in the area now defined by Calderwood Lake and Tapoca, North Carolina. Only a few miles north of Benton, the unbroken wall of mountains is marked by a deep V-shaped notch reaching from the crest of the ridge to the valley floor – a natural water gap – this one carved by the Hiawassee River. The course of the Hiawassee and its tributaries through these hills was later traced by the trails and roads, which allowed the settlers of Polk County to travel from one part of the county to the other, from Benton to Turtletown or Ducktown.

The landscape very quickly turns rough and wild from the point where the road crosses Lillard Creek and heads upstream toward Reliance. Lillard Creek is named for the man who became Colonel Lillard commanding officer of John Denton's Confederate outfit in the civil war. Reliance is now a crossroads community, which in the last century was a point of departure from the settled country to the backwoods and beyond. Reliance is cramped between the steep cliffs and ridges and the Hiawassee River. Some of John Denton's relatives owned land and lived in this wild part of Polk County at the time our family decided to leave.

Early in its move from Benton, the Denton family had to cross the Hiawassee River. This crossing could have been made at Columbus, which is about six miles north of Benton on the old federal road. There was a ford at Columbus, but this was probably too far west to have been the crossing of choice since the old federal road leads north up the valley toward Loudon while the Denton's were interested in breaching the mountain barriers as well as the river. From Reliance, which is further east and accessible by the natural gap cut by the Hiawassee, a crossing would have seemed more likely. It is not known if there was a ferry across the Hiawassee at Reliance in 1879, but even if there was one it would have made little difference, because Granddad Charlie, who was eleven, tells us the river was at flood stage when they arrived and they had to wait three days for the waters to recede before crossing. He has also told us that while waiting at the river's edge, farm animals, both dead and alive, were floating downstream. Charlie and Great Granddaddy John braved the flood waters, caught a hog, and brought it ashore. The hog happened, by providence, to be a sow and bore the family a litter of pigs.

Copper had been discovered in eastern Polk County in the 1840s near what are now Ducktown and Copperhill. This part of east Tennessee became known as the Great Copper Basin and the mining industry had a great impact on the development and history of the region. To transport the ore a road literally had to be cut through stone along the vertical cliffs facing the rushing waters of the Ocoee River. The "copper road" as it was known provided a grueling two-day passage for the mules, the drivers and the wagons from the mines in the Basin to the mills in Cleveland. The "copper road" along the Ocoee is today one of the most picturesque drives in eastern America.

Granddaddy Charlie was not specific in his account of exactly where the family crossed the Hiawassee, but geography dictates that it had to be crossed if they were going to reach Graham County, North Carolina. In the oral history handed down through the family, the river crossing was a significant happening. Certainly there were many assumptions about where this occurred, but there are no documentations. Some family members thought that this frightening and remarkable event took place somewhere along the Little Tennessee River below the point where the Cheoah River joins it at Tapoca, North Carolina. However, since the family was traveling from Benton northeastward toward Graham County, there would be no reason to cross the Little Tennessee since all of their movement would have occurred south of this river. If for some reason their journey would have brought them up the gorge of the Little Tennessee in the Calderwood area, one crossing would have required a second crossing to put them back on the trail to Santeetlah Creek – a decision that would seem most unlikely.

Water still flows from John Denton's spring – in fact, it is an abundant spring, which now supplies the drinking fountains and restroom facilities at Joyce Kilmer picnic area. This spring is a steep seventy-five yards from the home site down in a narrow hollow below the house. Grandmother Albertine, perhaps with the help of some of the children, carried wooden buckets of water up that steep trail to the log house. Some modern Dentons venture that if John had to tote the water, he would have located the home down the ridge from the spring. One hundred twenty years after this family finally found its nesting place on that high ridge, it is still possible to sit on a log close by and join them as they go about their activities. Most of them are still children, playing and laughing as they help out with the making of a home here among the trees. There is even a softness in the wild eyes of John Denton with the memories of those hateful weeks dug into the bluffs above the Mississippi, enduring the endless bombardment by the enemy, and the ultimate bitterness of capture when Vicksburg finally fell back in '63. Gone finally are the sounds and smells of the lockup in Benton, Tennessee where he served as jailer. Living quarters had been built into the jail building for his family, and this is where Granddad Charles was born. As jailer John had to contend with the low life during this treacherous time of reconstruction among the carpetbaggers, deserters, federal "regulators," and common thieves in the "over hill" country following the Civil War. In this present life, John was frequently forced to preserve his reputation as a fighting man. It seemed there were always those looking for an opportunity to prove their manhood by whipping John Denton, which like the gunfighters of the west who often ended up dead trying to out draw the "fastest gun around." Details are sketchy, but there had been a fight, perhaps at a dance, in Benton at the time the family moved, and Denton had bested a number of the locals. There had been enough war, enough hating, enough fighting, and now the veteran of so much brutality could rest here among the hemlocks and the hickories where the only sound of gunfire was the crack of his own squirrel rifle.

Still sitting on a log close by, the moving mental picture of this first and last family of Europeans ever to live in this pristine wilderness evaporates. The sounds of children's laughter and Granddad chopping wood drift off on the breeze, and become lost in the quiet stirring of leaves turned golden. The stillness is interrupted only by a squirrel cutting hickory nuts and casually dropping tiny pieces of the shell. The log home of John and Albertine Denton was strong and warm like those who built it. Those who tore it down were not able to finish the job. The Forest Service tried in 1944 and even with the help of dynamite could not destroy the essence of John Denton's vision, which had already survived Cumberland Gap, Vicksburg, and a hundred other bloody battles before John Denton found this place and gave his vision substance with his own hands. From my front row seat on a log close by, I was granted a passing visit with my people who lived before me and with the place which gave them succor and peace and which they gave permanent identity. Looking still at the remnants of the stone chimney and stone foundation, I feel I could conjure again the home in its fullness and warmth. Yet this home and the people who built it rested so gently upon this mountain that it must be sensed and felt before it is seen. The Joyce Kilmer Wilderness was not sullied by the Cherokee or the Dentons who were their neighbors a century ago. Late twentieth century hikers pass within feet of the gray stones hardly noticing the gentle terraces marking the places where a potato patch or a flower garden or some farm-related outbuilding once stood in quiet harmony with the majesty of this mighty mountain and trees which hold its life-giving soil in place. Surely John Denton and his brood found what they were searching for when they crossed over from Tennessee and spent that first night resting under the hemlocks with the gentle singing of Santeetlah Creek their lullaby.

Granddaddy Charles and Grandma Vienna Harwood Denton

Mom and Dad – Mr. and Mrs. Gwynn Denton

The six brothers and sisters: Charles Edwin (with guitar), Mary, Graham Noell, Gwendolyn, David Morris, and Joanne, about 1935

The six brothers and sisters about 1975

Transition

In just a few weeks members of this far-flung family will be making their way one more time to Little Snowbird. Some of us will come in pursuit of that wish that we all have to be able to go back to another time, a simpler time when things were more certain. Some of us will be coming back to become reconnected for a few hours, or for a day or two, with those people who have given us a name and an identity. Some of us will be hoping to fill up some of the empty places in our lives by being with, and a part of, our own. Some of us will be searching for a clearer understanding of just where and how we fit in with the larger group. Every season the patterns are repeated, but one thing is always constant, and that thing is the inevitable changes that occur between July and July...the appearances and disappearances of pieces of the family network.

Never has the reality that life is a transitory experience been so real to me as it has over these past few months. Coming back to Little Snowbird then becomes even more significant because the family reunion promises to help reestablish more solidly our ties with the things which we treasure most, our people. Transition marks the nature of our existence. The appearances and disappearances mentioned a moment ago are the natural order of things. This phenomenon is sometimes difficult to understand and accept as a reality because it brings us right up close against the shortness of our tenure as a family member. The appearances and disappearances become milestones and landmarks by which we measure our movement through time and space, from one reunion to the next, from "before daddy died" to "when Hannah was born," from the marriage of a daughter to the death of a sister.

Sometimes the process of transition is difficult…1989 hasn't been a wonderful year so far. In the same week, almost on the same day, we learned that Peggy's mother had pancreatic cancer and hepatitis, and we learned that brother Charles had lung cancer, seemingly inoperable. We looked one way and then we looked the other, and then we simply stood not knowing what to do, and then we said…this is not right; this is not fair; we have already been introduced to the reality of malignancy. What about Mary and what about Graham, and isn't that enough? After the anger had been disposed of, we looked at the reality of the moment. We set ourselves to the real task before us, that is, the task of living to the limit in the face of that bitter and threatening malignancy. In calmer moments we can say with some degree of understanding that this is nothing new and we are not alone. This is not the first family ever to experience loss; transition is reality; transition is natural. The important point is not to be chilled into a state of inertia. The important point is to become energized by the celebration of the very fact of living…if only for awhile.

This spring has been full of lessons. On the one hand my work with deaf people has brought me a degree closer to an understanding of the profound isolation which deafness imposes on the lives of individual people…being cut off by a wall of silence from those whom we need most, from those who need us most. Maybe the heart beat of our work in the education of children who are deaf is the release of human potential through the struggle out of the isolation of deafness into the embrace of others, through the wonder and the power of human communication. Deafness isolates babies from their mothers, and sisters from their brothers Deafness is invisible because you can't see it; it's elusive because you can't touch it and measure its influence. In education of the deaf, we can't restore hearing…no magic in our work…no mirrors…no casting out devils…no spiritual healing in the sense that the T.V. preachers would have us believe. The wonders we work all involve the simple act of touching and connecting. To see the first conversation, as limited as it might be, between a deaf infant and his mother, to witness the sense of discovery on the face of a child when he learns, for the first time, that he can capture in his mind a totally original idea, shape it and frame it with his hands, and then share it with another human being, is in some ways to witness the wonder of God.

By now, you the reader, are probably asking what is the connection here, what does deafness have to do with the family reunion on Snowbird. First of all, the connection is personal. Out of my direct and personal involvement with the lives of many deaf children, I have come to appreciate increasingly the pain of isolation and the power and wonder of being connected. Deafness affects not only the individual whose hearing is impaired, in many ways it tends to render all of us mute. It cripples us in our attempts to understand and to be understood, to communicate, to interact. Deafness isolates family members, thus one of our most important responsibilities is to focus our time and attention, our energy and our resources, upon the habilitation of the deaf child through the habilitation of the entire family. A deaf child who can interact freely, a deaf child who can communicate spontaneously with his family members is a free person. My involvement with deafness helps keep me, more or less permanently, focused on family.

In the workings of my mind I am always drawing parallels, I am forever seeing analogies. As an educator I have come to understand that learning, that becoming, are processes not events. In the lives of the children who move through our system, who graduate and go on and function as citizens in the larger world, we are able to mark the milestones of transition. We are able to witness a lessening of the extent of isolation and segregation the child's experiences, and we are able to measure growth in the level of involvement, participation, connectedness, as the child becomes one with his family and with his peers.

This spring, in addition to bringing us face to face with matters involving serious family illness, has brought us face to face, in our professional lives, with another equally frightening but considerably more subtle malignancy. This malignancy, however, is in many cases not ever known or understood by those who will ultimately suffer its most pervasive influence. This malignancy that I am talking about has been sold to the public as a happy illusion even though it is fundamentally destructive. The illusion is that the matter, the process of educating the deaf child is simple and can be accomplished essentially by placing that deaf child in a regular classroom alongside children who are not handicapped, and somehow out of this experience the deaf child will become less handicapped because he is "integrated" into the mainstream. The hidden nature of the malignancy is, in many cases, that it remains undetected even by the child's parents until the ultimate power of its isolating, segregating, handicapping influence can no longer be ignored and must be dealt with…much too late. As the popularity of this illusion has increased across America. Its influence has moved beyond the countless deaf children who are directly affected and it has come to touch a whole network of educators of the deaf across our land. In response to the growing sense of isolation of leaders in this profession all over America, we planned and hosted a sort of "professional homecoming" for our people on the campus of the Maryland School for the Deaf this past April. The concept of hosting a national conference to deal specifically with this most controversial matter was, I guess, almost a response to needs and urges which we instinctively felt. We simply had to bring our family home for a time for healing…for becoming reconnected…for tapping into the strength and nourishment of our brothers and sisters. This professional homecoming, I believe, accomplished what we believed it could. Our people came home, not to Little Snowbird, but to a place that is becoming increasingly important in a symbolic sense. They came home for a couple of days, deaf and hearing, parents and professionals, to the Maryland School for the Deaf because they too responded instinctively to the need to become connected. The need to break this awful inertia and the need to stem the spread of this malignancy, which is so happily promoted as a glittering illusion.

It is possible that this conference would not have developed in the same way that it did had it not been that some of us were simultaneously involved in the search for that other sense of connectedness…connectedness with our own kind. Yes, coming home this year is particularly important. Some of the milestones in the transition have already been passed this spring. Peggy's mother survived the surgery and is recovering, and we look forward, with her, to some time together; we don't know how much, but we are grateful for any and all of it. In the meantime, providence brought us a sparkling new granddaughter. With brother Charles, we simply don't know yet, but we have resolved to accept those things which we can't change, but to be sure and fix those things which we can fix.

I have already talked with Charles, I have written about him and to him. I have told him how I feel and he has told me how he feels. It is from his wisdom and his serenity as a very special soul that I have learned, that I am learning, maybe, to understand and to deal with the ultimate reality of transition as we experience it. In a conversation with my son David, who has always idolized his uncle Charles, David expressed openly to him his love, his gratitude for all the special attention that Charles had shown him, and his sense of hurt in the knowledge of what his favorite uncle was facing. Charles looked at him through a soft mistiness in his eyes, smiled and said, "David, don't feel sorry for me."

David immediately responded with a statement which captures the power and the deep human value of the relationship between them. He simply said, "Charles, I feel sorry for me." There is so much that we don't know and don't understand, but at this moment there are a couple of things which are wonderfully clear in my mind and in my heart. First of all, there is nothing which yet needs to be fixed between me and my brother Charles and secondly, I simply want to come home and become connected one more time.

David M. Denton
May 1989

...And Through the Woods

Santeetlah Creek was sparkling this morning, as it always does – singing too – wrapping us in a blanket of white noise, which filtered every harsh and coarse sound not of nature's making. This spot where we crossed Santeetlah is called Rattler's Ford, named for a forgotten member of the Cherokee family by that name, or for that polite fellow who crawls on his belly, but never strikes without signaling his presence, the timber rattlesnake. The early settlers crossed Santeetlah Creek at Rattler's Ford, and all those since who have chosen to enter this sanctuary, the Joyce Kilmer and Slickrock Wilderness, have breached this portal.

This was not just a trip to Grandmother's house during the holiday season. This was a search, and, yes the house of my great grandparents was at the end of it, but beyond that almost nothing was known or familiar. Not a lone soul among my great grandparents living descendants had ever seen the house, and perhaps no more than a dozen of them had ever been to the site where it stood. What was known was that this place marked the beginnings of our family in Graham County, that they had built a substantial house of logs and created a farm out of old growth forest, that they had raised a large family and lived peacefully here in this wild and beautiful place for several decades before relocating to Little Snowbird. Did they secure title to the place? To whom did it pass? When the Denton homestead was taken over by the U.S. Government in 1936 what kind of settlement was made? Why did they choose to leave Santeetlah and move to Snowbird?

If this was a search, what was being sought and why? Was it possible that something longed for would be revealed? If so, would it be recognized? Would this walk back in time lead only to a jumbled pile of stones scattered among the trees, the only tangible evidence that a family once lived here? Maybe this long and rugged uphill walk was born of a yearning to uncover a part of myself. Was this yearning to be hollow and pointless, or might there be a lessening of the want that is its own reward? This experience had been planned for two years and postponed out of necessity. Anticipation of this morning had produced troubled sleep and a generalized anxiety not well understood. Perhaps it was because the Denton homestead was now part of a federal wilderness area, and I felt like a trespasser, or worse, carrying a rake into this protected place in hopes of being able to locate the outlines of the homes foundations or the approximate location of its corners hidden under a deep cover of leaves accumulating since 1944. Great Granddaddy's home had been dynamited by the Forest Service in 1944 because there was concern that someone using the cabin might set the woods afire and destroy the ancient hemlocks and poplars. Resentment rose in my soul with the thought that I could not search freely among the stone artifacts of my family's labors here – stones hauled up these steep mountains on sleds pulled by oxen. The yearning to know increased with my frustration at the strictures, which prevented a search below the surface of the ground where the detritus of a family's struggles and secrets lie buried under the stones and decayed timbers that once sheltered them.

It is a matter of significance that the trail through this ancient forest was laid out by the man who was sharing this rare experience with me, Jim Birchfield, a man who has spent most of his life among these trees, now retired after 35 years with the Forest Service. There is no person to whom the purpose and meaning of this search would have more poignancy and urgency than he. This trail was not planned as the route to a destination. The forest through which it meandered was the destination, and it led the hiker to places of unexpected beauty and interest, places that only a man with the soul of Jim Birchfield would recognize and want to share with those who passed this way. As we made our way among the trees, standing and fallen, we stopped frequently to examine a plant or leaf or rock. The waxy leaves of galax were here and there on the ridges, and it was noted that the local name of galax is "colt's foot" because of the shape of the leaves. Since this was mid December, the tiny partridge berries reminded us of Christmas. Partridge berries are bright red and grow on a small vine with tiny green leaves, round and growing close to the ground. At one point I picked up the empty hull of the fruit of one of the wild magnolia trees, which grow here. Looking at the empty seedpod, which was shaped like a cucumber, I wondered aloud which species this was. Jim searched among the leaves on the ground and picked up one of many magnolia leaves scattered around. He observed that if the leaves had "ear lobes" at their base they came from a wahoo tree. In my lifetime of noticing such matters, it had escaped me that the so-called ear lobes on the leaves were an identifying characteristic of the wahoo tree, but not Jim. It was important to him that among the hundreds of varieties of trees growing in these hidden mountains, each was unique from all the others, and its differentness was an enhancement and made it special. As we stood Jim's eyes searched purposefully out across the tops of giant trees growing below us, and then lifted to take in the majesty and wonder of the Haoe Lead bathed in morning sunlight and towering almost a mile into the pale winter sky. He was a son and a student of these old mountains, and it was more than curiosity that allowed him to see and appreciate what others might overlook. It was his sense of responsibility to be aware, to wonder, and to be discerning with respect to the richness of nature's gifts and lessons surrounding him.

The trail was narrow as it skirted the edge of a ridge face almost vertical and led unexpectedly to a great outcropping of pale gray rook. This cliff face stood like a monument on the side of the mountain carved by wind and weather and the forces of time and gravity. Jim told me that it would have been much more convenient to locate the trail further up the ridge where the going was easier. "But the people would have missed this," he stated seriously sweeping his arm and his gaze up the contours of this irregular wall of stone. The trail was not to get you "somewhere;" the trail led you through "somewhere."

Underneath an overhanging ledge of stone was a protected dry area and a bed of leaves. I told Jim that a fellow could rest or even sleep there and be out of the wind and weather. Jim said, "Yeah, long as he didn't bother the big coon that lived there," smiling and pointing to a dark hole in the stone a few feet from the bed of leaves.

The trail continued through the old growth forest gaining elevation and offering new vistas with every change in direction. As we rounded a ridge and moved into a shallow but beautiful almost open glade, the nature of the forest changed. It became more open and one could see a definite demarcation between the huge hemlocks and poplars of the old growth and this younger forest. The trees were mostly poplars of a uniform size, probably around 60 years old. It was obvious that this land had been cleared in times past and intuitively I knew by whose hands it had been done. We were crossing what had been Great Granddad's fields or maybe pastures. The land lay less steep between the ridges and rose gently upward to a low saddle, allowing the winter sun to bathe the spot in golden sunshine. Had I ever walked in a place more lovely? ... Had I ever been stirred so deeply as by the floating spirits of family members, never seen nor known, yet recognized? Ghosts, of family, living and dead, separated by a century, were connected by blood and shared vision of our kind, pausing together for a moment on this familiar crossroad, and then dispersing in all the directions of the compass. Now, I knew the place as never before. I saw it through eyes that responded to the signals of the soul as well as the brain. Since it was winter and the leaves were off the trees, so much more was visible than during the summer months. The contours of small patches, the remnants of old farm roads, and locations of probable barns and sheds suggested themselves. Yet there was something more; something deeper just yards away, instantly recognizable, a home site seen from a different perspective. Then we walked up to the remains of the fireplace and chimney, a jumble of stones, if not a flag representing the magnetic pole of a family since the 1 870s. Within me, a yearning stirred, and as I rested on a stone and looked northward and upward along the expanse and to the backbone of magnificent Haoe Lead, the yearning lessened, and I felt exhilaration. No longer need, I wondered what brought John Denton here.

With the leaves off and the forest open to the sky, the scant remnants of the family home suggested more than could be revealed. What couldn't be seen was nonetheless insinuated by the altered landscape and by the arrangement of subtle, half-hidden clues, which when viewed together with the cabins broken skeleton, a crumbling chimney, and scattered stones tracing the direction and dimensions of old walls and foundations, an image emerged. A log house with oak shingles facing east – bathed in the sunlight pouring through the low saddle gap behind me. Surely this image was more than a phantom conjured up by deep yearning to see the place and touch it, part of it was transported on the current of human emotion and spirit flowing through and across generations. Jim must have felt a reverence for the place, too, because for several minutes the two of us walked slowly about the site without speaking. His expression was one of seriousness and expectation. He moved with caution and care born of a deep respect.

We rested while gathering our thoughts making mental notes of what was being observed. In the space just in front of the fireplace a tree about a foot in diameter had grown up. In recent months it had fallen over with its roots sticking up rudely in the space once occupied by living, breathing beings, bearing DNA and dreams identical to my own. Where the tree had fallen across the foundation of an outer wall, it had reached across the trail, which the occasional hiker passed. The caretakers of this federally designated wilderness had sawed the trunk in two and only a length of about 6 to 8 inches remained attached to the roots. My impulse was to yank it out of this deeply personal space and cast it down the mountainside.

With the rake I began to remove accumulated leaves from the foundation and by the end of perhaps two hours, the basic outline of the cabin could be determined with some certainty. A partial wall of stones could be traced along an embankment on the side of the structure built against the mountains. On the backside of the wall there was a space, now filled with soft earth and decayed matter, which extended a few feet reaching a much higher embankment. It appeared that this might have been a root cellar or other storage area built against the bank, the roof timbers of which had long ago caved in and rotted. The embankment angled away from the side of the cabin and upon study appeared that it might have been caused by the uprooting of one of the forest giants in times long ago passed. It is accepted as fact that John Denton fashioned a lean-to against a huge chestnut log to shelter his family that first winter after arriving on Santeetlah in 1879.

With the leaves removed from the traces of foundations it was possible to locate corners and to roughly determine the size of the house. I had brought in my coat pocket a 25-foot Stanley rule. If our crude measurements were approximate, the cabin was larger than we had thought. It appeared to be about 24' x 36'. From the north wall, the land dropped off abruptly and it seems that the chimney was located in the center of the west wall. In front of what would have been the east wall was a smooth, almost level area, which probably was a yard. On an earlier visit a couple of years ago, two stones, one placed upon the other had been discovered in the area that now seemed to be in front of the cabin. These stones had been put there, and we imagined that they might represent where the corner of a porch had been. In looking at the only known photograph ever taken of this home, one can see part of the Denton family in front of the log structure. Those in the front row are seated and those behind are standing. It had been thought that the family was gathered on a porch. Closer examination of the old photo now showed clearly that they were on the ground, not on a porch. Hoping to find some other clue, I raked the leaves away from the stones thought to be a porch support. There were no other stones in that area, and a search of the place where the other porch corner would have been revealed nothing. Puzzled, I continued to look in the area surrounding the stacked stones. The rake struck something solid but not rock. With my hands I searched in the soft wood's dirt and found a piece of wood about three feet long and about six or eight inches in diameter. It had been split from a larger log and was dense and heavy. The two stones were resting upon it. Raking some more, I found a second wood beam adjacent to the first and much like it. The fact that these two similar pieces of wood had been buried for an unknown time and were still solid suggests that they were locust. I raked some more leaves and then stood several feet back and studied the place. The second piece of timber was located across the trail down to the spring at the point were the level ground in front of the cabin dropped abruptly. Now it started to come together. This flat-sided timber was a step at the top of the trail from the spring where it entered the yard. There were probably several steps here at one time because that spot is fairly steep and anyone mounting the slope with heavy wooden buckets of water would have had to struggle mightily without steps. The trail down to the bountiful spring was clearly visible on this winter day. As for the stacked stones at the top of the steps, their purpose must for a while remain a mystery.

It was now past midday and time to make our way back to the trail head at Rattler's Ford. With full hearts we started down the trail meandering back through the old fields and orchards stopping again in that lovely glade with the sun now to the south of us and creating shadows and hues different from what we had witnessed earlier in the day. Shifting my vision from distant to immediate environments, I noticed a few feet off the trail a smooth depression in the leaves. "Something has bedded there," I was saying as I turned toward Jim.

Simultaneously he was commenting as he turned to face me, "An animals been sleeping there…probably a big bear." We agreed that it was a beautiful place to rest for bear or man.

Upon leaving what had once been farm fields we reentered the old growth trees of Joyce Kilmer. On the point of a ridge below us we stopped to admire the tallest white pine tree I've ever seen. To survive among these towering hemlocks and poplars, this white pine was destined to reach far beyond its kind and claim its portion of the sky and the sun. It is the power of sunlight which sets in motion those basic processes through which the tree converts one energy source into another. Those narrow needle leaves of the pine must find and secure full exposure to the sun's energy to survive while the rhododendron is content to occupy more modest places in the shade and broken sunlight, yet is able to flourish here as nowhere else with its waxy leaves broad as a thousand pine needles, claiming its portion under the arms of those grander species with whom it shares the mountainside. When we first entered the woods this morning, the leaves of the rhododendron were drooping and curled like so many dark cigars, wrapped around themselves reducing exposure to the penetrating bite of the frost.

Back at Rattler's Ford we stepped out of the trees and into the twenty first century. We walked to the truck and stopped to look back. One has to know where the trail enters the woods to see it. Jim planned it that way. Its obscurity helps protect its secrets from those who might pass this way with indifference. To those who search with purpose, it leads all the way from now to yesterday.... through the woods to Grandmother's house.

Stecoah Gap- about three miles from home

Yellow Creek

Mom (Growing Up in the Shadow of Old Humpback Mountain)

Over the years much has been written about the Denton side of the family, partly because we grew up where the Denton family lived and have, as a result, been somewhat isolated from Mom's side of the family. There is little question, however, but that the blood of the Englishes and Averys was at least as powerful in shaping the lives of family members as that of our Denton ancestors. Possibly another reason why more hasn't been written about Mom is that she chose to assume a supporting role rather than a leading role...at least it appeared that way. In recent times though, we have been able to measure the true power and force of this woman's personality and character. Since we did not live near Mom's people, we have missed opportunities to learn first hand more about the kind of people they were and, in effect, the kind of people we are.

During these past few days there have been moments when we could sit quietly and just talk about the past. When pressed just a bit, she is able to reveal with remarkable clarity memories of people and places from those early years. It is most pleasant to go back with her and touch one more time those pieces of her childhood. In listening to her, and in questioning her about those distant experiences and forces, it becomes clearer that the Englishes were different people than the family of Dentons into which she married. First of all, the Englishes had settled in that protected valley generations ago. They were a people of some means, not wealthy, but with land holdings of considerable value. They were a settled and genteel people who had married well and had lived well. Granddaddy Ed English built his home on the last large farm in the upper reaches of the valley. Beyond Granddaddy's farm, the valley narrowed quickly and the land became steep and unfriendly. Mom remembers with obvious pleasure sitting on the floor playing with the shavings while her daddy put the finishing touches on the trim work with a large, hand-held plane. Ed English was a merchant and a farmer. Most people living in the mountains at those times were farmers at least part of the time; although, most of the family income came from the General Store. It must have been the kind of family farm that we read about today in *Country Journal Magazine* or some similar publication. It provided all of those good things that make the difference between living and living abundantly. There were, of course, the main crops of corn and wheat; the corn primarily for the feeding of the livestock and the wheat for baking. There was an old roller mill not far from the Ashford Railroad Station, and home-grown wheat could be taken directly there from the farm and ground into whole wheat flour or a pure white, refined flour for cakes and other specialities. Granddaddy English loved fresh fruit, so the orchards and vineyards were extensive. The remnants of those orchards remain, and they bring back memories from earlier generations, including the annual sack of dried apples that would arrive each Christmas by train, thanks to the graciousness of Granny English. She must have peeled ten bushels of apples to end up with a single bushel of that wonderful dried fruit, which was made into fried apple pies.

Surely, the power of the natural world has its effect on all of us and surely Mom was affected by the raw natural beauty of her childhood home. First of all, she grew up in the shadows of Old Humpback. So imposing and so mysterious was this mountain that at times it seemed almost forbidding. The cow pasture crept up the bottom slope of Humpback, and scattered throughout the pasture were huge pieces of stone that the forces of nature had broken off this side of the mountain at some point back in history. Many of these stones were half as big as a house and they still rest in the very places were they fell. Mom could stand on the front porch and look squarely into the face of Humpback; but, that was not an easy thing to do because one's eyes had to be lifted upward and still upward to see the top. At any time of day, there were dark places on the face of Humpback not reached by even the mid-day sun.

Behind the house was still another world, a world which gave witness to other kinds of geologic forces. The land was not steep and overpowering like Humpback Mountain; but, instead sloped gently and the hollows were literally filled with hundreds of huge, broken stones. Mom remembers that someone had remarked that the devil himself had stumbled and spilled his sack of stones, and they still lay jumbled and broken and scattered among the trees. My own memories of this place are enchanted memories because I walked there as a boy, and I hunted there in later years as a man. Those journeys into this wild and wonderful place, which I made as a lad, were perhaps only a few dozen yards, because there was an element of fear about the place. It was dark among the rocks and trees and my imagination painted all kinds of pictures based upon the stories which my Mother told about the Wild Cat Way and the Witches Wash Bowl. Although I have never actually seen these places which Mom enjoyed as a girl, I can still picture them in my mind much as I did when I was 8 or 10 years old. A couple of nights ago, we sat and talked about some of these places and she re-introduced characters from out of the past whom I first came to know years ago when Mom's childhood recollections were still quite fresh. She talked about old Mr. Huger, who was a friend of the family, or perhaps more properly, a boarder in the English household. Huger was a man of mystery, perhaps someone who had been disappointed in love. He loved those enchanted places among the rocks, made trails from one to the other, and wrote poetry on the face of Written Rock; he gave names to other favorite childhood haunts of Mom and her sisters and brother. One of these places was the Castle, an unusual rock formation that could easily assume whatever form a childhood imagination would want to give it. Huger even made a ladder so that one could climb into the upper stories of the Castle. Local history, from the point of view of my mother's childhood memories, was divided into two parts…before and after the road came. Before the road came, Mom remembers a cave-like opening among the rocks in which her brother, Jay, found the remnants of an ancient fire, an ax and a pipe left by the first Americans who lived in that part of the valley. There was also the Cave in which the English children played on many a summer day. It was cool inside and damp, and if you went far enough into the side of the mountain, you came to a place where you had to get down on all fours and crawl under the overhanging rocks in order to get to the next part of the cave. Mom didn't like the feeling that tends to overwhelm one in such circumstances. The Cave, of course, became commercialized and has been for perhaps over fifty years known as Linville Caverns, a favorite tourist attraction.

Mom talked freely about Sam McGee and his lovely wife Lura. She said, matter-of-factly, when Peggy asked who Sam McGee was, that he was a part of the property. Peggy laughed and asked what she meant by that and Mom explained that Sam McGee was a fixture on the place. He was a tenant and helped out with the farming; but, more than that, he was someone for whom the family felt a sense of responsibility. I was aware as Mom talked that the mental pictures painted of Sam McGee this week were different than the pictures painted of the same man I remember Mom talking about fifty years ago. Sam McGee, I learned, was a periodic drunk…basically not a bad person, but not a first-class citizen either. At any rate, Mom and the other children loved Sam McGee and occasionally when he was on a drunk, they would walk him home at night for fear he would stumble and hurt himself.

Then, in his inebriated state, he would want to walk back home with them because it was dark. Mom talked a lot about Sam McGee and his seven children and Lura, and she speaks with obvious tenderness about the flood of 1916. Among the strongest memories associated with my childhood and going to Granny English's house were memories of the flood of 1916 as related by Mom. There was another flood in 1942 which created great destruction in the valley. My memories of that flood are quite vivid and personal. I could see firsthand evidence of the raw power of rushing water. The 1916 flood had changed the course of the creek and the flood of 1942 returned the creek to its original channel. Walking with my cousins across the torn landscape in the aftermath of the '42 flood was a startling experience, and it brought to life those descriptions of the sights and sounds and smells described by my mom as she and her family lived through the trauma of the flood of 1916. It is almost possible to experience with her all of those sensations associated with this violent act of God. I can imagine standing on the porch looking across the valley toward Humpback. The level of the water was almost up to the old road which means that the current highway would have been covered by several yards of rushing and roiling water. For several days it had rained without stopping. The land could soak up no more and in places on the steep sides of Old Humpback huge sections of land, trees and boulders had simply slipped off the face of the bedrock underneath and came sliding and crashing and tumbling from the cliffs into that ocean of dark water. As the rocks crashed and ground against each other, there were sparks and smoke even though the whole world it seems had been drenched by relentless rain. She remembers the sounds which continued right on through the night: the thunderous roar of surging waters, the crashing and breaking and tumbling of trees which had been uprooted and swept along by the torrent, sometimes tumbling end over end. There were smells, too. The shattering and grinding of trees and other vegetation, the gouging and opening of the earth released into the damp atmosphere those unmistakable smells associated with a violent flood. Mom also remembers the human dimension of the flood. Sam and Lura McGee had been flooded out, their home washed away, and they sought refuge with the English family. This was all quite normal and natural, as Mom said, "They were part of the place and we took care of them." It is strange and interesting how the powerful emotions associated with an event experienced by those in one generation can be transmitted with all of their power to those born in another generation.

These conversations with Mom during the past few days revealed other clues to an unlocking of the rich character of this woman. Mom went away to boarding school. When the kids were small, Mom talked a lot about "B.I." Brevard Institute was a fine school, and the young men and women from the better families in that part of the world had been receiving an education there for generations. This school became Brevard College and it still has a fine reputation. Those days it was both a boarding high school and a junior college, and those completing the curriculum were fully qualified to teach. This happened to Mom's sisters; but, Mom's story turns out somewhat differently. Mom had been frail as a child; they almost lost her when she was little, and throughout her youth she was plagued by recurring bronchitis. She feels that her mom and dad spoiled her and all of us can fully understand and appreciate the reasons why. She can remember with great feeling a time when she was suffering from bronchitis and having extreme difficulty in breathing. Each time she opened her eyes all through the night she would look up into the face of her father who would not leave her side. She could see his eyes filled with tears and the pain on his face…a father helpless to relieve the suffering of a sick child. She also talked about those terribly difficult weeks following the birth of Charles when she again faced what seemed like certain death. She was at home during this period of illness and again her mom and dad were a part of those difficult and life-shaping experiences. As we relived these experiences through the power of memories and words, I was fascinated with the somewhat different interpretation that Mom provided at this telling as compared with earlier tellings of the same stories. For example, Mom talked with frankness and feeling about an event which occurred about two years after the end of World War I.

While a student at Brevard Institute, with parental permission and with the permission of collegiate authorities, she spent the weekend with Lucille Hubbard. The two of them rode to Lucille's home on the train and then returned to Brevard by train on Sunday afternoon. On arriving at the station, they decided to take a little walk downtown to the drugstore. As luck would have it, they bumped into a couple of boys who had an automobile, and they were invited for a ride. Since there was still plenty of time before the 6 o'clock hour when they had to be back on campus, they decided to go. They drove to the home of one of the boys and spent a couple of hours dancing and in general enjoying themselves. Mom was a free spirit and saw absolutely nothing wrong in what they did and, of course, there was nothing wrong. As it turns out, however, they were a little bit late arriving back on campus, but they assumed everything was all right because they passed Professor Orr on their way to the dormitory and were greeted with a smile and a polite exchange. It was not until several days later, at a faculty meeting, that they realized the seriousness of this infraction. This matter was presented to the faculty and the decision was reached that this breach of institutional policy should result in severe punishment. Mom was sent home for the remainder of the semester. This was a painful experience for her and it is difficult to know its ultimate meaning to her down through the years. She, of course, returned to Brevard Institute and learned that the school authorities themselves felt that they dealt too sternly with this innocent infraction. She also learned that Lucille's mother didn't much want her daughter hanging around with Mom. She chuckled as she remembered this childish reaction.

Life was sweet in the Ed English household and comparatively settled until the young highway engineer became a temporary boarder. He was tall and with his high-topped boots and riding pants he must have attracted considerable attention, especially among the three sisters. It is interesting to imagine what it must have been like during those several weeks, especially since the story has probably been embellished a bit after a thousand or so tellings. The middle girl was somewhat surprised when the young engineer directed his attention toward her because she has assumed that he was more interested in her slender and beautiful older sister. The youngest sister was not party to the competition for the attention and favors of this young man from somewhere west in the wildest and most remote part of North Carolina. Perhaps she was more a cheerleader and a spectator, though, laughing and teasing and enjoying that small measure of interest which she was able to get from this person who had so thoroughly gained the attention of the entire family. As it turned out, Dad chose Mom, the middle sister and this was not the last victory in a long and full life not considered easy by any measure; but, one in which the difference between surviving and failing was determined by an indomitable will. This will and instinct for survival has served her well and has been tested countless times, not only in those early years of loneliness and separation from Dad; but, during the depression and World War II and especially during those times, unplanned for and unexpected, when at first a daughter, and then a son, and then her mate of over sixty years, and then another daughter were taken from her.

Mom was never conquered by adversity. All of the painful and difficult things that have happened to her over her long and rich life certainly have been enough to break a lesser person. Possibly her early illnesses and some of the other childhood trauma which she experienced would have a lasting influence on her life. Mom has always had a tendency to worry and many of her worries have been health related, even though she looks toward her 86th birthday with the benefit of comparatively robust health. So many of the difficult times in her life she has faced alone. When Charles was a baby, they moved to Bat Cave. Dad was a construction engineer when what we know as the Hickory Nut Gap Highway was under construction. This winding road we now know as Old U.S. 74, between Asheville and Lake Lure. At some point during those months at Bat Cave and Tuxedo, Mom and Dad decided to move to Robbinsville. They moved into the home which Great Granddaddy Harwood had built years and years before. But before they moved into that house, they lived for awhile with Grandmother Denton. Mary was born during this interim and Mom describes, with considerable feeling, those first months in Graham County and getting used to Grandmother Denton. One can only imagine the difficulty faced by this young mother in attempting to establish her own presence in so powerful and so different a household. The house of Ed English and the house of Charles Denton were not at all the same. Graham County was new country, a bit raw around the edges and terribly isolated, cut off from all that was familiar and comfortable. This was in the mid 1920s and for most of the time between then and the outbreak of World War II Dad worked away from home. His absence only increased her loneliness and the experiences of surviving alone in the mountains with a houseful of dependent children only added to the strength of her stubborn and charitable character. She had some help, such as it was. There were the two daughters of Maude Lail who stayed for awhile and then there was Lenna McIntyre. Lenna was hardly more than a child herself. But mostly Mom had to contend with such characters as Jim Davis and Mr. Will Nanney. Will Nanney was one of those rare persons who sort of drops out of the sky belonging to no one in particular but claiming for his own whoever will provide food and a place to sleep. Mr. Nanney was known to the Englishes, but because of some family misunderstanding, abruptly left the Cove and came straight to Robbinsville. Mother didn't need the likes of Mr. Nanney, but she generously put up with him anyway. Then there was Uncle Bud Bumgarner. Bud Bumgarner was a kind old drifter who belonged to the human race, but who lacked the benefit of a permanent home. Mr. Nanney could tell stories and entertain people with his dramatic abilities while Uncle Bud Bumgarner was mostly just handy around the place. I remember sitting on his lap while he peeled apples for me when I was still too young to play with a knife. Mom and I talked about that winter when he came to our house because he had nowhere else to go. He was already wracked with the fever of pneumonia. As if she didn't have enough to do or worry about, she now had this additional responsibility. To make it worse, Mr. Bumgarner could be stubborn and difficult even though he was a very sick man and the weather was awful. He insisted on going out into the snow across the creek to the outside toilet. The last couple of days of his illness were particularly hard on Mom. Dad was gone as was true so often in those years and Mom was trying to look after a dying man plus her own family. A stove had been moved into the original part of the old house to provide warmth for Uncle Bud. There was an old bed in the corner of the room, a tall bed, probably made by hand in Granddaddy Harwood's shop. It had a rope bottom and the corner posts were tall and had been turned on a lathe. On that particular day, I believe I was about five years old, JoAnn and I were the only two children home; the others were in school. Mom was sitting in a chair in that corner room so that she could keep an eye on Uncle Bud. I understood death only in an abstract kind of way; but, the talk among the adults was that he was going to die. Mom had nodded off at perhaps mid afternoon and I remember telling her that I thought Mr. Bumgarner had died. I did not understand clearly what it meant, but I was aware that his labored breathing had stopped. Dr. Crawford had been looking after him the best he could. I suppose the memories of this old country doctor, with his mysterious bag, his glasses and those hands with their ceaseless tremors, will never fade. The facts are unclear to me, perhaps Dr.

Crawford confirmed what we already knew, or perhaps his passing was officially confirmed in some other way. But, Uncle Bud had died and people from the neighborhood skilled in the art of wood craft were summoned to make his coffin. I believe this was done on the front porch near the door to the kitchen. At any rate, it was made of poplar and it had the configuration of the traditional coffin, broad at the shoulders and tapering toward each end. He was buried near the family section of the cemetery.

This is just one of Mom's trials and tribulations, and she accepted it as she accepted all the others. In those times when the whole world seemed to collapse, Mom always responded with a calm sense of peace and acceptance of the hard and bitter side of reality. It was the same during the war years when Audie Wilcox, a sort of honorary family member, was killed in action. I remember Mother receiving a gift from him just before he was shipped overseas. He had been assigned to the famous 30th Division and the gift was a satin cover for a cushion, bright red with the insignia of the 30th Division on it. This was a common practice in those early war years. G.I.'s would send home to their mothers or girlfriends the company's colors. Mom accepted with the same quiet resolve the enlistment of the two older boys in the Navy. She never knew if they would return, and she never questioned but that they would serve.

As we sat the other evening and talked about times past and a little bit about times yet to come, I was struck with the sweet and settled presence of this person for whom life had held so much hurt and happiness. Mom has somehow been able to balance the forces in her life. She had to be not only strong but shrewd and determined as well to deal with life as she experienced it. In addition to her strength, determination and shrewdness, she inherited an abundantly happy disposition, perhaps from her mother. That serenity in time of travail, I believe is something of her own making, and I think more than anything else, it represents the deeper character of Mom. Perhaps she took the lessons of religion and applied them in a very practical way. If the Bible meant what it said, then she helped it become sort of a self-fulfilling prophecy – God would never put upon her more than she could bear, etc. She also interpreted the evangelical charge in a very direct and personal way. I believe every letter I have ever received from Mom, from the time I left home at age 18 up until now, and every personal encounter with her in those years since, has included at least an expression of concern, if not an admonition, regarding the state of my soul. Mom takes her religion seriously and within it she has certainly found refuge. There cannot be one more worthy of respect and devotion than this woman. I wonder, had she known what the past 15 years would hold for her, could she have had the courage to go on? But then, as I see her reach instinctively and stroke the hair of her great grandson and speak to him with a soft feminine voice which has soothed the hearts of so many, I know without questioning that she would.

David M. Denton
December 1987

The Light Upon Her Face

It must have been late fall, maybe November, because at mid afternoon the sun was already angling toward the western sky. It was warm in the kitchen of the old house. There was a good fire in Mama's wood burning cook stove, and the tub I was sitting in was in front of the stove and bathed in the sunlight pouring through the window at the end of the room, which faced the corncrib. As I soaked peacefully in the washtub filled with piping-hot water, I studied the oven door on the stove. The center part of the oven door was made of white enamel with an eagle imprinted on it in blue. Below the eagle was blue lettering. Mama told me it said "Rome Eagle," and then in smaller letters, "Eagle Stove Works, Rome, Georgia." To the left of the oven was the fire box, and to the right was a water reservoir. From the reservoir Mama had dipped hot water for my bath. Between the stove and the window was a wood box filled with oak stove wood and a stack of chestnut kindling. Along the wall in front of the stove was a meal bin made years before by Granddaddy Harwood. The lid on top of the meal bin provided a flat work surface for rolling out biscuits or stirring up cornbread. When the lid was lifted it exposed two bins separated by a divider, one for flour and one for cornmeal. Along the wall above the meal bin were shelves covered with a variety of food items, cooking utensils, and of course dishes, At the end of one shelf was a battery radio about a foot tall with an arched top. Further down that wall was a window looking out on Mama's flowerbeds near the smoke house. At that end of the kitchen was the dining table with a bench built against the wall on the upper side with a moveable bench on the other side. When my brothers would make their way between the table and wall, the brads on the pockets of their overalls would make a scraping sound against the poplar boards as they slid onto the bench. To me that was a grown up sound, and I wanted overalls with brads on the pockets. For now, though, my bath had to be finished because someone else was waiting for the tub.

The radio was on and music was playing. The song was quite typical of what would be heard on the radio in the southern mountains in 1936. "I'm Just Here To Get My Baby Out Of Jail." This is my first absolute recollection of a specific song and it moved me in a most unforgettable way. Its sadness was its appeal. To me it was a beautiful sound and I wanted it to continue. The concept of a baby in jail bothered me, but Mama explained that the baby in the song was a grown up son. She liked the song too and we shared this musical interlude with all the meaning that the love between a boy and his mother can feel and express. As we listened to the closing notes of this song of heartache, Mama bent to help me finish my bath. While she checked behind my ears and stroked my head, I studied her expressions for a long moment. With the light upon her face from the warm afternoon sun, she was beautiful beyond measure. As she leaned toward me, her dark hair tumbled around her face. It smelled of her and was luxurious in its fullness and texture, deep brown among the waves and a glint of copper reflecting the sunlight around the edges, like a halo encircling her countenance.

Autumn had slipped into winter perhaps eight times over since that transcendent experience in the kitchen of the old house. It was probably January 1944. World War II with all the forces of hell was threatening civilization as we knew it, in both the European theater, and the Pacific theater. Charles Edwin had just received orders that his crew was shipping out of New York to the Pacific by way of the Panama Canal. With only hours between receiving his orders and his ship's departure, my bother went AWOL determined to see his family for what might be the last time. He appeared in full-dress blues like a stranger in the night. He couldn't have been there for more than two or three hours, and he was gone, not to be seen again until the war was over. Mama and her oldest son sat side by side in front of the fireplace speaking softly.

Dad was at Fontana Dam. I sat a few feet away wanting to be close, but not wanting to impose upon an experience that I sensed was filled with purpose and one which belonged to Mama and her son who in moments would be gone. My brother stared straight ahead into the fire. The red coals cast a warm, soft light on my brother's face. Tears welled up but he controlled them as best he could, hardly daring to look directly into the searching eyes of his mother. Tears were not to be denied and from moment to moment one would sparkle like a diamond as it traced a path down his cheek. The flickering of the low flames cast shadows on his handsome face. He held Mama's hand as they shared a treasured moment, facing the promise of a warm fire and the question of a future that could only be imagined. With the light from the dying fire yet warm but softer now on Mama's face, I saw the closest thing to angelhood that mortals are permitted to witness. As her eyes stroked, caressed and fully enveloped that image of her baby, her boy, her son, in uniform – an image that would sustain her through the strength of the sacrificial devotion that this experience captured and portrayed by the light upon her face.

It was another night in the wintertime, but four others had come and gone since Mama's oldest boy had stolen a few hours to be with her before disappearing into the darkness to take care of unfinished business behind the guns of a destroyer in the South Pacific. The second son had followed the first and he too wore the uniform of blue. When the war was over, Mama's boys came home. Events unfolded and plans were made….some things changed, but not all things. On this night in 1949, Edwin and Noell were in Raleigh, at North Carolina State. Edwin was married and so was sister Mary. She and her husband Bob lived in Chapel Hill. Sister Gwen was at Cullowhee, a freshman at Western Carolina. Dad was working for Lindsay Madison Gudger and Associates out of Asheville, building a school or a hospital somewhere in western North Carolina. Jo Ann was asleep upstairs. Though it was late, there was no sleep for Mama. A bronchial infection had pretty well gotten the best of me. Mama said I was delirious and feverish. It was a bad case of the croup, and I was having a struggle with breathing when I lay down. Mama had wrapped me in quilts sitting upright in the old rocking chair. We no longer used the fireplace but kept the house warm with a large, wood-burning heater sitting on the hearth. Mama took her place beside me and leaned forward with a hand on my forehead. She had already rubbed my chest with Vicks salve, and still each breath came with a deep wheeze. I could see the growing alarm in Mama's face and she mentioned the dreaded thought of pneumonia. She was troubled but acted with calm determination. She had me swallow a small amount of Vicks in the hope of loosening my breathing. It was cool and eased the raw burning in my throat but didn't seem to help the breathing. Then she did the most remarkable thing. The only light in the room was a kerosene lamp on the table beside my chair. She held a tablespoon of Vicks Vaporub over the globe of the lamp until it melted into a liquid. This, she held in front of my mouth and nose helping me to inhale the warm menthol vapors. It worked and I gradually slipped into blessed sleep, bathed in the soft warmth and love of my mother's face illuminated by the flickering flame of a kerosene lamp.

Today is July 3rd, 2002. I'm sitting in a beautiful spot near the head of the pasture. This is a place Mama loved too, and in summers long ago, we picked blackberries together here. As I sit here trying to record these thoughts, the images of Mama's face become increasingly vivid. Tomorrow is Independence Day, and the next day will be the one hundredth anniversary of her birth. From her present place of peaceful abode, she celebrates with us. Reunion of her people, our people, us – her! Of this I am certain, because in my last conversation with her, there were at least three generations present. As I approached her bed in the nursing home in Charlotte, I called to her. With instant recognition of a family voice, she rose upright. Her hair white as a wreath of snow framing a countenance as bright as that of a child, as warm as that of a mother, as wise as that of a matriarch who had survived two world wars, had buried her mate and four of her children. As I sat beside her on the bed, her eyes searched my face. "Garvel," she said with a sparkling smile.

"No, it's not Garvel" I answered.

She leaned closer and with certainty said "Jay."

"No, its not Jay," I stated. "It's your son, Morris."

Without any change of expression or mood, she smiled and said, "Oh, Morris." All within the span of a short moment she had greeted three generations of her family. She had spoken to and touched an older cousin, a brother, and a son. This time the light upon her face shone from within.

David Morris Denton
7/02

No. 49 (Some Numbers Are Special)

Sometimes the value of numbers is considerably greater than their mathematical worth. No. 1 has come to represent the very best in our culture. No. 49 derives its value from the specialness of the person with whom it has become associated. Were it not for the exceptional qualities of Charles Denton, No. 49 would mean no more than any other number. It is the person who makes it special.

The excitement and tension had been building for a couple of days. It was the kind of tension associated with those truly wonderful things that happen in the life of a kid of nine. It was Friday at about 1:30 in the afternoon. All classes had been dismissed in Robbinsville Elementary School and in the high school, too. People from the community were lined up in the shade alongside the old stone gymnasium; because it was September the sun was bright and it was quite warm. Football was a big thing in Robbinsville in those days, and still is. Football games are the one activity which bring together the entire community. In addition to being able to see in my mind's eye the things that were happening there that afternoon, I can even experience all over again the same emotions.

This was perhaps the second year that Robbinsville High School had fielded a football team, but what a force this had become in the life of that isolated and remote settlement. Perhaps 90% of that first football squad served in World War II, maybe more than that. Football activities were suspended in 1942 and not resumed until the Fall of '46 when some of the ex-GI's returned to complete the requirements for a

THE DENTON EXPERIENCE: FAMILY AND FRIENDS – FACES AND PLACES

high school diploma. It is uncertain who the other team was that afternoon; that really wasn't important because the thing that really mattered was to see my hero come onto the field with the other members of the Robbinsville Blue Devils. While we waited, I can remember seeing clusters of teachers standing near the corner of the gym talking and laughing, the principal with his grey suit, and important people from the community like Ed Ingram, the druggist; Patton Phillips, J. J. Snider, merchants; and a scattering of others. The windows of the gym, which faced the football field, were open and one of the older students was taking care of the sound system. The "Washington Post March" was being played on the PA system and the strains of this popular march by John Philip Sousa put the finishing touches on the most important event of that year in my life. It was 1940. From behind the old gymnasium came the visiting team. My lord, these people looked huge. I don't know if it was Sylva or Murphy, but it seems to me that their colors were black and gold. All of the pants of the football uniforms of that day were the same color; a canvas-like material somewhere between beige and gold in color, pretty much like a cotton-seed meal sack. Members of the visiting team gathered at the other end of the field and started doing calisthenics. It felt like my heart would fracture my ribs such was the excitement when the student announcer on the microphone started introducing the members of the "Blue Devils" team. These names still stir a lot of emotion when people get together over a cup of coffee, or at a class reunion, or at Fourth of July Homecoming to talk about football and the old days. I remember Josh Howell practicing his punting, and then I enjoyed the drills of the linemen of that team. Tony Ayers, John Siler, "Popcorn" Stiles, Lacy Slaughter, "Krueger" Beasley, I.G. Rogers, and Neal Webster. One of the fellows playing the end position has faded from my memory, but it was such a splendid joy to watch them run their pass patterns. It could have been "Buffalo" Orr. After a few minutes of warming up, the first team started running a series of plays up and down the field. The formation of the day was the old single wing. It is hard to say how good the Robbinsville team was that year, but that is really a secondary matter. They were wonderful as far as I was concerned, especially No.

49. Every time I would hear his name called over the PA System, I would feel like turning to all the people near me and saying, "That's my brother." No. 49, of course, was fullback Edwin Denton. It's funny how all three of the boys were called by their middle names during the growing up years, and then as they became different people in a different world, they took on different names, their first names. But to me, Edwin never changed.

Those first Robbinsville football teams had power both inside and outside…it was a thrill to see Leonard Jordan circle wide on a sweep and then cut back and race for 25 yards or more. But that thrill paled in comparison to those power plays up the middle in which "Denton picks up three yards and a first down." There simply was no greater glory than to be able to see and feel the accomplishments of my brother, especially in the presence of so many people. The blue jersey with the white No. 49, that was the object that I searched for during every play.

The helmets of that day were much different than the hi-tech, protective head gear that football players use today. They were part leather and part something else, a pressed material that was designed to yield upon impact. The helmet worn by No. 49 with the name "Edwin Denton" written several places inside stayed around the school up until the late 1940s as a symbol of the glory of that first team. The crown of this helmet was crushed from repeated contacts with the crowns of other helmets, shoulder pads, hip pads, not to mention the hard-baked surface of that old football field. So far as anyone knows, Edwin Denton was the only player from Robbinsville who played so hard that he actually caved in the crown of his helmet. When I went out for football as a freshman in August 1946, that helmet was still in the basement of the old gymnasium, and it remained as a symbol, not necessarily of power football, but more properly as a symbol of that deep and profound love of the game, that masculine craving for aggressive physical contact, and that commitment to whatever the team needed at the moment. My love for football was borrowed from these early experiences and that desire to be as good as he was kept me in high school. Take that away, and the future could have been very different. It wasn't just his class as a football player that gave my brother such powerful importance to me, it began much earlier than that and it was based on much simpler and more basic factors. I was special to him; I always sensed that even at times when I felt that I wasn't special at all.

Perhaps there was enough difference in our ages that all elements of rivalry, competition and jealousy were removed. Almost everyone has a big brother, but not many have the privilege of that unique bond. When we lived in the old house, he would find ways to involve me in his play and in his work. One summer he was enjoying a red wagon, like all boys. These were depression days, so we had one wagon for all the boys. It was red, it had the words "Radio Flyer" on each side of the bed, and it had a wooden-stake body that could be installed or removed depending on what you wanted to do. Charles loved to place one knee in the wagon and push himself along at high speed with the other foot. He would circle the old house at a high rate of speed making all the appropriate car or truck sounds as he raced along. The wagon was also used to haul stove wood and fire wood, and best of all, it was used to haul me. I remember one experience when Charles was pulling me as fast as he could run around the house. I was sitting in the bed of the wagon holding on with both hands. We rolled between the chimney on the upper end of the house and the fence, and as we came around the corner near the front porch, the wagon turned over because he had turned too sharply and I was thrown some distance across the yard. I was both hurt and frightened but soon stopped crying because of his excitement about what a wonderful wreck that had been. He carefully measured the distance from the point were my small body left the wagon to the point were it landed and announced with considerable pride that I had "flown" 13 feet. I stifled the tears because I felt that I should somehow be happy and proud because he was so happy and proud, when the truth of the matter was that it hurt like hell and I really wanted to bawl. This kind of thing happened time and again down through the years and on almost every occasion my hero was able to talk me out of tears and somehow would end up making me feel proud of how much pain I could endure without crying. Most of all, I think I simply wanted to do what he did and to be like him.

I probably would never have learned to play the guitar if he hadn't played the guitar first. Music was always a very satisfying element of my life and I still find myself moved by the same sentimental qualities that I remember responding to in music coming over the radio in the 1930s. I can still feel the same way when I think about that old Jimmie Rodgers record of "Moonlight and Skies." Gene Autrey also recorded this song, but that was the first one I remember my brother singing and playing on the guitar.

During those years before the war our friendship with the Elliott boys became almost as deep as if we were blood brothers. That association continued during and after the war when Charles was no longer at home, but before he went away to college and then enlisted, he was the catalyst. Friday afternoons in the early fall would find us with Dad's .22 and the 410 which belonged to Charles, making a quick hunting trip through the fields on the England property over the hill and down to the Elliott's house. Sometimes we would lean the guns up against a tree, find a smooth patch of ground, and play football for a half hour or so before we had to return home to do the feeding and the milking. On occasion, we actually played football with a walnut.

The summers of childhood have a way of all running together, so it's hard to know exactly in which summer certain things happened, but one stands out as particularly memorable. This could have been Charles' last summer at home before going away to Western Carolina and then into the Navy. As I recall some of the things that we did, there seemed to be a certain urgency about the activities that we were involved in…there were so many things that we wanted to do, so every day was packed. One of our favorite places to go camping was the "Cody Flats." I am assuming that we had permission to camp there because we took over the place as if it belonged to us. The Flats was a fairly open meadow about half-way up the mountain, very level, and near the outer edge, where the land dropped off sharply, was a cluster of walnut trees and large poplars. We selected a place under the limbs of the walnut trees and built a cabin, of sorts, out of chestnut fence rails which we carried from a place farther up on the side of the hill where an old fence had been forgotten and allowed to decay. Apparently this rail fence surrounded fields which had been under cultivation at some time in the past, and this would have accounted for the level field that was comparatively free of trees. We carried enough rails and stacked them one on the other until the structure was high enough that we could crawl inside through an open front. We made a thatched roof of sorts from pine brush which we cut from young trees scattered around the open field. This campsite remained there for many, many years, and I am guessing you could go back today and find some evidence of the creative energies of that group of boys. On all of our outings we carried guns, most of the time a .22, often a shotgun, and every once in awhile one of Daddy's high-powered rifles. Charles took empty 30-30 cartridges and drove them into the end of some of the chestnut rails on the front of our cabin and these became markers which we would remember and search for years and years later.

The open field, with the help of a little grubbing and cutting, became a football field and we even erected goal posts on each end from tall straight maple saplings. In remembering back, I guess the point of the whole thing was to make the football field because we spent considerably more time working on it than we did actually playing football. On those balmy days in mid-summer, after the hay was in and the corn laid-by, we could spend several hours on the mountain working a while, wrestling for a time, and then engaging in some other spontaneous activity. One of the things that became a particularly enjoyable sport was to shoot the dried seed pods out of the top of one of the tall poplar trees and watch the "wild geese," as we called the unusually shaped poplar seeds, as they floated like helicopters, or wild geese, to the ground. Each seed had its own wing, about 3/4" long and, as it would fall through the air, it would spin on its own axis, settling softly on the ground, perhaps 50 yards from where its flight began. We must have shot millions of these poplar seeds out of those trees, and today there is a grove of full-grown poplar trees which covers every square foot of what was, in that dreamy summer in the early part of the war, a football field.

When the war was over and Charles and Graham were back home, we walked a time or two back to the Flats to relive some of those special moments and were amazed at how quickly those poplar seeds sprouted and grew into young trees. In one-half dozen years the open meadow was gone and we had to search to find what was left of the cabin. But, when we rubbed the moss off the end of the chestnut rails, sure enough there were the spent 30-30 cartridges as we had left them in another time. Except for our memories, the one thing about the Cody Flats which lasted the longest was the iron cooking surface of an old wood stove which we hauled on a sled pulled by one of Dad's horses to the gap, and then wrestled, foot by foot, the remaining distance to the campground. We were the only campers in all of the southern Appalachians with their own cook stove. Charles, of course, was the central figure in this group of developing young men. He organized our activities, set the standards for our conduct, and was the one we looked up to. After the war, some of us camped at the Flats a time or two, and we even took along a hammock stamped U.S. Navy which Charles brought home with him from the South Pacific. It was never the same again. What had been lost, of course, in addition to our youth, was our innocence. The war changed all of that.

In thinking about the war...it became such a powerful and overriding force in the lives of all of us. Maybe that is why so many memories involved that time immediately before the long separation which took Charles and our, sort of, honorary brother, Audie Wilcox, and later Graham, from us for the duration. Audie never came back. After Charles had gone to Western Carolina, and perhaps even after he had enlisted in the Navy, he went opossum hunting with us one last time. As always, we took the dogs, gathered our lanterns and Dad's five-cell flashlight and started up the branch. We turned onto the old logging road, crossed the stream where the waterfalls flowed over those moss covered stones... that quiet little place that we all enjoyed. Then up the hill and along the remnants of that path along which thousands of cords of firewood had been pulled.

We stopped to rest at another favorite camping place where Charles and the Crisp boys had built platforms several feet off the ground where trees had grown up close together. We sat for a while on logs and stumps and talked, and then turned the dogs loose and waited for one of them to strike a hot trail. They worked their way around the area for perhaps 30 minutes and finally one of them barked "treed." We made our way through the woods, the rhododendron thickets, and over fallen logs all the way up to that unusual place called the "trough."

This strange peach orchard which had been planted between two sharp ridges forming a natural "V" by some of the members of the England family held a lot of attraction, especially during August and September when the peaches were ripe. We didn't like the Englands...we didn't know why...the dislike was inherent, and the flavor of this stolen fruit was especially sweet when we knew we were getting by with something.

Just below the trough was a patch of rhododendrons, a scattering of maples and poplars, and a tangle of wild grape vines. Years before a huge chestnut tree had fallen across this narrow ravine, and I remember Charles walking across this log and cutting the young tree where the opossum was hanging on with his tail wrapped around a limb just inches away from the reach of the dogs as they would leap and snarl. This is perhaps a disconnected event of no real importance, except for one element that the passage of time would cause to be registered forever in our memory. About two years later, in the heat of World War II, some of this same group of boys came back to the trough to capture another opossum treed in the same area. As we searched for those phosphorescent eyes in the darkness with a flashlight, we found something much more important. There, hanging from a grapevine, was a scarf which Charles had lost on that earlier hunt. I can't imagine what it is about this event that makes it so important, unless it is simply that this article of clothing connected me, at least in my emotions, with the person whom I admired most and whom I missed so deeply.

We were surprised and, of course, happy too when Charles unexpectedly showed up at home. He was AWOL. I knew it was serious because the sheriff or some important person came to our house with a message for him. I knew it was serious too because of the sense of anxiety surrounding this short but wonderful visit. Charles' ship, I believe, was docked in New York and they were preparing to ship out to the Pacific. He instinctively knew that this would be the last chance to come home for many months and he made his way back into Western Carolina for those few hours with family. Of all the memories of the wartime years I think this one stands out as vividly as any other. It was late and apparently it was winter time because there was a fire in the fireplace. Mary must have been at Cullowhee; Dad I guess was at Fontana, and I am really not sure about the others, perhaps in bed. Charles and Mom were sitting directly in front of the fireplace, a kerosene lamp was burning on a table somewhere across the room, and I was sitting over at the right nearer to the doorway leading into the kitchen. They were talking quietly. Charles was in his full-dress blues and was leaned forward in his chair. I was aware of the reflections from the fireplace as they played across his face; perhaps I was more an observer than a participant…most of all, I just wanted to be there. In thinking about the thousands of experiences which make up a relationship between two brothers, this one stands out as capturing all those special qualities of whatever existed between us. From time to time he would look away from the fire and turn his face in my direction and for a moment would direct his attention to me, perhaps without speaking, but with a soft expression in his eyes which I have come to associate with everything good about my brother. In my adolescent way of looking at life and people, I saw him as being near perfect. He was everything that he should be, and more than any goal in my life at that time was the wish to be like him. It was a long time before he was home again.

Perhaps there is a wisdom in children that gets covered up with experience and hurt and cynicism. Perhaps I saw the quality of my brother Charles more clearly and more precisely than would be possible in the world of adults. My affection for him was direct and uncluttered by any negative emotions or bad memories. It included admiration and was based on the absolute certainty that he thought I was okay. It wasn't until years later, when I was the one who was returning home from a tour of military duty, that my idealized perception of Charles came into painful conflict with a new and unexpected reality. Not that he changed…it is just that I was totally unprepared for his critical and, perhaps somewhat abrupt, judgments about me and what I was going to do with my own life. It occurred to me slowly and painfully that during all those years in military life I had carried around in my heart and in my mind an assessment of members of my family that was far too idealized. I really don't know why this happened. Perhaps it was that the separation from the people whom I loved and admired most took place before I had learned through experience and necessity to appraise people in a more practical and critical manner. To say the least, I was unsettled by the very different way in which I was being judged now as compared with 1942. In response to the heat I was getting for not getting myself in college or developing a future or whatever, I developed two very different responses. The first was a series of unhappy and abortive attempts to be what I thought other people were asking me to be. The second and later response was one of withdrawal, and it wasn't really until I went to Kentucky, found a place that I liked, and gave myself the freedom to be me without responsibility for the mud and unending hard work of that damned hillside farm in Graham County, free of the need to be like anyone else except me, and free for the first time in my years to reflect on the joy and wonder of the things taking place around me and the joy and wonder of my own personality, discovered or rediscovered. This was a time of growing and perhaps healing some, but most of all understanding… understanding that Charles' life couldn't be my own, understanding that as wonderful as he really was, I was different, understanding that the differences didn't matter, and understanding finally that I could be me and he could be he and the magic of our brotherhood could be as it had always been.

And now. The place is different, it's not the Cody Flats or the Robbinsville High School stadium or a stream bottom in July on Little Snowbird, but the feelings are all the same. He sat facing the sunshine rather than the fireplace. He was looking out across time, this time from the present to the past, and that time from the present to the future. The face was the same, only a little bit thinner. Occasionally he would turn in my direction and the eyes were the same, as soft and dreamy as then.

His life had gone in one direction, mine in another, but as we sat and talked and remembered and felt, everything came full circle. I could still look at this man and know that I wanted to be like him.

David M. Denton
March 1989

A Flower Cannot Hold Its Fragrance

It is not uncommon for persons to expend great energy and effort to influence the lives of other persons. Some people seem to measure their own worth through their influence upon the lives of others. It is wonderfully satisfying then to know people who have had, and who continue to have, a marked influence upon the lives of others without undue thought or effort on their part. The everlasting good that people of this kind render occurs incidentally and not by design or intention. The process is incremental and cumulative, but the effect is profound and permanent. I dare say Mary and Bob seldom, if ever, have thought about themselves in this way and I have concluded that they would be somewhat startled to realize fully the warm and happy difference they have made in the existence of others. Let me speak personally.

In those early days of my memory, Mary was the ultimate in terms of what a sister can be and, I suppose, should be. Her presence as an older sister was more a presence that suggested support than one that suggested control. It wasn't anything that was talked about; it was just a manner of being and behaving. First of all, she was such a nice person to look at, tall and athletic with soft expressions, capable and in-charge in a self-effacing way. When she went away to college, I felt a real sense of loss, and those rare weekends when she was home for a visit things were okay again...more than okay...I always felt that she singled me out for just a little bit of special recognition and attention. Without question, other members of the family felt she had singled them out, too. This capacity to make everyone feel special became a part of Mary. It was not so much a "gift" as it was that inclination of mind and heart that by nature put the feelings of others first. Anyone who could make another person feel so nice and warm and appreciated was certainly worthy of admiration, and my admiration for Mary simply knew no bounds! Going away to college was, of course, symbolic…Mary was grown, a woman now…and I was awe-stricken with her beauty. It was an all-inclusive kind of beauty and I guess I idealized her. As a benefactor of so much that was good and full of promise, I didn't fully grasp in those days my sister's capacity for feeling hurt or rejection. To lesser persons, I am sure, those feelings of hurt, which she experienced in those difficult and stressful times overlapping the Great Depression and World War II, would have become crippling and limiting influences. With Mary, personal suffering has been used as a motivation for increasing the happiness in others. Mary's character and personality have never been diminished nor limited by the pain in her life. Having personal knowledge of the meaning of hurt, she had no desire nor inclination to pass that on to others. Instead, she grew beyond the ordinary and developed a huge reservoir of understanding and caring which all of us have tapped from time to time, and which continues to flow without limit! One of the incredible things about this woman is that she continues to be propelled into self improvement because she wants to be better than she sees herself as being. This is a remarkably unselfish response to the tugs and pulls, stresses and fractures of life, of surviving and trying to become whole!

Since this is a personal statement I guess it is okay to talk about the unique involvement of the lives of Mary and Bob with the lives of Peggy and me. Strangely, this unusual association has not been controlled by geography. During most of the thirty one years that Peggy and I have been married, we have lived some considerable distance from Mary and Bob. This association, of course, goes all the way back to Kentucky, and even beyond. Let's go back then to December, 1954, and my discharge from the United States Air Force. As I said earlier, I tended to idealize Mary and, for that matter, I tended to idealize the whole family! Throughout those four years of separation from the family when I was a part of the military, I continued to embrace those perceptions of my parents and my siblings which I had carried with me from my childhood. A somewhat larger-than-life significance was given to each one of them, and in many ways that practice has continued to be a part of the way I think about my family. My high school years had been so completely dominated by work and responsibility that I really hadn't had an opportunity to reflect on what was happening in the lives of individual members of the family except in an idealistic sort of way. The four years with the Air Force were, in a sense, a continuation of the same thing. First of all, time and distance have an effect upon the way we see and think about and feel about others. During those high-school years, it was me and the farm, the cows, the crops, the winter's wood, and my own personal life…the guitar, football team, my friends. That was the way things were and I accepted it. The older brothers and sisters were away and Dad was away. The war, college, TVA, new in-laws, new nephews and nieces. Life was hard, but life was not bad. I felt needed, I felt responsible, and I guess I felt a sense of certain importance. After all, this was now and it was necessary; the future for me would be like it was, or as I perceived it to be, for my older brothers and sisters whom I continued to admire and look up to.

When I came home from the Air Force, I expected things to be different, but I really didn't know in what way. For the first time in my life, I found myself both without an anchor and a rudder. I hadn't changed, but everything else had. The thing I was least prepared for was the sense of disappointment conveyed to me by those whom I held in such high regard. This was an unsettling experience, because it felt like I was trapped in a time warp. My little sister was already out of college and all the rest of my brothers and sisters were married and settled and "successful." Work and responsibility were certainly no stranger to me and suddenly I had neither! In response to the compulsion to do something important and to regain acceptance and status within the family fold, I twice enrolled in college and then withdrew, drove a milk truck, traveled with a country music band, played the guitar for square dances at Fontana, sang for drunken sailors in Georgetown, D.C., built C-130's at Lockheed Aircraft, helped coach football, and helped make one last crop on my daddy's farm…all of this within the course of a year! This just wasn't the way things were supposed to turn out.

And then it happened. We left home fairly early in the morning in Dad's old green International pick-up...Dad, Mom and me. We drove through Deal's Gap and down through those switch-back turns on Highway 129, past Calderwood on through Maryville and Knoxville, and Clinton, Tennessee and then up through the desolate coal mining country between Habersham and Jellico, Tennessee – where the tar paper shacks cling tentatively to the sides of the hills and are surrounded by gray rubble left over from the strip mines. These flimsy homes were almost always in the company of one or two old cars jacked up on Royal Crown Cola crates with all of the wheels missing. Where we were going didn't really seem to matter as much as that we were going somewhere...anywhere! How could I know that it was a trip into providence? The only thing for sure was that Mary and Bob lived in Corbin, Kentucky, and we were going up for a weekend visit. The fact that Dad and Mom and I were making a trip together was something left over from another time. Not much conversation on this trip, but I do remember Dad clearing his throat and knocking his pipe out on the dashboard of the International pick-up while half-burned tobacco flew all over the inside of the cab. Dad would periodically relight his pipe and offer statements directed at no one and maybe everyone. Mom said little but showed much in her face. Maybe she and Dad sensed that this trip might lead somewhere. As we rode, I remember thinking about the unusual rock strata in the road cuts, and in the north facing areas there were sheets of ice cascading down these steep banks where moisture had seeped between the layers of coal and shale and stone and trickled down the face of the cliff. The fact that it was winter made the landscape seem even more raw and desolate. Sometimes the ice had taken on a strange color because of the presence of chemicals leaching out of the open and unhealed wounds of the land. We were on Highway 25W...that was the road that took the skinny boys from the hills to places like Cincinnati and Cleveland and Detroit and Chicago. That was the road out of a lean and hungry struggle for survival from the coal mines and cornfields and logging camps to that first real job working on the assembly line making Buicks in Flint, Michigan. And this is the same road back home! This road symbolized the link between two worlds…the way from an unacceptable reality to a dream. Too often that dream was smothered on an icy road in the middle of the night after too much beer in one of the joints in those little border towns. Or maybe the dream just simply rusted away in the weeds outside some godforsaken shack hanging desperately to a steep hillside like a '49 Ford automobile with a rod through the side of the engine and broken springs growing up through the upholstery. For me though, this was a road upward and outward…a road of discovery and light. Route 25W meandered along the bank of the Cumberland River up an incline with a sheer vertical cliff which exposed millions of years of history in the formation of the world. Later, I was to stand under the face of this cliff evenings and thumb a ride back to Corbin. Across the river from this cliff was the town of Williamsburg. You could see the spires of a least two churches as the town crept up the side of a hill. You could also count a thousand households by the coal smoke hanging heavily in the damp winter air. Somewhere over there on the side of the hill was Cumberland College but that would be another story for another time.

Mary and Bob lived in a comfortable rambling house in Corbin. It was open and airy like the two of them…warm, too. I liked this place. Before supper Bob and I went to a sporting goods store in Corbin and someone was showing off some huge fish that had just been caught in Lake Cumberland that afternoon. The sun was out even though it was well up into the afternoon and I thought about fishing. My God, how long since I had taken the time or had the time or allowed myself the luxury of going fishing! Going fishing is a symbolic activity. It doesn't really have much to do with catching fish. It has a lot more to do with thinking and feeling and being. Yeah, I was beginning to settle and to like this place and we had only been here two hours! I don't know if Dad and Mom brought me to Kentucky for a purpose or even if they had thought about it. As far as I had been concerned it was no more than a weekend visit…something to look forward to…yes, because a weekend with Mary and Bob was always something to look forward to. But beyond that, I was surprised at how I was beginning to feel about the place. We had a great weekend visiting Cumberland Falls and seeing some of the country there. And then Sunday afternoon we drove a few miles out of town with Mom and Dad, stopped for a while at a picnic area along the road, said our goodbyes and watched them drive off in that faded green pickup. They seemed content as they left and I felt a sense of wholeness that I hadn't experienced in a long, long time. That feeling is a hard one to describe because it's equally hard to understand, but it has something to do with the relationship with Mary and Bob. A part of it is the element of unconditional acceptance. Never was there any need for justification or rationalization. Never was any reference made about what I was doing with my life, what my plans for the future were, when I was going to get enrolled in college or when I was going to do something with my life. By accepting me unconditionally, Mary and Bob helped me make that critical investment in myself because they accepted me as I was and even made me feel very, very special. I let go and experienced the most glorious summer of my life! I experienced an element of freedom and unrestrained joy that I had always assumed was possible but hadn't, until that time, fully experienced. There had been other similar acts of unusual consideration that I remembered when I was fourteen or fifteen…tall and skinny…and with few clothes other than what I was able to buy for myself at the end of each summer…a couple of pairs of dungarees and some poplin shirts from Sears Roebuck. I felt responsible for myself and don't remember particularly feeling unfortunate. It just seemed natural that if I could do the spring plowing for Uncle Blaine and get paid for it, that I would buy my own clothes. Then at Christmastime the unexpected would happen. Mary and Bob, more aware of my state of poverty and need (emotional as well as economic) would give me presents that Mom and Dad couldn't afford and which were much beyond my means. I remember things like a knit turtleneck shirt or something of that kind…totally unexpected. And here I was in Corbin, Kentucky, a part of that happy household and within a matter of days I had a job at Cumberland Falls. This was pure ecstasy! I watched springtime return to the southern Appalachians. I had, and I guess I took, the time to watch and feel this wonderful transition take place. I often stood on the patio of DuPont Lodge and looked up the Cumberland River as it wound its way among the ridges. In the early morning it was like a glistening ribbon twisting and turning silently. As the sun would rise over the more distant ridges I could see the changing shades of color. As the sun grew higher in the morning sky and as the promise of spring became the full-blown reality of summer, I was profoundly moved by these experiences, and I felt rich and happy, and I belonged, and Mary and Bob were always close by somewhere in my mind or in my heart, or there with me in Kentucky. The story goes that Daniel Boone wept because his dying son who was killed at Cumberland Gap didn't have a chance to see and enjoy the beauty, the essence of Kentucky. But I was lucky, and it was all mine!

That spring and summer in Kentucky I found peace and I found more. I found myself, and I found my wife, and I found a life. Bob would drive by Cumberland Falls and pick me up in his two-tone green Ford, and we would spend a sunny afternoon living life in the hills of southeastern Kentucky. Bob liked me and he accepted me as a peer. That was refreshing and surprising, too, because I had come to believe that peerage was something that I had to earn over and over again. My, how things had turned around. I bathed in the sunshine of love and acceptance. I reveled too in the wonder of my own accomplishments. Yes, I was a man of the southern hills…I was a singer…and I had stories to tell.

A year before I was a peripheral person. Deep in my being I knew that there was something special out there somewhere, but it seemed so remote and all of a sudden I had it all! And I explored every dimension of living that summer. And then Peggy came along. I discovered her or she discovered me. We bumped into each other or the whole thing was providential, and this was the time and place for it to happen. But happen it did and I was the first to know it. It's strange; however, maybe even more than strange, the part that Mary played in this association. It's not that Mary and Bob liked and passed judgement on Peggy…no; it's not that Mary picked out Peggy and thought that she would be a fine wife for her brother…no! I found Peggy…I picked her out and Mary's role was one of affirmation. In speaking of providence, it would certainly be safe to say that Mary and Peggy were destined to meet each other and to become friends because the closeness and the character of that relationship is one that is rare among people that I have known. Again, in thinking about the twists and turns of my existence and the influence upon these twists and turns of Mary and Bob, it has always been an influence felt through warm support, total acceptance and availability in times of need. Interestingly, it seems now, as I look back, that I turned to Mary and Bob even when I didn't realize at the time that I was turning to them.

Our lives came together again in Albemarle, North Carolina. Mary and Bob had relocated from Corbin to Albemarle, and Peggy and I were struggling along in Chapel Hill. That summer in Albemarle is one for the record books. We lived with Mary and Bob and, at least as I remember that summer, it seems most of our time was spent in play or if not play some happy diversion that made the world of work seem like play. I was selling Standard Coffee door-to-door. Peggy was pregnant with David, and Mary and Bob had a houseful of white-headed boys.

The next encounter, perhaps the most providential of all because this encounter gave access to what has become the most compelling, the most fulfilling, and most challenging part of my life, my work in education of the deaf. We were in Macon, Georgia, and it was wintertime. I was in law school, and we were in desperate need of money. At that time, money and Macon, Georgia, were unknown to each other! Law school was fine and we were happy. We had no thoughts of making a change in the direction our lives had taken. But in our search for survival we found at the end of each corridor a door firmly closed. Illness intervened...mine and my son's. We needed work...there was work in Morganton, North Carolina. And, while I was looking for work there, we had stayed with Mary and Bob. In the meantime, of course, they had relocated to Morganton. Like that trip to Corbin, Kentucky, the one from Macon, Georgia, to Morganton at the time certainly had no particular significance. It was just a trip to find a job for a few months and then back to Macon. If, during that summer at Cumberland Falls, I found myself and realized that there was something special for me, it was in Morganton that I learned what that special thing was. Mary and Bob, of course, had nothing to do with education of the deaf nor with my decision to invest my life in that cause, but they were there and they were a part of the circumstances surrounding that remarkable discovery and decision on my part. It's simply a matter of history that the turning points in my life have, in one way or another, involved Mary and Bob.

In looking back over these thirty-odd years, our lives have become linked not in binding, limiting, or controlling ways, but through deliberate choice and without any form of restriction. One of the rare and precious things about Mary has been her capacity to maintain a relationship of complete trust and acceptance, and one that has made no demands! Whatever is shared in either direction is freely and generously given...free of expectation that anything is owed. Even though our lives, mine and Peggy's and Bob's and Mary's, have taken dramatically different directions, and even though the two households may embrace divergent philosophical or ideological points of view, the association and unique bond has maintained and become stronger. The quiet and sustaining presence of Mary and Bob, unaffected by time and distance, has been a source of spiritual nourishment for us. Always eager and willing to share a happy point of view without forcing it, like flowers whose sweet fragrance is free to all who come within their realm, they have lent much to the happiness of others. I feel like I am in position to speak from considerable experience!

David M. Denton
Summer of 1987

Herding Fish (Lessons from a Brother)

Some of the most interesting discoveries made by students attending Sweetwater Elementary School were made on the way to and from class in the white frame building that sat where the Sweetwater Baptist Church is now located. All of the pupils walked to school, and it was on these journeys between our homes and the schoolhouse that the big lessons of life were learned and the memories, which last a lifetime, were made. Children from down Sweetwater, from England Branch, from Pinhook, from upper Sweetwater, and from both prongs of Beech Creek arrived long before the first bell. If the weather was decent, kids engaged in play until the second bell, and then ran from all directions and lined up like the ladies and gentlemen they were. Funny, but kids who walk to school are never late! In mid-winter we would go inside and gather around the stove, cooking our backsides until the teacher arrived. Some of the older boys had the responsibility of kindling a fire and carrying in the morning supply of wood before classes began. Sweetwater School served children grades one through six. There were three rooms and each one accommodated two grades. Sally Shope taught grades one and two, and she was a dear woman and one of the best teachers I ever had. Lonazelle Brewer taught third and fourth grades and my sister, Gwen, was in her room. Herbert Carpenter taught fifth and sixth grades and was also principal. The older boys who built and took care of the wood heaters were fifth and sixth graders, which meant that they were eleven or twelve years old. They were our heroes. One of them, Fred Garland, hit a sawdust-filled baseball so hard it burst and sawdust went everywhere. I wondered if I would ever be that strong and wonderful.

Brother Noell was in the fifth grade, so he was one of the grown-up boys. He didn't care much about baseball, but he knew how to make a band guide better than anyone at Sweetwater. Rolling bands was one of the favorite activities among boys in the hills and it was a major sport at Sweetwater. In the books we read, bands were called hoops and were guided with a stick. The bands we used were from the hubs of old-fashioned farm wagons. Most of them were about a foot in diameter and the metal bands were about an inch wide. With a good guide, they were easy to roll and it was possible for a boy to run full speed keeping his band on the trail uphill, downhill, and around curves. We had long and intricate band trails laid out, and competition was fierce. Noell really knew how to make a good band guide, and some of the boys, like Jack Payne or Arthur Ray Millsaps or Ray Williams, were envious.

To make a good band guide, you start with an oak shingle about 30 inches long. Most of the buildings around the area had roofs made of oak shingles, so they were in good supply. The shingle was whittled into the shape of a paddle. The broad end of the paddle was about three inches wide and the other end was shaped to fit comfortably in your hand. The guide itself was made from a Prince Albert tobacco can. Both ends of the can were removed and the seam, which runs up and down one side of the can, was separated. Now the can could be opened into a flat sheet of metal, about 4" by 8". The ends of the piece of tin were bent upwards, forming a U. The base of the U was tacked to the broad end of the paddle and the band guide was now ready for use. The band was rolled and kept moving and directed with the guide. The uprights of the metal U kept the band going in the right direction, and a good band roller could easily maneuver sharp turns without losing control. So successful was the Noell Denton band guide, that by the time Sweetwater Elementary was closed and band rolling faded into memory, no one had come up with a better guide. Once, during recess, Noell was challenged physically by one of the bigger boys. The matter was settled when my brother was forced to use his band guide as an instrument of defense. He hit the bigger boy on the side of the head with the band guide, leaving two parallel scratches on the boy's cheek from the upturned edges of the Prince Albert can.

By road, it was only a mile from our house to school, but that could easily be stretched into a meandering journey twice that distance. This was especially true on our trips home after school. Mornings, our trips were pretty direct, especially on cold days, exploring was fun, but the thought of that old wood-burning heater drew us pretty quickly to the schoolhouse. Noell, Gwendolyn, and I sometimes walked together, but often, Gwendolyn would walk part way with her best buddy, Marilyn Brewer, who lived just up the road from us. Marilyn's mother happened to be their teacher. Edwin and Mary were already attending school in Robbinsville and JoAnn had not yet started, so much of the time Noell and I had all the time in the world to find our way home. Sometime during that year, Gwendolyn had a problem with fallen arches. Fortunately one of the young lady teachers at Stecoah happened to be going right by Sweetwater School on her way to Stecoah, and it was arranged for Gwendolyn to ride with her for several weeks. As Miss Blankenship and Gwen would drive past us, Gwen would pretend that she didn't see us, gloating all the while. Gwendolyn took a lot of teasing about her fallen arches. Miss Amanda Blankenship had a 1930 Model A Ford that was a dark green color. I can still visualize it maneuvering the deep ruts up the long hill below George Cody's house. The log trucks on their way to Milltown kept the Sweetwater Road in terrible condition during those pre-war times.

In those days, everyone had cattle and for the most part, they were allowed to range freely. The open hillsides were cris-crossed with cow trails. Even the wooded hillsides had many trails and the underbrush had been browsed by cattle, so it was easy to make one's way through the woods in those days. There were still hundreds of chestnut trees and many of them were still bearing nuts. Higher up on the ridges, thousands of the giant chestnuts still stood, killed by the blight but not yet fallen. They had lost their bark and marched like so many skeletons among the hardwoods and evergreens. We knew where all the chestnuts, which still were alive and bearing were, and we sought these out, filling our pockets with the shiny, brown fruits. We also knew where all the neighbors' fruit trees were and when they were ready for harvest. It was understood and accepted that anyone passing was welcome to apples, peaches, or pears from a neighbor's tree. We knew it was perfectly all right to pick up fallen fruit or even to pluck an apple from the tree. We knew, too, that we were absolutely not to climb a neighbor's tree or to shake it, or to carry away fruit except for a spare apple in the pocket. There was a rich variety of apples then and we knew where all the favorites grew and when they were about ripe. Wild fruit was in abundance, too, especially grapes and plums.

Noell knew about unusual things and places that went unnoticed by others. Everyone was familiar with chestnuts and most of us knew where the trees were that were still bearing, but few indeed knew where to find chinquapins. One fall afternoon, in the balmy sunshine, as we happily made our way down the road, Noell said he would take me to a chinquapin tree if I would keep it a secret. I must have been as good as my word; because this is the first time I remember telling anyone where it was. As we walked past George Cody's barn, he said that we had to be real quiet and try not to let anybody see us. We sneaked through the fence just below the road and followed a farm lane used by wagons, sleds, other farm machinery and, of course, the cattle and horses. The lane continued between the road and a cornfield. At the end of the cornfield the lane turned to the right and continued in the direction of the creek. Where the farm lane turned toward the creek, it moved along the edge of a small hill, leaving a bank of exposed red clay dirt. Bushes and briars grew along the top of the bank and it was here that my brother said to start looking for "chinky-pin" bushes. We crept along and suddenly, there on the ground, were dozens of burrs, like chestnut burrs, only smaller, scattered along the lane and up the bank. At the top of the bank were two or three small trees with leaves shaped like those of a chestnut tree, and with smooth bark that was brown and shiny. These chinquapin trees were full of burrs, some of which were beginning to open and exposing the round nuts, which were like chestnuts, only more round and smaller. They were a rich brown color, smaller than a marble, and very shiny, like polished leather. The chinquapin trees, or shrubs, were seemingly unaffected by the blight which was destroying the much larger chestnut trees, and they were much scarcer. I remember seeing very few of them in my life, so this first experience was special. Noell smiled brightly and his blue eyes literally sparkled. As he stood there in the sunshine with his light brown, almost blond, hair tousled and a few freckles scattered across his nose, he told me that not many people knew about this place and for me to keep it a secret. It was not too far off the road and we didn't want such a treasure to fall into the wrong hands. His happiness in sharing this wonderful new discovery with me was contagious and the memory of that moment of pure innocent joy still feels the same. We filled our pockets with the sweet brown nuts, and he showed me how to open a chinquapin burr with one's heel – minus shoes. Barefoot season continued as long as we felt we could get away without wearing shoes. Noell could open chestnut burrs with his heel, but when I tried, I ended up with the burr stuck to my ankle, rather than my ground-toughened heel. Looking into Noell's face, I could see the scar, which ran diagonally from his right eye across the bridge of his nose. The scar was the result of an accident. He had quietly walked up behind Edwin, who was splitting stove wood with an axe. As Edwin raised the axe over his shoulder, the blade struck Noell in the nose and he carried the scar all his life. When he was a boy, the scar had a slightly pink tint, but as he matured, it lost that color and became another feature of the character on his handsome face.

Once the weather got warm in the springtime, Noell took me on some of the most unusual explorations that could be imagined. Beech Creek flowed past Sweetwater School and just across the fence bordering the school ground, cool water poured over the spillway of Arthur Deyton's gristmill. The roar of the flowing water provided a musical backdrop as the children played and studied in the white schoolhouse. On mill days, that sound was replaced by the low grinding of large cog wheels being turned by the force of water pouring over the mill wheel. In winter, I could look out the classroom window and see icicles ten feet or more tall, hanging from the spillway all the way to the creek bed, like crystal stalactites. The mill was a place of great interest and mystery. Not a half-mile down the creek from the school was another mill. This one belonged to Fannie Rogers, and it was located where Pinhook branch runs into Sweetwater or Cheoah

Creek. Just past the point where the creek runs under Sweetwater Road, a hand dug canal branches off from the creek carrying a substantial flow along the canal or millrace. The creek continued to flow along the floor or the valley while the millrace traced its way gently around the side of the hill, arriving at a spot near the mill, where its flow was directed into a flume and arrived above ground by a wooden trestle. At the end of the trestle was a gate, which could be lifted to allow the water to pour over the huge mill wheel, thereby turning the mills grinding mechanism. When the gate was closed, water from the millrace poured over the side in much the same manner as was true with Arthur Deyton's mill. The millrace and plume being several feet higher than the creek at the point of the mill's location gave the water flow ample force to operate the mill.

One of the most delightful activities that Noell and I shared was wading the millrace from the point at which it branched off from the creek all the way to the mill. We would wade slowly, side by side, bending over to make larger shadows and herding the many varieties of fish down the millrace to the point where the closed gate stopped the flow of water until the flume was full and its level had risen until it poured over the spillway. When the gate was open, the entire flow of the millrace was directed over the wheel and the level of water in the flume and race was lower. Usually it was possible to keep the fish moving ahead of us, and only occasionally did one dart past us and escape upstream. Sweetwater Creek hosted many small fish and a few that were quite big in the eyes of a boy. There were "hog suckers," "silversides," "knotty heads," "molly crawl bottoms," "red bellies," "red eyes," and "bass," but they were wily. Our hope was to corner the fish at the end of the millrace and to snatch them with our hands. Sometimes we did. If we were lucky, we could put what we caught in our lunch buckets. Lunch buckets were usually lard buckets. Sometimes, we would disturb a brown water snake, and this would cause great excitement. More often the exotic species captured were spring lizards, crawfish, bullfrogs, or some little water creature that we didn't recognize. There were snapping turtles in Sweetwater and rarely a "water dog." The "water dog" or hellbender is a primitive salamander-like creature with gills. We often talked about them but seldom saw one. When we approached the gate at the end of the millrace, the situation became chaotic. The first fish to reach the gate would turn and head back toward us, startling the others. As the number of fish in front of us became more concentrated, the fun increased. Fish were darting in all directions, running into each other, running into the sides of the flume, and running into our bare ankles. The bottom of the flume was slippery and as we dodged and leaped and fell, fish were everywhere leaping over the sides, leaping into our faces, darting between our legs, or escaping upstream. The hilarity didn't last long, but it was sheer joy while it was happening. If a knotty head or a hog sucker ended up in our pocket or in our lunch bucket that was a bonus. The millrace was there for many years. Fannie Rogers' mill was still in operation when I enlisted in the Air Force in 1950. During all that time, to my knowledge, only two human souls had the privilege of herding fish in the millrace. Noell showed me how it was done.

Fannie Rogers lived in a house across the creek from the mill and during the Sweetwater school days, her son, Porter, lived with her. Fannie had several daughters, but I think Porter was her only son. There was a store where Pinhook Road turned off Sweetwater Road and headed down the hill toward the mill. Porter had a brown Chevrolet car about 1935 or '36, which he parked at the store or sometimes, under a sycamore tree near the mill. Sweetwater Road rounded a curve directly above the mill, so as we walked past we could look directly downward to the mill and see Pinhook Road Bridge where it crossed the creek in front of the mill. It was fun to throw rocks from the road above and see if we could throw all the way to the creek. As the rocks fell, we could hear them striking the large leaves of the sycamore and poplar trees. One afternoon, Noell felt particularly exuberant and thought he could throw a rock all the way over the sycamore tree, under which Porter's car was parked and into the creek. Sometimes my brother's nature worked against him and this was one of those times. Today we would say he was pushing the envelope. With a mighty heave he let go of a sizeable piece of gravel and we watched expectantly as it arced outward and downward, stripping leaves off the sycamore tree and leaving a fist-sized hole in the very center of Porter Rogers rear window. It seemed to take forever for that rock to fall; it almost hung there between the branches of the tree before being pulled magnetically toward the one place that we didn't want it to go. We suffered through that eternity knowing for certain that the sin had already been committed. Noell looked like he had been struck by a rock himself as the realization took over his faculties. For a moment we stood looking at each other before my brother broke to run. There was no way I could keep up with him and was lucky just to keep him in sight until we had covered half the distance between the scene of the crime and home. As soon as we got to the house, Noell told Dad what had happened. Dad sternly looked at us. I felt guilty too, and Dad told my brother that the first thing he had to do was retrace his steps back to the Rogers home and tell Porter Rogers that he had thrown the offending stone and was sorry, and ready to take his punishment. It was unclear exactly how the details of the matter were handled, but without question Noell was required to make payment for his indiscretion through some kind of physical labor. In the years that followed, we often recalled the experience and shared a moment of laughter together, but we also remembered with a bit of emotional pain that profound lesson, the self knowledge of a wrong done, or a mistake made is evident even when the act is occurring and remains forever woven into the fabric of the experience itself. I am glad that we were raised this way, and I am gladder still that the brother from whom I learned so much taught by example. His striking countenance always told me how he felt about a matter before he had uttered a word.

Another of our favorite excursions on the way home from school involved a trip up the branch from Flora Cody's house to the log landing, a place where the timber cutters had snaked the logs for loading onto a truck a few years earlier. As the trees were cut on the higher ridges, teams of horses were used to drag them down the narrow hollows to the landing area. A platform was built of earth and logs that would allow the trucks to pull alongside and loggers to roll them from the platform onto the truck beds with a peavey or cant hook. The log landing consisted of a couple of acres of open area which was fairly level. From the landing trails led in several different directions. One of them led up a long hollow to a spring below the Flats. Another led around the ridges through pines and poplars and ended a short distance above the Sweetwater Road. An old chestnut tree with only the bottom limbs still alive sort of marked the end of this trail. From that point we could easily climb over an old rail fence, slide down the bank and be back on the road. In the edge of the woods below the log landing near the branch, fox grape vines grew among the alders and young maples. Fox grapes are large wild grapes with a thick skin or hull and a very distinctive flavor. Fox grape jam was treasured among local people and families would gather them by the tub full.

After playing at the log landing for awhile we would make our way along the trail which leads to the Holloway Cemetery and around the hill and down to the little orchard. Depending on the time of day when we were on this trail, we sometimes rounded up the cows and drove them past the little orchard and down to the barn. There were some buckeye trees growing along this trail, and we enjoyed picking up the brown buckeyes and would carry them in our pockets for days at a time. The word was that buckeyes were poison, so we never tried to eat one, although they looked like large chestnuts.

As golden and happy as these memories are as they come floating back, there are also memories of sadness, even tragedy. One of them had to do with a boy who in my experiences existed only as a name connected to an experience related to me by older siblings. The name was Ed Lail, a boy from Pinhook, one of a family of several children belonging to Sam and Mattie Lail. I knew most of the other family members, but Ed had been killed the year before I started to school at Sweetwater. On my first day as a student Noell, Gwendolyn, and I walked excitedly up the road filled with anticipation and wonder. As we came nearer to George Cody's house, Noell started telling us that we were almost to the place where Ed Lail was killed. With my heart in my throat, I walked with my brother and sister over to the edge of the road where among the weeds, Noel pointed out part of the wreckage of an old car. He explained that Ed was riding in an open car, probably a Model T Ford, which was driven by someone else. The car ran off the road, turned over and little Ed Lail was killed by a spear of broken glass from the car's window. Noell searched around in the weeds and picked up a large shard of glass, perhaps a foot long. That spot, there on the roadside, became forever connected with the death of a boy whom I never knew, but have visualized and thought about on a thousand different occasions when I walked past this place. The lingering hurt and sadness related to Ed Lail and his short life was rekindled into a sense of chilling tragedy a few years later when Noell and I drove several dry cows and heifers up Pinhook to the Davis place for summer pasture. As we neared Sam Lail's place, we could see dark smoke billowing up over a small ridge between us and their homestead. As we topped the low hill, there before us was a picture of desolation. The family, from babies to full-grown children and adults, was huddled under an apple tree looking hopelessly at what was left of their house. The women and children were weeping while Sam stood silent and broken as the smoke rose from the ashes representing the hope and labor of a lifetime. What was to have been a joyous and carefree summer sojourn for two brothers, a few cows, and a country road has remained in memory juxtaposed against a picture of extreme heartbreak.

The differences in my two brothers became obvious to me early in these years when we wandered the fields and hillsides making play and adventure of even the most tiresome chores. Edwin was the big brother, in charge, extroverted and charming. Noell was thoughtful and serious, less social but equally warm in his interactions. For me it was the best of all possible worlds because I adored them both, and the richness of our activities and experiences was enhanced and sharpened by the contrast of their personalities. These differences in nature, character and age were also the source of the inevitable sibling conflicts. Noell and I were close enough in age that we sometimes fought with considerable passion. If necessary, Edwin would intervene. Similarly,

Noell and Edwin were close enough in age that they would find themselves in determined conflict. I hated to see them fight and it didn't happen often, but occasionally it did happen. Once Noell lost his temper, he was very hard to control. Humor was Edwin's best friend in defusing such situations. Once we were working in an unplanted field on Slaybacon. The ground had been plowed but had not yet been harrowed and was uneven, making walking difficult. For some reason, an argument started and tempers began to escalate. A couple of the Elliott boys were there, too, and their presence called for both brothers to show as much bravado as possible. Noell swung at Edwin and landed a pretty good blow to the upper body. Edwin was caught off guard and Noell's aggressiveness surprised him. He angrily responded, shoving Noell backward into a freshly plowed furrow. Now Noell was really angry and he looked around for some object that he might hurl at his bigger brother. He reached for a rock partially exposed in the dark earth, but it was larger than it appeared and required both hands. As he bent to lift this rock which was much too large for a boy his size to heave, he grunted mightily, stumbled and pitched forward into the brown dirt, face first. The tension broken, we all laughed, but that was a mistake. Now Noell was not only mad, he had been humiliated too. Swann and John Elliott sensing the graveness of the situation quickly held Noell trying to help calm him. Meantime, Edwin literally rolled on the ground trying to control his laughter. Once Noell was able to get his temper under control, he stopped crying and finally stood between his best buddies who still clung to him. He smiled faintly while huge tears washed the fresh dirt down his face leaving white trails. It was over! We all laughed with relief and good feeling and bragged about how big that rock was that Noell almost threw at his brother.

In addition to the actual adventures that we experienced, there were also the stories we had heard and witnessed in our graphic imaginations. A story heard and imagined in most cases is more dramatic than the actual event. We had vast storehouses of such adventures, heard and imagined, that we could share and relive again on a moment's notice. One of these involved Noell and our bird dog,

Kate. Kate was an English Setter with the tangerine and white color combination. Like all Setters she had luxurious, long hair on her tail, ears, and legs. She was a pretty dog and had a gentle disposition. The story took place at the bridge across Sweetwater Creek on Slaybacon Road.

After World War II, the bridge on Slaybacon Road was rebuilt and the creek bed under the bridge was lowered. Before that, the creek sometimes flooded, completely covering the bridge. The old bridge floor consisted of wide planking, which rattled when a vehicle or wagon crossed. The ends of the planks were uneven and the timbers underneath were resting on an old stone foundation, giving the appearance of a structure that was not too safe. Nevertheless, the bridge was an interesting and exciting place. Large maple trees grew on the creek banks and alder bushes hung over the water. Just downstream a ragged fence of barbed wire and wood was stretched across from bank to bank to prevent cattle from the fields below escaping up the creek. When the creek was up, the lower wires were under water and it was interesting to watch to current work against the wood pieces, which were connected to the wires to keep them the correct distance apart. The constant and irregular movements of the make-do fence was interesting to watch. The bridge was a good place to rest in the shade, and we would often lie flat on the planking facing down the creek and stare into the water, watching for darting fish or other objects floating on the current. After a rain, the creek was muddy colored and its level would rise. These were the times when I would think of how Kate, the bird dog, saved my brother Noell's life. Noell and Edwin were on their way home from Granddaddy's after a summer thunderstorm. When they got to the bridge as always, they decided to stop and watch the swirling water. Staring at moving water sometimes causes dizziness, or according to my brothers, "It'll cause your head to swim." Well, Noell's head began to swim, and he toppled into the rushing creek. Kate barked excitedly getting Edwin's attention and then she leaped headlong into the swift water, grabbing Noell's overalls in her teeth and struggling against the current. With the dog's help, Edwin was able to pull Noell to the bank where he could grab alder bushes and pull his brother out of the water. Noell was helpless against the current and, with his loose clothes, would have been swept under and carried downstream had it not been for that wonderful dog and an older brother, strong beyond his years, in the face of an almost certain tragedy. In the years that followed a mere crossing of that bridge generated feelings of closeness among us and a special affection for dogs. Even now when I look at moving water, I know to hold on in case my head starts to swim.

When Noell was a senior in high school there were only eleven grades rather than the twelve grades common today. The nation was deep in war and times were pretty serious for citizens of all ages, including adolescents. Every family was touched personally by the war and it seemed that every home up and down Sweetwater had a flag in the window with a white star for each family member serving in the Armed Forces. One family on Beech Creek had a flag with four white stars and a fifth son not quite old enough to serve. Boys Noell's age were focused on the war and most of them were drafted at 18 or volunteered as soon as they reached legal age. Noell turned seventeen in January and enlisted immediately in the U.S. Navy. Being under 18 his enlistment required his parents' written consent and, of course, both of them willingly agreed out of a sense of duty. It must have broken their hearts to see him go. I know it did mine. When Noell enlisted, there were two stars on our window flag. We really could have had three, because Audie Willcox was thought of as a family member. Audie's star would have been gold, because he never came home from the war and rests somewhere in Italy.

Robbinsville High School suspended football at the end of the 1941–42 school year for the duration. There simply weren't enough boys in the small schools to field a team. Those who didn't volunteer were drafted. It is difficult to know if Noell would have played football had there been an opportunity. His interests seemed to go in other directions, particularly in the area of science. He and a classmate, Donald Allen, were forever experimenting with whatever could be scrounged from the school lab or any other possible source. They learned to make black powder and concocted some wonderful explosions that were bragged about for years to come. They also had a lot of fun playing with a carbide lamp like the miners used. They would scorch their initials or clever sayings on the unfinished walls of the upstairs rooms. The carbide lamp also provided illumination in the attic where Noell fashioned a table where we would construct model airplanes from kits of stamped balsa wood, glue, and paper. Noell's nature was inquisitive and the world was literally full of opportunities for exploration, experimentation, and discovery. The simplest, most straightforward activity could be turned into a spellbinder. For example, splitting acid wood with the help of homemade black powder was a lot more fun than splitting it the hard way with an axe or hammer and wedge. First of all, the acid wood log had to be split part way to provide a crack into which black powder could be packed. Often as not, there would be nothing more than a bright "flash in the pan" when the powder was ignited. There were, however, some practical applications for things Noell had learned about, or just imagined. One of these was the use of a hangman's knot. Somewhere he had learned how to fashion a hangman's noose with a common piece of rope. Since there was nothing that needed hanging that would require something as strong as a rope, Noell had to adjust his thinking downward. A camping trip and dynamite blasting wire provided the opportunity. Dad had brought home from Fontana Dam, dozens of feet of blasting wire which is small, flexible copper wire covered with a layer of soft insulation. This wire served many ordinary uses around the farm, but my brother imagined a new purpose for it. He found that the wire was flexible enough, and sturdy enough to be wrapped and twisted into a small, but authentic, hangman's noose. An opportunity to use it was no farther away than a camping trip to the Cody Flats. It was our custom to quietly snatch a chicken from the roost as we left for our night in the woods. Even a laying hen is pretty good when you are really hungry and cooking your own supper over a fire. Full grown roosters are to be avoided if possible. We didn't have to "steal" a chicken; we would have been welcome simply by asking. Somehow that didn't seem as sporting as snatching a sleeping chicken from its perch. Ordinarily we would wring the chicken's neck, or do the deed with an axe and chop block, but a new and different possibility was staring us in the face. Noell conducted a tribunal, at which we found the chicken guilty of being a chicken, and the sentence was to be a hanging. He carefully wrapped and tied a noose from blasting wire, all the while explaining why he was doing what, until the noose was ready. The main event required the help of the rest of us. We helped boost the hangman onto the lower limbs of a large tree and there he placed the noose over the chicken's head, tightened it and dropped the chicken. The hangman's noose worked, but it was a frightened, chastened, and shamefaced group of boys who struggled through the most disappointing chicken dinner of a lifetime.

In high school, Noell became friends with the shop teacher and enjoyed helping out on practical projects that this teacher might be called upon to do. Electricity was most fascinating to him and once he found himself helping the teacher with a wiring problem in the crawl space above the ceiling in the high school classroom building. The high school building was a long, low building made of native stone. A hallway ran the entire length of the building and there were classrooms and offices on each side of the hall. Ceilings in the classrooms were made of a lightweight fiberboard material. Working above Herbert Carpenter's classroom, Noell and the shop teacher struggled in the darkness with only a flashlight to guide them. Noell stumbled or tripped and fell forward between the rafters. The fiber board shattered under his weight and with a great clatter, Noell, a dozen square feet of broken fiberboard, several year's accumulation of dust, and a flashlight dropped through the gaping hole in the ceiling and landed squarely atop a long oak table in the back of the social studies classroom. Noell, dust covered and startled, but unhurt, rose like some specter from the rubble and looked around. In this scene of chaos, the head of the shop teacher appeared in the hole in the ceiling with an expression of extreme alarm. The students in the room were huddled against the walls and pure silence reigned. Herbert Carpenter, realizing no one was killed and wanting to regain control of his classroom approached Noell and said, "Well, Mr. Denton, we hope you will drop in again sometime."

My middle brother had a profound sense of duty all of his days. Is that the reason he came back to the place he was born for those last but painfully significant years? Certainly the light of his leadership never burned more brightly than during those struggles when he taught by example, shared dreams through his own creative initiative, and caused a broken people to generate new confidence in themselves in a county with the most limited economy in the state. My brother's people, my people, our people had endured isolation, neglect both benign and cruel, and the abuse of their resources for generations. And he helped them look toward a horizon, which had been elevated by hope and possibility. A portion of that hope had been upon the shoulders of Graham Noell Denton. And when he fell in 1981, his dreams not yet finished, he accepted with rare grace and stoicism, what he couldn't change, and offered comfort to his bed mates there in the Veterans Hospital even as he died. The price he paid for the good that he brought turned out to be the ultimate sacrifice.

None of us can know with certainty the private burdens he endured. And none of us can fully grasp the grandness and the promise of the dreams he held...dreams that he fashioned and framed like lovely paintings only to give them away. Noell believed that a dream fulfilled, a dream realized was a dream shared! Can anyone of us ever know the depth of the responsibility that Noell felt about being near at hand during the declining years of Mom and Dad? His little sister, JoAnn, needed an ally beyond the unconditional love and support that her parents offered. Noell was there during the critical times. His presence, his steadfastness, his self sacrifice were gifts beyond measure to Mom and Dad and JoAnn. We can only speculate about what was in Noell's mind and heart when he moved his family back to Graham County. As witnesses to the footprints that he left, we can determine with certainty that every change of direction was carried out with purpose and stirred by a sense of duty. His seventeenth birthday had scarcely passed when he forsook the warmth of home and mother and enlisted. No one asked him to go, and no force outside himself brought him back home for the sunset years of his parents and his sister. Sundown for him came earlier than expected.

Waiting for Toby Dog

It was after supper and late in the day – almost dark. We were sitting on a couple of blocks of wood perhaps a foot long and about as wide. There were piles of stove wood and kindling already split and ready for the wood box behind the cook stove in the kitchen. The wood yard where we were sitting was between the lane and the branch which originated with a spring way up in the Harwood Cove. Great Granddaddy Harwood had settled this land in the last century. He and his family had prospered, acquiring much mountain land and operating the largest grist mill and saw mill anywhere in Western North Carolina. That mill stood until 1947 when my brother Noell and I tore it down plank by plank so Daddy could use the material to build the large dairy barn he had dreamed about all his life.

The old house, as we called it, was built by Granddaddy Harwood and that is where Grandma Denton was born. The old house and several outbuildings along with 28 acres of land became Mom and Dad's home in the 1920s. It was here that most of us were born, all of us were loved, brooded, and nourished like a family of partridge until it was time for us to leave the nest and scatter. Like the partridge we each found our own nesting places, many of them far away, but we never forgot the way back to the old house.

A pathway led from the end of the upper porch to the fence which enclosed the farmstead. The pathway divided a few feet from the house and led either to the spring house or to the small gate. The wooden gate was perhaps three feet wide and attached to one post by hinges. The gate was light enough to be pulled open by a child and was self closing by way of steel plowshares suspended by a piece of rope. Each time the gate was opened or closed the clanking plowshare and squeaking of rusty hinges signaled to all of us that someone was coming or going.

Just above the wood yard was a foot bridge that crossed the branch and a path led to two outdoor privies underneath a large white oak tree. On the bank of the branch were two large holly trees which added color, aroma, and beauty at any time of the year. Pig Pen Branch danced and sparkled as it made its way past our house and on to the creek and ultimately into the Gulf of Mexico.

Sitting there in the wood yard we could look at the soft light coming through windows on each side of the stone chimney. The chimney was covered with English Ivy and became in a moment's imagination the rude and dark features of some being which existed fleetingly in our minds with the windows and their warm light forming the eyes of this specter – taking away any fearsome thoughts. Inside, on a summer night when the windows were open we could listen to the happy sounds of the branch as we drifted into the perfect sleep, reserved by the Deity for children who lay curled in the arms of a brother or sister.

The shadows grew longer as we continued to sit looking down the lane toward the road. We were waiting for Daddy to come home from some far-off place which we knew only by name – Altavista, Virginia, or possibly Lynchburg. Daddy didn't get home often in those days, but when he was expected we would wait for hours listening for the slow crawl of an automobile making its way through the deep ruts of Sweetwater Road, or at last headlights turning up the lane past the mailboxes, up to the wood yard where we sat. As we waited, our imaginations ran wild and we talked of many things. Suddenly, a small dog trotted by not far from where we sat and continued down the lane toward the road. Though we called and probably chased it, the small dog continued until it was out of sight and gone. We never saw that dog again, but it assumed a presence in our lives that continues to this day. That experience brought Toby Dog into our lives. Toby, along with his litter mates, provided hours of wonderful escape into that world occupied by children and animals with remarkable names and habits, each unique and capable of all things which can be imagined, including funny ways of speaking. Toby Dog's siblings had names like Dinner

Dog, Supper Dog, and Breakfast Dog. Sometimes there were others with names not related to mealtime, and these lesser characters were played by friends while Toby and the mealtime namesakes were reserved for blood brothers and sisters. Both of us could testify to the actual existence of that small dog which granted us that brief and happy chase in his twilight world. Yes, he was there, so close, just barely beyond reach. Not to be denied, Toby Dog was created by you out of that experience and he embodied the spirit of your free ranging personality and sense of self direction which continue to mark your manner of living . The little black and white dog that for a moment entered our consciousness was never seen again. Though we never touched him we have been able to claim him as our own forever, and he lives yet, sometimes in the gray shadows of twilight as when we first glimpsed him, and at other times in the burst of bright sunshine and in the happy echoes of children's laughter.

Possibly no experience is as defining as the creation of Toby Dog in the lives of the two of us remaining. At once it describes many of the elements that have remained central in the way we constructed our lives intellectually and spiritually. Remember, when he visited our senses for those few seconds, we were waiting for Daddy. We knew he would come, it was only a question of time. Besides it was the joy of gratification postponed that we treasured perhaps more than the event itself. We were able to touch what we couldn't see, and to hold and embrace for a lifetime something we may never have been able to claim in reality. Not only in Toby Dog who came to us even while we waited with certain and expectant hearts for something else worth treasuring – Daddy in his sweet magnificence, more adored from afar than up close – but in a thousand other experiences down through the years when we were able to discover that the unspoken certainty of becoming what we were at times only able to reach for was enough to allow us to endure what seemed beyond endurance as we lived through and beyond the deaths of our brothers and sisters and parents. Somehow, my sister, we have been able to look beyond what has been and fasten our minds and souls on the possibility of what may yet be, or more properly, what will be.

I recall a gray Saturday on the upper porch of the old house. I can smell supper cooking in the kitchen, and I can see the zinnias and marigolds in Mama's flower garden with the rock border between the porch and the chicken house. In the corner next to the kitchen door was a small wooden table with a galvanized water bucket and a blue speckled enamel wash pan where the grown-ups and sometimes the children would wash their hands before meals. I'm certain I can still smell the Lifebuoy soap and see the spot of bare slick earth near the flower beds where family members would toss the wash pan of dirty water when they were through. There were straight back chairs on the upper porch and a rocker where Bud Bumgarner sat and peeled apples with his pocket knife and told tales.

On this Saturday as on most others we were waiting for the *Asheville Citizen* newspaper with the "red funnies." You would say, "I want Tille the Toiler," and some other child's voice would cry, "I want Maggie and Jiggs," and a third would state, "I get Little Orphan Annie first." Ordinary events among ordinary people? Hardly! It seems to me that in that remarkable household there was always the ability to transform the ordinary into the sublime. That old house held generations of hopes and dreams fueled by a love of family unique among people anywhere.

As I mentioned before, the first song that I distinctly remember hearing on the radio was on another Saturday after baths in the kitchen near the cook stove. The song stirred me then and even a fleeting memory of that moment brings it all back. Possibly it is and has been music that has set us apart and helped define a central characteristic in us regarding how we perceive, interpret, and respond emotionally to everyday experiences. The song on the radio was " I'm Just Here to Get My Baby Out of Jail." It was the melody which carried the message and not the lyrics. I'm sure I did not understand the intended meaning of the words, "Here to get my baby out of jail," but there is no question whatsoever about the chord progressions and the melancholy melody's impact upon my whole being. On another day it would be Vernon Dahlhart singing "Flowers from My Angel Mother's Grave," his spectacular tenor voice transported to us through the old, hand-cranked Victrola. (Vernon Dahlhart was a famous opera singer in the 1920s who supposedly became one of the first million sellers with his recording of the crossover country melody, "Prisoner's Song.") On yet another evening my senses would be helped to transcend mere mortal experiences as I sat mesmerized by sounds of a full orchestra with strings bringing me "Humoresque" or a Viennese waltz in a corner bedroom upstairs at Aunt Carrie Harwood's. As a boy I often stayed overnight there after feeding the animals, bringing in wood, and taking care of the milking.

Much of the pure joy that I have experienced in my life has come to me through the music of my early years. It has been replayed a million times in a million different places. It is always the same, wonderful, profound, and unexpectedly moving whenever it is heard or felt.

At other times we looked down the lane toward the road in anticipation of a brown package on the ledge beside the mailbox. Sometimes, but not often, there would be two packages, one of them on the ground. Packages came from places like Sears Roebuck, Montgomery Ward, and occasionally from somewhere called Spiegels. Packages were awaited at our mailbox generally twice a year. Most years Mom would send out an order in August for school clothes. When we were younger, an August package could mean a pair of overalls, flannel shirts or long underwear for both girls and boys. Shoes were usually not ordered, but boots were, and boots with heels and hooks were really special because the men and big boys who logged or cut timber always wore them.

Although the end of summer meant school, waiting for a package was something looked forward to for months. It didn't really matter what was in the packages since not all packages contained something for each child. Knowing that a package was coming was the source of our pleasure, and that happy circumstance has served us for a lifetime. What a blessing to have been conditioned early in life to draw pleasure from what might be, and to have had the wellspring of hope and belief so carefully and thoughtfully nourished while we were yet too young to have been beaten down by loss and disappointment. Since our very hopes and dreams were so central in this kind of thinking and expectation, when the storms and tragedies that befall all families began to overtake us, we were able to remain anchored, for the most part, and never permanently cut adrift as so many around us have been.

Spending two years in the seventh grade served to prolong the singular disgrace that I had heaped upon my family and myself. Even while it was happening though, it was not to be allowed to kill the seed of what I was to become – someday. During that period of aloneness and shame, those few precious constants in my existence became to focus of not only my energy, which was expressed in brutally hard and endless work, but more so in my spiritual and emotional existence, which remained centered upon those deep and warm sentiments which I felt and experienced through music, imagination, anticipation, sharing and being connected through football, loving and being loved. Through those scattered minutes and memories, I constructed a multi-colored mosaic of dreamlike experiences and wishes, which for me became a patchwork piece of heaven while I was too busy becoming to risk the very real possibility of dropping out.

A glimpse into this little visited universe might include a scenario such as this: More than one day drew to a close during those critical years with these thoughts and feelings providing the blanket which warmly enveloped me as I blew out the kerosene lamp and drifted into tomorrow. As I undressed and sat for a moment on the side of the bed and looked around the room, the pale light of the lamp created shifting shadows on the dark, coarse, unpainted boards of the wall and ceiling of my room upstairs. There was a calfskin rug on the floor that was soft and comfortable to my feet. In those days saying my prayers was serious business, so I would get down on my knees and pray in much the same way I had done since I was first taught a children's prayer. Sometimes I would wonder what I would do when I was in the Air Force or Navy and it was time to say my prayers.

Reading was always considered important in our home, and I think all of us developed the happy habit of reading in bed. Flora Cody operated an extension of the county library in her home just up the road and the delivery man came every two weeks, so I was never without a good book. Good books included everything written by Zane Grey, Edgar Rice Burroughs, James Oliver Curwood, and Jack London. With my head filled with the description Zane Grey painted so dramatically of the great southwest, and my soul set aflame with the account of Arizona Ames, our hero, meeting and being overcome with the beauty and wonder of the new school teacher who had come to settle in the Rim country, I drifted quietly into a state of semiconscious bliss, my senses massaged with the thoughts and pictures in my mind, and my soul touched and soothed by the sound of a lovely voice and the mellow ringing notes of the piano. If the notes and chords and movements had been created in my own imagination, they could not have settled more harmoniously upon my soul than those I remember and hear even now.

David M. Denton
January 1 998

The Two of Us...

The fountain in front of the old stone schoolhouse was a gathering place. I suppose that was common practice in those days…it was just an ordinary fountain at an ordinary school. In my memory it was octagonal in shape, with perhaps eight heads projecting out of the stone, each one of them spouting a small stream of water. It was just before dark, and to enter the auditorium one had to walk past the fountain, either to the left or right. There was a handful of kids and a few adults, standing around. It is strange why the memory of things like fountains remain plastered forever on the walls of the mind, when the memories of other things far more worthy of being permanently stored away evaporate in time and space. From each of the little spigots there was a trail of color on the stone where the minerals from this good mountain water had left their trace. The streams of water mixed with grime from dirty hands, spit, and an occasional smattering of blood from a nosebleed left over from a playground fight would flow, mixed together, to the grate in the center of the fountain and disappear. The design of the fountain was imperfect and there was always a trickle of water spilling down the outside wall. In the wintertime this would freeze. Also, as the pupils drank, and played, and splashed in the water the area around the fountain would become wet, and this too would freeze and was a favorite skating place.

As we walked into the auditorium, one of those instant associations moved quickly to a level of consciousness…the association between the smell of oiled hardwood floors and school buildings. Other remembered associations with schools include the smell of new denim, the smell of chalk, and the smell of new cedar shavings and graphite from the pencil sharpener. Some of these associations assume a mildly positive response, while others provoke negative feelings. The smell of denim in those early years made me homesick because it meant the end of summer and a time of separation and uncertainty from things that were familiar and secure. On this night, however, the smell of oiled hardwood floors was pleasant because this was a very special experience.

In reality, the seats in the old auditorium were hard and uncomfortable, even though they were contoured to fit the anatomy of the bottom side. Maybe it was because I was skinny, but the contours didn't help. The excitement of the upcoming program was distraction enough that I didn't even think about discomfort. The houselights were soft, and I remember the old maroon colored stage curtains.

With the introductory notes from the piano, she stepped toward the microphone, and taking a quick breath I moved toward the edge of my seat. The song was "Indian Love Call" and the voice was something that the walls of this old auditorium were unaccustomed to. The other students who had performed were good...aaaaah, but this was something quite special. The sound system, although archaic by modern standards, gave pure power and range to this developing voice, and the place became deathly quiet. This audience was unaccustomed to this kind of performance, this kind of music, this kind of quality; but, I smiled inwardly with the quiet knowledge that this is what one could expect when a Denton came onto the stage. She was the fourth of six children, and I was the fifth...both of us blessed, or more properly cursed, by being middle children. Although close in age, separated by about nineteen months, we were never particularly close as brother and sister. Oh, we got along well and there was no real problem between us. It was that she was just, well, different. For one thing, she was perhaps the most attractive of the six children, and that hasn't changed. She is as striking today as she was then. As she stood facing the audience, holding lightly to the microphone stand first with the one hand and then the other, relaxed and in complete control, I thought to myself that this must be the ultimate experience for a kid. She was so beautiful and so indifferent to that reality. That voice was so rich, so trained...so unexpected. Nothing ordinary about this event.

Music was already a central force in my being, and experiencing such skill and power with the art on the part of my sister, simply added truth and meaning to the whole thing. The frames of this video, as they are played back in the front of my mind, spring loose memories of other experiences, some of them to be repeated a hundred times over. During my adolescent years I found deep-down joy connecting the experiences shared with me vicariously by Zane Grey and the actual, real life pleasures of the sound of her voice and the piano drifting up the staircase and through the cracks between those rough-sawn boards in my bedroom directly above the living room where she "performed" as it were, for my joy alone…at least it seemed that way. Some nights I would play along with my guitar and we would sing together, but it was always as if she were the pro and I was the novice.

Our association during those high school years was pleasant. The activities in which we found ourselves involved together usually included music, in some form or another. Most of the time, however, I was the spectator and she was the event. Her friends were my friends, up to a point. Her boyfriends were fellow athletes, or friends with whom one could make music – a couple of years older, but nonetheless compatible. Her girlfriends were obviously a couple of years older, too, and the source of some fabulous fantasies on my part. One of them in particular I remember would stay overnight at our house, and on occasion she would walk up behind me and put her arms around me saying nice things in my ear and squeezing me softly against her well-developed breasts. She tended to wear knit sweaters and wool skirts which did a lot for my well-developed feelings of sexual discovery. One of these girls used to come and spend several nights at a time with us, and we would sit around the living room kidding, playing set-back, and smoking cigarettes after Dad went to bed. This was during my senior year in high school and just a matter of weeks before I enlisted in the Air Force. Gwen was already in college at this time, but she was home between quarters or something. I figured if I was going away to war, I was old enough to make other decisions on my own; thus, I found the courage to light my first Camel in Dad's presence. He said nothing but maintained a very severe expression of disapproval which lasted perhaps thirty seconds, but it could have been thirty minutes from the way it felt. But, what was new about that?

The next four years in the military, and away from home, changed a lot of things, and perhaps changed nothing at the same time. Sometimes time and distance heighten and sharpen one's objectivity. In other cases they just stir the fog of illusion. During my absence from home, friends and everything dear, I idealized my family to the degree that that idealization interfered with the establishment of more practical realities in later years. Perhaps there were fewer illusions maintained regarding Gwen than any of the other brothers or sisters. First of all, she doesn't project illusions, and secondly, there was always a distance between us that was never quite closed…not an uncomfortable or strained distance, understand, but more probably a silent statement of her sense of privacy and apartness. This quality I respected, even if I didn't understand it; maybe I still don't. In terms of raw intellectual potential, Gwen is probably the most capable of the group. Her brightness was not particularly evident from her grades in high school, nor from her grades in the early years in college. It was not until later when she was on her own…down and out, divorced and responsible for three kids that her mental toughness and stubborn resolve moved in and pushed aside such characteristics as self-pity, and even such realities as poverty. When I remember back to those years, I still can experience some of the hurt that I felt for her…not about her, but I remember with equal clarity, and perhaps with even more emotion, the admiration and the respect that I felt for her. I am aware as I sit here thinking that a smile just moved across my face displacing some other expression. This smile is an acknowledgment of my sister's tenderness which underlies her toughness. Her eyes are the source of this modest betrayal of a will to beat the odds when the odds seem unbeatable. Wasn't it enough to simply have to rear three kids without a husband and a father? Wasn't it enough to have to fight and struggle for every damn penny of support? Wasn't it enough to be kicked in the teeth? The agony of her struggles, the ecstasy of her kind spirit…these are reason enough for the smile to prove worthy of conscious reaction. Wasn't it enough to have to go back with your face in the wind, your chin slightly elevated, your fatigue expressed only by an ever so slight droop of the shoulders…to have to go back and complete that under-graduate degree. Wasn't it enough?…Apparently not! The under-graduate degree would have satisfied the need to prove to oneself that it was not only within reach, it was also, by God, in grasp. The motivation was more complex than to prove…and deeper too. So the years of commuting to the University of South Carolina in Columbia, and the years of commuting by Amtrak, by automobile, and by plane to the seminars and workshops at Georgetown University became a part of the history in the intellectual, ethical and professional development of a very unique woman. And then the master's degree, and then the family practice. Toughness was beginning to pay off with a soul full of intuition, with a head full of knowledge, and with a briefcase full of credentials. She converted a struggle into a life, into a career with meaning, with dignity, and with reward. If one doesn't understand the nature of things, they sometimes appear to exist in contradiction. For example, it is hard to imagine those tough, dry six foot tall ferns of asparagus in mid-winter as being just weeks away from that tender, succulent and innocent delicacy that we can snap with our fingers in May. No contradiction at all, they are one and the same. The only difference is time and the process. So it was with her. The wonderful thing about the whole scheme is that the tenderness is never lost, and in the case of my sister Gwen, we don't even have to wait until springtime to experience it. But, the toughness is also good. Without it she would long since have been fractured, or maybe even worse, bent and twisted by the forces against which she wrestled.

She remains true to herself and to the sweet and tender things which shaped her…most of all, music. It is now more than forty years since those nights when I would lie in the darkness listening to the piano, almost able to anticipate every number that she would select…many of them were her own compositions, and those were the ones that I loved most of all. Perhaps I have come to understand the meaning of the words "blood is thicker than water" when I think of the bond between us. It is deeper than the simple genetic tie. It is stronger than the similarity of eye color and hair texture…yes, it is thicker than water. In fact, it is almost as heavy and as dense as honey once the water has been evaporated from the nectar and it has been allowed to distill and settle...sweetness too. I could pull the old straight-back chair up near the piano and we could move from song to song, from melody to melody, from composition to composition without missing a chord, without dropping a note. This was not a measure of our musical skill, but an expression of a common quality sensed and understood, although never stated in words. During all those years of upheaval, of hurt and disappointment, of struggle and sacrifice, she maintained her claim to that central part of her character, her music. We can hock the television, but the piano stays. How many times I have wondered about the music which has always been the common ground which the two of us share. She likes the kind of music that I like, and I like the kind of music that she likes. In all probability, I couldn't explain why, but in all probability I can listen to a song once and know whether or not it will become one of hers. Strange, too, I can still pull up a chair near the piano, with all of that time which has come and gone separating then and now, and instinctively play along with her, sensing a chord change, a shift in tempo before she gives away the first clue.

She is my sister; she has been since 1931. It has always mattered, but now it really matters. The two of us...sometimes I feel like it's the two of us, and the rest of the world, with all of those hellish forces bent on finishing off this generation. How puzzling because it hasn't been so long since we walked hand-in-hand up the branch without shoes, and with the full warmth of summer sunshine on our faces, happy and free, and waiting for the wonder and the discoveries of another day in that little remote, shut-off from the rest-of-the-universe world in which we lived. Oh...life would go on forever. There was Mom and Dad and six of us kids. Well, my sister, life has lost some of its glitter, but it is still full of surprises. The pain which we understood only in a detached and distant way has come home to roost not once, but several times. Still, there is sweetness and always, at my election, when I close my eyes and depress the play button, I can see the light coming in from that strange window in my bedroom. (Even standing on tiptoe, I couldn't see over the windowsill; why would they build it that way in the first place?) No, that is not the important thing; with my eyes closed, yes, I am aware of the light coming in the window, but I can see, too, the boards in the ceiling, the nailheads and the knots. I wait and my pulse increases, and then the first strains of "Song of India" or maybe "La Paloma" will be the first one that she plays tonight…and then oblivion. I float unconscious, undisturbed, carried softly on the sounds which soothe and caress before they fade entirely.

My sister, this is not just a memory, it is a statement of reality, it is also a celebration of now. Even today as much as I know about you, as much as I have studied and thought about you, there is much that I don't know. That really doesn't matter. My sense of certainty, my sense of peace and security rest comfortably on my love and respect for you. You are a survivor and a fighter. You are also a peace maker and a counselor. Sometimes you are a bit clinical in your approach, but always you come at life, and you come at people with a desire to know the truth, to look at it squarely in the face, and then simply to go on and do what you have to do. You are still awfully pretty, and besides that, I like you.

David M. Denton
January 1990

Unfinished (Remembering a Sister)

In February 1963, we were living in Reseda, California, perhaps a mile from the campus of California State University Northridge. I was enrolled in a graduate program at the University entitled "Leadership Training in the Area of the Deaf"; being one of ten persons selected in national competition. The program involved thirty-two semester hours of course work and a variety of field work experiences available at that time only in a place like California.

One Saturday morning Macon Richardson showed up unexpectedly on our doorstep. Macon was my sister JoAnne's husband and he was on his way to join her in Mountain View, just outside San Jose. She had recently moved there from North Carolina, and I assumed Macon had gotten our address from her. In looking back it appears obvious that their marriage was going through a rocky stage, though I was not really aware of it at the time. That morning Macon and I drove to Van de Kamp's bakery and coffee shop on Reseda Boulevard so we could talk freely over coffee. Mary was two and David was five at the time, so adult conversation would have been difficult at the house.

Macon was not someone whom I knew well, but he was intelligent, charming, and seemed generally interested in working things out with my sister. He stayed overnight with us and left the next day for the Bay area. I never saw him again, and in the years since 1963 have had no contact with him or even any news as to his whereabouts. I guess I had expected that he would remain in the family and that we would stay in touch because I had given him my Gibson guitar. He had expressed an interest in it, and although it meant a great deal to me, for some reason I wanted him to have it. Subconsciously perhaps, I really wanted to do something for JoAnne. The answer will probably never be revealed, but it doesn't matter because I have complete contentment about the matter. The significance of the guitar needs to be explained, however, since it has already claimed a place in this attempt to commit to paper some thoughts and feelings about my younger sister which are long overdue in finding adequate expression.

Shortly after arriving in Corbin, Kentucky, in the early months of 1956, I saw this instrument through the window of a music store on North Main Street. A Gibson guitar was the instrument of choice among the artists of the day whom I admired, and this model J-50 was a real treasure. This is the guitar that I played at Cumberland Falls while entertaining the guests at the DuPont Lodge between shifts at the front desk. This was the guitar that I was playing the first time Peggy and I sang together. It really got a workout that summer. Evenings during the annual month-long appearance of the Pioneer Playhouse, a buddy who played bongo drums and I would play a set before curtain call on the terrace of the lodge overlooking the Cumberland River. One night while playing and singing down on the riverbank above the falls, the music stopped only when I was down to three strings remaining. Musically, the summer of 1956 was a landmark. Peggy and I settled into a serious relationship, which revolved around our unusually close harmony and shared love of the art. Unexpected opportunities came along too, but eventually they had to give way to emerging new priorities in my life; Peggy and the matter of an adequate education.

The owner of the Campbell House in Lexington was a brother of the Director of Kentucky Parks and Recreation who had heard me perform at the lodge. He was involved in an effort to buy a suburban hotel in Palm Beach, Florida, and wanted me to join him in this new venture as a roving troubadour moving among the tables and entertaining his guests. He didn't buy the hotel, but I was given a suite at the Campbell House for a weekend with meals in return for serving as guest entertainer.

A woman from Cincinnati who became a frequent guest of DuPont Lodge that summer became interested in promoting me and was able to secure an audition on the Arthur Godfry Talent Scouts' program. This culminated at just about the same time that I registered at Cumberland College in Williamsburg, about twenty miles away. Another frequent visitor to Cumberland Falls was a pianist with Ray Block orchestra. He guaranteed me full employment and an opportunity to really get my career going if I would return with him to New York. It was kind of flattering to have such interest expressed in my talent, but I realized before committing to a trip to the Big Apple that the musician might have his mind on something other than my guitar and my voice. There was another offer that was harder to turn down than the one from New York. Three young women from Lexington who were associated with radio station WLAP offered employment at the station, immediate and full with other enticements, never stated, but expressed in a rather transparent manner. I declined, and thus a glorious summer came to an end.

That guitar served us through many beautiful and satisfying musical experiences in the months and years that followed. While at the University of North Carolina in 1957, Peggy and I had the privilege of appearing weekly on WTVD channel 11 in Durham. The show was *Saturday Night Country Style* and we did mostly calypso numbers there. That old guitar remained a daily companion until our move to California. Before returning to North Carolina, we bought a lovely Mexican classical guitar in Tijuana for sixty dollars.

During the summer the other graduate students and I were located in San Francisco Bay area for about ten days of fieldwork in a variety of agencies which provided services of one kind or another to deaf people. We roomed at the California School for the Deaf in Berkeley during this visit and spent our days moving from agency to agency throughout the metro area from San Francisco down to San Jose and between. I had told JoAnne when I would be in that part of the state, and she had invited me for dinner and a visit one evening mid week. Peggy and the children were back in the San Fernando Valley, so I made the trip down the peninsula to Mountain View alone. JoAnne's apartment was in a lovely area and I remember being amused at the names of the streets. It seems that I turned off Montevideo Blvd. onto Monte Vista Street, in the town of Mountain View, all three of which mean the same thing.

We had a very pleasant and meaningful visit although the atmosphere was charged with a sense of mild melancholy. I remember thinking at the time that this feeling was that the two of us, brother and sister, were together for a time in such a distant place under the most unlikely circumstances. I'm so glad I was there. We did not talk much about Macon, scarcely at all, but it seemed clear that he was gone from the marriage. JoAnne was in fine spirits and really looked beautiful. She was robust and happy and her apartment reflected the loves and passions of her life. Samples of her art were everywhere, as always tastefully displayed, and quite eclectic in variety. Her artwork included several lovely samples of ceramics. Naturally, there were books everywhere and they too represented broad and divergent tastes. Most of her reading was hardcover, very few paperbacks, and I don't think there was a single romance novel or common thriller in the place. I knew I was in the company of someone not ordinary. This small and intimate environment which she had created for herself mirrored the best and the noblest of her character. As we sat and talked after dinner, the music from her fabulous record collection settled upon us like a soft, warm blanket. There was not to be another opportunity for intimate intellectual and spiritual connection between us, expressed and understood without a word and without a touch. We visited for a couple of hours in this realm, both of us aware, I am sure, that this was a rare and transcendent experience touched by just a hint of uneasiness. Around midnight, I left and returned to Berkeley for the remainder of our fieldwork.

The Leadership Training Program ended in late August, so with a Master's degree in hand, we headed back across the country to Morganton where I assumed duties as Coordinator of the Lenoir Rhyne College program in Deafness at NCSD. It was good to be back in North Carolina, although I did not see JoAnne for some time. Later she returned east and lived for a while in Morganton. It was never clear to me what happened between her and Macon.

In December of 1954, I was discharged from the United States Air Force. Thirty-seven months of my four-year enlistment were spent at

Luke Field, Arizona, and it was there that I received my discharge. My old buddy Joe Mulvaney and I headed out across the desert one evening in mid December on our way home. I had bought a 1942 Buick automobile in Phoenix and everything the two of us owned on earth scarcely covered the back seat of the car, but we were civilians and that made us rich beyond measure. In a particularly desolate stretch of desert in New Mexico late at night, the car overheated and then the lights began to dim. Uh oh, this looked bad, but my experiences as an aircraft mechanic made me think that the problem must be the fan belt since the fan belt drives both the water pump and the generator. Joe remembered seeing a fan belt in the trunk so we began searching for a service station or any place where there might be water. Out of the darkness appeared an old roadside building with an ancient gas pump. We pulled over only to find the place closed and deserted. We did have tools and a flashlight and fortunately, there was a used fan belt in the trunk. With Joe holding the flashlight, I put on the belt, adjusted the generator support, tightened everything down and then we were ready, except for water. We searched around the old building and finally found a water spigot. Now we had water but nothing to carry it in. Our search produced nothing, not even an empty oil can. We had heard of people carrying water in a shoe, and thought about that. Then I remembered my Garrison hat. It had a plastic lining and would hold more water than a shoe. After several trips to the spigot, the radiator was full, and we were ready to go. We laughed deliriously, at our predicament, our ingenious solution, and most of all at our newfound liberty.

We arrived in western North Carolina a few days before Christmas, stopping first in Robbinsville. We stayed overnight at home and I drove Joe to Asheville the next day. At this time, JoAnne was a sophomore at Mars Hill College and from Asheville I drove on to Mars Hill, so I could bring her home for the holidays. It was still a couple of days before the Christmas break began, so Jo arranged for me to stay in the guest room of her dorm. Since I was still in uniform, the housemother was gracious to me. JoAnne, some of her girl friends and I had a delightful time about the campus and she was able to introduce me to college life. It was a great experience, and I was very impressed with the school especially the art lab. JoAnne was two years younger than me, and here she was halfway through college, and it seemed to me that I was hopelessly behind. In the years I had been away, she had grown up . . . was a woman now with a life of her own and talents quite beyond anything I had expected. She had a broad circle of friends, was deeply involved in the life of the campus, drama, music, art, academics. Four years ago when I had enlisted, she was only 16, not only young, but innocent and unaware. Or perhaps I was remembering back to what my life had been there on the farm and a world away. There had always been something just a bit unconventional about JoAnne. She had the soul and temperament of an artist and her intellectual compass inclined her toward an exploration of those things which stirred her imagination and spirit. I've often felt that if she could have been born at a different time or in a different place her emergence from the chrysalis which sheltered her there in the hills might have been seen and recognized in the fullness of its potential beauty and wonder. It was almost as if she had to test those glorious but fragile wings before they had time to dry and harden for the journey which lay ahead. For those who knew her well, however, there was a gift in her presence though it was as fleeting as the season of a romantic butterfly.

After graduating from Mars Hill, which was a two-year institution at that time, JoAnne secured a teaching position at Mountain View Elementary School, which served children in the remote northern part of Graham County. It was here that she began to build a legacy which still thrives and continues among those who came under her influence as a teacher with the hands of an artist and the heart of an angel. I believe it was here that she and Marilyn Brewer began to form a friendship which lasted to the end of their short lives. I knew Marilyn, and indeed had known her my entire life. She lived just up the road when we were children and she and Gwendolyn were bosom buddies all the way through school. Marilyn and I dated a few times following my Air Force years; happily she shared my love of music and we would sit for hours listening to her collection of Eddy Arnold records. JoAnne and Marilyn spent a year living together and teaching in Marathon,

Florida, one of the Keys. This was somewhere between the time of the beatniks and the flower children who took center stage in the sixties, but living and teaching in the Florida Keys was exotic enough of appeal to these free spirits who wanted to reach out and embrace life. For some, reading about living isn't enough.

For the next few years there was very little contact between JoAnne and me. In 1955 alone, I lived in Charlotte; Florence, South Carolina; Robbinsville; Marietta, Georgia; and Washington D.C. It wasn't until I made a weekend trip to Corbin, Kentucky, early in 1956, that I finally found what I was looking for and the unending search seemed to end. Once I got enrolled in college, things began to stabilize and by 1959 we were living in Morganton, North Carolina, where my career in education of the deaf got underway. JoAnne came to live with us for awhile on East Concord Street. David was a little fellow at this time and was quite fond of her. She always had music going, and of course, her room with its treasure trove of pretty and interesting things, attracted him like a magnet. From time to time he would go to Jo's room uninvited and she would good naturedly but firmly invite him, "Out, out, out!" One day he turned the tables on her and while imitating her pose, he pointed dramatically and shouted "Out, out, out." She remained in Morganton for awhile working in a law office before moving to the Chapel Hill area

She enrolled in the University of North Carolina and completed requirements for her degree. It was at UNC that she met Macon Richardson and they fell in love and were married. They remained in Chapel Hill until early 1963 when her move to Mountain View, California, took place. There was more than coincidence in the parallel moves which JoAnne made and the moves made by Peggy and me during those years. She had come to live with us in Williamsburg, Kentucky, for awhile when we were first married. This was in 1957 when I was at Cumberland. When we came to Morganton in 1959, she joined us there, and then in 1963 we moved to southern California and learned shortly thereafter that she had moved. I never understood the reason for these moves, but have always felt that they represent part of what seemed to me to be an unfulfilled search on her part for something that was missing in her life – A search for that deep and certain connection with someone close – A need to be near that blood connection – The need to claim a place within the fold never quite achieved or claimed. I thought about this at the time, and I've thought about it ever since, and it remains unresolved both in my mind and in my conscience. In later years after her health had failed and we would only see each other from time to time at a family gathering, I would find her looking at me with a profound hunger or need in her eyes. Always, she would quickly look away and the moment would settle into unexpressed uncertainty. What was it that she wanted to express? What was it that she wanted to feel? Was she craving some familial validation that could not be granted? Why was she denied the sense of unconditional belonging at the family table? How could such questions remain forever unanswered? Or more properly perhaps, why would such questions remain unasked?

The various households of the extended family were pursuing their separate dreams and responsibilities during the late sixties and seventies. We had moved to Maryland in 1967, our careers had taken off, our kids were growing up and life was good. Much the same could be said for the other brothers and sisters. All of the siblings managed to get together at Robbinsville perhaps once a year. Members of the other households got together periodically for a few days at the beach.

During the summer of 1978 Charles and Frankie, Mary and Bob, and Peggy and I with all our children were to rent a house and spend a week together at Kitty Hawk, North Carolina. For some reason Gwen and Jody and also Graham and Mary Jo never took part in our beach excursions. The same was true of JoAnne who at this time was living in Robbinsville next door to Mom and Dad. By mid-afternoon Saturday everyone had arrived and we were all settled into the beach house. Late in the day, Graham was able to track us down by telephone to break the news that JoAnne had died. Graham was living in Robbinsville also and the entire responsibility of dealing with the aftermath of her death had fallen upon his shoulders. He had a difficult and frustrating time finding out where we all were and finally finding the numbers of the realtor on the Outer Banks. The news traumatized all of us and it was not until the next morning that we were able to get on our way to the mountains. Certainly, this was one of the longest one-day trips in memory. From Kitty Hawk to Robbinsville is more than 500 miles, and the enormity of the emotional upheaval which we were experiencing made it all like an unending bad dream. She was 44 years old – where was the rationality in this death? How could it sneak upon us so unexpectedly? Or, did we know that JoAnne's internal flame had become a flicker and just couldn't deal with the terror of this potential reality? The hours were filled with minutes each one stretching longer than the one before it, like the road starting at sea level and climbing tortuously to 4,000 feet with whatever was ahead always hidden by the next curve. This small caravan of automobiles transported family members on a mission of duty and sadness. Meantime, brother Noell was dealing with the hard and bitter consequences of the unexpected death of a sibling in a more personal, face-to-face manner. Even our imagination cannot fully convey the weight of the lonely burden that he bore for himself and for us. Thank God, Mom and Dad were there and they could care, and that helped. Noell in his characteristic dignity never said a word; he just did what had to be done.

There is disharmony in the fact that the youngest member of a family is the first to be taken. Maybe the unconscious choice of the term "first to be taken" rather than "first to go" expresses disharmony, too. I don't know. In so many ways, the loss of family is beyond reason, unexplainable, incomprehensible, but in the end something that is acknowledged and ultimately accepted as final. With my little sister, JoAnne, there is still something about this dramatic, colorful, and ultimately fragile personality that never quite achieved expression – a tiny piece of unfinished business

David Denton
02/01

An Unexpected Brother

The Robbinsville Lion's Club sponsored the annual Mike Brown Bear Dinner for a good number of years. Local members and spouses as well as representatives from Lion's Clubs all over the district would attend this popular affair. Bear meat and other less exotic entrees were on the menu, and a special program featuring music or other appropriate entertainment was included. Peggy and I had been asked to provide a program of folk songs and other close harmony selections that we were doing in those days. We had driven down from Morganton, so this would have been the late nineteen sixties. We had a chance to greet a number of old friends and were warmly received by the Corpenings. They were the parents of a former girlfriend, and I remember thinking at the time that their graciousness must have been an expression of relief that I had married someone else's daughter. It was a very pleasant experience and largely so because throughout the meal and proceedings leading up to the program we were entertained by a shadowy figure playing classical music on a nylon stringed guitar. This was more than a pleasant interlude, an unexpected bonus of sensory pleasure presented without a word. When the evening's events were concluded, the classical guitarist was gone, but his presence lingered. I felt something warm and lifting inside, something of significance, though not expressed. Walter's music drifted and flowed a soft enhancement to the conversation and goodwill being shared around the tables created there in an obscure spot near the back of the room. A singular experience with sound and color and feeling registered and recorded in two souls, kept and embraced in a sacred state for decades, only to be simultaneously acknowledged and expressed as these same two souls are again joined in common experience and common perception.

This time we were sitting on a log in a quiet hollow among large trees not far beyond the edge of a meadow in Cades Cove. It was October and the Smokies had never been more beautiful. It was perhaps 9:30 in the morning and we were slowly making our way around the loop road. Pulling over onto the shoulder of the road to take in this beautiful expanse of woods and fields, attracted by movement, we both glanced in the same direction to see two large buck deer in full antler engaged in violent conflict. This was truly a rare event. We watched for a full ten minutes as the bucks charged each other again and again. As their antlers would crash together each would thrust and shove trying to knock the other off balance. The sounds were otherworldly and the picture unforgettable. They panted and gasped and bellowed and their breath came in great bursts of steam, hot against the cool autumn morning. Finally, as if by some telepathic signal, they stopped fighting and each drifted quietly into the woods. Walter and I made our way through the open field into the woods near where the two bucks entered. It was a beautiful spot and we found a seat on a log under the spreading arms of a big, white oak. In years past this glade had been part of a pioneer farm; remnants of wagon roads and terraced fields were in evidence.

Some few weeks before this trip to Cades Cove, Walter and I had been together for the first time in years at Mom's funeral. Following those times of closeness during the sixties and early seventies, we had shared a common love for our particular brand of music and an appreciation for the beauty of a well-chiseled rifle stock. For a span of almost three decades, our destinies had led us in directions profoundly different. Maybe it was the high emotion surrounding Mom's memorial service; or maybe only providence, but there was a compelling urgency to our emotional reconnection after so many years. After all, it had been during this protracted separation that the direction and substance of our lives and careers had been determined and essentially accomplished. That this was a reunion of note did not fail to register, with some significance, in the souls of each of us, but it was not until later that it found expression. A message came to me via the hand of Walter; maybe it was a letter or maybe a fax. Whatever the form, when I read the message I felt I was staring in the face of my own ghost. I guess we were both deeply moved or even shaken by the experience and talked about it by phone. It was then we decided to spend some time together in the mountains. We met at his place in Knoxville.

The rest of that morning in October we spent there on that log. It was less a matter of catching up on the events that had filled up two lives which had gone in such completely different directions, and more a matter of revelation and discovery of deep life forces, of passions and visions, of insights and yearnings, of thought and purpose, of hurt and healing, forces of family, blood true and undeniable in the oneness of their origin. New discoveries, unexpected moments of déjà vu arrived on a flow of questions, not statements. By the time we resumed our drive around the perimeter of Cades Cove, we both understood why we had come to this place. For almost thirty years the urgent, searching journeys we had made, as well as our casual meanderings, had unalterably brought us here to this place, at this time. What we shared in common, what we sought as brothers provided the impulse and energy. Navigation was predetermined and our inner compasses yielded always to the pull of the magnetic pole of family – of spiritual connectedness.

Our careers, though as different as the two sides of a coin, were yet separated by only a couple millimeters of metal forged from common ore. The tasks were different; the reasons for doing them were the same. That morning we revisited the early imaginings of two boys whose hearts and minds grew among different faces and different voices though separated by only two ridges and the England Branch. Most of the voices falling on Walter's young ears dropped from faces already old and weathered. He drew the attention of his grandparents and he spent not much time in the company of others of his generation. He was quiet, alone, sometimes indifferent. I didn't know him well. I did know, however, that he was comfortable in the presence of his grandparents and that they showed unrestrained delight in him; and that was good enough for me. He was family. Here, on Sweetwater, the faces and the voices were younger and considerably more numerous. Among many siblings our sense of belonging came more from the necessity of settling into a small niche that became our own, than from the individual attention we might get from adults. There were simply too many children and too few adults. Since Dad commonly worked away from home, it was usually Mom who had to divide her time and energy among members of the brood.

The fact that we grew up in different ways with different experiences and different responsibilities in no way diminished the influence of what we shared in common that cannot be witnessed and measured. The debate over whether, ultimately, it is nature or nurture that tips the scales in one direction or the other, may never be settled, but it seemed to us that the striking parallels which emerged as we shared that singular morning on a log were more than coincidence and were expressions of a message arriving in two different souls from a single source – a message born with in the genetic code.

We each learned that there had been moments of triumph, moments of pure ecstasy in careers acted out on stages worlds apart. We wept with startling realization that we had endured, separately, experiences of heartbreak of betrayal in the extreme. We learned of the birth of new knowledge of breakthrough, of enduring search and occasional discovery. We shared visions and dreams and nightmares. We lived again those moments of unexpected acclaim and we endured again the hours of loss and ruin. Always and again, we thrilled at the prospect of renewal. As we wiped away the tears born of hurt and disappointment, we felt their salt water evaporate on our cheeks, bringing cool refreshment on the breath of a soft breeze. As we walked back to the place where the car was parked, we smiled without speaking, each knowing that this interlude was still another example of the charmed lives we had been granted.

We tuned our guitars and Walter drifted easily into the Marty Robbins classic "Man Walks Among Us." I guess it is our shared appreciation for, or more properly our fascination with, certain kinds of music that identifies one spiritual kinship. Perhaps there is nothing that stirs more deeply nor more completely than the music which Walter and I enjoy. In a way it is puzzling how we learned accidentally of our mutual admiration for the music of Marty Robbins. In 1951 when I was transferred to Luke Field, Arizona, Marty was just getting his start on local radio and television in Phoenix. His first record was released that year, and I immediately became an admirer. His home is in Glendale, Arizona, which is between Phoenix and Luke Field. Years later, I learned of Walter's similar admiration for Marty. Perhaps it isn't really puzzling that the three of us are attracted to the same themes and sounds. Maybe Marty is another cousin.

So many of the experiences which Walter and I have shared have developed into moments of discovery. Not always, but often, discovery yields the unexpected. Discovery also causes us to look backward searching for matters such as cause and effect. Our revisiting of those two divergent careers provided many moments of discovery. If the forces driving Walter's career and the significant experiences of his life's work, and the same elements of my own were screenplays, though acted on different stages in venues distant from each other, they were penned by the same author. Similarly, if the elements of energy and insight, of passion and vision, of caring and concern, of gaining and losing were woven into tapestries of strong colors and bold symbols, they would hang like flags on the wall – of North Carolina and Maryland – dignified by contrast. A closer search of their fabric would tell us that those diverse and multi-colored threads were spun from the same yarn. Among all the discoveries made on that October morning in Cades Cave was the discovery of an unexpected brother.

Just a Weekend Visit

Perhaps within every family there are certain matters which are accepted without question. In my family one of those givens was that we would go to college. In the area where I grew up, the matter of going to college was certainly not a given condition among most families and perhaps not even more than a remote kind of dream for many of them. I was born and grew up in Robbinsville, North Carolina, and those early years for me were the depression years. Dad was a Civil Engineer and his work took him to such places as Altavista, Virginia, or Lynchburg or some other such place which reduced his contact with the family to occasional weekends during those difficult years between the Crash of '29 and Pearl Harbor. When he did get home, there was a celebration, of course, but it was short because he had to turn around and leave again. Dad wasn't much when it came to things like pitching baseballs with his sons; but, he was good at such things as dreams and the future and things of high principle. He had visions of his family of six all holding college degrees. He had another dream too; but, more about that in a moment. Mother lived with the harsher reality of trying to raise six children during the depression on a small mountain farm when her husband was away most of the time and reliable help was hard to come by. But, Mom was faithful to the dream also. Even though no one had answered the question of how this dream was to be realized, each of us held stubbornly to that ideal which we had inherited.

World War II came along and added its own measure of chaos to the lives of people there in the hills, not to mention its effect on humanity in general. In a way, the War helped Dad's dream come true, at least for the three boys in the family. The G.I. Bill, from a very practical point of view, made it possible for us to graduate comparatively debt free. For the three girls, the situation was different and that is a story within itself. Dad and Mom struggled and my sisters struggled, and increment by increment the dream was realized, but not without exceptional sacrifice on the part of each one. Dad lived out his days with the joy of knowing that his children were educated, and he died with the hurt in his breast that he had not been able to do more.

Since I was the only male home during the War years and those years following World War II, it was in the natural order of things for me to take over the management of the family farm…a reasonably heavy load for a skinny adolescent, but there was no particular reason to dwell on that at the time. As a matter of fact, it was not something that I thought about very much at all. One of Dad's other dreams was to develop a profitable dairy farm. In looking back, it's easier to understand now how I figured into that particular dream. At the end of the War, my brothers came home and enrolled first of all at Western Carolina University and then transferred to North Carolina State University; both of them majored in Dairy Manufacturing. During my high school years, when I was fully in charge of the farm, (Dad was working for an architect out of Ashville, North Carolina) Dad would make periodic comments about my attending North Carolina State University and majoring in Dairy Production. I am certain now that he envisioned a dairy operation with my brothers handling the management and sales end of the business and me handling the production end. This was not something discussed, Dad did not engage in private discussions very often with his offspring, instead he talked about things that were important to him in a much more detached and abstract kind of way. Each week, or however often he was home, he would lay out for me those things which needed to be done within the next several days and the list of responsibilities typically went beyond what had to be done on our own farm and included taking care of the second cutting of hay for Uncle Patton or mowing, raking and stacking Charlie Garland's hay on shares. One of the things which I looked forward to in the time spent with Dad was his unspoken sense of approval of what I had been able to accomplish. He often referred to me as "old man" and I interpreted this not only as a term of endearment but more than that – one of respect as an equal. It was hard to know what he was feeling because he never talked about his feelings, and I sometimes found myself searching for recognition or understanding or approval of those parts of my life which were more personal and not related to the farm and my duties there. Athletic competition was very important to me, and I was able to play football and basketball all four years of high school. At the time it didn't register, but my Dad never attended a single game. I have never felt that this was because of any indifference on his part but most probably a reflection of his own preoccupations, about which I knew little. Dad was a complex man…I knew he loved me and respected me because he placed few, if any, restrictions on me and turned over to me at a very tender age responsibilities beyond the strength of many mature adults.

There were times when my daddy's dream became an almost unmanageable burden for me. I flunked and had to repeat the 7th grade, and I was the only member of my family to carry the weight of such disgrace. Ironically, I can look back upon that awful year as the one year which most profoundly shaped my attitude toward children and learning. What I learned from that painful and bitter experience has served me well a thousand times over in dealing with the lives of children who may be struggling in their own way to live out a dream, theirs or someone else's. There were two factors which worked together to keep me in high school, because in looking back I can remember still that feeling that what I really wanted to do was take my failure and disappear quietly off the face of the earth. Those two elements were football and the compassion and good sense of my family never to mention my 7th grade tragedy.

The Korean War broke out in June 1950, and the possibility that Daddy's dream would be interrupted by yet another War was very real in my mind. I had enough credits to graduate; but, I also had one more year of football eligibility. So the decision was made to go back to high school and wait for the draft or, if my luck held, to enroll in college. I had read a lot about Berea College and had had a cousin who attended. Berea had tremendous appeal because it was possible to work your way through, and money, at that time in my life, was a genuine problem. During that fall of my senior year, life was good. Something big was just around the bend, but I didn't know what – Berea or Korea, college or war – but for the moment I was captain of the football team and I could pick the guitar and sing. Who knew what great promises life held for me? By the time football season was over, winter was settling in. The War seemed closer than ever, and Daddy's dream had to be put off for awhile. So I enlisted in the U.S. Air Force in November with the understanding that I would report December 26th, the day after Christmas. December 26th was gray and awful. Fog had settled in the mountain valley and there were intermittent downpours. I kissed Mom goodbye and Dad drove me to catch the bus. Dad had on his old, faded and torn hunting coat and a cap with dark sweat stains around the base of the crown where the bill is attached. He didn't say anything but smoked his pipe and cleared his throat. When we got to the Courthouse corner in Robbinsville, the bus was already there and several other boys from Graham County were gathered around. Most of them had been drafted and were being taken to the Induction Center. Two or three of us were volunteers, the Denton's had always been volunteers. I was filled with a confusion of feelings, and I just wanted that bus to leave and get away from there. I climbed aboard and settled into a seat next to the window and in that next couple of minutes before the Trailways bus pulled away, I allowed myself to look out the window at a picture which has ever since remained clearly fixed in my memory and in my heart. It was pouring rain and my dad, apparently only at that moment fully realizing that the last of his sons was leaving and that his dream or at least a part of it was over, leaned against a utility pole, lowered his head against his forearm and started to cry. I could not hear him, but I could see the sobs. I couldn't bear to look at him, and I couldn't look away. The finality of my decision to enlist began to settle coldly in my being. The bus pulled away and I was gone. Dad seemed so old, so tired and suddenly so broken. Why hadn't I seen these things before? Dad's dream of a family-operated dairy business had evaporated. I suppose I knew that even before I enlisted; but I didn't think Dad allowed himself to see and understand that reality until that climatic act of putting me on the bus was accomplished. But, there was another dream.

Berea College, of course, would have to wait. The Korean conflict and the U.S. Air Force sidetracked the normal course of things and created a four-year hiatus. Maybe with the G.I. Bill I could afford to go to some place like North Carolina State University; so I freely put aside the notion of attending that small college in Kentucky where mountain kids could earn their way to a degree. There was no way of knowing, of course, how strongly Kentucky would figure into my life…another campus in another small town in the hills. During those four years of separation from familiar things and people, I thought often of family members and our shared dream, the one that Dad had given us. One thing was certain, however, that I was getting behind. All of the other members of the family, including my younger sister, were "through" college and succeeding or were on their way to completing a degree. I still clung stubbornly to the notion that I, too, would complete a college education, but I had no clearly defined plans and the idea was quite general, even nebulous. In talking about the future after military service, my standard response was I planned to go to college. There was a tendency on my part to over idealize my family and exaggerate their successes and accomplishments. Whenever my tour of duty was over, I would return home, get a job for awhile, put away some money and enroll in college. It was simple, or at least it seemed that way, until I was introduced to a radically different reality than the one I had conjured up in my mind and dreams during the past four years. Almost immediately I began to feel the pressure, subtle and nonintentional but pressure nevertheless, to do something with my life. So, I began immediately to satisfy my own sense of increasing anxiety about my abilities and my worth and to live up to the expectations of my parents and my brothers and sisters. Within a week of my discharge, I was driving a huge, worn-out truck for Biltmore Dairy in Charlotte, North Carolina, making an endless circuit of the major supermarkets around the city filling the display cases with homogenized milk, buttermilk, half and half, chocolate milk and Biltmore's wonderful double-heavy whipping cream. I would pick up the empty cases at each of the stores and stack them in the back of the truck and rumble up and down the streets of Charlotte. Civilian life wasn't at all what it was cracked up to be. A dog rushed into the street and, try as I might, I couldn't bring that lumbering piece of machinery to a halt. The dog was crippled and I agreed to transport the animal to the office of a local veterinarian to the relief of the distraught woman to whom this furry little animal belonged. In the days to follow, I stopped by to check on the dog and, to everyone's amazement, it recovered. I thought I had done the right thing and was quite unprepared for the less than gentle reprimand I received from the sales manager with the dairy. But, that was only the beginning. After completing my rounds late one January evening, I parked the old Ford truck where I always parked it, firmly depressed the brake pedal, and flipped the switch controlling the brake lock to ensure that the truck would remain parked on this steeply sloping parking area near the garage. When I returned to work the next morning, I was immediately confronted with the foul tongue of the sales manager who accused me of deliberately parking the truck without locking the brake. If the accident would not have resulted in my dismissal, I am certain that my well-chosen remarks to my boss would have. So I quit on the spot and found myself broke, out of service one month, without a job, and another failure to contend with.

From Charlotte I went to Florence, South Carolina, and joined a country music band. Music had a deep and powerful meaning to me and I had often toyed, kind of on the edges of my dream, with the idea of being a singer. I was really afraid to fully embrace this idea because of some of the things my dad said about "guitar pickers," but I was grown now and on my own. We played six show dates per week at schoolhouses, firehalls, V.F.W.'s and an assortment of other places throughout the low country of South Carolina, always ending up at the Pavilion in Myrtle Beach on Saturday night. We also did six 45 minute live-radio broadcasts out of Florence, taped a couple of shorter segments, and did a 30 minute live television program each week. In addition to all of this glory, I was paid $40 per week – or at least I thought I would be paid $40 per week. As each payday rolled around, the band leader would plead some horrible financial difficulty he was experiencing and would promise better days just around the corner. The band was made up of a pretty fair group of musicians, each holding onto the dream of making it big someday and each too broke to escape this dismal situation. When I had had enough and left the band, I had to hock my steel guitar to have enough gas money to get home. So I returned to Robbinsville with my tail between my legs only to confront additional pressure from those who loved me most. Things just weren't turning out well at all, and I was profoundly puzzled and anxious. Within the months that followed, I twice enrolled at Appalachian State University only to withdraw. I helped coach the home football team, without pay of course, played three nights per week for square dances at Fountana Village and laid in one last crop on my daddy's farm. With the arrival of winter, I sold my car, my only possession that I couldn't carry in a B-4 bag or strapped across my shoulder, and joined two buddies in forming a country music band in Washington, D.C. We might have made it if we could have held on long enough to eat and pay the rent both, but that wasn't to be. So for awhile then I helped to make C-130's for Lockheed Aircraft Corporation in Marietta, Georgia. A year earlier I had been working on B26s for the U.S. Air Force and gone full circle accomplishing nothing except, from my own perception, to have registered a list of failures. The harder I tried, the further away I seemed to drift from the realization of that dream. And then it happened.

My oldest sister and her husband had relocated from Carolina to Corbin, Kentucky. Her husband was branch manager of the Corbin office of the Home Finance Company, specializing in automobile financing. In their letters to Mom and Dad, Mary and Bob described the beauty of southeastern Kentucky, often mentioning such places as Cumberland Falls, Cumberland Gap and others. Dad had always been interested in history and frequently talked about "the dark and bloody ground" as the Cherokees called Kentucky. I was aware of the familiar Kentucky associations such as the bluegrass horse country, the Hatfield and McCoys feud, and even "Bloody Harlan." Since I had willingly put aside the dream of attending Berea College years before,

Kentucky hadn't figured into my future at all until now, and this was only a weekend visit. Had it not been that I had sold my car, that providential trip to Whitley County would have never occurred. I was without transportation and agreed that it would be pleasant to drive to Corbin and visit with Mary and Bob for the weekend. After passing through Knoxville, Clinton, and Lafollette, we entered a different kind of country, lean and hungry, gray and desolate. The hillsides were horribly scarred from strip mining, and it seemed that everywhere one could see heaps of rubble left over from the gouging of the earth; dirt, low grade coal, overburden, each heap leaching poisoned and foul smelling water into the mountain brooks and creeks. In the narrow hollows and along the steep hillsides were occasional tar-paper shacks propped up with spindly poles clinging desperately to the slopes. On the narrow porches of these homes were Maytag washing machines and coon dogs with their ribs and hip bones showing through their brindle markings. As we drove through places like Habersham and "the narrows," we saw these pictures repeated…rusted out automobiles with bullet holes through the doors, propped up on Nehi Cola crates with all four wheels missing. This was Highway 25W, the highway both of promise and broken dreams. This is the road that leads out of the hills to places like Cincinnati and Detroit, to jobs and assembly lines and second-hand Fords. This is the highway of too much speed and too much beer from a State Line honky-tonk and dreams lost forever on some switch-back curve on this narrow and treacherous ribbon of asphalt. We passed through Jellico and into Kentucky and it was not without its beauty. I remember the road cuts and the layers and layers of stratified stone and coal, each layer a different shade. Some of these cuts were quite deep and millions of years of our earth's history had been opened up for examination for any who cared to take a look. Highway 25W passed by Williamsburg. I remember looking across the Cumberland River and seeing clusters of homes creeping up the hillside with the spires from two or three churches and the dark smoke from a thousand chimneys hanging over this quiet town. I didn't know it at the time, but somewhere up the hill among those houses and church spires was Cumberland College.

Kentucky for me was the beginning of a dream unfolding in all of its glory and in a most unexpected way. Approximately 75 years earlier, my great grandfather and his oldest son had ridden on horseback to Cumberland Gap to dig young apple trees to use as stock for grafting an orchard in the hills of North Carolina. My great granddaddy fought at Cumberland Gap during the Civil War and recalled seedling apple trees growing there. He thought Kentucky was grand country and returned with his son years later. It is said that Daniel Boone wept at the death of his youngest son who had been shot by the Indians on the Tennessee side of Cumberland Gap. The story goes that he wept not only at the loss of his son, he wept too because his son never had the chance to see the beauty of Kentucky. But here I was, I was free to choose and it was all mine. An unplanned weekend visit began a change of direction in my life. In less than a week I was working at Cumberland Falls. From the back terrace of Dupont Lodge I watched spring return to the southern Appalachians and seized for the first time in my life, the opportunity of being free and being me.

The decision to remain for awhile in Kentucky represented more than my immediate good feelings about the place and the people. It was most probably a determination to finally give myself that opportunity to settle in for awhile and find out who I was in terms of that dream out there. That spring and summer in southeastern Kentucky held, without doubt, the most satisfying experiences of my life up until that time. The sense of comparative failure when I thought of myself alongside members of my family began to evaporate and in its place came a growing sense of wholeness. This was the way things were supposed to be. Yes, I was a man of the southern hills and I had songs to sing and maybe some stories to tell, and certainly a pocketful of favorite dreams that I clung to mostly in the privacy of my own thoughts. Frequently in the spring months I worked the 11:00 p.m. – 7:00 a.m. shift at the desk in Dupont Lodge. At the first promise of dawn, I enjoyed walking out onto the terrace and looking up river and watching the changing shades of light as the sun slowly rose touching first of all those distant ridges and wrinkles of the Cumberlands and glistening on the ripples and eddies and quiet places on the river. I would think back on stories from history books and from ancestors, stories about the Cumberland River and Kentucky, and here I was, a citizen of that place and liking it very much. The perspective of the Cumberland River winding its way among the ridges of the Cumberland Mountains from that particular spot must have impressed the Dupont family who made this land a permanent gift to the state of Kentucky with the understanding that its beauty and character would remain protected, because it certainly had a powerful influence on me and my emotions. As the spring season matured, every week brought new delights, deepening shades of green, a profusion of redbud blossoms, the dogwoods and finally the full-blown glory of summer. Having grown up in the mountains not really too many ridges away, I was familiar, of course, with all of the natural things happening around me. But now, instead of simply accepting without conscious thought, these things as a part of one's ordinary existence, it was almost as if I had come or been sent to witness these remarkable things. The spring drifted into summer and peace was mine to the fullest extent. New forces had entered my life, forces like a newfound measure of success as a singer and the approaching possibility that the college experience may actually happen, and then there was another force, or perhaps more properly, there was another presence which certainly speeded up the process of finally making decisions about such things as college, direction in my life, and what I would do with myself. This presence was in the form of a striking woman who was no stranger to the hills and hollows around Cumberland Falls. Peggy and I first of all had become friends and then we sang a song together. That experience altered everything from that day forward. I was shaken, I admit, to my very shoe soles and was startled as I understood more fully what a chance weekend visit to my sister in Corbin was becoming.

It was already August and I had a day off. Bob invited me to ride with him to Williamsburg where he planned to call upon two or three automobile dealers there. I also recall attending on that day a Rotary luncheon in Williamsburg with Bob. I remember feeling uneasy among these professional and successful people. There had been considerable talk among Bob, my sister Mary and me about college in these last few days. No pressure, mind you, except a self-imposed measure of stress prompted by the growing knowledge that a decision had to be made soon. Before returning to Corbin, Bob thought we should drive up W. Main Street, and in so doing we drove right through the campus of Cumberland College. I had heard of Cumberland because some of the young people working at the Falls were students here. The campus was quiet because it was between the last summer session and the regular fall session. We walked around campus for a little while and bumped into a couple of faculty members. We walked into what appeared to be the newest building on campus…it was the Gatliff Building…and we found the President's office. I knew we were down to the wire and I was frightened out of my wits. Bob turned to me and with a smile said, "Why don't you go ahead and register." I remember the feeling of increasing panic and embarrassment and I indicated to him through gesture that I didn't have any money. He then did one of those wonderfully kind things which he has continued to do down through the years, he paid my registration fee until I could repay him. A thousand disturbing questions were racing through my mind…was I really college material…could I really keep up with the academic demands…had I been out of school too long…was I well enough prepared to succeed in college? At least a couple of these questions were tentatively answered during the next couple of hours. A kindly member of the faculty, Professor Vallandingham, took me to the second floor to an empty classroom and administered a battery of exams. After an initial period of uncertainty, I settled into the task and found that maybe I could go to college after all. We hung around long enough for Professor Vallandingham and Dr. Boswell, the college President, to tell me that I could attend classes there. Some more papers were filled out concerning such things as the G.I. Bill, preregistration for a series of basic courses, etc. The drive back to Corbin was accomplished in a fog, although a happy one. It had happened, that hurdle had been crossed and I simply overflowed with a generalized good feeling. During the first several weeks, I hitchhiked back and forth between Corbin and Williamsburg; but, by mid-semester I had found a room at Mrs. Agnes Perkins' place. The basement area of Mrs.

Perkins' home had been divided up into boarding quarters for a couple of college students. There was a small sign leading down the steps to my new home. The sign bore the words "Seldom Inn." The college experience could not have meant more to anyone than it was meaning to me. I was in love with every course that I was taking, my grades were excellent, and I had the distinct impression that everyone of my professors had taken a very special interest in me. Generations of Cumberland College students have experienced many of the things that I experienced and carry with them these warm and happy memories. I shall always be convinced that for me, these experiences and memories were profound…even such simple and wonderful things as the evening meal in the old student dining room where food was served family style and a few hundred young people from the hills had a chance to come together and fulfill a dream reserved in many places for those with greater means. Cumberland was more than a way out for kids from the hills; it was a way onward and upward. Maybe it was because I was somewhat older than the average student, although there were other returning G.I.s, I understood in the most personal way the significance of Cumberland College's determination to remain true to its fundamental mission. I look back from time to time and wonder how differently things might have turned out if it had been Appalachian State University or North Carolina State University which came forward with an institutional response to the unique situation facing one frightened boy from North Carolina. I certainly hadn't been bold enough to question or change what seemed providential…I had come to Kentucky for a weekend and I had found a life, and I had found a wife, and I had found a thousand reasons for living well.

Peggy and I were married in November. We ran away to Georgia because there was no waiting period and because we had so little time…just a weekend. She was in nursing school in Knoxville but decided to put her college career on hold until we could somehow get me through school. I missed a Monday morning convocation and had to report to the Dean's office for this infraction. That was standard procedure in those days and Dr. P.R. Jones conducted that brief session with a stern countenance until the last possible moment. When I explained to him that I had missed a day of school because I was getting married, he asked me in a most solemn manner if I thought getting married was more important than attending Chapel. When I answered yes, he smiled briefly and then, with an expression of mock concern, reminded me that I should never put another similar blemish on my college record.

Peggy and I felt a need to build a life on our own, away from her family and away from my family; so, we transferred to the University of North Carolina in Chapel Hill for the second semester. Carolina was a great school, of course, but it was huge and lacked the intimacy of Cumberland. As luck would have it, Peggy became pregnant and we found ourselves at the end of my freshman year needing work, expecting a baby, and with little chance of being able to survive financially at the University of North Carolina. And then a strange and providential thing happened. Almost in desperation I was looking for a source of income that would allow us to bring a baby into the world and perhaps live a bit better than we had been able to live up until that point. The American Casualty Company was looking for persons with certain qualifications to be trained as special agents. I applied, survived the initial screening, and was offered an appointment with certain requirements. There would be twelve weeks of training in Reading, Pennsylvania. I then would be assigned to a site somewhere in the east, probably Richmond, Virginia, be given a new automobile and a salary of $5,000 per annum. This seemed like an answer to our immediate need and $5,000 per year and a new car was several thousand dollars and a new car beyond what I was earning at the time. Before leaving for Reading, we returned to Williamsburg so that Peggy, who was well along in her pregnancy, would be able to stay with her family until my training was over. She was due in the later part of October, which meant that I would be gone right up until or beyond the birth of our baby. Before leaving for Reading, I walked over to Cumberland College and had a visit with Dr. Boswell. When I told him of our plans, he seemed most thoughtful and even sad. I remember how he appeared at that moment; he was leaned forward with his arms on his desk. As I rationalized our situation, he said "David, don't do it." And then he said, "Do you know what you will have if you take this position?" I, of course, didn't answer, but he answered for me by saying, "If you take this job, you will have exactly what they offered you…$5,000 a year and a new car." He looked thoughtfully at me and said, "Are you willing to settle for that." My response was immediate and firm and the answer was no! He then reassured me, as he must have reassured a thousand other students looking for a way to pay for a college education, by saying to me, "David, if you will stay in school, somehow we will find a way to make it possible." We shook hands and I turned and left. Peggy and I got in that old Studebaker automobile, which her dad had given us, and drove to the Williamsburg Cemetery to a spot which overlooked the Cumberland River and the distant hills. We sat for a long while, talking and mostly just crying and holding onto each other. The moment which I remember most clearly is the one that Peggy said through tears, "David, I don't know how in the world we can do it; but, if you are determined to go to college, we will find a way."

My next trip to Cumberland College was a matter of a couple of days later, and I guess I was asking Dr. Boswell to live up to his promise. We had found a little frame house not too far from where Peggy's family lived on W. Main Street (that house is now gone and in its place is a huge excavation through which Interstate 75 runs). That house was available for $25 a month, but it was empty except for a coal-burning stove. We had not one stick of furniture. My request of Dr. Boswell was simply to ask him if he knew of any place where we might be able to find some kind of temporary furniture. He directed me to the attic of Mahan Hall and indicated that whatever discarded furniture I found there I was welcome to use and keep. Well, under layers of dust, pigeon manure and mouse nests, I was able to locate a steel-frame bed complete with springs which could be folded into a single army-type bed or opened into the semblance of a double bed. I also found a couple of discarded chests and some straight-back chairs which we painted a flat black. Peggy made cushions using foam rubber from automobile seats covered with an attractive paisley pattern with a ruffle around the edge and tied them to each side of the chair back. These chairs really turned out to be very attractive and we were most proud of them. The bed problem was simple; all we had to do was put a mattress on top of this extraordinary find from the attic of Mahan Hall. The chests were touched up and refinished. Peg's mother lent us a round oak table, and we were able to setup housekeeping in short order. It is strange even now, to think about it, in that there was no feeling of regret or uncertainty to remain at Cumberland and turn down the job with American Casualty Company. That second year at Cumberland College was equal to, and perhaps surpassed in some ways, my first year there. David, our first child, was born at home in that little house on W. Main Street on November 2nd. I was with Peggy the entire time thanks to the kindness and understanding of Dr. L.X. Brown. That second winter at Cumberland was filled with its own special challenges. Work was hard to come by, but we were able to manage nicely. I guess if we had thought fully about our state, we would have been scared half out of our minds; but, it all seemed quite normal at the time. Mostly I worked construction during free hours, digging septic tank holes, mixing concrete, pouring footers…whatever had to be done. A friend and fellow student and I managed to keep one day ahead of a fuel crisis by scrounging blocks of coal from a variety of locations around the county and hauling them home in the trunk of his car… one block for you and one block for me, and so on. Three of us Cumberland students who happened to be ex G.I.s, always arrived on campus early in the morning and immediately went to the Wigwam for coffee. Coffee was 5 cents a cup and, on those days when we only had 10 cents, we would order two cups of coffee and the loan of a third empty cup. The ladies who worked in the snack bar couldn't have been more understanding. By the end of the second summer, all course requirements for a pre-law background were completed and I was set to enroll at Mercer University. That was the summer when the present dining room was being built, so I was able to work part days with the contractor on this new building and finish up my last courses at the same time. The separation from Cumberland was difficult, but I was well prepared for law school or whatever other directions my life might ultimately take. In my own estimation, it still seems remarkable that at the end of that summer, scarcely 2 ½ years from that fateful weekend when I sort of dropped out of the sky into southeastern Kentucy, I was able to leave that little town with a wife, a baby, a diploma from Cumberland College, debt free and with the knowledge in my mind and the firm resolve in my heart that I, too, was going to be able to add my share to the fulfillment of my dad's dream. There have been many other experiences that have occurred in my life in those years since Cumberland, but it was those experiences, there in that small college, that set the direction of my life that was not to be reversed or sidetracked. I could not have imagined nor hoped for a career such as the one that I have enjoyed over these years. I was led, it seems, providentially into education of the deaf and it has been in this, of course, that I have found ultimate satisfaction and the ultimate reason for being and for doing. Dr. Boswell could not have known that I would be an educator of the deaf but that really doesn't matter. Dr. Boswell and the institution which he directed saw in me something which I was unable to see in myself at that time, and Cumberland College became the enabler for the good things that have happened since. When I think back on my educational experiences, there are two that stand distinctly apart from all the others. One of these was that awful time when I was a 13 year old failing the 7th grade, disgracing myself and my family, and the other one was that warm and wonderful time at Cumberland College where I experienced education in its most fundamental sense, that being the release of buried potential. It was not so much what Cumberland College did to me or for me, it was more the opportunity Cumberland provided me to learn how to be free and the personal support which Cumberland offered during the process. No other school has meant so much to me.

David M. Denton, Pd.D.
Maryland School for the Deaf
Frederick, Maryland 21701
September 1987

The Author just out of the Air Force 1955

Peggy West – "Why I went to Kentucky." 1955

Peggy West Denton – "Why I stayed in Kentucky."

The Author at Cumberland College 1956

Camping at the Flats

In the hills of western North Carolina, there was no diversion among local boys as wonderful as going camping. Life in the hills is life filled with work and responsibilities and perhaps that is why an evening and night in the woods let us feel as completely free and uninhibited as the creatures who lived there. We enjoyed sleeping there under their trees and awakening to a shower of hickory nut hulls raining down from above as the squirrels feasted before it was yet full light on this Saturday in mid-October. As the mist rose and the sun first touched some of the eastward facing ridge tops, the morning symphony of birds began. The first to grace our senses were the wood thrush. Their liquid notes floated from the deeper woods at first light and were heard again as the shadows began to lengthen in the evening. Wood thrush offered a rolling phrase something like "tyro lee, tyro lee." These shy birds were almost never seen, unlike the gaudy blue jay and the cardinal. The cardinal's song is not as lovely as that of the thrush, but it is pretty enough, and the fact that "redbirds" are so numerous and bright makes up for any deficit in voice quality. Blue jays don't know that they can't sing well even though, according to legend, they, in times past, had the loveliest voices of all. They were so flashy and had such grand voices that they were greatly admired by the other forest creatures. This admiration by others led to increasing vanity on their part. They became so taken with their loveliness that they preened and primped and sang all day and found themselves with the coming of winter without supply of nuts and acorns. In their conceit they felt that the other birds and animals owed them a living because of their loveliness. Thornton Burgess, author of the *Mother West Wind Stories* tells us that the blue jay stole the gray squirrels' winter storehouse of nuts and acorns and denied doing so Mother West Wind allowed Mr. Jay to keep his lovely coat of blue and white and black but, ever since that time when the blue jay opens his beak to sing, all he can produce are the sounds "thief, thief." As the morning symphony progressed, the timid thrushes their voices lilting one thousand fold were joined by myriad warblers and chickadees and sustained by the solid performance of the cardinals; this symphony settled over woodland like a soothing blanket of sound. Among the countless other voices the call of the blue jay was no more than a muted trumpet. Percussion was provided by the pileated woodpecker and, at regular intervals, punctuated by the ruffed grouse as he sits on a log nearby spreading his tail feathers like a fan and drumming softly.

We always camped with the Elliott boys and would plan in advance a particular day, almost always a Saturday, and would look forward to this experience with increasing excitement. On many occasions I remember looking up from my fieldwork or wood cutting and glancing upward toward the "Flats" and imaging what it would be like in a few hours to be there. If possible, we would try to terminate the fieldwork a few minutes early and then hurry through activities involved with feeding, milking, etc. When the chores were done, the Elliott boys had arrived and we would quickly gather our camping supplies and tools before heading for the woods. The lantern would be filled with kerosene; we would grab the axe, a gun, call the dogs and be on our way. The first stop would be the smoke house where we would cut off a slab of bacon and a pound or two of cured ham or shoulder. On some occasions, we would also stop at the chicken house. By this time it was late in the day and the chickens were already on the roost. Trying to be as quiet as possible, one of us would sneak into the chicken house grab a hen off the roost and quickly exit without creating a ruckus. Mom and Dad surely knew we were snitching chickens and meat, but it was something we never discussed.

We made our way up the branch, over fences, through the pasture to the old logging road leading to the gap. The logging road was pretty easy walking although steep. About halfway to the gap, a huge chestnut tree had fallen across the logging road and we had to climb over it. It was about four and a half feet in diameter and we had chopped steps into the side of the log to make crossing easier. We usually rested here for a moment. At the gap, the trail narrowed considerably, and we had to make our way through a laurel thicket and a very steep hillside for a couple hundred yards.

At this point the trail crossed a little branch and upward of the trail a few feet was a pool of bubbling water, a natural spring that supplied all our drinking and cooking needs. From the spring the trail turned steeply upwards for the last few hundred feet to our camping spot. After reaching our place and unloading our gear, a couple of us would retrace our steps to the spring, fill a couple of buckets with water and return to camp. The trail from the spring up the hill to our spot meandered through some scattered walnut trees, small pines, and a scattering of poplars. Abruptly the ground leveled and to our right was an open, flat meadow comprising perhaps an acre. To the left along the edge of the flat area stood a couple of large walnut trees and perhaps three large poplars. Our campsite was under these large trees and facing the open, flat meadow. Beyond the clearing, the ground turned steep and was once again covered with thick woods. What a delightful spot we had discovered! Among all of these steep, rugged, tree-covered ridges was this perfectly level open, grass-covered area with a grove of sheltering trees at the western edge. Maybe this had been a cultivated field at one time. Beyond the field where the land turned upward and at the edge of the woods, we found the remnants of an ancient rail fence made of chestnut.

Back in the forties when we "discovered" this place we knew we had found the world's most perfect place for camping. We selected a spot under the large walnuts and poplars for our camp. Searching the woods we found enough rocks of carrying size to make a couple of fire rings for heating and cooking. The rail fence gave us an idea, so we made trip after trip carrying chestnut rails across the meadow under the big trees and there we made a lean-to open in the front and large enough for several people to crawl inside for sleeping. The structure was made rainproof by covering it with pine boughs. These had to be replaced from time to time, but we had a camp with a real fence rail "lean-to." During the "construction" period, before Charles went off to college and then into the Navy, we spent many happy summer hours fashioning our camp. We could actually play our own brand of football in the open area between sessions of carrying rails to make our cabin. The place simply became known as the "Flats."

In October of the year 2000 I made a pilgrimage back to the "Flats." A few years ago, we prepared a site to place our travel trailer on what is now our piece of the Denton farm. Some grading was done, a septic system installed, electric power connected, and a gravity flow water system was hooked up. Our piece of the homeplace includes what we call the head of the pasture. The property includes the old logging road leading up to the gap. A couple of summers ago, Peggy and I trimmed the bushes from the old logging road making it passable. Today it looks very much as it did in the forties; remnants of the old chestnut log are still there.

On this day I stopped at the gap to rest as I had done so many times as a boy. The trail from the gap through the laurels to the spring is still recognizable, although not as easy to negotiate as it used to be. Since this was October and the summer had been dry, the water flow from the spring was low, but it was still there. I turned up the hill toward the Flats and continued my quest. As I looked around, the hollows and ridges looked the same. The hills and woods are timeless in the broader picture. The immediate landscape, however, required some study. Over there were the remains of a huge, leaning hickory, decaying pieces of the trunk and larger limbs. I had taken squirrels from that tree more than once. Apparently it had stood until it died; too crooked for lumber, a landmark, however, and in my memory it rose again. Upward the trees thickened; not trees that I remembered, these were pines and poplars. I knew I was going in the right direction; I've been here too many times to be mistaken. Then I noticed the ground – it was level, but I was standing in a thick grove of poplars and pines. *These were grown trees – where is our meadow?* I needed some time to settle myself.

For several minutes I walked among the trees searching the dimensions of a place I knew like my living room. This would be close to the place where we built our fence rail cabin – no trace – no big walnuts or poplars – but a stump and another. Then I stumbled catching myself on a pine tree. Looking down I saw the cause; there were several rocks of carrying size among the leaves. This was a fire ring. Now maybe I could figure it out. Through triangulation, I could reestablish the relationship between the fire ring and the largest poplar stump. Now I knew where to look for walnut trees next to our cabin. Not there – but remnants of a tree trunk, dark wood…yes, walnut. I dug among the rocks and leaves, and touched the twisted lid of a metal cooking pot. Walking around some more, I stepped over something dark. It was metal, fairly large; this was part of the firebox of a small cook stove we hauled here on a sled during the War. As I scratch around in the leaves, I found another man-made object. It was a piece of metal about one foot by one foot covered by enamel-like the old wash pans. This was one of the doors from the warming closet of the old cook stove. I remember very well the details of how that cook stove came to be here, but how did the Flats come to be taken over by a forest? How did our meadow, our little football field, come to be covered with full-grown pines and poplars? Some of the pine trees a foot through had died and fallen and are decaying under foot. The pines were being crowded out by this forest of tall, straight poplars. It looked as if someone seeded the Flats on purpose – and then I remembered.

At about the same time that we "discovered" the Flats and began our project of making the ideal camping place, we made another discovery. At the time Dad bought the additional acreage from Cleveland Cody, there were two old frame houses and several out buildings standing on the property. One of the houses was adjacent to Marty Holder's place and one of the chimneys is still standing. In earlier times different families had lived there including the Emanuel Jones family and the Jeff Crisp family. When the last family moved out of this house, they left behind a small, wood-burning cook stove. While involved in some sort of farm work one summer day near this old house, it occurred to someone that we could use that stove in our camp. Ours would be the only camp in North Carolina with a cook stove. We were probably hauling rocks that day because we had a horse and sled with us. This particular sled was what is called a "lizzard" in the mountains. A lizzard is a small, low sled made from a single tree – a forked tree. Lizzards are almost always made of sourwood, because sourwood is dense and doesn't tend to split. People in the mountains in those days were always searching for a forked sourwood. To make a lizzard the sourwood was cut below the fork. About 5 feet above the fork each prong was cut. This left a single piece of wood shaped like a "V". The point of the "V" was the front and it was there that the horse was hooked. Heavy boards were nailed across the two prongs of the "V" forming the bed of the sled. Because the sled was pointed, it was easy to pull and because it was low to the ground, it was impossible to turn over.

We dismantled the stove, removing the legs and the warming closet. The main part of the stove including the firebox, oven, and cook top was in one piece. We loaded the stove and its parts on the lizzard and tied them down with rope. Then we headed out across the pasture, up the old logging road, around the fallen chestnut tress and on to the gap. The next part was the most difficult. The lizzard didn't overturn as we navigated the narrow trail around the hillside through the laurels. The horse was handled by Charles while the rest of us placed ourselves on the lower side of the lizzard heaving and pushing and stumbling in an effort to keep the stove components on the sled. Finally we reached the spring, rested and let the horse drink before continuing up the remaining ridge to the Flats. We unloaded the stove near the big walnut tree and set it up on a foundation of rocks.

In the months and years that followed that stove served us well. Most of the cooking we did was frying; eggs, meat, potatoes, onions, flapjacks, so cooking on a stove top was much to be preferred over cooking over an open fire and contending with ashes, soot, and popping coals. We did try to bake cornbread and an occasional squirrel in the oven. We could bake potatoes and once we tried to bake a hen, but only once.

We camped in the summer and fall and even after camping season was over, we would use the camp while possum hunting at night in the late fall and winter. In the fall after the leaves have fallen, the large poplar trees were filled with thousands of seed pods about two or three inches long. Once the pods had ripened the seed were dispersed by the wind over an extended area. Birds and animals also fed on the seeds. Each pod contained hundreds of individual seeds which floated to the ground whirling like a helicopter. One of our favorite past times was shooting at the ripened pods with a sling shot and watching the wild geese flutter to earth. Even better than the sling shot was shooting the pods with a .22 rifle. When a bullet struck a pod, it literally exploded, sending hundreds of wild geese spinning to earth. Month after month for a few years, we enjoyed this activity. It was especially enjoyable at night. In the brightness of a strong campfire and against the blackness of an autumn night, we brought untold thousands of our "wild geese" to rest on this mountainside meadow like so many delicate snowflakes. In our blissful innocence we were seeding a forest. And then we were gone, most of us never to walk among the trees we had planted. The face of the mountain has changed. The little flat meadow on the side of a hill hidden there just for us can no longer be discerned even by one who stands at its center. To return to the "Flats" one must float above the trees like the "wild geese" set free from their roost at the top of the tallest poplar or drift on the morning mist with the song of the wood thrush not seen or heard but conjured up by an undying dream to hold forever something once treasured.

D. Denton
12/2000

Note to a Buddy

When the Elliotts left Graham County and moved back to Madison, Georgia, around 1948, they left an empty house on Slaybacon and a vacant feeling in my soul that seemed as deep and huge as one of the dark hollows in the mountains of western North Carolina. Actually it was only Sam and Dixie and Cramer who had moved, but their leaving had a finality about it because all the others were away from home anyway. John joined the Air Force in about 1947, Swann was living with his older sister, Azalea, near Robbinsville, and Tine, the older sister, was living in some far-off place like Chicago.

Few experiences in my memory, up until that time, hurt as deeply as the loss of the Elliott boys. My own brothers and older sister were gone, and Dad worked away from home, and now Cramer was gone, too. In a practical sense the time and energy demands of a hillside farm during those years consumed most of the waking hours. There wasn't time to reflect upon the loneliness, but the reality of genuine and increasing isolation was inescapable.

Since there was no one to make music with now, I learned to feed that profound longing for musical expression though private introspection. Mostly, I would sit in my spot in the kitchen near the cook stove where it was warm and secure, singing and playing guitar. Mom was often there and would sometimes sing alto with me on some of our favorites. Thus, music became for me, during those years of searching and wondering, the very coin of exchange through which I felt, interpreted, and expressed life and the world around me. Alone, but full of hope, I listened to and sang those sad, sweet ballads; those songs of tragedy so loved in the hills and the gospel songs and hymns, which could transport a lost soul all the way to the protecting arms of the good Lord. Life was captured and distilled in all its shades and dimensions by Jimmie Rodgers singing "Moonlight and Skies," or Vernon Dalhart singing "Flower from My Angel Mother's Grave," or maybe Hank William's "Wedding Bells Will Never Ring for Me." Some things are internal, especially those which become woven into the very fabric of our lives and personalities. Powerful and unforgettable is the mental picture and indelible emotion of Cramer sitting on a cot in a tent at Lackland picking a borrowed guitar and singing, "Cabin in the Hills of Carolina." Days later we were sent in different directions and had no more contact for almost four years.

In a way, I suppose, people like Tom Barnes took the place of my buddies during those months in the late forties. They were from another generation, yes, but it was those persons with whom I spent many waking hours. I thought Tom was delightful in an unusual sort of way. We spent many days together sawing wood and hauling and spreading manure. It all had to be done by hand in those days, which meant we had to fill the bed of the wagon with pitchforks emptying each stall all the way down to the hard-packed earth. By the end of winter, hay stems, corn stalks, and manure had accumulated two or three feet deep and the cows and horses literally had to climb up into their stalls. All of this had to be loaded and spread pitchfork full by pitchfork full. Tom Barnes helped make a game out of this dirtiest job. And I can now see him doing a little buck dance on the empty wagon bed on the way back to the barn for another load. Tom was on older man who wore pants several sizes too large around the waist, but they always seemed a little too short. He had spindly shins which would show above his shoe top, and his socks were always crumpled and falling down over his ankles. With his oversized shoes and skinny white legs, he looked like the Graham County version of Lil' Abner. Yet, he was a wonderful and rare human being.

Tom Barnes also helped with the gathering of corn. In late fall we would pick the corn after it had matured and dried. Each ear would be stripped from the stalk and tossed into a pile between the rows. Later, with a team and wagon, each pile of corn would be tossed into the wagon bed until it was full and then hauled to the crib where it was stored. The horses were gentle and well trained so it was not necessary to pick up the lines as we moved from pile to pile – a simple cluck or a whoa was sufficient to start or stop them. Tom and I would race each other from corn pile to corn pile, and he loved to trip me with one of his oversize brogans. He would laugh uproariously as I sprawled among the corn stalks and his baggy pants moved loosely around his spindly legs.

Tom bought a new cow, which he often bragged about. She was a brindle cow, one of the last of the old pioneer breeds now almost extinct. Once, I remember, he brought her to our farm to be serviced by Dad's registered Jersey bull. It was my responsibility to take care of such activities, and I recall commenting that his new cow was quite skinny. Without a change of expression, he was quick to explain that she was "skinny on the outside, but on the inside she just had rolls of fat." I was amused but even then recognized this as part of an attitude of acceptance and survival. People like Tom and his dear wife, Omie, made the best of what they had, finding a little laughter in even the most unlikely situation. We were separated by a couple of generations, but fate threw us together and for awhile he took the place of the buddy I no longer had.

Work was the defining reality during those months, and happiness became a matter of looking forward to a future, which I blissfully believed would be better. I learned to look for the good outcome of things; thus, hard work and faith was enough to sustain me through an otherwise difficult and lonely time. In the absence of my brothers and the Elliot boys social relationships were pretty tenuous and revolved around the working hours spent with neighbors such as Fred Lail, Herbert Crisp, and the irrepressible Tom Barnes. I learned to respect these fellows, and I learned to care deeply about them, because we shared more than common labor; we shared in each other's struggle to survive.

One afternoon in August, I was hooking the team of horses to a hay rake at Uncle Patton Harwood's barn across the road from our place. I heard a familiar voice and looked up to see Cramer Elliot making his way over the fence up near the road. I was moved by a feeling of absolute joy and we visited for a while.

Cramer had come back to Robbinsville to finish high school being somewhat disillusioned with the schools in Georgia. As I recall, he was living with Azalea down near the mouth of Mountain Creek, so we were able to spend some time together in school up until the time we enlisted in the Air Force in December 1950. The memory of an evening that fall continues to grow despite the passage of time. It was a Sunday, I believe, and Cramer and I were sitting on the bars where we let the cows into and out of the pastures from the barn lot. It was late in the day and we talked seriously about the future. Somehow we felt we had a special insight into life's secret and meanings. Perhaps we did. Events, not even imagined at that time, would tend to verify that we each lived with an intensity and sense of energy a little beyond the norm.

For three and three quarter years following basic training, we had no contact. And then one day in August 1954, I picked up a note in the Orderly Room to return a call to a certain number in Phoenix. I was stationed at Luke AFB, Arizona, and had been since June 1951 except for a couple of TDY assignments at Chanute and Amarillo. So for the last few months of my tenure with the USAF, my lifelong buddy and I were back together. Actually, we were assigned to the same crew, working on Douglas B-26's, which were being used as target tugs. Not only did we work on the same crew, we shared a room in the barracks with T/sgt Bill Holloway of Anniston, Alabama.

At that time I had a small band and we played at some of the local honky-tonks around that part of Arizona. What I remember most is sitting in the Cactus Club in Glendale, listening to the jukebox, and getting reacquainted after all that time. I can still experience the same feelings when I remember us listening to Kitty Kallen sing "Little Things Mean a Lot," or Pee Wee King and Red Stewart doing "Backward Turn Backward." I can clearly envision the intense expression on Cramer's face – his eyes would narrow a bit revealing a passion for the music and a level of emotions unusual in its dramatic power. There would be a tightening of his mouth revealing the scar across his lip – not a blemish, mind you, but an enhancement offering a mark of character. In those days he loved to drink "Moscow Mules," and from time to time would express his feelings with a softly spoken, "Damn," as he brought his fist down gently against the table. We both marveled at how quickly we were able to reestablish a friendship that was beyond the bounds of expression or definition. Each of us even at that time realized that our lives were taking dramatically different directions, yet we shared a kinship that was mutually understood, even though not necessarily stated.

The Cactus Club was a bar operated by the American Legion in Glendale. My band played there from time to time and Cramer enjoyed catching our performances. It was during one of these evenings that I wanted to sing "A sad song about folks a dying." This became sort of a standard expression between us having its own significance based upon a shared moment.

Cramer went on to complete a distinguished career with the USAF spending 30 years of active duty followed by a period of work with the Air Force as a civilian. For me, providence allowed an entirely different set of circumstances and opportunities. Roughly 35 years were spent in the fascinating search for an increased opportunity for the education of deaf children.

Tales That Wag – (Isaac, Poco, and B.J.)

ISSAC

Isaac Motter from all indications was a fine man, and a member of one of Frederick's old families. Mr. Motter probably had other namesakes, but the one I knew could stand alone in almost any gathering. In fact, his name alone was enough to distinguish him; it was Sir Isaac Motter. His registration papers do not indicate whether he was actually knighted or if he became Sir Isaac on the basis of his membership in a noble lineage. He was surely the pick of the litter. I knew three of his siblings, and would venture that members of the households with which his litter mates were identified would agree that Isaac was a cut above his brothers. They were English setters, each one a different combination of the traditional colors of the breed. Isaac was black and white and as handsome a specimen of this old and famous breed as one is apt to see. Isaac and his brothers grew up on a lovely farm on Crickenberger Road near New Market. They had hundreds of acres of fields and woods to roam, and the benefit of this rigorous exercise helped them develop the one characteristic by which they became legendary, if not famous. This characteristic was stamina.

One of Isaac's brothers belonged to Arthur Potts. Arthur was a member of my board so we often had chances to compare notes on our bird dogs. Arthur told me that he and his dog made several attempts at obedience training. I often saw them together in Baker Park, walking briskly, one behind the other. It was sometimes difficult to determine if Arthur was just flushed from the excitement of their daily walk, or, if he was having difficulty keeping up. Apparently, the obedience lessons helped, because Arthur consistently maintained the heel position just a step behind his dog. Arthur's dog was lighter colored than the others, being a soft combination of tangerine and white. He was not as robust as Isaac, but he had learned to survive on only a small amount of oxygen. His lungs must have been powerful, because you could hear him wheezing from a block or more away as he leaned enthusiastically into the collar, as if his whole purpose was to pull Arthur as fast and as far as possible.

Judge Claytor Smith and his family had another member of Isaac's litter and this one was the most easily recognized canine in Frederick, if not the most popular dog outright. He knew the town and its people and it is said by many that he was most comfortable in the historic district. Although he traveled everywhere in the city from Fort Detrick to the Victorian homes on Clarke Place in south Frederick, he was most at home near where the old money resided. With his easy-flowing trot, he covered the miles with ease, in light or heavy traffic. He seemed oblivious to the clamor and noise about him and intent only on his destination. People spoke to him from their cars or from the sidewalk, which they shared momentarily with him. He might give one a quick glance of recognition, or even a wet kiss if close enough. His expression was one of pure delight and determination – a happy dog on a daily mission – a mission of being seen in all the places that mattered at least once in twenty-four hours.

The James McSherry family had Isaac's third brother. He was what is called a tri color, the most in demand color combination found among English setters. He was probably as handsome as Isaac, but I was never around him enough to really know his personality. He certainly was not as boisterous as Arthur's dog and was not nearly as well traveled as the Smith family dog. The McSherry dog was greatly outnumbered by females in the household, as was Jim, of course. I believe there were a dozen daughters in the McSherry family, and this factor alone could have a lot to do with the quieter and more disciplined demeanor of the dog who shared the large home on East Second Street.

It was mid afternoon in August, and both the temperature and humidity were high. He was barking as if he had an animal treed or cornered in some way. He was on the pasture hillside behind the house and by the time I made my way to him, both he and I were overheated. Isaac was maneuvering back and forth to keep himself between a monster groundhog and the animal's hole. This went on for awhile longer, and then as if he was tired of the contest, he quickly rushed forward and caught the animal before it could reach either the main entrance or the back door to its den on the hillside. Typically, woodchucks, or groundhogs as they are called locally, dig a maze of underground chambers all interconnected. Around the main entrance is a large pile of earth and rocks easily identifying the location of the animal's home. But somewhere close by, hidden in the grass, is an exit or escape hole. There is no fresh dirt around this hole since it is removed from underneath, thus allowing a trapped animal to slip out the back door and even sit and watch a hapless dog digging away at the main entrance.

In this instance, the groundhog was caught before he could reach either entrance. Isaac simply grabbed the animal between his jaws and lifted it into the air. He grasped the animal about mid body so its head was on one side of Isaac's muzzle and its back end on the other with the four legs pointing forward. With both his head and tail held high, Isaac easily trotted down the hill with the stunned woodchuck being transported ungracefully to an end it could not have imagined. I eagerly followed the dog and his prey down the hill, and through an opening in the fence where the well-trodden path used by our horses and other animals led to a small creek. The creek was several feet wide at this spot, and there was a pool where the water was perhaps a little over a foot deep. By the time I got to the creek, Isaac was already in the water alternately lapping then panting with his pink tongue dribbling water and saliva. He was shifting his position one way or the other, keeping the groundhog in the deepest water and unable to escape. I now realized that Isaac had chosen this unusual way of disposing of the groundhog because he was too hot and needed to cool off in the fresh water. The groundhog was "in over his head" and struggling to stay afloat while Isaac was in ecstasy, stretched out full length in the water with only his head and the tip of his tail showing. He was fully alert, however, and the groundhog's every move toward escaping was countered by a shift on Isaac's part, cutting off any avenue of retreat or escape. When sufficiently refreshed, Isaac quickly and mercifully dispatched our groundhog. This was one of perhaps a dozen groundhogs that Isaac caught that summer. Almost certainly there were others that we didn't see, but Isaac kept us informed of his success by bringing dead ones home and leaving them on the lawn or in the flowerbed as a token. On one occasion, he overstepped propriety of placing a particularly large one in his bed under the steps in the garage. That incident almost cost me a good dog and a marriage.

Isaac brought home other things, too. Some of the treasures that we found in or near his bed were of more than passing value. We would have praised him except for the uneasiness, we felt that some or most of these items were gained through larceny. Like his brothers, Isaac covered a lot of ground, just how much we could only imagine. Over time his reputation was known far and wide. We hoped that having him neutered would remove some of the incentive to travel, but we misjudged the animal and the source of his wanderlust. The reduction in hormones was surely replaced by a freedom of conscience, because his roving only increased in the years post surgery. Maybe his innocence helped to feed his growing enthusiasm, because he was never covert in the manner in which his wandering occurred. Everything about his movements was out in the open, and I tend to believe at times that he was able to take on phantom qualities.

On two occasions, he brought home five-pound, unopened bags of dry dog food. This was quality stuff, Purina or equal, and not the store brand sold by the discount houses. Maybe these bags of dog food had been given to him, or at least he thought they were his. Why else would he bring them home? Of course, he got to eat what he brought. It still puzzles us, though, that he was able to carry these bags home from somewhere without tearing them and spilling the contents. He would occasionally bring home treats from a local butchering, and turkey bones were commonplace at our house around the holiday season. During hunting season he brought us bony parts from deer. Isaac would chase deer, but I don't think he was ever able to catch one. Once our niece, who lived close by, announced to her mother that "Uncle Denton's dog ate a whole cow." Dutifully, the mother followed her daughter to examine the evidence and, sure enough, there Isaac lay gnawing on the leg bone of a cow, complete with hoof. "See, Mommy," the little girl explained, "it's all gone but the foot." But, beef and turkey were not the only domestic meats that Isaac liked. Imagine our surprise at finding a complete country-cured pork shoulder next to Isaac's bed. The shoulder weighed about ten pounds and had not been cut or even chewed. There were only faint markings left on this piece of meat by Isaac's canines. This was one experience that we didn't really want to talk about. No one is apt to get upset about a neighbor's dog carrying off a beef bone, or even a five-pound bag of dog food now and then, but people have been shot for raiding the smoke house. In a way, I was proud of Isaac. He was showing exceptionally good taste, but at the same time, I was afraid if I made a fuss over him, he might go back for a ham next time.

Of course, Isaac was acquainted with all the dogs in the various neighborhoods where his sojourns took him. Since he was such a free spirit, some of these dogs envied him, always on the move, stirring up excitement, and then quickly disappearing. An older couple who lived not far away had a pair of beagles. The beagles were kept in an enclosure, but they really liked Isaac. He loved to visit and enjoy the attention these smaller dogs gave him as he viewed their world from his position of assumed status because of the unlimited freedom he enjoyed. For a while the owners of the beagles enjoyed Isaac, even feeding him on a couple of occasions. His visits became a source of disagreement between this couple. Finally, the matter was placed in the hands of the animal control department. Twice, I had to spring Isaac from jail, and twice, I learned that it was because of the beagles.

One man in the neighborhood had a pack of dogs that were used for hunting. These were not the "wannabe" type hunting dogs, but were the genuine article: mixed breed, aggressive, ill tempered and large. They were also a little on the trashy side, and they didn't like Isaac. The feeling was mutual, and things would have been all right except that Isaac could not leave well enough alone. When he was on one of his runs, he just had to swing by this house and get this gang all stirred up. Up against these mutts one on one, or even one on two, Isaac could dispose himself quite well, but against the group, no way. One afternoon, Isaac and I were out with a gun walking through the fields and woods with the hopes of jumping a rabbit or even a pheasant. Isaac's hunting style was fast and free ranging, and before long I could tell from the ruckus that he had gotten this pack of dogs upset. I was moving along an old farm lane at the edge of a field calling Isaac, hoping he would get away from this crowd before it was too late. The noise told me that there had already been a couple of brief encounters and feelings were running high. By now the whole pack was headed in my direction with barks and yowls from half-a-dozen different dogs. Just then, I saw them. First, I saw Isaac with his ears laid back heading in my direction with the speed of the wind, but he was followed closely by the mongrel pack, which seemed to be tumbling head long toward me. At this moment, Isaac saw me and heard me calling his name. Infused with new hope and energy, he began to open the distance between himself and his pursuers. When Isaac got closer to me, I instinctively stepped forward toward the pack of tormentors, yelling at the top of my voice and flailing my arms and the gun. My actions startled this pack of dogs hell bent on getting even with Isaac, and they skidded to a halt, bumping into and falling over each other. By now Isaac was even with me and emboldened by my presence and the noise I was making, he suddenly whirled and went on the attack. The neighbor's dogs panicked and fled in bedlam. Isaac followed them a short distance, turned to look at me with that noble head held high and then scratched the ground with all four feet in a dramatic display of assumed dominance as if to say, "Man, we showed them."

If I walked out the back door with a coat and tie on, Isaac may or may not get out of his bed to greet me. If, however, I came out the back door with a cap and what he recognized as fun clothes, he was immediately at my side, waiting to see which direction I took. Similarly, he was aware of the differences in vehicles. If I walked to the state car, he returned quietly to his bed. If I approached the pickup, he was there and would enter the cab from whichever side the door opened first. Best of all, he liked it when I walked to the tractor shed. While I was on the tractor mowing the pastures, he would hunt in wide circles, jumping small animals, birds, an occasional deer, or in the 70s or early 80s a pheasant or two.

Isaac didn't take well to the short period of training he was given to show him how to be an English setter. The whistle was supposed to be the key to maintaining control over his movements, etc. He ignored the whistle completely either when used by me or the trainer. Isaac knew what he loved and that was to range about the fields and woods in wide interconnecting circles, moving at a determined pace and flushing his prey a hundred yards ahead of the hunter. If he happened to encounter a groundhog, and he encountered many, he was in most cases able to catch the animal before it reached its hole. Since Isaac's passing, groundhogs have repopulated the farm in staggering numbers. The grandest chase of all, however, usually involved a full-grown deer, sometimes two or more in a group. One November morning, Isaac and I were working a thicket of multiflora rose and such along a small stream bottom. On one side there was an open hillside covered with grass, and on the other side a hill sloped gently upward toward the woods. This hill was covered with standing corn. Suddenly two large doe exploded out of the cover in front of us, and Isaac quickly engaged them. For the first hundred yards, I could see all three animals streaking single file through the dry corn stalks. I could also hear the rustling, but beyond that point, I could not actually see the deer or the dog. Instead I could see three separate spots of motion like waves moving through that sea of corn stalks.

Isaac liked to ride in the truck, and even more he loved to ride on the farm wagon. As mentioned, if I was on the tractor, he was content to go about his earnest hunting returning quickly to my side if I stopped for any reason, even to open a gate. He liked to sit high up, as high as possible, on top of whatever load was being hauled. One winter weekend, David West was visiting from West Virginia. It was a pretty day, though cold and with almost a foot of snow. David and I decided to take the tractor and wagon to the top of a hill where I had snaked several dead trees to be cut up for firewood. We took along a couple of chainsaws, an axe, a bucket of fuel, hand tools, and headed out. Isaac quickly joined David on the wagon as I drove the tractor. After a couple of hours, we had managed to saw and load the better part of a cord of wood and were ready to head back toward the house. The load of wood was stacked quite high and the tools placed among the blocks of wood. We were on top of an open hill, which sloped sharply in the direction we had to go. The wagon tongue was connected to the tractor draw bar with a simple pin. Ordinarily the pin was kept in place by a cotter pin, which prevented it from bouncing or being pulled out. Neither of us had noticed that the cotter pin was missing as we prepared for the down-hill journey. Isaac, of course, was perched at the highest possible point enjoying the most commanding view available. David West had cleared a spot on the front end of the wagon bed and was sitting with his legs hanging over the bed so as to be able to quickly jump off if necessary. The weight of the wagon and load of wood pushed the tractor forward as we started down the incline. I knew that with gravity at work plus the snow, I would not be able to hold the load back with the brakes and would have to depend on the gears. Glancing back and forth while trying to control our descent, I happened to see the pin connecting the tractor to the wagon bounce out of its hole and disappear into the snow. I yelled at David to jump and turned the tractor sharply to the left to avoid being overrun by a load of wood and a dog. David easily cleared the wagon as I brought the tractor to a stop. We watched as gravity took charge and the wagon picked up speed hurtling down the hill toward an old barbed-wire fence and a thicket of small trees including a cedar about 15'–20' tall. Isaac sat perfectly still facing straight ahead with his ears blowing gently back alongside his head. By the time the wagon struck the fence and the cedar tree, it was moving with considerable energy and speed. The noise of screeching barbed wire, breaking timber and tumbling blocks of wood provided a violent backdrop of sound to a visual image which seemed frozen in time, slow motion tragedy and comedy. The entire cord of wood lifted into the air as the wagon bed slammed against immovable objects and the back end of the wagon was thrust upward. Above and in front of all of this was a black and white English setter propelled with all the force of the wagon and the wood plus his own energy released instinctively as he leaped to clear himself from the tumult all around. He disappeared into the underbrush just as a huge cloud of snow rose like a thunder head engulfing everything. David and I made our way quickly to the scene knowing for sure that we had lost more than a load of wood in this remarkable incident. As the snow cloud settled and as individual blocks of firewood rolled downward through the snow, Isaac climbed out of the snow and bushes, shook himself and trotted busily around the area as if in charge of the whole matter and just checking things out.

As Isaac became older, he became mellower and seemed to enjoy his quiet moments of togetherness with me. Sometimes when I was out doing some chore around the farm, Isaac would conduct his own business close by. For example, if I was working on the corral fence, he would busy himself not far away, but when I stopped my activity for whatever reason, he would quickly appear and stand or sit close to me so as to be touching. I remember very well when we had to build the small horse barn after the old shed had burned down in 1984. The barn project consumed many evenings after the regular workday, and Isaac always wanted to be nearby as we completed the different phases of this job. When I would sit down to catch my breath he would be there within seconds with his head upon my knee.

One experience is especially memorable. It was a Saturday in October and I thought it might be fun to walk through the woods taking advantage of the colors and perhaps even see a squirrel or pheasant. Isaac seemed as happy to go hunting as I was to have him join me, so we set out. It was a lovely day, bright and crisp with plenty of fall color and sunshine that added gold to everything it touched. After an hour or so, we found ourselves at a favorite spot. The woods were open and the trees were mostly large oaks and a few scattered hickories. There were dead trees here and there and woodpeckers were busy breaking off pieces of bark searching for beetles or grubs. I sat down with my back against a large white oak and watched as Isaac searched out every stump and hollow log. It was such a perfect setting that I began to feel drowsy. I guess after awhile I must have dozed off. As a sense of awareness returned, I slowly opened my eyes. My head was tilted slightly forward and I looked into the soft brown eyes of my dog. I had not known he was there, and as he sensed that I was awake, I felt the movement of his body against my leg as he wagged his tail.

Isaac had made friends with an old gentleman named Shoemaker who lived alone over near Highway 26. We were aware that Isaac was getting extra food somewhere because he was gaining weight even though he was eating less at home. One night in February 1985, a man knocked on the door and explained to me that he thought he might have struck my dog over on 26. He described the dog and indicated that when he stopped his vehicle after the accident, an older gentleman approached him distraught and crying, and told him who the owner was and where he lived. The man who had hit Isaac was very apologetic and explained that he simply could not avoid the accident. He told me where the gentleman lived who had seemed so upset about my dog being killed, and he explained that Mr. Shoemaker had told him, "If you don't tell the man about his dog, I will." All along we had known that something like this was inevitable. Peggy and I drove in the darkness over to the busy intersection on 26 and Old Annapolis Road. While we were placing Isaac's body in the bed of the truck, Mr. Shoemaker, alone and old, walked up to pay his last respects to a friend that had brought him immeasurable pleasure down through the years. We learned that Isaac made nightly calls to the home of Mr. Shoemaker, scratching softly at the door and waiting to be invited inside for a few moments of tender and priceless affection, followed by a second supper.

POCO

At the end of the holiday break, parents were returning their children to the North Carolina School for the Deaf on a Sunday early in January. This was around 1965 and we lived on campus. Late in the day, Fred Rusmissel, chief of maintenance, stopped by the residence and told me that a family from down in Eastern Carolina whose son was a middle school student had decided to return home without their small dog which escaped from their car earlier in the day. It was an eight to ten hour drive to their home, and they reluctantly left only when assured that school personnel would make certain that the little animal would be given a good home. The lost dog was a little black Chihuahua, which remained hidden for two days under Goodwin Hall, a large dormitory.

Fellows from the maintenance department were finally able to catch the frightened and starving dog and I was called to make some determination about what to do. When I got to the maintenance shop, I found the tiny dog cowering at the bottom of a barrel. They were just trying to make certain that he didn't run away again. When I picked up this trembling creature, it seemed to weigh almost nothing and its eyes seemed much too large for its body. I knew then that I would keep the dog, so I took him home. So frightened, so hungry, and so small, we called him Poco.

We were never certain how old Poco was, but he never grew, so he must have been an adult when he made the trip to Morganton that January. He had two sets of upper canine teeth, which we noticed when he first arrived. We thought the first set would soon drop out (baby teeth) and he would have a regular smile or snarl, but they never did. He lived out his days with a toothy grin and seemed to understand that it gave him an appearance of fierceness that served him well. He bonded quickly with family members and was seldom separated from us. Wherever we went, Poco went, and he traveled in every manner of public conveyance: sometimes in a pocket, sometimes in a ladies' handbag, sometimes in a picnic basket, or under a sweater. Being so small, he was easy to sneak into hotel rooms, and he visited some pretty exotic places.

On one of our regular and frequent trips from Maryland to Kentucky we stopped at a Gulf Station at Inwood, West Virginia, where Highway 51 connects with Interstate 81. After filling the gas tank and using the restrooms, we piled into the car and headed down the Shenandoah. After perhaps twenty miles, someone asked about Poco. Mary and David both looked startled and immediately blamed each other for leaving the dog behind.

"You were supposed to get him!,"

"No, you were supposed to get him,"

"Oh, Mama, what can we do?"

Tears started to flow, some yelling occurred, and then we searched for an exit and headed back up the Interstate. By the time we arrived at the station, we were all on the verge of an emotional explosion. Pulling up in front of the building, I shut off the engine and we all piled out. As we stepped inside, we were greeted by a tiny black Chihuahua occupying the manager's chair and very much in charge. The manager told us that Poco had claimed the chair and refused to let anyone sit down. When approached, he would bare his impressive canines, both sets, and whoever was there would quickly back off. The people at the gas station enjoyed our family reunion, and we happily went on our way with David and Mary both trying to carry the little dog at the same time.

In 1971 we bought the first 21 acres of the farm where we now live. Having the farm, of course, meant that we would soon be involved with horses. Poco never really liked horses. At best you might say he tolerated them. He enjoyed the farm, though, and loved his visits to the open spaces. Being involved with horses meant that we were also involved with vets. This was especially true once we began breeding horses and having young foals to care for. Poco had no experience with vets except his required shots. These visits were perfunctory, so there was never an opportunity to discuss particular problems or concerns about his health. Once when Dr. Lee Miller was at the farm treating one of the horses, I remembered to ask him something that had bothered us for a long time. As Poco became older his impacted teeth contributed increasingly to a breath problem. "Dr. Miller," I said, "What do you do for a dog that has really bad breath?" Innocently, I assumed he would recommend some simple remedy, or ask specific questions.

Without looking up from his task, Dr. Miller replied. "Don't get your face too close to his mouth."

As I stood there holding the horse's halter, it occurred to me that Dr. Miller had exercised a sense of humor developed over years and years of experiences in fielding questions whose answers were self-evident. After he left, I leaned against the board fence and laughed until I was exhausted. Poco never lost his impacted canines. I never gave him breath mints, and every time I got my face too close to his mouth I smiled quietly.

David had several G.I. Joe toys including a large number of plastic soldiers about two inches in length. These items made excellent chew toys for Poco and many of them disappeared for a time only to show up later as nondescript pieces of mutilated plastic barely resembling the commandos or paratroopers they had once been. It was a common matter for these little treasures to be found between the cushions on the couch, under the beds, on the carpet in the TV room, or wherever a bare foot may land in the darkness. There are still some of Poco's favorite toys hidden away in the nooks and crannies of the house on campus even today, more than thirty years later. One of these thoroughly chewed soldiers was found with a small tooth still imbedded in it. I don't remember if this one was found shortly before or after Poco died, but it quickly became a symbol of both the pure sweetness and the heartache that a small dog can bring into the lives of a family.

When we moved to Frederick, we arrived late that night. The movers would not arrive until the next day, so in the absence of furniture in the superintendent's residence, at the school, we stayed at the Frances Scott Key Hotel in downtown Frederick. Poco, of course, stayed there with us although it was probably illegal. He was stowed away in Peggy's handbag while we registered and made our way to the room. Perhaps there were other dogs who had been guests at the old FSK down through the years, and then, maybe not. We all slept soundly that first night in Maryland, sharing a bed and a mood of excitement with a little black Chihuahua. Poco slept in many hotels and a couple of times flew tourist class on one of America's major airlines.

Baker Park was the location of a family festival one summer. Children and adults were strolling everywhere listening to music, picnicking, feeding the ducks or simply resting in the shade. Poco was enjoying the festival with the rest of the family when we came upon a contest for pets. Mary immediately decided that she wanted to enter Poco. She chose the category of "Most Unusual Pet" and took care of the registration procedures. There were judges and others handling the contests, and there were photographers and reporters from the local papers. One of the handlers asked Mary what was unusual about her pet, and she replied happily that he was Poco, the talking dog. Mary was holding Poco in an upright position with her right hand cupped underneath his bottom and her left hand around his chest with his paws hanging over her hand. He appeared to be quite comfortable perched there securely and facing the crowd with great interest. People gathered around and a photographer focused his camera while the contest handler asked Mary to have to dog talk. Almost immediately Poco's lips curled back exposing a mouthful of teeth including two sets of canines, and from his throat came a gravelly growl. Flash bulbs popped and the crowd roared. Poco and Mary were on a roll and for the next five minutes or more the talking dog was the most popular venue at the family festival. What the crowd didn't know was that each time Mary wanted Poco to speak, she would gently squeeze his bottom with her cupped hand and he would immediately bare his teeth and give forth a throaty growl. Poco was a little dog, but he had testicles large enough for one of the standard size breeds. For whatever reason, he was sensitive about being touched there, and Mary had accidentally discovered that he would growl and bare his teeth if anyone put a hand in the wrong place. The following day both issues of the Frederick paper featured a grand photo of the talking dog, winner of the most unusual pet ribbon. Both Mary and Poco were smiling broadly. We still have the newspaper clipping, but the secret of the talking dog was buried with Poco.

Since we never knew exactly how old Poco was when he came to NCSD and inadvertently in to our lives, we never knew his age when he became infirm and passed away. For the last two or three years he was with us, he had become quite gray around the muzzle. He maintained his zest for living and his aggressive Chihuahua attitude right up until the final weeks of his life. He was an unusually affectionate dog, much more so than any of his breed. Chihuahuas can be nervous and ill tempered, but Poco was a laid back and outgoing fellow.

He developed congestive heart disease the last couple of years of his life. We first noticed this condition when on occasion he would become overly excited and suddenly collapse. When this happened, both his heart and his breathing would stop. We discovered, almost by accident, that by massaging his chest it was possible to get his heart started beating again and then breathing would resume. This happened many times and as time passed the incidence of attacks became more frequent. Each time it happened, it was extremely upsetting for us and for him. Following an episode he would want to be held and comforted. The knowledge that we were going to lose him seemed to endear him to us the more. How can one ever know what a dog is feeling or thinking? It's doubtful, I guess, but it really seemed that Poco understood the fragile nature of the bond among us, and our affection and need for each other increased with every close call. The day finally came when the inevitable would occur. Peggy and the kids were at Ocean City, and for some reason I had remained on campus. Maybe it was that I was to join them later. I'm not sure, but in retrospect it seems that the whole situation was providential. Poco was really beginning to fail, and that last evening he didn't want to be apart from me. His movements were slow and he seemed very tired. At least twice before bedtime, I had to resuscitate him. I was glad that the children and Peggy weren't there because it was becoming increasingly painful. When it was time to go to bed, I carried Poco into Mary's room where he always slept and placed him in his favorite chair on a soft pillow. As I walked out of the room, I couldn't help looking back only to see his soft eyes following me.

Next morning upon awakening, I walked immediately to Mary's room – the chair was empty. I stopped to listen and then I called for him a couple of times. Next I walked into David's room and then downstairs searching each room with a sense of increasing dread. Going back to Mary's room, I searched again and found the little fellow lying under her bed already cold. His heart had finally given out. The time had come for a passage, and I knew then what Poco had recognized hours before – sometimes a heart is just too tired for another resuscitation. Or maybe a heart that is full just needs a quiet, pretty place and enough time to rest undisturbed. The quietest and prettiest place I could imagine at that moment was under a huge and spreading white oak down near the creek on our farm. That is where Poco and I went that morning. I left him there under a blanket of rich, sweet smelling sod with buttercups growing close by. His rest is peaceful and complete, and his memory lends to the sweetness of the place. That is where I go when I need a quiet and pretty place to rest. I was there today.

D. Denton
2/02

B.J.

The first Jack Russell terriers I saw were at a horse farm n the Middletown Valley. Tom McFadden and I were on our way to Wednesday dinner at Camp Kanawha, so we swung through the valley to look at a couple of horses. We found the farm, parked near the barn, and were immediately greeted by two Jack Russells. They were wonderful to behold and I knew immediately that our next dog would be one of these dogs whose spirit makes them larger than life.

Isaac, our English setter, had been gone only a few months and we really missed the affection and warm attention given by a loving creature. I guess this would have been the summer of 1985, for Mary was still in the Philippines. The loss of Isaac had been hard for her, too, even though she was half a world away. Promptly a search was undertaken for a Jack Russell. I was referred to the Kay-Don Kennel in the Woodlawn section of Baltimore. It happened that Ron Sisk and I were attending a meeting in Baltimore and decided to stop by the kennel on our way home.

The owner of the kennel met us and led us around to the back of the house where the pens and cages were. A tiny Terrier puppy fell in behind us stumbling over tufts of grass, trying to keep up, all the while wagging the rear half of her tiny body along with the stub of a tail. I asked the lady if this one was for sale. She said, "Oh, that's Hazel and she is for sale." After this brief introduction, there was no point in looking at other puppies. My secretary was named Hazel, and although she was a wonderful secretary and a person, a dog named Hazel didn't sound right.

I gave the woman a check and Ron and I headed toward Frederick. This beautiful little tri-color terrier slept on Ron's shoulder, spitting up on his shirt only once. Ron didn't mind because he was as taken by her as I was. She was a Russell girl and the only other Russell girl I could think of was Jane. Jane was striking in her own way, so this little Russell became Baby Jane, or B.J.

B.J. quickly established herself as top mammal on the Silver Hill Farm including domestic as well as wild species. The fact that horses weighed more than one thousand pounds each went unnoticed, or more probably just ignored. A dog of any size or description was a challenge. It wasn't as if she had a bad disposition, it was more that she thought confrontation was fun. Once in the off-season, we were visiting Ocean City, strolling the boardwalk with her on a leash. We happened to meet others who were walking their dog, a Great Dane. As they approached, B.J. suddenly sprang at the large animal and when she reached the end of her leash, she was propelled at least two feet in the air where she seemed to remain suspended for a time. The Great Dane was clearly startled and quickly retreated behind his master. B.J., upon returning to the boardwalk from her airborne state, looked happily around and wagged.

She was drawn to any hole in the ground particularly one dug by a groundhog. She would disappear underground and engage any other animal she encountered in a bitter and noisy struggle. We could alternately hear the growls and screams of both animals. Combat would continue until a victor had been determined. We have to assume that B.J. was winner because she survived these encounters throughout her eleven-year life. On two occasions she dug herself in for three days or longer. This is not unusual behavior for a Jack Russell, we learned, but it is stressful for all concerned. When able to finally dig herself out, she would come to the back door and scratch. We usually found her covered with blood and grime, swollen around the face, with a new set of scars, badly in need of food, water, and rest. We tried to keep her on leash or inside, but from time to time she would escape and race directly to the closest groundhog hole. One winter night, about eleven p.m., Peggy and I arrived home and decided to let B.J. out to attend to her toileting without a leash. It was cold and blowing snow. B.J. sniffed around for a few seconds and then broke into a race for the tractor shed. There was a huge groundhog hole under the shed and she disappeared down it before I could grab her. Quickly echoes of the struggle reached our ears, and from the sounds, B.J. was winning. In winter groundhogs do not actually hibernate, but enter a state of estivation or slowed metabolism. It would be a mistake to say lethargy, because no lethargic animal is capable of the sounds made by this one. After what seemed hours, we decided to force both animals out with water. All my hoses were connected and were just long enough to reach from the garage to the tractor shed. The end of the hose was placed in one of the openings to the den and the water turned on. After about twenty minutes a very distraught and muddy groundhog emerged with B J. in rapid pursuit. Peggy managed to grab her. Both Peggy and B.J. required a bath and, as for the marmot, he had to move in and double bunk with a neighbor across the creek.

B.J. really enjoyed television and was especially fond of the Discovery Channel. She would watch with me and respond appropriately to whatever piece of drama was taking place on the screen. Once as a mountain lion stalked a deer she became so interested that she jumped from my lap and approached the TV. As the cougar and deer disappeared off screen B.J. followed them around behind the set growling and barking with every step. The commercial for Fancy Feast cat food provoked her; from any room in the house, she would bolt toward the television when she heard the tinkling of a fork against the crystal dish. As soon as the fluffy, white cat appeared, B.J. would charge toward it and then walk away indifferently as the picture faded. Cats were no good, and this one was particularly offensive.

Perhaps B.J. was the runt in her litter, because she was always small. She also had a habit, which led us to believe she might not have gotten all the nourishment she craved as a puppy. We gave her a soft green rug for bedding and occasionally she would go to the laundry room to her cage and drag the rug from the cage all the way into the family room. With her paws and mouth she would form a suitable "sugar tit" from a corner of the rug and then suck on it for long periods of time. She would place her front paws against the rug, close her eyes and nurse as if she was still cuddled against her warm, mama dog.

B.J. made several trips to Florida with us. Once on Sanibel, which is famous for good shelling, she created quite a stir. Tom McFadden had gone to the beach to do some shelling and had B.J. on a leash. She was so content and well behaved that he decided to release her. Apparently, she had already surveyed the situation, because, ignoring the dozens of happy people strolling and stooping to examine shells, B.J. ran directly to the most unpleasant person in sight described by Tom as "a little, angry, Jewish lady." Tom ran after as quickly as he could in time to find B.J. barking, jumping on the woman, and tugging at her towel. Finally grabbing her (B.J., not the lady) Tom offered voluminous apologies, and endured the woman's wrath long enough to secure B.J. and move quickly away bowing as he backed off. Tom walked far enough away that the woman was barely visible, just a speck among the many other odd shapes on the beach. Feeling safe, he put B.J. down. She seemed so innocent, but to his astonishment, she bolted down the beach through the throngs of people straight to the little woman with the large straw hat and unhappy disposition. By the time Tom caught up, both the woman and B.J. were in a frenzy. The woman was shrieking obscenities and threats of a law suit while B.J. leaped and yelped. This time Tom did not wait to apologize; it was more of a strike and retreat operation with Tom and the dog quickly disappearing into the crowd.

Later that morning, Tom and I, while searching for shells and remembering the incident with the lady, happened upon one of natures most fitting parodies. A group of perhaps thirty royal terns were milling around noisily on the sand as terns will do, but that is not all. Royal terns are white shore birds with bright orange beaks and black skullcaps, which extend backward making their heads seem larger and longer. Two of the birds claimed center stage while the others just milled around looking uncertain and a little embarrassed. One of them (a female, we guessed) very much in the face of another one (a male, we guessed). The female squawked and stalked aggressively in a relentless attack upon the male. The male tern would turn away and try to escape, but she would quickly maneuver in front of him squawking and pecking. Again, he would look away and try to walk off, but she wouldn't let him. Somehow the male took on a Groucho Marx appearance looking aside with one eye cast a few degrees off plumb. Tom and I literally rolled in the sand knowing that we had seen recreated for our pleasure the encounter between the Jewish lady and Tom. The large group of terns who looked on with nervousness and embarrassment represented the other people on the beach.

B.J. lived to be eleven and during her years provided three very special offspring. From her first litter came Denton, a tri-color like her. Tom and Vicki were so fond of B.J. that they were allowed first pick and Denton graced their household and their lives for several years until his sudden disappearance. (We think he dug himself into a groundhog hole.) Denton had a sister from the first litter who was sold to the people living in our farm house. She was called Megan. B.J.'s last litter was a single puppy who became the delight of our daughter Mary. Mary named him McFadden because of Tom's fondness of B.J. and Denton. McFadden has many of his mother's characteristics, especially her good nature and boundless energy.

As she aged, B.J. developed arthritis, which was especially painful in her front limbs. She was able to get some relief with occasional doses of phenobarbital, but this caused other problems. She seemed free of the pain when she was permitted to roam outside and find a woodchuck hole to explore. In the final weeks, she was wracked by pain and kidney failure. When it reached the point where she could no longer take water or eat, the ultimate decision had to be made.

In looking back over the years that Isaac and B.J. were a part of our lives, it is difficult to imagine life without their warm presence and unconditional affection.

David Denton
Summer 2000

Kinfolks Who Weren't Relatives

Mom and Dad moved to Robbinsville in about 1927. They had been living in Bat Cave where Dad was a young engineer helping build the road across Hickory Nut Gap down the mountain to Chimney Rock. That road is now old U. S. 74. Dad had met Mom when he was the engineer supervising the construction of U.S. 221 from Ashford up to Linville Falls. Dad was a boarder in the English household where Mom was the middle daughter. They fell in love and were married. When U.S. 221 was finished, they moved to Bat Cave. In March of 1924, Charles Edwin was born, and in October of 1926, Mary was born. These two oldest were born in Bat Cave, and the other four were born on Sweetwater. Graham Noell came along in January of 1928.

The house on Sweetwater had been built by Great Grandfather Phidelia Harwood. By this time Granddaddy Harwood was gone but Grandmother Harwood was still alive. I'm not sure what the financial arrangements were, but the house on Sweetwater with 28 acres of land became the property of Mom and Dad, and thus, our home. Because of the nature of his work, Dad had to follow his jobs to far away places like Altavista, Virginia. Dad's absences made it tough on the family, especially Mom. With our own place, the family could have a garden, fruit, crops, chickens, cows, pigs, and of course, there was plenty of wood for heating and cooking. Somehow, with Dad away and able to come home only every couple of weeks, Mom and the kids made it with sporadic help from some folks who became part of our family.

Jim Davis was one of these folks. Jim was one of those characters who sort of came and went. He would come stay with us for awhile, then something would happen and he was suddenly gone. When he was there, his presence was generally a positive force, but there was also an air of unease, which seemed to follow him. Maybe it was that he would periodically get drunk, and this would raise the level of tension in the household to unbearable levels. Jim could be pleasant and he was certainly handy around the place, fixing things, cutting wood, plowing or fieldwork, or just hauling rocks from the fields and piling them along the creek bank.

Jim was related to the Hardy Davis family who lived down Sweetwater about a mile, but they didn't seem close. Jim didn't have a wife, and Mom said he was too contrary for a woman to live with. It seems like he did have a daughter who was married to Garrett Riddle. Garrett Riddle got killed when a bulldozer fell off a cliff during the early days of building Fontana Dam. I didn't know what happened to his wife. I guess we were the closest thing to family that Jim Davis had. He was sort of crippled, and I think he had a bad eye. He had one good eye, though it was dark and reminded me of a pirate. He always smelled of tobacco, and for good reason, he smoked a crook-stemmed pipe that rested against his chin and he chewed tobacco. I used to enjoy his tobacco rituals. He always carried a twist that he used both for chewing and smoking. Twists of tobacco are no longer made, I don't believe, but were common in those days. A twist was several leaves of tobacco folded lengthwise and twisted around each other and looking like a large pigtail from some girl's hair. He carried the twist in the long, narrow pocket on the leg of his overalls where carpenters carried a folding rule. When he was ready for a chew, he would pull the twist from his pocket, open his pocket knife, and cut a piece about half as big as his thumb and push that into his jaw. Then, he would take his pipe from the front bib pocket and carefully cut smaller slices off the end of the twist and crumble them into the bowl of his pipe tamping it down with his thumb. By now his cud had been well worked and he would spit before putting the pipe stem between his teeth. Jim always carried kitchen matches in his pocket, and he would now grasp one with his right hand and pop the head of it with his thumbnail. Usually the match would light on the first or second try, and he would hold it to his pipe puffing and letting the smoke billow around his head. Occasionally in striking the match, a piece of burning phosphorous would lodge under his thumbnail causing dramatic flailing of his arm, and some language equally dramatic. Choosing to strike a match with his thumbnail, I am sure, was done for purposes of impressing the impressionable. I was one of those.

One Christmas while Jim was staying with us, something happened that touched me and taught me that family is sometimes more than blood relations. The fireplace was in the center of the north wall of the front room and on each side of the fireplace was a window. The tree was a cedar as was customary because the pasture was full of young cedars and they smelled like Christmas. Most of the family had left the front room and I remember only three of us remaining there. Perhaps the others were lingering over a Christmas breakfast in the kitchen, or out among the farm animals finishing the chores. Jim Davis was sitting in front of the fireplace staring into the fire with a sort of far-off expression on his face which I didn't understand. He said nothing. Dad, I believe, was trying to tune the old floor radio. Stations were few and distant, the mountains were a barrier to reception, and the old battery was getting weak. I remember the static sounds and the occasional voices, incoherent and hollow. Mom was walking around the tree with a quiet half-smile on her face. She stopped and reached into the branches of the cedar saying with mock surprise, "Why, there's something here! And it's for you." She pulled a popcorn popper from the tree and handed it to Jim. It had a stiff wire handle about three feet long, and the basket that held the corn was made of screen about two inches deep with a length and width of something less than a foot. In those days we popped corn over an open fire extending the basket over the coals and holding on to the long handle. Jim's one good eye sparkled with surprise and his hard face melted into a look of sweet gratitude. I don't remember anything about the other presents, but this was one fine Christmas. For the price of a wire popcorn popper, Jim became family. We grew our own popcorn in those days, and there was enough to last the winter.

Other memories of Jim are less pleasant than that special Christmas but as powerful in the emotions they evoke. One of these represents a sort of coming of age for my brother Charles Edwin who would have been about eleven or twelve at the time. Jim had probably been drinking, because he was loud and belligerent. Dad was away in Virginia, and Mom, surrounded by her brood, was trying to deal with this difficult man, now drunk and threatening in his demeanor. Mom looked frightened and pale, and suddenly Charles darted from the room, grabbed Dad's .22 rifle from its place in the corner and ran back into the room. He yelled and his eyes literally blazed with the terror and weight of the situation. I don't know what my brother said, but Jim paled, dropped his arms by his side and slowly walked out of the house. I'm not sure if Mom ever told Dad about this experience, but it was a long time before Jim Davis could muster the courage to come back and apologize. As for Mom and the six children, we simply grew closer and stronger.

Occasionally, Jim's presence or his deeds were a source of laughter. As already stated, Jim could be a lot of help around the farm. Charles Edwin was scarcely old enough or strong enough to do the plowing at this time and it, of necessity, fell to Jim or someone like David Holloway who Dad hired from time to time. It was late spring and the day before Jim had just gotten started with turning the sod in our bottomland. Apparently, Jim had a bottle of moonshine hidden away somewhere, because by the time we had harnessed Bell, a gray draft mare, and gotten her to the field, Jim showed up in a loud and abusive manner. He immediately started to take out his temper on the old horse. He yelled at her and started jerking her around. This was upsetting to my brothers and me, and we tried to get him calmed down. He then decided that she needed to be ridden, and that he would "learn her a lesson." No one to our knowledge had tried to ride her, and Dad had already warned that she was not to be ridden. Jim paid no attention to us but proceeded to unhook her from the turning plow, hang the trace chains over her harness and attempt to pull himself up on her back. She was a big horse with big feet and not at all graceful. Jim was holding onto the harness, one foot already lodged in the harness, trying to pull himself up with the horse now beginning to whirl in a circle, trying to get away from the man who was punishing her. Around and around they flew, Jim hollering with the one foot up and the other foot knocking clods of dirt through the air as it periodically touched the earth. Bell was snorting and emitting vast amounts of gas as the whirlwind continued over the uneven, plowed ground. With one mighty heave, Jim launched himself into the air and as it appeared that he would finally land astride her, she rose to meet the challenge thrusting herself into a full-fledged buck. With an arched back, they met in mid air, Jim Davis coming down among the chains and straps and harness. The impact forced every cubic inch of air from Jim's lungs with a resounding "whoomph." Every trace of alcohol from Mr. Davis's system was expelled with the air, because as old Bell's feet settled into the clods and her legs compressed like coil springs, she returned skyward and upon reaching the apex of this, the greatest leap of her life, Jim Davis and old Bell parted company. Seeking equilibrium while still airborne, Jim's arms whirled like propellers as he spread eagled into the freshly plowed ground. He was sober but didn't seem to be hurt in any mortal sense. Bell stood quietly as if thinking "well that ought to take care of that." She took little notice of Jim but waited patiently to be hooked to the plow again. That didn't happen and as Jim walked stiffly and uncertainly away, Bell slowly looked up as he disappeared in the distance and lifting her tail slightly she pooted quietly. When we were able to get ourselves settled down from this unexpected and entertaining spectacle, we returned Bell to the barn, unharnessed her and turned her loose in the pasture to enjoy a wonderfully earned day off.

Lenna McIntyre came to live with us while we still lived in the old house. She was in her teens, caught somewhere, it seemed, between being a child and a grown up. She could be either one, but by any standard she was a pleasant addition to the family. She was especially helpful to Mom, willing and cheerful about any task, and with a bright face with a big happy smile. Lenna's mother was a Hensley and that meant musical ability. All the Hensleys could sing or play instruments or both and she was no exception. In fact, Lenna looked a lot like June Carter when she was younger and had a similar personality. Charles Edwin had a guitar that Mom and Dad had gotten for him from Sears

Roebuck. It was a Silvertone and was a pretty nice sounding instrument. Lenna could play guitar, and I can still visualize her with that guitar which seemed too large for her small frame. Somewhere there is an old photograph of Lenna and the guitar. My favorite of the songs she did was "You Are My Sunshine" written by Jimmie Davis who became governor of Louisiana. I also loved to hear her play and sing "Born to Lose," a sweet country ballad.

In the days when Lenna lived with us, there were other persons who became a part of our lives. Essentially these were men or young men who were involved in one form of farm work or another. David and John L. Holloway were brothers from mountain creek who helped out periodically with fieldwork. They were as different as if totally unrelated. David was stocky and solid, while John L. was slender and rangy. They were different too in disposition. John L. was quiet and serious while David was easy going.

There were also the Crisp brothers from lower Sweetwater, Henry and Clint. Clint was Edwin's age and they were pretty good buddies. Henry was older and more of a serious work hand. Clint and Henry both liked to hang around, and it seemed there was always something fun taking place. The Crisp's had a friend or a relative, I'm not sure which, who visited from time to time, and this person was also musical. My memories of this person are scant, but on one visit this person or one of the Crisp brothers fell off the fence while playing Edwin's guitar and knocked a hole in it. Everyone was upset and an effort was made to patch it. A piece of unmatching wood was hand whittled to fit, and it was glued into place. This piece of wood was thicker than the regular guitar wood and was never finished with respect to sanding and varnishing. Nevertheless, this guitar remained in use for years to come. I learned to pick on this old, patched Silvertone.

Charles Edwin was pretty well grown up during the Lenna years and I think that she represented one of the early romances in his life. Lenna needed a separate and private place to stay, so the smokehouse was converted into a self-contained place for her. Originally the smokehouse had an earth floor and the walls and ceiling were dark from years of smoke and were unfinished. A floor, walls and ceiling of beautiful knotty pine were built and the end result was an attractive and lovely room for one extra sister. Lenna left about the time we moved into the new house in 1938. The smokehouse reverted to years of use as a meat house although we did no more hickory smoking there. I can't walk into the old place though with out hearing Lenna's sweet voice and the strings of Edwin's old guitar.

Cropland and pastureland were always at a premium on the small farms found throughout the mountains. Steep hillsides were not suitable for row crops like corn, because the soil once plowed and prepared for planting would erode rapidly during rainstorms because there was no vegetation such as grass to hold it. The hillside, however, once cleared of trees and shrubs were fine for pasture. Some of the fields used to grow hay were also pretty steep. The shortage of land that could be cultivated often called for multipurpose uses. Our vineyard had several rows of very productive grape vines, and every year between the vines we grew corn and beans. The soil in the vineyard was very rich but extremely rocky which made plowing and hoeing a challenge.

The best bottomland and the less steep open fields were used heavily for the production of corn or hay. Occasionally we grew wheat or rye on our cornfields and when it was harvested in May or June we immediately plowed the ground and planted corn. Corn was the principle source of feed for all our livestock; chickens, hogs, cows, horses, and for us. Corn bread was baked twice every day. Of course we also needed adequate space for our gardens, potato patches (sweet and Irish) and sometimes tobacco.

Since Dad was trying to improve and enlarge our herd of cows in order to have the dairy operation that he dreamed of, grain and forage for the cattle was a growing need. The dry cows, heifers, and young steers were moved to outlying pastures in the summer months to take pressure off the regular pasture needed for the milking herd. My brothers and I would move small herds of these non-milking cattle to the Harwood Cove or to the Davis place on the head of Pinhook for summer pasture. The Harwood Cove belonged to Uncle Patton Harwood and the heifers and young steers grew fat grazing and resting among several acres of fruit trees. The Davis place was owned by Granddaddy Denton and this remote farm was used primarily for summer pasture by himself, us or some mountain family needing a place to rent. We would carry bags of salt to the cattle in these far pastures once a week, and had many fine adventures doing so. When we returned the animals in the fall, they were sleek and fat and, having spent the summer on the mountainside, were wild as turkeys. The young steers were ready for butchering by Thanksgiving and the dry cows and heifers gradually took their places among the milkers.

My most vivid and happy memories of Audie center around the spring and summer we put in a crop of corn at Granddaddy's orchard known as the Riddley place. It seemed that Granddaddy had fruit trees everywhere and this good-sized orchard of several acres was hidden away in a lovely cleaning at least a mile from his home on Slaybacon. Audie Willcox came to live with us and work on the farm in exchange for room and board. He was a young man, single and certain to be drafted now that World War II had become a reality. Maybe this is why Audie came to be a part of our family. He had a brother, Porter Willcox, who lived with his wife and children on Beech Creek. There were no other family members since his parents were already gone. It seemed that almost every family was struggling in those hard times. Audie was in need of work and a place to take his meals, and we had both a place for him in our hearts and in our home.

He was a most pleasant fellow and he had a gold tooth in front, which sparkled when he smiled, which was often. He enjoyed teasing my sisters, especially Gwendolyn, and treated me like the younger brother he never had. I don't know where Audie had been in the months before coming to our house. Maybe he had been in the CCC because jobs in this part of the country were non-existent. His arrival almost seemed a providential thing in ways that I can't explain. He seemed happy, and his stay with us was a dreamlike interlude between the great depression and combat on foreign soil waiting just around the corner. We were family, we had each other, we belonged, and we had a cornfield to plant.

Most of the planting had been done, the first cutting of hay would wait a few more days and if the weather held we could plant this extra patch of corn in by weeks end. Audie knew farming so he got everything organized in short order and we were on our way to the Riddley place. We loaded the turning plow, section harrow, single foot, and corn planter into the wagon bed, along with corn and hay for the horses for a few days, hooked the disc harrow behind the wagon and headed for Slaybacon. Our plan was to take all our tools with us, and leave everything at the Riddley place until we were through, including the horses. There was fresh water there, some grazing, and we would make a small enclosure of fence rails where the horses could be fed and kept overnight. We would return to Sweetwater each evening on foot, complete the feeding and milking, eat supper and then repeat the process the next morning before returning to Slaybacon.

Audie and Charles Edwin handled the team taking turns with the plow or harrow. Graham Noell and I patched the fence surrounding the orchard, because there would be cattle foraging outside the orchard this summer and we didn't want them destroying our corn. We also carried rocks, cleaned up brush and briars, and made a sort of corral for the horses. It was our responsibility, too, to harness, unharness, feed, water, and curry the horses. Along about noon, either Gwendolyn or Mary would arrive with our dinner. This was a time of great fun. Audie would laugh and tease and brag on the food as we sat around under a walnut tree near the spring. Audie's favorite was Mom's fried pies made from dried apples. They were wonderful and still warm despite the fact that Gwen or Mary had completed a walk of something like two and one-half miles. Mom would also send country ham biscuits. I don't know where the idea came from, but Mom started spreading peanut butter on our dried apple pies. Audie raved about them, and I must admit they were really good. Sometimes Mom would bake a yellow cake with chocolate icing. Audie told Mary or Gwen to tell Mom that that was the best cake he ever tasted. He said, "Tell her this has to be a Merita cake, because homemade can't be this good." Mom always got the message because at supper there would be another "Merita" cake. Audie would just beam and Mom would, too.

Once the ground had been broken, the team was hooked to the disk harrow. The disk broke up most of the larger clods and finally both sections of the drag harrow would be used to smooth the soil in preparation for planting. For planting, one horse was hooked to the single foot plow for laying off the furrows while the other was hooked to the corn planter. The planter had two hoppers, one for fertilization and the other for shelled corn. As it was pulled down the furrow, the planter deposited a small stream of granulated fertilization and dropped grains of corn every few inches. Two metal prongs at the rear of the planter covered the corn and fertilizer with an inch or two of soil. Noell and I carried buckets of fertilizer to the planter to keep its hoppers full. Before the week was out there was a cornfield to be twisting in and out of Granddad's apple trees. We loaded the tools onto the wagon, hooked the disk harrow behind and climbed aboard. Audie said that he thought the horses would go all the way to Sweetwater without having to use the check lines. He told us that they would stop and start at the gates by voice command and for sure could make it all the way home without anyone having to touch the lines. We thought it was a great idea and set out. Sure enough they plodded happily and confidently down the crooked makeshift road all the way to Granddad's. Every time we came to a gate, the horses stopped automatically waiting for someone to open the gate. Maybe once or twice did Audie have to cluck to the team to get them started again, but not once did he have to touch the reins, which were tied neatly to a post at the front of the wagon bed. When we reached the smooth dirt lane going down past the Elliott boy's house, I knew we were home free. Overflowing with good feeling, we made our way up Sweetwater around the England curve and on up to the lane leading to the barn. The sounds and smells around the barn were comforting and the feeding and milking were a thankful time between hours of work and sanctuary around the supper table. Dad was home for the weekend and he was pleased with Audie's report about the new corn patch at the Riddley place. He smiled as he crumbled hot cornbread into a bowl of fresh milk. For dessert we had another piece of Mom's "Merita" cake.

Audie was drafted. He had been classified 1-A for a few months and then the announcement arrived in the mailbox that he was to report to the induction center. It all happened so quietly; he was there with us and then he was gone. From the induction center he was sent directly to boot camp probably at Fort Jackson. We got a few letters and then one day Mom got a small package from Audie. He had been assigned to the thirtieth division, and I don't know if it was an armored division with tanks or if it was a infantry division of foot soldiering. Audie had sent Mom a cushion cover made of a soft, silk-like material with the emblem of the thirtieth division on it. Such emblems of the Army divisions or air force squadrons were common gifts of G.I.s to their girlfriends or mothers back home.

We never did see Audie again. He was shipped overseas immediately and died somewhere in Europe. It seems that we were told that he was killed in Italy. A few weeks ago, I was back home for my aunt's memorial service. I arrived a day early and had a chance to walk among the headstones of Old Mother Cemetery where most of my folks are buried – brothers, sisters, parents, grandparents, aunts and uncles, and scores of friends many of them veterans. I thought of Audie. Not far from the graves of some of my family, I came across a tombstone for Jim Davis. It's good to know that he is resting near folks who cared about him. He had so much aloneness while alive, in a way it's ironic that he found his way back home in death. We don't know where Audie lies, because he never came back. His spirit is alive and nourished in the hearts of the family who claimed him, though his bones lie on some rocky hillside in Italy.

D. Denton
1/01

Audie Willcox

Jay-pan and Other Faraway Places

In the 1930s dramatic things were happening all over the world. In Europe the charismatic leader of the emerging Third Reich was moving crowds like some dark and unexpected messiah. His words and his message fueled hope, hysteria, hate, and fear, depending upon where and by whom they were being heard. This was such a short time after the "war to end all wars," and much of Europe was trapped by unpreparedness and disbelief. The shadow of war loomed dark as it drifted ahead of the forces propelling it.

In the Far East, the island nation of Japan was making similar noises and moves. The Japanese Navy, particularly its fleet of aircraft carriers and its network of strategic holdings, extended the reach of Tokyo throughout the Pacific world. Was Japan's imperial reach benign or did it have the potential of turning malignant? Perhaps the only obstacle in the path of Emperor Hirohito's advancing military was the United States Pacific Fleet in Hawaii.

Britain, just twenty miles across the channel* from mainland Europe, and its closest ally there, France, could see what was inevitable but couldn't do much to prevent it. England was talking appeasement, and France was searching futilely for someplace to hide.

America was beginning to struggle out of history's worst economic depression and was preoccupied with recovery. The Pacific threat was recognized by many, but it was so far away. No one doubted that war was coming, and soon, to Europe, but American shores seemed secure. The uniformed services of the U.S.A. were well under strength, and America's young men were not flocking to enlistment centers to join up. Thousands and thousands of these military age males were putting on the uniform of the Civilian Conservation Corps, or CCC, as it was known. The CCC's were building trails, bridges, and schoolhouses, though, – not tanks or battleships.

Meanwhile in Graham County, kids were collecting all kinds of scrap metal that was to be shipped to Japan. As always, our mountain people were kindhearted and generous to a fault. Adults and kids alike pitched in to help with the scrap drives. Down below the road on the other side of the potato patch where Great Granddaddy Harwood's barn was, there were several piles of old, broken, and discarded farm machinery scattered among the piles of timbers from the old barns and sheds. We happily gathered this treasure trove of iron and steel and helped load it on the trucks, which came to transport it to the railroad depot. All up and down the creeks, other folks were busy doing the same thing.

At George Cody's house on the way up to Sweetwater Elementary School, there was one scrap pile, which held undue fascination for the kids who walked past each day on the way to classes at Sweetwater. Alongside the road were the broken and crumpled pieces of a wrecked car. We would walk, uneasily, over to the torn metal and splintered glass, and stand there a moment looking at the place where Ed Lail was killed in the car wreck a few months before. Ed had died we were told, by a dagger of thick plate glass from the cars window. The blade of glass severed his heart and he had died there in the weeds. When the scrap metal from the car was hauled away, some of the horror of the place was hauled away with the metal and glass.

Over the mountain, on the Stecoah side of Graham County was a countryside of great mystery. There were literally dozens of small communities hidden away, remote and inaccessible, between the huge and steep backbone of mountains on one side and the deep and treacherous gorge carved by the Little Tennessee River and farther up near Almond where the Nantahala River joins the Tennessee. These communities and villages had strange names, and most of them are gone today, buried by the cold water of Fontana Lake. Perhaps being buried under water helped to add to the mystery. When the federal government, early in the war, was condemning this property, and the people were being moved out, an element of quiet tragedy settled over these little villages like the fog, which hangs over the waters of the Little Tennessee.

Through the auspices of the Tennessee Valley Authority the U.S. government was acquiring this land in order to build Fontana Dam. This proposed dam was to produce hydroelectric power for Oak Ridge, Tennessee, for the development of the atomic bomb and for Alcoa, a major producer of aluminum so critical to the war effort. Periodically, when the waters of Fontana are drawn down more than usual, chimneys, or rooftops appear like ghosts out of another time. Though buried and silent for half a century, they still speak volumes in the memories they cling to – or the memories that cling to them.

The names of some of these little communities still come up in conversation from time to time, and in a few cases there are surviving communities still bearing the old names, like Cable Cove and Almond. Others like Procter and Japan exist today in name only. Occasionally, an old timer will mention one of these prewar settlements and memories come flooding back. When I was in first grade at Sweetwater, the word Japan began to take on a new significance. In my child's mind Japan was a far away place like China. I thought of the two of them together because they were distant and the people who lived there looked different than the people who lived in Graham County, and now that we were collecting scrap iron, there were more and more references to Japan. At the same time, I knew there was another place called Japan, and it was not as far away as the place where we were sending scrap iron. This Japan was somewhere over the Stecoah mountain, but I had never been there. When I first started to become aware of two Japans, this was around '36' or '37 most people I knew pronounced both places *Jay pan*. Somehow I understood that Japan, over on the other side of Stecoah mountain, was not where the scrap iron was going. That matter was pretty well settled, but something else needed to be resolved in my small world. I had noticed that little trinkets such as small badges or buttons stamped out of thin sheet metal had the word printed on the back side – Japan. The little badges had a tab that could be bent so you could fasten them to a shirt pocket on the bib of your overalls. Sometimes these treasures were found in a box of Cracker Jacks. Assuming that these things were made in *Jay pan* over the mountain, and not in the other Japan, I thought *Jay pan* must be a very special place, because there was nothing like that on Sweetwater.

At our first grade Christmas celebration at Sweetwater School, each child received a small gift. It is still not clear to me whether the gifts were provided by the teacher or the children's families. At the time, that was a matter for Santa to worry about, not me. My present was wrapped in brown paper, and it was small enough to fit in the palm of my hand. I tore the paper off and found a little tractor not much bigger than a "match box" toy car, less than two inches long. It had two larger back wheels and was made of thin sheet metal, crimped and folded in the shape of a tractor. It was a bright color, and on the underside was the word Japan. I was sure it had been made over the mountain, and I thought how wonderful it would be to visit this great place called *Jay pan*, North Carolina. I remember talking to one or two of the other boys in my class and we all agreed that toys were made in our *Jay pan* and not that other one.

Time slipped by, and the depression morphed into World War II. My brothers, the Elliott boys, and I had spent a glorious Sunday afternoon riding homemade sleds on pine needles. It was milking time, so we headed home pulling our sleds behind us. On reaching the house we were immediately stunned by the news that Japan had bombed Pearl Harbor. Reality was turned upside down, and life as it had been was changed forever. Those innocent and happy perceptions of childhood were ripped away, or in some cases covered up by new perceptions and new realities. The sad voice of Gabriel Heater brought us the mounting reports of casualties and losses. During those early months of the war, it seemed that the whole world was ablaze. One evening after Gabriel Heater and after supper, I sought escape by rummaging through boxes stored in the small closet under the stairs. We kept old books there and from time to time Mom would put away boxes containing other items temporarily forgotten as time passed and our lives changed. On this occasion I came across a little crumpled toy made of thin sheet metal. I gasped, it was the tiny tractor made in Japan. It was barely hanging together and as I turned it over in my hands, one of the seams had separated and I could see something on the reverse side of the thin metal, a different color than the tractor. Puzzled, I pulled the sides apart and as the little toy unfolded, part of the emblem of a popular American beer became clearly visible.

By this time there was talk among folks about how the scrap metal we had collected and shipped to Japan had been forged into bullets and bombs and sent back against us as missiles of war. Well, I guess I had been really wrong back at Christmas 1937. There was only one Japan, and I was only now beginning to understand what it was and what it meant. As for *Jay pan*, it no longer exists. It got covered up like my innocence. As Fontana's turbines fueled Oak Ridge and Alcoa creating not only the bomb but the B-29 which dropped it. *Jay pan* quietly sleeps in her watery grave, knowing that one Japan is enough.

David Denton
1/01

The Prophet from Cable Cove
(Remembering Earl Cable)

In those days before World War II, the parts of the world that I knew about, and those in other parts of the world that I wondered about, were separated by elements of time and distance that seemed monumental in their vastness. Impressions and perceptions of "town" were powerful and dramatic, much more so than the actual recollections of specific events. These impressions were hazy and diffuse although moving and heavy in the manner that they settled on my consciousness and more so on my conscience. "Town," of course, was Robbinsville, the county seat, three and a half miles away but spanning centuries in my perception. My impressions dealt not so much with places as with forces. The world I knew about and the world that I wondered about were connected by the common thread or maybe the chain which connected good and bad, right and wrong, sin and salvation.

A few feet down the sidewalk was the barbershop, and it was outside this place of business that the most dramatic picture of that era is so indelibly captured and framed. Charlie Sawyer, the Chief of Police, walks fully into my field of vision and lingers for a full minute before entering a restaurant. The bulk of the man in his dark uniform, shiny like the blue serge suit, his face ruddy, and not unpleasant with a cop's garrison hat, his badge polished and bright over his heart, the image made complete and unforgettable by the .45 caliber pistol at his side. Charlie Sawyer had killed a man with that same gun, probably in that same restaurant, just weeks before. People said that he had to, that it was in self-defense, but a killing was an awful thing beyond understanding, beyond imagination. The contradictions that his memory evokes remain unreconciled more than sixty years later.

The England curve was one of the many sharp curves on the Sweetwater Road. On the lower side of the road was a steep drop off and from time to time a car would fail to negotiate the curve and would end up in Zimeri England's field down near the creek. Where the road had been carved out of the side of the hill, there was a considerable bank of red earth where we would sometimes play in the summer. Sometimes we would find Nehi or R. C. Cola bottles that had been tossed out the window of a passing car. These empties could be traded at Tumpy Elliott's store so we would save them. Once when I was alone and on my way to Slaybacon I picked up a Krueger Beer can on the side of the road. It was not made of aluminum and was much heavier than the cans of today. Also it had a short neck like a can of brake fluid. I had never tasted beer and I held the can to my nose to see what it smelled like. The sour, fermented aroma of barley and hops struck me as particularly offensive and evil. I could see the distorted face of the Reverend Earl Cable and hear the anguish in his voice as he related some dark and dreadful sin he had witnessed before being plucked from the jaws of death and destruction by the saving grace of Jesus.

Earl Cable was the pastor at our church, Sweetwater Baptist Church, a mile up the road from our house. Earl Cable was the best preacher I had ever heard and served a couple of times as pastor of our little congregation. His power as a preacher was measured by the force of the truth conveyed by his voice and his face. There could be no doubt that he saw and understood and felt the truth no matter how dark and ugly nor how gloriously uplifting.

His face was like magic, as gripping as if filling a wide screen, transforming the pure agony of a felt and feared hell to the beauty and release of a newfound paradise. All the time it took for a paragraph's worth of words to fall like music or thunder on the hearts of those assembled. This is the way it was when Pastor Earl Cable conducted the revival at Sweetwater. Two weeks at the end of summer, when the spiritual presence of this good servant, this mountain-bred John the Baptist drifted like September fog down the creeks and branches and hollows of this mountain community. Cable Cove sent us a prophet and we were changed.

Sometimes as he preached it seemed that all of us were propelled into a headlong rush, stumbling over each other in our reach for heaven, or in our blind flight from hell, never quite sure which it was. Perhaps it was both, and still is, aware and driven by the spiritual imperative, we hang on.

This was the revival when I would be saved. No more waiting until next summer. There was no escape…I must have been "under conviction!" I could no longer bear being "lost," being a sinner. And then the congregation started singing, "Oh, Why Not Tonight." Florrie Cody started walking back between the rows of pews looking at me. Her face was as sweet as an angel, as sweet a woman as ever lived, and I knew for sure that whatever she had in her heart, that's what I wanted. I didn't wait for her to reach my pew, I met her halfway and she guided me to the front of the church where I knelt by the mourner's bench. God knows I was trying to make it happen. Expecting something powerful and dramatic, I was at first distraught that it didn't occur. I reached and I pleaded. I believed with all the determination that I could muster. People spoke words of encouragement; there were soft whispers of praise; there were prayers; there were warm hands on my shoulder; and there was the unmistakable voice – Earl Cable and he touched my head, "AAA-MAAN!" Affirmation, grace, yearning – did it happen?? Was I saved? I didn't shout; I didn't jump up and down! I didn't feel a sudden rush of adrenalin to my brain. But I was standing, and I was smiling, and people were hugging me.

As I walked the gravel road from the church to home that night, I was aware that a big change had taken place. Being a Christian was serious business. Everything around me was the same – the chirping of a thousand katydids offered that comforting blanket of background noise so much a part of a mountain night in September. The occasional whippoorwill made me feel at home. But this night and every one thereafter would be different. There was a new and different inclination of the heart and mind. Things were the same, but I was different. An awareness of something called accountability settled into a new and serious consciousness. I didn't know if I could handle being saved and living a Christian life. At the same time there didn't seem to be any choice. It was kind of like having to keep up with all the farm work. It was mine to do, and nobody was about to accuse me of being lazy. But plowing and sweating was not the same as avoiding sin and dealing with shame and guilt and worse still, the gnawing doubt that I had even been saved. I would be ashamed to mention these private fears to anyone. I guess this is just part of the pain that comes with trying to live up to all that is required of being a Christian. How could I ever be sure? Imaginations of the meaning of heaven and hell were so extreme in my experience. I understood that rewards were earned with supreme effort and sacrifice. Could one ever be certain that he had measured up, or was the best effort still to be weighted down with doubt? I had real difficulty grasping the concept of "blessed assurance." Sure, I believed. Yes, I wanted a personal relationship with my Savior. I wanted to be changed! But in the peculiar way, my young conscience was constructed, one had to earn again and again, to prove on a continuing basis one's worthiness for the final reward. I understood the absolute certainty of separation and hell, but I was afraid to count on the promise of heaven until I was already there. Was perpetual anxiety just part of Christian responsibility? What about forgiveness? Is forgiveness as elusive as salvation? Does there ever come a time when doubt yields grudgingly to peace? How long does one have to wait?

Did I miss some significant lesson along the way? It's possible, but I don't think so. From this milepost and looking backward, was there some major course correction not seen that should have been made? If that one mile walk from Sweetwater Church to home could be made again tonight, would those same thoughts resonate through my consciousness? How differently, if at all, would the realities of these two nights, two moments in a lifetime, be perceived? Well, the whippoorwills are gone, but no doubt the katydids would still provide a soft cushion of white noise as a curtain for personal reflection. What I wanted that night, I still want. What I sought that night, I am still seeking. Minus the songs of the night birds things are pretty much the same. As for me, that new awareness of something called responsibility so striking that night long ago has not diminished, but grown. I am still struggling with the matter of being saved and living a Christian life. That new and different inclination of the mind and heart has not diminished, and that among all of God's gifts to me has determined how I would deal with the hopes and dreams and duties of one life balanced against the doubts and fears that at times sought to rob one soul of the everlasting promise. Hope for peace deep in my soul depends, in the first instance, on intentions that are compatible with my belief in right and wrong, and in the second instance, on thoughts and words and deeds that settle comfortably upon my conscience, a conscience fed and sharpened by the message of Earl Cable, the prophet from Cable Cove.

David M. Denton

The Rev. Earl Cable

The Upper Row

An interesting family lived just down the road from us. Nobody seemed to know much about the Englands except that they were different. It seems that three brothers and a sister moved into Graham County sometime before the turn of the century – not this one, but the one before. Only one of the four ever married, and that was Will. I think he was the oldest. He lived up the little valley now called England Branch. It was a narrow little valley, but pretty, and he raised his family there on a little hillside farm.

Will England's wife's name was Nettie. She was a quiet and lonely woman, seldom seen with not much to say. Will owned a lot of land up and down Sweetwater Valley and this fact always puzzled me, because the source of his wealth was obscure. Several poor and struggling families rented small, hilly pieces of land from Will England on shares. Sometimes he would sell some timber, but where his income came from was a mystery because he did not have a job, and money was not easy to come by in those times. He owned property adjoining ours, and we never felt comfortable on England land.

Will and Nettie had a tall son named Donald, and he was kind of strange like his dad. Their oldest daughter was named Bera, a nice person who grew up to become a teacher. The other daughter was tall like her brother and was named Zora. These unusual names interested me as a boy, and added a bit to the strangeness of the family. Nettie killed herself in 1943 by drinking Red Devil Lye. It was a horrible experience because she lingered several hours. Some folks said Will England just drove her crazy, and some said she simply couldn't stand being stuck up there in that holler anymore. I don't know what

241

happened to Will, but I guess he died somewhere along the way. Someone told me that Donald and Zora lived somewhere in the county, but I'm not certain about Bera.

Will's brothers and sister lived together in the next house down Sweetwater Road from ours. None of the three ever married. I don't know why this was; it seemed to me that it was a natural part of being an England. Zimeriah was sort of the head of the house and everyone called him Zim. The sister's name was Cornelia, but everyone pronounced it "Corneel." She took care of cooking and gardening and carrying in water and some of the farm chores like milking and feeding the chickens. Zim was kinda like Will. He didn't do much obvious work but bossed Cornelia and the other brother, Herschel. Herschel was slightly stooped and had a bad "hare lip." He had not only a cleft lip, but a cleft palate. His voice sounded hollow and since he "couldn't talk plain" most of the time, he stayed to himself. Herschel always wore overalls and on summer afternoons, the three of them would sit on the porch facing the road. Zim and Corneliia on one side and Herschel sitting on the other side alone.

From the front gate, a walkway led straight to the porch. A double row of boxwoods bordered the walkway and the yard on each side of the walkway contained beehives, perhaps 30 or more. Granddaddy Denton had bees and so did Dad, but they were gentle. For some reason the England bees were ill tempered. Herschel was the one who took care of the bees, and he could walk among them with impunity. This gentle and kind man never seemed to get stung, but it seemed that the England bees would deliberately hunt us down as we walked past.

But the England bees were not the only thing the Denton boys had to fear as we walked past our neighbors' house. In daylight hours the honeybees would chase us summer or winter, and at night we had to contend with that yellow cur dog named Kaiser. He must have been named for Kaiser Wilhelm or "Kaiser Bill" as he was remembered during these sleepy times between the world wars. Perhaps Zim and Corneel and Herschel had named their dog Kaiser after they learned what kind of disposition he had. Perhaps, too, they named him as a puppy and the name turned him sour. Whatever the reason he was a dog to be hated and feared, and along with these angry honeybees. They reminded us to tread softly when near the England place.

In the summer time Kaiser would lie in ambush under the boxwood bushes in the shade. No matter how quiet we were, and no matter how hard we looked to see where he was hiding, he always managed to surprise us, sneaking up behind with his head low to the ground and the ruff along his back standing up like a brush. With a deep-throated growl he would frighten us into panic. Maybe it was our frightened and hysterical response which stopped him, but somehow we escaped those slobbering jaws of death long enough to tell about it. Maybe Kaiser came to represent the strange and disturbing forces that seemed to define the Englands in our young minds. Anyway, I still would not want to walk by the England place at night. Zim and Corneel both dipped snuff, and Zim, who was not particular with his appearance, would have two brown streaks running down each side of his chin from the corners of his mouth. He also chewed tobacco and usually had a twist in the bib pocket of his overalls. Maybe he chewed and dipped at the same time; I never found out, but he did spit a lot. For some reason as I reconstruct these memories, I can see Zim with the side vents of his overalls unbuttoned. The tabs with the brass buttons on these vents were folded inward and his long handled underwear was exposed. Perhaps it had once been white, but now came closer to a deep tan in hue.

Corneel's garden was across the road from the house, or on the "upper side of the road" as we would say. She always had a large garden and I always thought of it as hers because she was the only one who worked it. I genuinely liked Corneel, although there were few things about her that I understood. She was very conscientious about keeping the place pretty and clean. She had many roses and hollyhocks during the summer. There were also beds of old fashioned lilies and in the spring the place was bright with daffodils and narcissus. Along the garden fence she also had flowers. Depending on the season, there were sweet peas, morning glories or tall zinnias.

If Corneel was in the garden when I passed, we almost always visited for a few minutes. We could catch up on the news, the apple crop, the lack of rain, or any of a dozen other topics. If there is one thing that immediately describes Corneel, it would be her glasses. They were ordinary wire-rimmed glasses that never seemed to be quite level across her nose – one lens or the other was always higher than the other. Maybe this lent to her slightly off-centered way of seeing the world, or her corner of it. She shared with me one morning a conclusion she had reached that still makes me curious as well as amused. As I strolled past she called out to me, and I walked over to the garden fence. She was sweating and the lenses of her glasses were so clouded that she could scarcely have recognized me. I greeted her and commented on her fine garden. But she was not happy. She responded by saying, "Well, I'll tell you one thing…this is the last year I'm gonna have the upper row in my garden."

Puzzled, I said, "What do you mean, Corneel?"

"C'mere, son. I'll show you what I mean!" She stepped over the rows of onions, carrots, beans and cabbage as I followed her to the upper side of the big garden. She stopped and pointed remarking, "Look at them weeds! Why they've took over the whole row."

She was right, the night shade, ragweeds and pig weeds were lush and had all but crowded out a few spindly plants of okra. "I'm tired of a pulling and a digging just to get a crop of weeds. The weeds allus claim the upper row, so next year I ain't gonna have no upper row." That'll put a stop to it." She gave no hint that she was teasing, no change of expression, no suggestion of a smile.

To say I was dumbfounded would be an understatement. I didn't want to seem either stupid or smart-alecky, so I finally said as she turned and walked back across the garden, "That's a good idea, Corneel."

As we reached the gate and she returned to her vegetables, she said to no one in particular and to the world at large, "Upper row ain't never worth nothing, no how!"

My relationship with the Englands, Kaiser, and the bees continued until I enlisted in the Air Force. When I returned to Graham County years later, the house was empty and they were gone. Maybe they died off or moved away, but someone else lived there. The place was different, kind of spiritless, and empty in a peculiar sense. The beehives were gone the big balsam trees had blown down. Even the old-time apple trees were missing. There was no sneaky yellow dog hiding under the dogwoods. The garden fence was down and Corneel's wonderful vegetable patch was taken over by weeds and kudzu, upper row and all. I felt a lump in my throat and, glancing toward the house, I saw a porch with three empty chairs.

I thought again of Kaizer and smiled to myself remembering one occasion when we finally got even: the end of the pitched battle between the Denton boys and the double-barreled threat of the England family – that devilish yellow dog and 30 hives of ill tempered bees. It happened this way. Dozens of times we drove the team and wagon past the Englands hauling hay or corn or machinery between our house and Slaybacon. One June while hauling huge loads of loose hay to the stacking ground near the barn, we had been harassed by Kaiser a couple of times. The horses were afraid of him, and we were a little bit afraid of a runaway or some similar catastrophe. We decided on a plan that was sure to be fool proof. We usually carried slingshots in our back pockets and decided that we would conceal ourselves in the load of loose hay, and one of us would shoot Kaiser with the slingshot as he emerged from under the boxwood. No one would know who did it because we would be safely hidden in the hay. We piled a huge load of hay on the wagon. It was really stacked high. Before starting up Sweetwater Road we filled our pockets with gravel, the perfect size for sling shot missiles. Noell would bury himself in the hay on the left side of the wagon, the side that would be facing the England house. I would drive the team with only my head and arms exposed from the top of the load near the front. I drew the horses to a slow, deliberate walk as we passed directly in front of the boxwoods and bees. The yellow dog crept out of his lair, ears back and stalking like a cougar. Noell let fly with a rock almost an inch in diameter. I heard the twang of the sling shot rubbers followed immediately by the whack of stone against wood. I jerked my head up from my nest in the hay in time to witness a cloud of angry bees from the hive, struck by the rock from my brother's sling shot, rise up and then settle around the head and ears of the hapless Kaiser. The sneaky dog yelped, pawed at his head, shook his ears like propellers, ran in circles, rolled and finally bolted toward the house bumping his head and yodeling as he disappeared under the porch.

One shot from a slingshot gone awry, a hive of angry bees disturbed and seeking revenge, and a yellow dog as cowardly as his name sake; these forces were turned finally upon each other. We continued up the road toward home safe in our nests of hay, our happy innocence betrayed only by our laughter. The honeybees had brought sweet irony to the end of a childhood conflict.

David Denton
Dec/2000

One Generation Is Not Enough Time
(Learning to Be a Dad)

My father was always teaching. He was a man of considerable knowledge and substantial ability as well. These matters were clear to me early in life. The setting could be somewhat controlled as when we were sitting around the dining table. Every activity provided an opportunity for instruction. At supper during the early forties, we were given the bonus of supplementing the war news from radio and newspaper with added history, geography, and philosophy of Dad's insight and understanding.

Sometimes as we traveled in the family automobile, Dad would offer a flowing commentary on whatever subject held his interest at the moment. He spoke to everyone and to no one in particular, his voice modulated by the degree of urgency he felt to get this piece of knowledge out for our consumption. It was left to us to pick and choose, filter and assess, or to ignore. He would gesture to the left or right, commenting on a house or the people who used to live there, clear his throat, knock out his pipe on the ashtray and sit for a few moments in quiet reflection.

As a youth I sometimes had the privilege of working with Dad on some farm-related project, or sometimes we would spend hours in each other's company surveying a piece of property deep in the mountains. On these occasions, he expressed his interest and knowledge of many and far ranging matters. He spoke without expecting an answer, and I heard and wondered without responding. He seldom talked about the activity in which we were engaged and when he did it was usually a specific directive like "Old man, bring me that ax," or "Hook up the team and ease on up to the Poplar Cove." Like as not he would quietly drift away without further comment.

My dad was a mystery to me. Our talk was impersonal and general. He didn't talk about me, or to me, or about himself. He talked about issues of importance and matters of principle. I knew something of his knowledge and ability, but I had not the faintest grasp of what he knew about me or how he felt. I would have done anything to please him, but I didn't know what pleased him, being much more certain of what he didn't like. My duty was to meet expectations which were never articulated to me, but which I knew must be very high. Were these expectations his or mine? Neither or both? They were there and they were heavy and urgent. Learning their source would have to wait awhile – a generation or two.

Technically, becoming a father is quite simple. The major responsibility falls to mother who incubates, nourishes, nurtures, protects and gives birth and breath to the infant. The matter of becoming a dad, however, is not at all simple. The contributions of a dad may not be understood or even recognized until a generation has passed. I am much closer today than at anytime in my life to the spirit of my dad. I have come to know, and sometimes even to engage his spirit, not on the basis of what he was able to express or show openly to me, but on the basis of what he believed, treasured, lived and died for. Becoming a dad is truly a multi-generational exercise in faith.

Name

Name – given to a baby son
The most precious of all gifts, or
An act of pompous self indulgence
The power to ennoble the bearer
And the risk to disgrace the same
A legacy that cannot be returned
Once it is given.

DMD 1991

In this verse one finds the contradictions inherent in fatherhood. It is not suggested that this is the way it was intended to be, and certainly not that this is as it must be. For you and I, son and father, have often visited this realm certain that for us it would be different. After all, we were able to venture to the very soul of the matter in our private discourse, each believing that for a concept to be so freely expressed, it must first be felt and understood. Yes, we have been able to search the hills and hollows of this curious and puzzling landscape, and to make some cross-generational discoveries of our own, different though they might be. We have together gained insight and accommodation, and have resolved that we would not be limited by what had come before. We knew what the barriers were which separated sons and fathers, and we had the understanding to remove them or at least to bridge them.

You have heard me say that when my daddy died, there was no unfinished business between us, that I felt reconciled with him. Yes, that statement is true – nothing can be changed anyway, but I never really knew the man, my dad, and probably he never knew me. He is gone, but the book is not yet closed. Every day I read new chapters in this story of a family, and it is still being written. His death was a passing, not an ending! Others of us must pick up the pen and write. It is our turn, but Dad continues to author unfinished verses. What they reveal will be clearer tomorrow. We can wait, can't we!

"How many hopes and fears, how many ardent wishes and anxious apprehensions, are twisted together in the threads that connect the parent and the child!" (Goodrich, Samuel G. 1793-1860 American author)

Perhaps neither of us should be surprised, because it seems that thinking men were struggling with the same wrenching agonies and sometimes ecstasies in the nineteenth century. Has anything been learned since? Maybe! But not by the masses – it is left to the sons and fathers of each succeeding generation to visit this field of dreams, or battleground, and struggle anew with powerful forces, resolving them for their times or passing on the burden unfinished! Strange, but history leaves no record of winners or losers, only a legacy of hoping and hurting.

Some of us are lucky, however, and are able to secure a measure of closeness, which deepens over time. Perhaps it is the searching and reaching which provides its own joy. Such may be the reward of good intentions felt, expressed, and acted. Do we ever get far enough away from the process to gain objectivity about the plan and nature of parenting and being parented? I wonder.

Name

Name, most defining word of all
To a baby, stronger than the generic mama or dada
A word with substance and distinct form
Like "me," strong enough to stand alone
Among a million others, first scribbled
In manuscript, Then yelled
With one's rank and serial number.

DMD 1991

Some acorns fall directly beneath the tree; some are deflected further away by striking a stone. Some are carried away and lost forever, and a few fall on sloping ground and roll downhill to a rich and sunny place where they can grow without being shaded by the tree which bore them, or bruised by the stones which lie everywhere. We all must grow – and grow apart too, though we need to remain aware of the distance between us and be able to close it lest it lead to separation rather than self dependence. Each of us sees things differently, though when as children we gathered meaning from what we were observing aided by the caring and discerning eye of a father, we acquire a bond which can never be broken, though never fully understood either. This is the connection through which ever deepening understanding flows. Or sometimes it becomes the point at which we engage each other in the classic inter-generational tug of war. I guess there is nothing instinctive about learning how to engage each other. It seems we all search and struggle in darkness generation by generation, family by family. Too many of us arrive at that time of crossing over – strangers still denied the joint celebration of the final victory.

Name

Name, a synonym for life's work
Like a shingle on the craftsman's door
The mark of his labor and skill
For a time they are one
And the same - inseparable
Until one is taken.

DMD 1 992

The mystery of my father – a lifetime of uncertainty and anxiety regarding what I meant to him, and how he measured me against standards which I did not understand, and which seemed always beyond reach, has left me not much wiser because he is still a mystery, but much more at peace. I am now secure in the faith that my dad was not unlike me – frightened and often alone; responsible and strong – committed to principles of the highest order – feeling more than he could show, and quietly embracing good intentions without proclaiming them. Even as he was awaiting death, he wept quietly, wondering if he had loved enough, not quite certain whether he had added luster or tarnish to the family name.

Well, David, you know and I know that Dad gave brilliance to the name Denton. In his own deliberate and understated manner, he is teaching us still. His latter-day influence is like a soft nudge to the shoulder, reminding us that this matter of being son and father is not yet finished. Have we not truly engaged each other in a joint reach for an understanding that will have satisfied the standards of even my dad?

David M. Denton
February 1998

Letter to Grandchildren

For the past few months you have been very much a part of my thoughts and my feelings. You occupy my thoughts on a regular basis, but for the past few weeks there has been an urgency felt deep inside me that wants and needs to be expressed. Two separate and very different experiences are responsible for my decision to respond in this particular way. The first experience occurred while Gramma and I were visiting in Santa Fe, New Mexico. The second experience occurred since we returned to Maryland, but it had its beginnings years ago, during my thirteenth year.

Our trip to the southwest in December was made in part to reconnect to a past part of our lives, which helped shape who we are today. I cannot tell you the details of this experience in this letter (we will talk about it someday), but it brought me face to face with some of the experiences which have most shaped my life, my personality, and my values. This experience involving a close friend was extremely painful and left me deeply shaken for several days. In a way it was like going back to 1944, the middle of World War II, the middle of the seventh grade, which I was failing, a time of isolation. (My brothers were in the Navy; Dad worked away from home; my oldest sister was in college.) I was taking on the responsibilities of the farm which was a man's load, and I couldn't talk about my fear or shame of failing school, so I had to deal with the situation alone. Perhaps one of the most important aspects of this experience was how I felt about my family. Family members seemed to me to be almost perfect, and it was my duty to be as good, as successful, and as attractive as they were…but that seemed to be increasingly beyond my reach. I knew that I was the only one in my family to fail a grade in school, and the shame and disgrace I felt were more than I could bear at times, especially since there was no one with whom I could share my awful secret. So it remained my secret, something pushed down and covered up, hidden under a mountain of unending physical labor. Taking over the farm at age 13 was the answer. Running the farm was a man's job and, if I could do a man's job, I was a man! There was no time to worry about whether or not I could do all that was expected. There was no choice; there was no one else to depend upon. Of course, I had no way of knowing what Dad expected of me because we did not talk about it. It was clear, however, that the running of the farm was on my shoulders, so it didn't matter so much what Dad or others expected; what mattered was what I expected. I did not wonder if I could do it all. I would do it all, and possibly a little bit more. This awesome responsibility that was mine, became my mission and my salvation. I became so concentrated on my mission, so focused on the future that I could move beyond the shame of what was happening in school and hold on to the certain belief that something special awaited me out there somewhere. Because I did not know the limits of my strength and endurance, I never reached those limits. There was always enough energy to see me through, and as I look back I do not remember being tired. . . alone, but not tired.

Work was not the only thing happening in my life at age 13, and it is now time to shift our attention to those elements of life responsible for the development of my spirit, my mind, my feelings, my values. Sure, the farm and those years of physical exertion developed and toughened my body and my will, but the other elements were what made life wonderful and full of meaning. At the beginning of the letter I told you of two experiences that had led me to write this letter. The first experience involved a very good friend and left me feeling much as I did when I was in seventh grade. You will remember that it was the responsibility of taking over the farm that allowed me to find peace in purposeful work, accomplishment, and satisfying my own self-expectations. In trying to resolve the experience in Santa Fe, it occurred to me that not much has changed. There is still within me a mission. It is not the farm anymore, but it is still filled with purpose, responsibility, and high self-expectation. This time it is the growing and nurturing, and cultivation of those I love and for whom I am responsible, my family...you!

And now for the second experience – a strange and unexpected one, but one full of soaring feelings and tender thoughts. Back in December, I read a review of a new CD by one of my favorite singers, Collin Raye. The article was very complimentary of this new record especially since it was created for families. After we returned from our trip to the southwest, I was able to find the record and upon listening to it I was deeply moved. Quickly, I felt that the music was speaking to me and I knew it was something I wanted to share with you. Let me try to explain.

Many of my earliest memories are of music, and those memories are still filled with the emotions that I felt as a child. I have distinct memories of hearing songs on the radio in the kitchen of the old house before I started to school. The kind of music that I love most deeply has not changed. When I listened to the Collin Raye record, my sensations were exactly the same as the sensations I felt listening to an old battery radio more than 60 years ago. All my life, music has been a central force in the development of my values and probably even my personality. There are some basic characteristics in music down through the ages that people from cultures all over the world seem to enjoy. These elements of good music involve particular chord sequences, movements, harmonies, and lyrics that show up equally in the classics and in the music of the common people throughout the world. Music has a civilizing and enriching influence on human experience. During those awful months when I was thirteen and struggling with the nightmare of failure in school, it was in music that I found sanctuary. Teaching myself guitar and sitting in the kitchen after supper, I touched the very soul of creative experience, learning old songs and sharing their harmony with my mother. The music bridged the difference in time and distance between two generations. Many of the songs had survived the breadth of the oceans and the separation of family members by centuries....still they stirred the same tender, noble, and sometimes sorrowful sentiments of individuals in every generation.

Especially during the second half of the twentieth century different styles and types of music have become associated with different generations. This is something that has had a very strong influence upon the development of differing attitudes and values between the generations. When I was a boy, there were not different styles of music listened to by adults and other styles listened to by youth. The music of the region during the depression and war years was the same for adults and youth alike. This is a significant matter because music has always been a unifying language across generations. With the growth of mass communication, particularly radio, television, and the recording industry, music has become less and less a common language shared and understood across generations. It is a little unsettling to realize that something that once united us is now a reminder that the languages of our music define our worlds, and those languages can separate us.

When I listen to this record, it speaks in sentiments and values and melodies that are universal and timeless. First of all, I hear music that is expertly and beautifully performed. Collin has a rich Irish tenor voice, and he maintains pitch that is pure and beautifully controlled. The Irish quality speaks to all sides of our family and conveys sentiments that we intuitively recognize as being our own. The theme or themes expressed in the lyrics and tones of these selections convey love and human value with a focus on children and family. His music conveys innocence, not just the innocence of childhood, but the reach and search for purity that never dies in our soul no matter how old we become. This is music of hope and faith that is never more beautifully or nobly expressed than in prayer. Finally, in listening, I became swept along with the melody and caught up in the creative process, becoming part of the magical experience. Few things, if any, in my life have been more deeply pleasurable than creating music. Sometimes, music becomes a sacred experience. It is almost remarkable to know, that at any age, now or when I was 13, I have the capacity to thrill throughout my being, to literally be lifted and to tingle in my senses with the boundless joy known through one of God's most personal gifts, the transcendent experience of hearing his message in the strings of my guitar or in the tones of a sweet and tender voice filled with yearning.

My children, if as you read this letter, and as you listen to the record, you are able to hear some of what I hear, and able to feel some of what I feel, then you will begin to know who I am and what family means to a grandfather.

A.W.O.L. (Traveling Light)

It had been almost twenty-four hours since I boarded this Trailways bus in Knoxville, Tennessee. This journey, since its beginning in Robbinsville had not been a journey of providence, to the contrary, it had been more a venture into darkness which was occasionally illuminated by an unexpected circumstance the meaning of which may not be revealed for years, or maybe never. We all face such a trip, now and then – a trip we really do not want to take, but one that must be taken.

It had taken a full day to hitchhike from Robbinsville to Knoxville, a distance of seventy-eight miles. Before me were two and a half thousand miles that had to be covered in a bit more than the forty-eight hours remaining on my first military leave. In my pocket was all the money I had – about forty-five dollars, and the rest of my worldly treasures were folded neatly in a small suitcase borrowed from Mom. It contained my uniforms and a couple of letters and perhaps a photograph or two. My shaving kit, socks, and underwear were in a small ditty bag.

I told the agent at the ticket counter that my destination was an Air Force Base in Nevada. Then I asked her how far in that direction I could go for forty dollars. She studied the charts, tables, and maps a while and then told me that I could purchase a ticket to Tucumcari, New Mexico, for thirty-nine dollars and forty-five cents. I asked the lady where Tucumcari was and she said that she didn't know, but it was in New Mexico. There were not many options that I had to consider, but I did feel that it would be helpful to know when the bus would let me off in Tucumcari. She again turned to her charts and tables and in a moment

257

answered happily that the time of arrival in Tucumcari was ten a.m. mountain standard time and that would be "the day after tomorrow." That meant that I would need to thumb the remaining distance (800 miles plus) by midnight that night, or be A.W.O.L.

As the bus rolled through the night somewhere between Little Rock and Oklahoma City, now about twenty-four hours after leaving Knoxville, I awakened from a nap and, returning to consciousness, my soul trembled as the letters A.W.O.L. echoed through my empty and frightened being. I started to change positions and reached up with my left hand to rub my eyes and felt something drop lightly against my chin and tumble onto my shirt. It was a crumpled five-dollar bill that had been placed in my hand.

She was a nurse dressed in a white starched uniform, a light-sweater, and the standard cap that nurses wear. She had boarded the bus a couple of hours earlier, I suppose, on her way home from work. She was older than me, maybe thirty, attractive, and very friendly. She took a seat next to me and we talked for a few minutes before I drifted off. I remember her asking about where I was stationed, where my home was, and the standard queries regarding how I liked the Air Force.

This nameless nurse, moved by some unseen force, touched the frightened spirit of another human for reasons she could not comprehend – for reasons she could not deny. Somewhere out there on old U.S. 60 she stepped out into the night leaving behind a gift.

There were other players on this unexpected stage, which rolled through the heartland. One of those with a major role never came out from behind the curtain, and not one of them ever took a bow. Both intrigue and mystery were introduced into this drama by one actor who lurked in the darkness, as it were, never showing her face, giving no hint of her motive. She had entered our traveling stage in Memphis early in the morning. She was bent on a purpose known only to her and she set about it in a manner as forthright as it was strange. Like a deadly spider, she spun her web, and certain in the knowledge that the prey would be hers, retreated into the shadows to wait. She made her exit in Oklahoma City without revealing her scheme, though if one could have noticed, her demeanor must have betrayed the hunger that was there –

a hunger and more – kept in check by an infinite patience fastened on the ultimate fulfillment somewhere farther down the road.

Tucumcari, New Mexico, in 1951 was not very big, and I would have missed it if the bus had not stopped. A harsher reality sets in as I begin to prepare for the rest of my journey totally at the mercy of passing automobiles and trucks. It was midmorning and sunny – a good day for hitchhiking. Reaching above the seat to the storage rack, I grabbed my ditty bag and felt around for the suitcase. Where was it? Stepping out into the aisle where I could see, I began a genuine search feeling panic, now in addition to the dread, which had marked this adventure. The suitcase was not to be found, so I enlisted the help of the driver and the agent inside the small café where the ticket office was. The driver emptied the bus, searched the interior as well as the storage bins, which are reached from the outside. Nothing! Finally the agent called the Trailways offices in Amarillo and Oklahoma City to put a tracer on the missing luggage. My name, address, and a description of the contents were given to the ticket agent, and with apologies the driver re-boarded the ongoing passengers and roared off in a cloud of diesel smoke. With my ditty bag, with my khaki summer uniform, and with what was left of the five-dollar gift from heaven in my pocket, I walked out into the New Mexico desert with my thumb in the air and my heart in my throat. At midnight tonight, I had to be at Nellis Air Force Base, or face the heinous crime of being A.W.O.L. Would it mean a court martial? Would it mean the brig? Would it mean a dishonorable discharge? At the moment it meant disgrace and more – but first I must catch a ride.

How did I happen to find myself in such a state of affairs? Surely I was a conscientious young man. More than anything I wanted to bring honor to my uniform and carry out my responsibilities like I had been brought up to do. Well, there was no great mystery about it. A voice from the last century offers a simple and timeless answer. "There are two rocks in this world of ours, on which the soul must either anchor, or be wrecked. The one is God and the other is the sex opposite." God was surely not the author (F.W. Robertson - Nineteenth Century English Divine) of this tragic-comedy, but he did have something to do with the creation of "A union of two spirits – to perfect the nature of both, by supplementing their deficiencies with the force of contrast."

When I enlisted it was November of my senior year in high school. I had more than enough credits to graduate, and as it turned out, I was eligible for a furlough at the same time my class was celebrating commencement. Basically, trying to go back and pick up anew with my classmates was a disappointment. The Korean conflict produced few heroes, and a self conscious G.I trying to cover the collar of his blue uniform shirt with a graduation gown was an embarrassment to himself and the rest of the class, except for one, maybe.

The days passed quickly and even as I was beginning to put aside some of the strange and lost feelings about being back home, it was time to go. I had allowed myself four days to get back to Nevada and certainly that would have been adequate, except – the day before I was to leave, I happened to be visiting with my former football coach. He had earned a commission in college and was now being called up as a sparkling new lieutenant in the U.S. Army. He mentioned to me that I could borrow his car to see my girlfriend. I was struck by his friendship and generosity, even though I really didn't have a girlfriend.

There was someone whom I had been fond of all through high school, but we had never really dated in the strict sense. Spending some time with her at commencement had given new meaning to the concept of the "Force of Contrast." This was something I hadn't counted on, and suddenly priorities became shifted and I granted myself one more day before returning to my military duties.

This was the evening most nearly approaching perfection up until that point in my experience. Clearly I believed that everything I felt, thought, imagined was shared impulse-by-impulse, heartbeat-by-heartbeat. This was like an extraordinary moment of discovery or regeneration – beautiful and wonderful in its promise and in its innocence.

The coach's car was returned and he was kind enough to drive me home. Scarcely had I fallen asleep then the alarm clock jolted me into a new and harsh reality. I now had only three days in which to cross the country with a heart full of new emotion to deal with. Within moments

I shaved, dressed, kissed Mom goodbye, pulled myself apart emotionally from all the ties of a lifetime and started walking down Sweetwater Road. A ride to Robbinsville was not long in coming, but once I headed down U.S. 129 toward Tapoco, traffic dried up and it took me the rest of the day to get to Knoxville, Tennessee. Initially, I had planned to thumb all the way back to Nevada, but since that first day had covered only seventy-eight miles, and since I had traded one of my days for an evening in heaven, it became obvious that bus travel would be necessary. How far can one travel on forty dollars?

Had it not been for the dark cloud of dread hanging over me, the miles through the wild and beautiful New Mexico countryside would have been enjoyable. It was not a bad day and sundown found me in Flagstaff, Arizona. The elevation of Flagstaff is over five thousand feet and as the sun disappeared, the mountain air became bitter. Even in midsummer there is snow on the San Francisco peaks outside Flagstaff, and now that my suitcase had disappeared with my winter uniform, I stood shivering outside the bus station watching darkness fall. With night the traffic slowed considerably, and soon I was forced inside.

At about eight p.m. I realized with cold certainty that I would never make it to Las Vegas in four hours. My wealth by now was down to a dollar and some change and it was decision time. At a pay telephone I got the operator and asked her to call the C.Q. in my squadron at Nellis Air Force Base. After a wait which seemed like hours, she said, "Deposit four quarters please." The sergeant who had Charge of Quarters duty at my squadron orderly room identified himself and took down the information I gave him, name, rank, serial number, etc. He could see from the orders before him that my leave was up at 12 p.m. and when I told him I was stranded in Flagstaff, Arizona, he reminded me that within hours I would be A.W.O.L. I asked the sergeant what he thought would happen to me. In response, he said, "What did you say your ranks was, son?"

"I'm a private," I replied.

"Oh, you'll be a private," he said, and hung up. With my last quarter, I had a cheeseburger, stretched out on a wooden bench and worried.

With the first hint of daylight, I walked briskly into the Arizona morning anxious to finish this bad dream and face whatever unknown punishment I would be dealt once back at my base. In less than an hour, a Lincoln automobile with Tennessee license plates pulled over to the side of the road and a middle-aged couple warmly invited me inside. They were on their way to visit a son in California and shared memories of earlier times when he had been in the military. To my surprise, this kind couple was going through Las Vegas, Nevada, which meant I had a ride all the way. With a sense of great relief, I quickly fell asleep.

The car slowed down, pulled off the pavement and I could hear the tires on a gravel surface. We had stopped in front of a diner in Kingman, Arizona, and my hosts were happily inviting me to join them for breakfast. By this time I had no money left and was embarrassed to say anything about that. I made an excuse and said I would stay in the car and rest. It was then that I realized that the woman had covered me with a very beautiful fur coat. I was deeply moved by this realization and, being quite hungry, I did join them for a wonderful breakfast. By mid afternoon we had crossed the Colorado River into the state of Nevada, and by sundown I was safely back in my quarters at Nellis Air Force Base. The punishment was not as severe as I had thought it would be – several days of extra duty, which to a farm boy from the mountains was easier than what I was used to. Best of all, I was back to my duty as crew chief of an F-51 Mustang fighter aircraft. In the days following, I tried to make some sense of the puzzling events that were still too fresh in my consciousness. I could not have known that the story was not yet ready for the telling.

On the same day about two weeks later, I stopped by the orderly room to check my mail and had two letters. I put them in my fatigue pocket and decided to wait until after chow time to read them. Later sitting on my foot locker, I opened the first letter. It was from the girl back home, and my heart felt like it was in my throat as I began. "I guess by now you already know that I am married." It was as if each word weighed pounds as their burden settled with a cold finality upon my senses. As for the other words in the letter, they might as well never had been written, because they remain, yet, unread. No explanation, no question. Returned to its envelope, the letter was folded twice dropped into the garbage can while I looked in another direction – no haunting final glimpse, no more.

The second letter was also addressed in a woman's handwriting bearing a name I had never seen before – Miss Faye Sample Vivian, Louisiana. The letter written on blue stationary began, "Dear David," that was unusual because no one except my G.I. buddies called me David. I had always been called Morris, my middle name. "I have your suitcase, and got your address from a letter to you from your sister which I found in the small pocket in the suitcase lid. You were sitting on the right side of the bus in row seven." The letter went on to describe in detail what I looked like, what I was wearing, what color my eyes were, and how badly she wanted me to come to Vivian, Louisiana, to get my suitcase and see her.

She had gotten off the bus in Oklahoma City to return to Louisiana. The suitcase and my ditty bag were on the rack directly above my head, and apparently Miss Faye Sample had reasoned that a certain way to get the G.I. who slept just inches away was to take something that belonged to him. With my suitcase, dress uniforms, and mail in her possession in Louisiana, certainly it would not be long until I was there, too.

Immediately, I wrote back, essentially ignoring everything in the letter except to state that I needed the uniforms, and would she please send them to me as soon as possible. It was June 1951 and before the month was out my squadron had been transferred lock, stock, and barrel, to Luke Air Force Base, Arizona. Shortly before the transfer, another letter in blue stationary from Vivian, Louisiana, arrived. This letter made no mention of the suitcase or uniforms, but dealt extensively with the state of her emotions, her loneliness, and her desperate need for my company. I wrote again repeating the message of my first letter.

In the meantime, the transfer to Luke was complete and my outfit was settled into its new home. The third letter from Miss Sample had been sent to Nellis AFB and forwarded to me at Luke. This letter was even more disturbing than the earlier ones and by now my buddies couldn't wait for the next bizarre chapter in this ongoing drama. By now, too, I had been required to buy new uniforms. Can you imagine having to tell the Commanding Officer about Miss Faye Sample? More letters arrived following and expanding the pattern already established.

August came and my letters became more direct and threatening – she had stolen U.S. government property and that was a most serious offense. Near the first of September, I received a note from Railway Express that they were holding a package for me in Phoenix, collect.

In the late fall of 1954 just a few days from my discharge, and a full three and a half years from the discovery that my suitcase was missing, I stumbled unexpectedly into the final chapter of this serial. While visiting my girlfriend in Glendale, Arizona, she introduced me to her new neighbor who was also in the Air Force and stationed at Luke Field. He was married and lived off base and had just gotten settled at Luke. I learned that he was from Louisiana, and jokingly asked if he had ever heard of Vivian, Louisiana. He indicated that his wife was from Vivian, and for a moment I was almost too stunned to respond. We were standing outside his house and he called to his wife. She came out, we were introduced and I asked if the name Faye Sample meant anything to her. She looked a bit startled and replied, "Why, yes. I know her. Everyone in Vivian, Louisiana knows Faye Sample." She went on to describe one of those rare personalities that we tend to meet only in movies or mysteries, a woman whose life had been touched by tragedy, beauty, loneliness, and a passion fueled by love unfulfilled. It seems that no one really knew Faye Sample. She was too much like those will-o-the-wisps she was forever pursuing to be known or understood. She was not altogether a creature to be pitied, either. Who knows the ecstasies that might have been hers, and who knows what ecstasies might have been theirs for those who dared follow the suitcase all the way to the spider's lair.

David Denton
3/98

Words, Senses, and Metaphysics

"Nothing we use or hear or touch can be expressed in words that equal what is given by the senses.... Was it not precisely the discovery of a discrepancy between, the medium in which we think and the world of appearances, the medium in which we live, that led to philosophy and metaphysics in the first place?"

Hannah Arendt 1906 - 1975
German born American Political Philosopher

Sweetwater Elementary School closed its doors for the last time at the end of 1937–1938 school year. This meant, of course, that the pupils were transferred to the big rock school in Robbinsville and for the first time were able to ride a yellow bus – #24 – a Chevrolet with a cut in the back door made by an axe. Robbinsville School was a long way off, but on a heavy winter day, one could hear the bell all the way up to Beech Creek as George Millsaps tugged on the rope. George always smiled when he rang the bell and his gold tooth sparkled. He smiled too when he fired the boiler and when he applied an old mop to the oiled floors of the schoolhouse. George Millsaps was one of the best things about leaving Sweetwater and going to the big school.

At Sweetwater, we walked to school at least a mile up hill in both directions. Six grades in three rooms, Sweetwater School for some of us was like a honey-coated baptism into that slightly elevated experience of wonder and learning. Perhaps heaven is a bit like that. That little community school was so central to the lives of the people served by it, that they tore down the old wooden structure and built a church on the exact spot. A stone church!

Every moment of the school experience was full and learning occurred wherever the children happened to be, especially during a protracted lunch hour in the woods and hillsides around the neighborhood. Every small incident, it seemed, had a golden purpose. Like the day when one of Arthur Deyton's hogs grabbed my sister's lunch bucket and made off with it. At first my sister cried, but then kindly Mrs. Deyton took her small hand and led her to the Deyton's house next door and fed her a warm and satisfying dinner with the Deyton family.

Time and distance are supposed to sharpen one's objectivity, but I am not certain that is true. It is still most difficult to look with detachment and a coldly critical eye upon the quality of the educational experience within the Graham County Schools in the thirties. Among all the years spent in education, those early years in western North Carolina stand apart from a veritable lifetime of most satisfying passages in our uniquely American system of public education. Whether in the role of pupil or teacher or teacher of teachers, my life as an educator was essentially set on course in the first five years of school. The experience itself was its own reward. The search was the object – the pursuit of the rainbow more precious, more compelling, than the ephemeral pot of gold. The rainbow was and is eternal.

Our classroom activities at Sweetwater were accompanied by the rhythm and groan of the old, water-powered gristmill just outside the window and across the creek. Tuesdays and Thursdays were mill days. We could hear the soft voices and hoof beats of local people arriving at the mill with sacks of corn on their backs, or on a wooden sled or farm wagon. The millrace carried water on an above the ground wooden trestle, which started about one hundred yards upstream and ended where the water poured over the top of the mill wheel, which was about ten feet high. When the mill was not in operation, the water poured over the side of the millrace. In winter, this would form into gigantic icicles creating a scene from some far-off yesterday.

The mill is gone too, but the water yet runs free, down the valley towards Robbinsville where the big Rock school sat on a hill.

Aside from our explorations into the endless wonders of language and arithmetic, history and the natural and social sciences, our senses were stroked by ennobling influence of art, music, and drama. I learned to sketch and color the likeness of tulips in a stone pot and for the most part, I was able to stay within the lines. Tulips were not ordinary flowers and I wanted my artistic creations to be as special as the flowers themselves. I don't know who taught art, but she was good. She brought us an awareness of color and form that helped transform children's early and humble efforts into true works of art.

The name of the music teacher has also slipped form memory, but not the music. She carried with her a portable, hand-cranked Victrola and a stack of 78 RPM records. She introduced us to the world of classical music, adding to our knowledge and appreciation of the music of our culture and our time. I discovered that there were similar emotional and spiritual qualities in the music, that musical harmonics is universal, and that some of the most poignant chord arrangements and movements in a Jimmie Rodgers ballad can be heard as well in a Viennese waltz by Strauss or in one of the many works of Bach. We learned that strings, when well played, can consist of dozens of violins and cellos, or an old Gibson guitar on some front porch up on Sweetwater.

At our weekly assembly in the auditorium, we always sang. We sang songs left over from World War I until World War II came along. We sang patriotic songs and songs of love. We sang in the Glee Club and we sang in class presentations, and of course, we sang in the Annual Operetta, which was a school-wide production of music, dance, and drama. It brought the entire community together in a spirit of pride and celebration.

Sometime near the end of school during my second grade year, our teacher brought our growing interest in words and language to a fever pitch by holding a spelling contest. One by one, pupils were eliminated and finally, at least according to my memory, there were two of us left standing, Mack Huffman and me. That last word was long and tough and I stumbled, giving Mack first place. His prize was a wooden paddle with a long rubber band attached to a small ball. The whole thing was wrapped in cellophane containing perhaps half a pound of candy. My prize was a small metal shovel such as a child would take to the beach. It too was covered with cellophane and contained candy. We didn't go to the beach that year, nor the next, nor the next, but I'm still playing with the words.

Mack Huffman had a fascination with language and even as a second grader could turn a phrase with adroitness. He still can, for that matter, though battling against the force of a brutal stroke. As a boy, he brought with him from West Buffalo a truly unique sense of humor, a bottomless curiosity, and a love affair with the language of his people – our people. It is more than happy circumstances that Mack, early in his development, benefitted from the encouragement, unconditional acceptance, and nurturing of a good family in an isolated but united community. His heart filled with these good blessings, his soul on fire with the possibilities of tomorrow, his tummy filled with hot biscuits and ham and saw mill gravy, Mack laced his boots, walked to Sam Stewart's, caught the bus, and carried a pocket full of dreams in his flannel shirt to the rock school in Robbinsville. It was dark when he left the house and it was dark when he got home, but he would spend his days in the care of a little mountain school, struggling financially and self conscious in its awareness of the awesome responsibility it carried, supported solidly by the community and the scattered families which comprised it.

Predominately, the values, attitudes and behaviors that the children brought with them to the school house door each morning were those of the community at large and the self-same values, attitudes, and behaviors as those embraced and promoted by the school system itself For those few pupils whose values and behaviors were an affront to the standards of the school and community, the situation was usually self-correcting. The school's responsibility was to reinforce, extend, and formalize the basic teachings of the family and the standards of the community.

As extraordinary as it may seem to many today, those WPA years, when the depression was winding down and the world was preparing again for war, were not without hope. First of all, the people were united in the struggle for a common destiny. In those isolated communities in western North Carolina, however, family after family had been tempered by the fire and ice of several generations of bitter struggle against poverty, ignorance, isolation, prejudice, and neglect. Our people had a deeper than ordinary sense of self. They knew who they were; they knew how they got to the mountains, and why they came in the first place. They knew well the stories handed down from another time…when the people had been pushed off the land in Scotland to make room for the sheep, or when they could no longer feed their families on the wages paid in the dark and dangerous coal mines of Wales, or when their peat bogs and rocky hills of coastal Ireland were too poor to put potatoes on the table. Many found their way into the wrinkled hills of the new country seeking only to be able to worship free from the oppressive reach of the church, the government, and the ruling class locked together in an unholy alliance. Some of us found our way to Graham County from ancestral homes on the continent of Europe across the channel and a bit to the east.

Whatever their country of origin, and whatever trail they followed to get here, our people arrived together in this small place, struggled together, and struggled quietly, patient in the certain faith that here, here in the mountains we at last held destiny in our own hands. Where there is hope, where there is a future, dreams postponed a generation or two is more an inconvenience than a calamity.

And so it goes, even as we prepare for the next millennium, not much has changed, at least as far as the world outside is concerned. We are affronted by the rude perceptions of our home as a forgotten backwater. There is really no point though in protesting too loudly. There is a difference between a rock and a diamond though they appear the same to the eye less discerning.

How to Mix a Metaphor

Among all the generations down through history, we must certainly be the most blessed. With late twentieth century technology, it might even be possible to "make a silk purse from a sow's ear." Well, stranger things have happened without so much as provoking a blink among our sophisticated contemporaries. Consider the blurb on Fox on ESPN a day or two ago regarding the medal count at the winter Olympics in Nagano, Japan. These major communications networks have invested millions for the rights to cover these games, which celebrate the ultimate in human achievement brought to you courtesy of Miller Lite or the Bud frogs. Oh, the blurb – that was about the Canadian snowboarder who was stripped of his gold medal because he tested positive for marijuana. Speaking of the news, what about the American G.I. onboard a U.S. Carrier in the Persian Gulf who was watching with his buddies a Presidential press conference featuring President Clinton and British Prime Minister Tony Blair. The President and prime minister were meeting primarily to discuss the precarious situation in Iraq. U.S. Secretary of Defense was visiting the Gulf for the same purpose, and while visiting our troops, he was asked by the G.I. mentioned earlier why the two heads of state did not have a chance to discuss Iraq. The answer, of course, is evident, though startling, and deeply troublesome. Representatives of the nation's preeminent news processions were simply unable to get their heads above the swill that was mostly of their own making and in which all of us, including them, are drowning. We can always consider such matters as American troops abroad after we have finished our tryst with Monica. Well, one good thing, our overseas military forces, not to mention the rest of us, can bathe in continuous, uninterrupted, satellite enhanced TV coverage of the Lewinsky crisis while Saddam slowly poisons the other half of the world. After all, what would you rather watch? With late twentieth century technology, the medium is the message.

As more and more of us are able to make our way up the on ramp and merge tentatively with the swelling traffic on the information superhighway, it seems that we are already being overtaken by millions of others who are chasing their own micro-bytes of power, or at least, the illusion of it. In the competition and confusion of changing lanes, swerving and braking, we may forget where we were going, miss our exit, and be swept along with the others lost in pursuit of the traffic on the superhighway that leads only in a circle.

Superhighways are not destinations, and information is not knowledge, despite the assertions regarding computers with memory and sense. Knowledge involves reason, experience, judgment, energy, and expression. Information may be no more than undifferentiated data until it is gathered, measured, compared, enriched, modified, and applied through reason and judgment toward a purpose. What about smart bombs? The data programmed into it determines the limits of its smartness, and it is able to go only where directed by the controlling computer. Unhook the computer or shoot it down, and then the smart bomb is dumb as hell and twice as dangerous. Powerful, but devoid of judgment or a conscience. The Unabomber is smart, too.

Although we are bombarded with ever-growing volumes of information, we seem yet confused. This confusion is noticeably revealed in the way we express ourselves through the medium of language, in private conversations, public discourse, and entertainment (TV, movies, etc.). Mainstream language has become coarsened by falling standards of propriety, the influence of impersonal mass communication, increased dependence upon technology, and instantaneous contact with others worldwide. The focus is on the medium rather than the message.

Language impoverishment may be just the tip of the iceberg. Language has been described as a vehicle for thought. Does impoverishment in language result in impoverishment of thought? Does one suggest the other? Which one comes first? What is the true nature of the connection between thought and language? Does faulty language expression lead to faulty thinking? How important is accurate linguistic construction and expression to the development of precise cognitive function? Is the clarity and preciseness of thought governed by the clarity and preciseness of the medium that expresses it? The answers seem to be self-evident. It would be most difficult to measure the clarity of thought when meaning is distorted, hidden, or lost by a defective code.

Would a generation of citizens comparatively underdeveloped in the mastery of their mother tongue pose a risk to the nations survival in the next millennium? Dare we ponder the future of a society in which the masses possess the basic skills and knowledge provided through technology, but who are ethically underdeveloped?

A vivid thought may remain hidden by the absence of fit and vivid words to paint it. I wonder if out thinking might remain frail or become crippled until nourished and liberated by robust and fully ordered language. Emerson tells us, "thought is the seed of action; but action is as much its second form as thought is its first. It rises in thought to the end that it may be uttered and acted."(Emerson, Ralph Waldo 1803 – 1882) What if the utterance only half reveals the thought? Can it be fully acted? Is the thought rendered faulty due to faulty utterance?

Language and thought are interdependent in another sense as well. It is through language that our thoughts are revealed so they may accumulate and add to the wisdom of the ages, or at least reveal to future generations the state of our development. Language has been compared to amber "in which a thousand precious thoughts have been safely imbedded and preserved." (Trench, R. 1807 – 1886 Eng. Divine)

Without language to give clarity and expression to our thinking, without language, which like amber, holds and keeps "a thousand precious thoughts" from ages past, without language the creations of the noblest human minds would be but as the blinking of the firefly: here for a moment and then gone, swallowed by the darkness.

February 1998

A Shrunken World in a Miniverse

"We shall not cease from exploration and the end of all our exploring will be to arrive where we started and know the place for the first time."

T.S. Eliot 1888-1965
American-born English poet

Perhaps nothing that has happened in the twentieth century has shaken and altered the foundation of our understanding of the universe as much as has space exploration – in particular the Apollo series of moon shots by which man was transported to the moon and successfully returned to earth. In addition to the expected new knowledge produced by the space program, this extraordinary scientific undertaking has spawned whole new industries. These secondary benefits of man's search for meaning "out there" have possibly done more to shape contemporary attitudes about the nature of the universe than the core knowledge being sought in the first place. In view of the potential for remarkable new insights and new understandings gained from new discoveries, our grasp of the nature of our world, its inhabitants, and the larger universe is unexpectedly disappointing.

Our lives have not only been touched by telecommunications, computers, and a host of other new technologies, but our lives have also been changed, maybe even deluded. The rising flood of new information, its mere volume, its immediate accessibility, its here and now aspect has overtaken the lives of latter-day Americans and given rise to the concept of a shrinking world. Existence on the Internet, life in cyberspace, become arrogant cliches and conceal from us the possibility and promise of new knowledge and new insights into a universe infinitely larger and more complex than imagined.

As we venture onto the "information superhighway" armed with laptop, cell phone, and pager, we may risk becoming part of the gridlock on the mean streets of the "miniverse" in touch with everything but our own humanity. Perhaps it was the words of the astronauts themselves that allowed us to begin to think of a world that could be seen in its entirety, from the vantage point of the moon. That "blue and white ball" cast against a "curtain of absolute blackness," provides a vivid and stirring perception of what was, to the astronauts, their introduction to a new reality. Glimpsing earth from the moon was like peeling back a single tissue of opacity from their senses, only deepening their wonder at what would be revealed with the lifting of the next tissue. One astronaut, in describing his thoughts and feelings on "looking up at the earth" from the moon, stated that for some unknown reason he lifted his open hand and to his astonishment realized that it (his hand) completely hid the world from his view. He did not say that he suddenly perceived the earth as being small; he said instead that for the first time he saw the world as a single community. (Colonel Charles Duke-Apollo XVI Astronaut.) He saw the continents, but without the boundaries which separate nation from nation. He said that with new appreciation he looked at earth realizing that the barriers, which separate the children of the earth, are erected in the minds and hearts of men.

It has been suggested that the only manmade feature on earth visible from the moon would be the Great Wall of China. This wall is evidence of mighty effort, but no one has suggested that it was either a bridge to understanding or a stairway to heaven. I'm not sure about the "information superhighway," since it was constructed after our last manned moon shot. Perhaps when we are able to secure a definitive satellite photo of our shrunken world, it will reveal that the information superhighway is a road without a destination, going only in circles.

While Colonel Charles Duke, member of Apollo XVI, stood outside the lunar module, and looked with awe at his home planet, the earth did not change nor become smaller. He did not see a world no larger than his open hand, a shrunken world in a miniverse. In terms of time and distance, vis a vis the universe, Colonel Duke's point of view was altered only by inches and seconds. His journey to the moon and back allowed him to "arrive where he started and to know the place for the first time."

David Morris Denton
3/98

Letting Someone Else Do Your Thinking

Some current television commercials are perhaps more instructive than their creators imagined, and in ways completely unexpected. A commercial for Motrin caused me to smile the other day, and finally to shake my head in disbelief. Apparently this 30-second exercise in deception is working because it plays often. The theme is that Motrin users are "tough" on pain. These characters, wonderfully macho in their demeanor, "don't mess around" with pain, but at the merest hint of a headache, they "kick butt" by downing a Motrin or two. There is a huge stretch between the message and the image; in fact, the two are contradictory. "Not messing around," "getting tough," and "kicking butt" are good in politics, professional football, and movies, and in much else of America's contemporary obsession with youth and flat abs. Is wimping out to a simple headache by chasing the nearest analgesic or non-aspirin pain killer, an act of self directed toughness? What is one to do with the glaring contradiction between what is said and the imagery used to distort it? Pondering this problem was giving me a headache, and since there was no Motrin in the household to provide relief, without thought to my dilemma, I "wimped out" and actually thought about it. I concluded that to really make it in the image and label-driven culture that owns us, we simply have to give over our thinking to others. It's already been done, and there are labels, images, and code words a plenty to handle almost every situation with no thought at all. It has even been suggested that we give simple numbers to all our favorite jokes, so that the telling is no longer necessary, and once you have called out "#6," everyone laughs on cue.

In our most recent national elections, one politician referred to his opponent as "A Card Carrying Liberal." Millions of potential voters shuddered in horror at this utterly damning revelation. The unfortunate politician, so-labeled, was unable to defend himself against such an imagined indictment, so he committed suicide. Someone said that a small group of "compassionate conservatives" almost cried as they cheered. I went to the library to try to learn all I could about the nature of "Card Carrying Liberals." Not a single reference to this subject could be found in print in any library here or abroad although we went almost all the way back to Gutenberg. Realizing that I must be searching in the wrong place, I contacted the editor of the local newspaper. Being a tough and macho kind of editor, he set me straight quickly by stating, "Hell, if you want the truth you have to go right to the source?"

" Of course," I said, "But where is the source?"

"You some kind of an intellectual?" he said hoarsely. Without waiting for a reply, he continued, "If you want to know what *Real Americans* think about them liberals, go to the Rash Gumball chat room on the net." It should have been obvious to me earlier that if you want answers or images, without the discomfort of thought, go to the net.

Things were becoming clearer now, even an incident that took place a few years ago could be remembered and enjoyed with new enthusiasm. It is amazing, the things you can learn from people who let others do their thinking. First of all, these persons are so free in sharing what they haven't thought about. Since their conclusions have been reached without the messiness of deliberate thinking, they are unbending in their commitment to one of the processed "truths." Television and the Internet help us merchandise images with the speed and volume of Wal-Mart.

The incident alluded to earlier was a candidate's forum involving individuals who were running for seats in the state legislature. I was a candidate for a seat in the House of Delegates. One of the others on the speaker's platform was a young man from an adjoining county who was seeking a seat in the State Senate. This seat was being vacated by a highly respected gentleman who had served in the Legislature for many years. This was 1994, the year of the "Gingrich Revolution" and the young Senate candidate was a perfect caricature of the kind of politician making up the "Contract with America" movement. He brought with him to the forum a considerable following of true believers. Throughout the evening, one young woman of the group supporting the young Senate candidate caught my attention. She applauded loudly at every one of her favorite candidate's comments and looked with disfavor on any remark that strayed from the popular conservative themes of 1994. Several times during the course of my own remarks and responses she looked uncertain. She would look at her candidate and then back at me nervously. When the formal part of the program was over, the candidates mingled among those assembled, shaking hands, and answering questions, etc. As I moved about the floor, this young woman approached me. She still looked puzzled, and as I extended my hand she said, "Dr. Denton, you really surprised me tonight."

I said in response, "How did I surprise you?"

Pleasantly she replied, "Why, you had some very good things to say tonight."

Surprised I said, "Why did that surprise you?"

Without blinking or hesitating, she said, "Because you're a Democrat."

The conversation went no further. It had all been said: labels were more important than ideas. If you'll simply turn your thinking over to someone else, the convenience of being able to hold onto your favorite assumptions is guaranteed. Minds and attitudes and opinions get changed on the basis of confronting new understanding and new evidence. Like the woman said, I was a Democrat and, knowing that, it was unnecessary to understand any thing else. Thinking gets in the way like a headache. The next time someone says something provocative, something that stirs your imagination or something that pushes a question deep in your mind almost to the level of consciousness, don't mess around with reasoning, be tough, "kick some butt." Thinking can rob you of the happiness of knowing simply by looking at the label.

D.Denton
1/01

Religion, Reason, and Being Right

In every neighborhood, there in the mountains were individuals who possessed special knowledge or skills, which were highly useful to people throughout the community. For example, there would be someone who knew how to rive oak shingles for roofing. Someone else in the neighborhood held all the secrets about capturing a swarm of honeybees and introducing them to an empty hive, thereby increasing some family's winter supply of sourwood honey. These good folks with special skills made life imminently easier for others in the community. Among them perhaps no one was more basic to the every day functioning of the families up and down the mountain valleys than the man who knew how to sharpen a crosscut saw. Filing the pairs of cutting teeth and drag teeth to the proper angle and point was not the most difficult part; properly setting the teeth was the key. Setting involved inclining the points of the pairs of cutting teeth outward, in both directions, so that the narrow strip of wood cut and dragged out of the tree with each stroke of the saw was wider than the thickness of the saw itself. Otherwise the saw would bind and be impossible to pull. Mr. Quilliams knew how to file and set a saw, and his services were very much in demand among farmers up and down the creek.

On this occasion I had brought one saw with me and was to leave it and pick up a second saw left for sharpening earlier. Mr. Quilliams suggested that I wait while he filed the saw just brought, and I could take both of them home at the same time. He offered me a seat in a straight-backed chair there on the upper porch while he set to work on the saw. I knew him to be a stern man who took his responsibilities and his religion seriously. He was a member of the Sweetwater Church and he had children both younger and older than me. Adults in the neighborhood in those days didn't hesitate to express themselves openly to the children of neighbor families especially on matters of the soul, or such things as smoking those nasty cigarettes. Mr. Quilliams questioned me about my religious condition and then briefed me on the state of his own soul. He told me that he had been sanctified and had not sinned in the past year. Today it is my belief that he was speaking with absolute certainty and conviction. That is what made the whole thing so scary. He had absolutely no grasp, I am certain, of the weight of the burden his declarations placed on my fourteen-year-old shoulders.

By now the saw was finished, and it was getting on toward milking time. Crosscut saws are flexible steel about five feet long and with a width that averages from about five inches on the ends to about eight inches in the center. A crosscut has a handle on each end, and it takes two men to manage one. The two saws were pretty heavy and difficult to carry considering their length and exposed teeth more than an inch long. Making my way carefully down the hollow from the Quilliams' house I was soon walking on the loose gravel of Sweetwater Road. As I walked, the two saws carried over my right shoulder would bend and sway with my footsteps, resting harshly on bony shoulders. This made for a difficult burden, but it could compare, in no manner, to the one that Mr. Quilliams had dropped upon my soul. The load I struggled under could not have been more oppressive had it been a tow sack filled with creek stones. I felt like a pitiful excuse for a Christian, hardly able to ponder the awesomeness of living a year without sin. But that is what he said! And he had been sanctified. I was familiar with the term and had a vague understanding that it had to do with being cleansed and thus freed to some degree of the desire to sin. But how does one become sanctified? How did he accomplish it? Why was my state so different from his? A year without sin! I wasn't even certain I could make it for 15 minutes. As I trudged along with the crosscut saws hurting my shoulders, the words of this good Christian man beat against the eardrums of my soul. I would have thought his words would comfort – lift. And then, before I had even made it past the England curve, I sinned again. The thought surged through my brain and my emotions that maybe his year without sin had ended suddenly when he declared self-righteously that he had been sanctified and had not sinned for a year. I knew that thoughts could be sinful and I was guilty as hell, because it was my thought and I claimed it! And now I was guilty of another transgression for almost feeling good that maybe I had caught him in a big one.

That this incident has been lodged in my memory since 1947 speaks to the seriousness that I attached to the man's words, not to mention the struggles with feelings of self doubt which it wrought as I questioned the state of my soul in light of his pronouncements. I wondered why it was so important for this neighbor man to be right in laying out his religious claims in the presence of someone who was as ill equipped as I to question the truth of what he stated. After all, he had been sanctified!

Quite recently another incident occurred which reminded me that all over the globe millions of people are caught up in bloody conflicts waged in the name of god. It is written in the lower case here because I believe it is hateful to the Deity to do harm to others to prove a religious point of view. The mother of one of Peggy's former students called one evening during the first week of the recent war in Iraq. Since Peggy was not home, this woman and I engaged in conversation for several minutes. She asked me how I felt about the conflict in Iraq. I told her that I was sure that our Maker was weeping in the knowledge that in that part of the world where three of mankind's major religions were born, millions of people were divided by bitter hatred and people of all faiths were being killed ostensibly in the name of God. I'm sure this good woman had heard my words, but something had prevented her from considering their meaning or intent. Because she blithely replied, "What those people need is Jesus!"

A few weeks ago, I was given the standard reminder that I was responsible for the invocation at the Rotary Club on April 23. In view of world events, the thought of public prayer led to the thought of religion, which led to the thought of war. Was this a paradox in themes? Religion and war? Prayer and persecution? Or, was it something more subtle? Prayer and religion exist in the realm of faith. Maybe that is what religious freedom implies. I thought of the comfort and peace brought by a secure belief – a belief in something that cannot be proved. Believing is an act of faith. Proving is an act of force. The thought these words provided at first startled me. Believing is an act of faith – proving is an act of force. Then came a hint of illumination, then peace. Then this prayer was breathed: "Let us, for a moment, break free from the need to be right – or to prove – and wrap our souls in the warm blanket of blind faith, daring to touch what we cannot see – to claim what we cannot own."

Religion was a central force in the life of the neighboring farmer who sharpened my saws in 1947. He was certain in his pronouncements of sanctification and the absence of sin from his life for a year. Perhaps he had revelation, but what was it that was missing? Why couldn't the certainty of what he had be revealed as clearly to me? If not clearly, then why couldn't revelation be mine, even if it was murky? Maybe the missing element was reason. This is no longer 1947, but for some souls the need for reason, even in the faith-based world or religion, is a continuing and growing need. "Revelation may not need the help of reason, but man does, even when in possession of revelation. Reason is the candle in the man's hand which enables him to see what revelation is." (Simms, William Gilmore – American author 1806 – 70)

What would I have given for a candle that evening on my way home, carrying both the weight of two crosscut saws and the heavier burden of spiritual unworthiness and doubt? Or, could I have heard or read the words spoken at a time still earlier: "He that takes away reason to make way for revelation puts out the light of both…" (Locke, John, English philosopher 1632-1704). But there was no candle to provide illumination that would allow me to glimpse, even faintly, the revelation that so emboldened my neighbor to declare his freedom from sin – no words to hear or read that could anchor my faith now adrift. At that moment, religion was the over-riding force. Revelation and reason would have to wait.

The Years We Spent in Georgia
that Semester

Though unexpected, the Cumberland College experience, as it was coming to a close, had been idyllic in what it had seemed to promise for the future. That last summer in Williamsburg found me doing construction work on the new dining hall at Cumberland where I was taking my last classes. At that time, Cumberland was a Junior College and I had pretty well exhausted the course offerings there and was looking to move on to the next level. In a most enjoyable Business Law Course, I had learned of Cumberland's affiliation with Mercer University in Macon, Georgia; in particular Mercer's Walter F. George School of Law. Mercer offered a four-year law curriculum to students completing Cumberland's two-year A.A. program. Upon application to Mercer, I was quickly accepted and preparations began for truly significant change.

When Peggy and I eloped to Georgia and then returned to Kentucky to begin our lives together, where I was enrolled as a freshman at Cumberland College, her dad made available to us a little Studebaker Champion automobile which had been wrecked and given new life in his auto body shop. This car served us well throughout this time though we literally drove the wheels off it back and forth between Williamsburg and Cumberland Falls State Park where I worked nights until our son David was born. One day the little red and white Studebaker sort of died on West Main Street in Williamsburg near the college. Peg's dad suggested we sell it for whatever we could get out of it and that turned out to be eighty dollars. It happened that Peg's dad, Wade West, had towed a badly wrecked 1950 Ford car to the lot behind his house seven months before. The wrecker bill and storage amounted to more than the car was worth, so the owner gave Wade the car to cover the bill. Wade suggested that I use the eighty dollars to buy parts for the Ford, fix it up myself, and perhaps end up with fairly reliable transportation. He said the Ford had a pretty good engine.

Peggy and I were very pleased, and Wade let me use the wrecker to tow the Ford to the back of his shop where I began to dismantle it. I enjoyed mechanical work and this task would be a real challenge. From a local dealer in used and wrecked auto car parts, I was able to acquire two doors, a left front quarter panel (fender) a hood, a grill, complete wheel and tire, and a front end assembly including control arms, shock and coil spring, spindle, bearings, etc. It was my job to take the parts off the various carcasses, but this helped reduce the cost. The 1950 Ford was black, and I ended up with two green doors, a blue quarter panel, and a maroon hood. With initial assembly, this was a strange looking automobile. Wade smiled knowingly, but he was gracious enough not to laugh aloud in the presence of me and my new wheeled acquisition. All of the used parts cost me around sixty-five dollars. Wade and his men in the shop helped with such things as front-end alignment and adjustment of ill-fitting parts. I did the rough sanding, filling with bondo, and Wade's men did the priming and painting. This Ford had a good motor and Peg and I found ourselves in possession of a pretty good car.

The Ford had been bought in Tennessee and had a title in that state. When Wade acquired it, the title was signed over to him by the original owner, and he then signed it over to me. The state of Kentucky at that time did not have a titling law, so a bill of sale and the original Tennessee title were enough to get the car current Kentucky registration and tags. This was the car we were driving when we made our move to Macon, Georgia.

We were living at that time in a small, white, frame house on West Main Street in Williamsburg, just a few doors from Peg's parents. That is the place where David was born.

Not too long after we moved, the house burned to the ground taking the life of a small child. That spot is now about twenty feet above the surface of Interstate 75. We had accumulated quite a bit of used furniture there, much of which had been salvaged from Cumberland College. Our first move to the University of North Carolina had been made in the little Studebaker. Small as it was, it held our worldly possessions. Now, our move to Macon would require a U-Haul trailer; but we had a car that would pull a trailer.

Arrangements had been worked out earlier regarding a place to live in Macon, so the move itself was accomplished in thirty-six hours. Peg's cousin, Bud McDaniel, helped with the first load from Williamsburg to Macon and back, and the second load I was able to handle alone.

The 1950 Ford handled a small U-Haul trailer very well, so all our household belongings were in the little apartment in Macon the evening of the next day...a Friday. Peggy's sister was getting married that weekend, and she and the baby would be making the trip Sunday by Trailways bus. Meanwhile, I temporarily arranged the old furniture in our new home.

Our apartment was in a government subsidized, low-rent project. It was one of perhaps a dozen such units in a single, long building. Construction was essentially cinder blocks and steel with a stucco-like coating on the exterior. The downstairs floor was concrete and the stairway was metal. The upstairs floor was vinyl over something hard. In front of the apartment building was an open area, part grass and part gravel, which was our yard and parking lot. Facing our building was a series of duplexes of the same style and construction. Affordability was the primary attraction that the place offered, and as we would come to realize later, the only attraction.

Our comings and goings were observed and studied carefully by our neighbors during the first few days. We were approached with caution, even suspicion, when the word got around that I was a student at Mercer University Law School. This development was not far from the University, but the two institutions might have been on separate planets. The housing project was racially segregated, meaning this was a classic "white trash" enclave. The residents seemed to share a monolithic view and attitude of "folks from somewhere else," like us.

That little black Ford had the only out-of-state license plate in the parking lot, and Kentucky must have seemed pretty far north to our neighbors. There were a few children in the Project; some skinny little boys and a precocious little girl from across the street who practiced often with the hula hoop which had just exploded on the American market that year. The little girl was cute, and like her mother seemed quite aware of that fact. Her mother, I believe, was a waitress, but she might have had some other business interest, perhaps in sales, because persons called at the residence on a fairly frequent basis. This housing complex was built for low-income people, so Peggy and I did not have a problem meeting the qualifications. The one common denominator in this neighborhood was poverty, although we learned, over time, that even that is something that exists in varying hues, tones, shades, maybe even perceptions. Our experiences there over the next several months were highly instructive and broadening, and in some cases unsettling to our idealism.

When we arrived in Macon, it was still several days before classes were to begin at Mercer. It would be a few weeks before my G.I. Bill checks started arriving, so Peg and I both set out to find work. She was able to get a job quickly doing bookkeeping and related work for a clothing store owned by two Jewish brothers. I followed up on an ad in the newspaper and met a gentleman by the name of Andy Nichols in the coffee shop at a downtown hotel. He was a flamboyant fellow, almost charming, and he was heading up a regional sales effort for one of the major encyclopedia companies. He conducted an interesting orientation and then set out to offer hands on sales experience in the neighborhoods surrounding. Andy was of Greek descent and his last name was Nicholopolous, or something close to that. He had shortened and anglicized the name to Nichols, but to hear him boast, he was stuck emotionally somewhere back there in the Greek classical period. At first I liked Andy, and we had grand conversations. After a while, though, his mouth and his behavior began to weigh on my sensibilities. First of all, our entire pitch to potential customers was that they would get an entire set of encyclopedia free by agreeing to purchase one yearbook each year for ten years. Each yearbook sold for nineteen dollars. When all payments had been made, the customer would have a set of encyclopedia free and could look forward to receiving a new yearbook every year for ten years. The current yearbook (1957) was on hand as a sample and it was indeed very nice publication – obviously worth the nineteen dollars it would cost, and more. The beautiful set of encyclopedia was a gift! Can you believe all of this for only one hundred ninety dollars? This was an offer you couldn't refuse, especially if you had children. Children were plentiful in those days.

Andy and I hit the road to make the people in central Georgia aware of the gift that keeps on giving. Our first sojourn was in the community of Warner-Robbins, Georgia. This was the bedroom community for Warner-Robbins Air Force Base, populated by hundreds of young couples most of whom had school age children. Andy asked me to drive my car. I soon realized this was a pattern and that he did not even own one. When the market for nineteen-dollar yearbooks and free encyclopedias had been saturated, Andy would be on his way to Mobile, Alabama, or Dayton, Ohio. We called on several homes and I would watch Andy perform his sales magic; it was good. Soon he would give me one side of the street and he would work the other. During the second or third visit to Warner-Robbins, Andy abruptly said, "Stop here," and pointed to a driveway on the left. I pulled into the driveway and stopped. Andy got out of the car and asked me to wait a minute. He went to the door, knocked and was invited inside. After a few minutes, he came out of the house and a woman stopped at the door. Andy was flushed and excited, and suggested that I move the car and work the other side of the street. He suggested that I come back "in a while." In about twenty minutes I returned to the house where I had left him. It began to dawn on me that, although Greek and handsome, Andy was not Adonis, and this was not a wild boar hunt. Andy might be in danger of getting shot by an angry Airman if he happened to show up about now. I found it hard to believe that Andy and the woman were talking about yearbooks. It also began to dawn on me that I may be seen as an accomplice. I moved my little black Ford with Kentucky tags down the street and waited for Andy there.

Eventually he came out of the house, looked around in surprise, and spotting the car came hurriedly down the sidewalk. Well, I didn't make a lot of money giving away sets of encyclopedia, but I do remember this as one of a number of unusual experiences occurring during those years we spent in Georgia that semester.

The course work in law school was interesting as I had hoped it would be. All of my classes were over by 1 p.m. Afternoon hours until Peg got home from work at about five thirty, were spent in study. Often it was necessary to continue study after supper. Study consisted mainly of reading and doing case briefs. Peg's work was boring and difficult; our son David was growing and changing though not yet a year old. We found a woman who lived near the project to care for him during the day. David became very fond of Mrs. Marable. We did not particularly like the circumstances of our new home in Georgia, but I believe we were basically happy. We just accepted the fact the life would be difficult while we were preparing ourselves for the future.

Free time was limited during those months, but we did manage to pay some visits to the Okmulgee National Monument along the river near the edge of town. There had been a large Indian settlement at Okmulgee for centuries, and the Department of Interior had done a creditable job in preserving and restoring many of the artifacts including ceremonial mounds, burial mounds, earth lodges, and others. Occasionally I would walk the cornfields and cotton fields down by the Okmulgee River in the late afternoon searching for arrowheads and pottery shards. Some mounds, not yet excavated, stood among the trees near the river. One such mound had been cut in half like a loaf of bread by the Central Railroad of Georgia. This regrettable piece of destruction occurred before the government intervened. Later in the fall, I would walk along the river with my twenty-two rifle looking for the occasional rabbit or squirrel. These glimpses into the life and times of the first Americans provided a happy counterpoint to my hours spent in the study of law.

The children in the project were as curious and delightful as kids everywhere. They were especially interested whenever I left the apartment with my rifle. One Saturday in November a neighbor and I had planned to go deer hunting. He knew of a place in Jones County a few miles north of Macon where we could hunt. All I had was the twenty-two which was not suitable for deer, but what I really wanted was a day in the woods and fields. Getting a shot at something would be a bonus. We found the place and it really did show a lot of deer sign. There were heavily used trails and many young trees where the bucks had rubbed to remove the velvet from their antlers. On the backside of a beautiful wooded patch, the area opened up into old fields covered with broom sedge and young jack pines. There was a sizable lake in the old fields, maybe a couple of acres. The bare earth above the water line was covered with deer tracks. I found a comfortable spot with a good view of the area and sat down under a small pine to wait, watch, and listen. Pretty soon I heard water splashing around a bend in the lake. I listened carefully and the sound continued. Growing more curious, I decided to sneak a little closer and see what was there. Softly, I made my way through the sedge and as I peeped over a rise and looked down toward the water's edge I saw a long bamboo or cane pole which was stuck in the bank bending and jerking like it would break. The water was being splashed and roiled by a sizeable creature and I watched for several minutes. It was obvious that the pole had been set and baited, so I waited for the owner to appear. The owner did not appear and by late morning, when it was time to meet my hunting partner, I decided to see what was making such a fuss in the water. As I lifted the pole I could feel the weight of something live, and with a little effort a sizable, blue catfish was pulled from the water. It had struggled until it was worn out, but it was a pretty nice fish and would make a good meal. Since the legal owner of this prize was nowhere in sight, I claimed it for myself, removed the hook and placed this game in the pouch of my hunting jacket. The weather was cool so the catfish didn't spoil in my pocket but continued to wiggle periodically until we were back in the project. As we pulled into the parking lot several of the kids came running up to the car. Excitedly they began asking questions.

"Did you catch a deer?"

"Did you shoot anything?"

Remembering the prize catfish, I reached into the back of the car and retrieved my hunting coat. "Well," I said, "I didn't get a deer, but I did shoot a fish." The boys stared at me, and then at each other. Finally, one of them said, "Ah, you can't shoot a fish."

I smiled under my breath and replied, "Well, you can if it's a catfish and if it is in a tree."

The boys looked startled, then doubtful. Again, the boldest one said, "Fish can't climb a tree."

Then I said, "What about a catfish? Why do you think they call them catfish?" With that, I reached into my game pouch and pulled the catfish out. About four pairs of eyes became even wider and rounder. Pointing to the pink area in the fish's gill I said, "Shot him right there. And it came our over here," I said, pointing to the other gill.

With that the boys scattered yelling and laughing, "Mr. Denton shot a fish out of a tree."

"Yes he did, too." — "It was a catfish?"

After the crowd dispersed I walked to the apartment and told Peggy all about our hunting trip. It was late and we were both tired so we turned in early. The catfish had been placed in the sink when I arrived home and was promptly forgotten. Next morning Peggy was faced with a bloated catfish floating in a sink full of water.

Living in this project provided some experiences that were unusual in the least and in some cases downright strange. We had never lived in a place where attitudes of suspicion and distrust were as pervasive as here. It seemed that persons from "somewhere else" were especially suspect as where people who had plans for the future or who were here for only a short time. I remember thinking that this neighborhood was different, and then I realized that it was not a neighborhood at all. This was not a community where the residents were united by a shared set of values or attitudes. This was more properly a place where the residents shared in common only proximity and discontent. Did the people in the other units see Peggy and me as different, as outsiders? We never really knew because most of them were pleasant when we would meet face to face, yet we would hear gossip and things would happen that gave us pause. One afternoon I left the apartment to make a short trip to a little grocery store a few blocks away. As I walked toward my car I noticed a policeman in his cruiser parked near my Ford watching me closely. As I pulled out of my space and was leaving, I noticed in the mirror that he was still watching me and was now using his radio. Upon returning to the project a few minutes later, I saw a second police cruiser. When I parked, the second car moved so as to prevent my driving away, and I was approached by the officer. He asked me several questions such as who I was, where I lived, what I was doing here, etc. Answering each question, I finally had a chance to ask him why I was being questioned. He told me that I fitted the description of a criminal they were searching for. By that time, I became aware of several sets of eyes watching from doorways at various places around the project. A few neighbors stood in groups of two or three watching intently. Shortly the little interrogation was over, and I walked back to the apartment with my bag of crackers and peanut butter. The neighbors vanished immediately.

Late one night not long after the experience with the police officers, we were awakened by an awful pounding at the door and loud voices yelling, "Open up." Jerking on a pair of pants I ran quickly to the door and opened it. A huge fireman in full regalia burst in brandishing his fire axe. "Where is it? Where is it?" he yelled.

"Where is what?" I asked.

"Where's the fire?" he answered.

A little upset now, I said, "What fire…there is no fire here."

"What's the number of this unit?" he asked.

"103," I replied.

"This is the right place," he stated, now beginning to become impatient.

"Go ahead. Look around," I said with resignation. He and another fireman carefully searched the apartment. Of course, they found nothing, and finally told me that someone in the project had called and reported a fire in our unit.

It was only a few days after the false alarm that we were again awakened late at night by a pounding at the door. This time the caller was a policeman. Before I could ask him what he wanted, he asked me, "What's your name?" I told him and he quickly asked, "What kind of a car you got?"

I said, "A black 1950 Ford with Kentucky tags."

He said, "Where is it?"

Pointing to the parking lot, I said, "It's right out there."

Quickly, he cut me off saying, "No, it's not!"

Dropping my arms a bit frustrated, I asked, "Well, where is it then?"

"It's over on the other side of Macon," he explained, now seeming to enjoy himself at my expense. Once the harassment was finished, he drove me across town where the little Ford had been abandoned on a dark street. The car was littered with Dixie cups, cigarette butts, candy and chewing gum wrappers, but otherwise okay. The car started okay, so I thanked the friendly cop and returned to the project. It appeared that a group of teenagers had taken the car, had some fun, and left it.

David had his first birthday while we lived in Macon. He was a rapidly growing boy and a real joy to us. In looking back on those times it is clear that he, too, dealt with some hardships.

As he was learning to walk, he took many a tumble in the little apartment. Like some other Dentons, David had a prominent forehead and it always seemed that the first part of his anatomy to strike those concrete floors was his forehead. He endured a big blue "pump knot" in the middle of his forehead for weeks. He also had to suffer the indignity of his first haircut when Granddaddy Wade came for a visit. Wade had a thing about haircuts and couldn't sit still until we had searched out a local barber who gave our beautiful son his first "one size fits all," Lonzo-style haircut. Those lovely, honey colored curls were swept into a corner and we brought back to the project a boy who seemed eons older. Haircuts and bruises to the head weren't the only injuries he suffered. Mrs. Marable, the lady who looked after him while his mama worked, had an unusual way of dealing with a runny nose. In a manner it was ingenious, but David protested in the only way he could, he squalled. Mrs. Marable would use an ear syringe to extract copious amounts of mucous from his tender nose. It worked, but it was not a pleasant thing to watch or to experience. Nevertheless, David loved Mrs. Marable.

In those days, it was possible to have fresh milk delivered to the doorstep every day. Each morning we would bring in a quart of whole milk fresh and creamy in a clear glass bottle. It seemed so much better in a bottle than in cardboard or plastic. Later in the fall, the milk started disappearing. This was really upsetting, and the realization that someone would actually steal milk intended for a baby unsettled something deep within us. One evening I walked out of the apartment with my twenty-two rifle. Purposefully I looked around the area stopping to gaze upward to a small window directly above the doorstep. Two or three neighbors were outside sitting on their stoops or on lawn chairs as was customary this time of day. I leaned the rifle, which was unloaded, against the door and turned around so the people who were outside could hear me. In a strong voice I said, ''I'm going to be sitting right up there behind that window with this gun because I'm tired of some thief stealing my baby's milk!'' It was not necessary to wait for a reaction, so I turned around picked up the rifle and went back inside. Not another bottle of milk was stolen from our doorstep.

The household to our right was an unusual one. I don't remember if there were children, but I don't think so. The man worked for one of the Macon newspapers as a stereo typist. As I understand it, a stereo typist makes plates which are used to make metal castings for the printing process. The woman was friendly and willing to talk, perhaps more than she should. We learned much more about these people than we wanted to know, more even than we would have imagined. Neither of them seemed "put off" by the things shared about them by their partners.

We learned, for example, that the husband had offered to his boss the "intimate services" of his wife in return for a raise. It was made clear in the telling that "she was good." We never learned whether or not this unusual form of barter was consummated, but there was not much evidence that his wealth had increased, because he continued to "hit me up" for a twenty from time to time. He also borrowed my twenty-two when we went home to Kentucky at the semester break. I was not able to get it back until we had settled in Morganton, North Carolina, months later, and then only with the help of the Police Department and the rifle's serial number.

The first semester ended successfully and as soon as grades were posted, Peg, David and I were on our way to Kentucky for the holidays. The little Ford ran well, but as soon as we got north of Atlanta and darkness fell, we began to get cold. I think the thermostat had been removed earlier, and with nothing to slow down the circulation of the coolant, engine temperature remained low and the car heater was ineffective. A piece of cardboard box was placed between the grill and the radiator. This helped some, but not enough. For the last couple hundred miles Peggy had to place her body over David with her mouton on top to keep him from chilling. We never did know if this exposure contributed to the horrible attack with Asian flu that David came down with as soon as we were back in Macon. It seems that we had no more than arrived back at the project when David became seriously ill. Twice we had to take him to the emergency room with a raging fever. A particularly powerful flu virus was making its way across the country that winter referred to as Asian flu. We had to administer alcohol baths, and it seemed that the struggle would not end. About the time classes were to resume at Mercer, I came down with the flu. I misjudged the severity of the illness and went back to class fearing the danger of getting behind. That was a mistake, because there is a period of time about which I still have no memory. Peggy was faced with the burden of taking care of two seriously ill persons, and had to quit her job to do so. By the time I was able to return to Mercer, the Dean of the School of Law, Dr. Quarles, told me that the only reasonable thing to do was to take the semester off, get well, and come back in the summer.

At the time I contracted the flu, I had parked the car on the street just outside the project. The starter was dragging and the battery was down. By parking on a slight hill, it was possible to roll the car off and start it with the clutch. Once I was back on my feet and could not return to school I decided to do the next best thing and see if I could find work. When I got to the place where the car had been parked, it was gone. How long it had been gone, we still do not know. I searched the area, asked questions, but learned nothing. Finally, I returned to the apartment exhausted and discouraged. I told Peggy the car was missing and we finally decided to call the police. The desk sergeant answered and I told him my story He asked several questions and I could hear papers rattling over the phone. He asked again what kind of car was missing. When I told him it was a black 1950 Ford with Kentucky tags, he slowly said, Yeah, Mr. Denton we have several charges against you!"

I asked, "Oh?"

He said, "Illegal operation of a motor vehicle, illegal registration. The title and tags don't match. Illegal parking. Besides, there will be towing and storage."

I thought to myself, "This can't be happening. I must be delirious with the flu." Reality settled coldly upon me and I finally said "Where is the police station; I'll be right down." He gave me the address and I walked downtown to the police station. I introduced myself and he repeated the litany of charges. Finally, it was my time to speak and I explained that the car's original title was from Tennessee and he had the title on his desk.

He said, "But it has Kentucky tags."

"Yes," I said, "Kentucky does not have a titling law, and you have the Kentucky registration in your hand, and it is current." He looked at the title and then the registration. Again, I explained that the car was originally titled in Tennessee, was now registered in Kentucky which did not have an auto titling law, and the Kentucky registration and tags were current.

Again, he studied the papers before him. In a moment he asked, "Could I see your driver's license?"

"Certainly," I said, reaching for my wallet. He looked at my driver's license, glanced at the other papers and a smirk began to express itself in the corners of his mouth. "Now, we're getting somewhere," he asserted. The smirk forced its way into something else, almost a smile. Knowingly he said, "Tennessee title, Kentucky tags, North Carolina Driver's license, and hell, you're living in Georgia." His expression was wonderful in its certainty.

I could almost see him flexing his chest muscles. He waited for me to explain. "It's simple," I said, "I'm a transient."

Before I could go farther he blurted, "You a what?"

"I'm a transient," I repeated. "My permanent address is North Carolina, so I have North Carolina Driver's license. I've been in college in Kentucky where I got the car from my wife's father, and now were living temporarily in Macon where I'm a student at Mercer – I'm a transient." He looked almost overwhelmed for a moment, then I continued, "Oh, by the way, I parked the car, so I could roll it off because the battery's dead and the starter drags." Now his expression was one of disbelief. Feeling a hint of returning hope, I thought I ought to finish stating my case. "My baby and I have both had the Asian Flu and my wife had to quit work to take care of us," I started again. "We didn't even know the car had been impounded until today." Finishing I said, "I can't believe the police department would tow my car without informing me. It doesn't seem right."

He asked me to wait while he discussed the matter with others. Shortly he came back and told me that all charges had been dropped, and that I could pick my car up, but I still had to pay storage. I paid the storage bill and then walked to the lot where the car had been impounded. This was January; it was cold, and there was about two inches of dirty snow on the ground. The battery was dead as a doornail and there was no way I could move the car. The storage lot was operated by a service station, so one of the attendants suggested that I get a rebuilt starter from Wards, which was only a couple blocks away. I walked over to Wards and found the automotive department. The clerk told me they had rebuilt starters, but I had to have the old starter with me. So, I returned to the lot, got my toolbox from the trunk, crawled under the engine and disconnected the old starter. Returning to Wards, greasy and muddy, I made the exchange and returned to the lot. While I was flat on my back in the mud installing the rebuilt starter, I felt someone kick the bottom of my feet, and the unmistakable voice of my neighbor settled harshly upon my ears and my spirits.

"Hey, Denton, I need to hit you up for a twenty."

It was not yet time for lessons of living in Georgia to be finished, so we persevered for awhile. Our intention was to use this semester to earn a little money since I could not attend school. We hit the streets in the most literal sense. We completed application forms by the score, registered with every employment agency, public and private, and followed leads in the classifieds until we were heartsick. Providence intervened once again in the manner of a late night telephone conversation with my sister, Mary, who had moved with Bob and the boys to Morganton. She said there was plenty of work there and they had just moved into a large home with extra space. Peg and I talked it over and decided to make the trip. We piled a few things in the car and headed for North Carolina. There could be no way of knowing that this would be perhaps the most significant trip we would ever make. We had no plans other than trying to find employment for a short time, and then a continuation of our unfinished sojourn in Macon. Mary was right; work was no problem and before the weekend was over I had secured a position with Icard Cordage Company, a cotton mill manufacturing braided cotton cord. Meantime Dad and Mom were living in Shelby where Dad was involved in the construction of a plant for Pittsburgh Plate Glass. We reasoned if we could swap vehicles with Dad, it would be possible to rent a u-haul and with his pickup move our things to Morganton in one load.

The trip back to Georgia was uneventful. We felt a sense of relief that we had employment, and it would be easy to pick up where we had left off in Macon with some change in our pockets. Upon arriving in Macon, I rented a U-haul and backed it up to the little apartment in the project. We had just started packing when we were paid an unpleasant visit by someone from the housing authority. This individual informed us that it had been reported to him that we were attempting to leave while owing back rent – in effect that we were skipping town. The words, "too much is enough" rang in my head. After all the lousy luck, this turn of events would have to be responded to with blunt force, so to speak. "Let's go to the office," I said. Together we went to the housing office and I asked to see the superintendent. As the unpleasant scene came to an end. The Housing Authority gave me back $28.00 and an apology.

That afternoon we left Macon and headed northward. Everything that we owned was loaded onto that small trailer and the bed of Dad's International pickup. We knew only that there were lessons in the events which had sort of overwhelmed our lives during these past months. We didn't know yet what those lessons were, and certainly we could not know that the hand of the Deity had figured in some of them. After all, if the Deity is to be credited with the creation of creatures such as us, doesn't it stand to reason that he would have a sense of humor?

As we approached the little town of Madison, Georgia, later that day, we decided we needed to make a pit stop for all of the standard reasons. As we pulled into a little country store and filling station, it started to sprinkle. I pulled the pickup over near the front of the store, so Peg could get out without getting wet. As I pulled the pickup and trailer around making a second approach to the pumps, I happened to look up and see Peggy doubled over in laughter in the doorway of the little store. She told me later that as she watched that old green pickup and that small U-Haul trailer circle the pumps in front of this little country store, groaning under a load of jumbled furniture, she realized that she was watching the real live version of what could have been Norman Rockwell's *The Local Junk Man*.

Were it possible to make that trip again, now, all these years later, I can imagine pulling out of the hard-packed clay parking lot in front of that little store and heading up US 29 toward Athens. In my imagination it occurs to me that it was next to impossible that so many events hopeful, frightening, funny, evil, fateful could occur within so short a span of time. Yep, we remember with feeling, those years we spent in Georgia that semester.

David Denton
4702

How the Triple A Fixes Flats

Sometimes it can get pretty cold in mid October in the hills of east Tennessee. This was one of these times and we had awakened early on this Sunday morning so we wouldn't miss a minute of the last day of the International Storytelling Festival in Jones borough less than ten miles away. During the night I had dreamed that the left front tire on my pickup was flat. Still anxious about the vivid dream, I hurried around to the backside of the motel to check on it, and, sure enough, the left front tire was flat. Walking over as if I knew what I was looking for, I spotted the hex head of a bolt about 3/8 of an inch buried between the treads. My mood sagged because the morning program at the festival got underway at eight and we would surely be late. Besides, it was really cold.

I hurried back to our room and broke the news to Peggy. At first she looked disappointed, but quickly brightened and reminded me that we had AAA membership, and this was the time to use it. Grabbing my wallet, I hurried to the front desk. The young woman at the desk was exceptionally helpful. She helped me locate the AAA number and placed the call. At first I reached the main number for the eastern U. S. – I think it was in Richmond. I gave the agent all requested information, which took a few minutes, and then she said she would have to transfer me to a regional office in Knoxville. She did so, and again I provided all requested information. It took a few minutes again, and then I was transferred to someone in Johnson City, which was near the motel. This time the voice was male, and the information requested was more specific, like what kind of vehicle, what year, what was wrong with it, where was the vehicle, where was I, what is the nearest highway intersection. We went through this data again and I was absolutely certain that he knew that it was the left front tire on my blue, 1996 GC Sierra 4x4 with Maryland tags, which was parked in the back lot of the Sleep Inn which is located on Old Jonesborough Pike at Exit 36 off I-181 near Johnson City. He said someone would be right out.

At the end of the first hour of waiting beside my truck I started to get cold and maybe a little bit impatient. As the second hour began to tick by, a white van parked in the rear lot not too far away. A big guy got out of the van and after looking all around started walking toward me. Man, he was one big guy. He was taller than me and looked to weigh about 260. He made me think of Chad Brock, the ultra macho country singer, because his head was shaved and slick as a billiard ball. He also reminded me of a number of NFL defensive linemen. He appeared to have an abscess in his jaw, but it turned out to be a cud of chewing tobacco instead. I asked him if he was making a AAA call and he said. "Yeah." Then he said, ''Where's your car?"

I said, "Oh, this GC pickup."

Then he said, "What's wrong with it?"

I said, "It has a flat tire."

And he said, "Which one?" I showed him, and he looked at the tire before responding, "Yeah, it is!" He seemed puzzled, and it was then that I noticed the van he was driving belonged to some locksmith service. The situation was already strange, but quickly became stranger when he turned to me and asked, "You got a jack?"

Not really believing what was happening, I said to him, "Yes."

As if waiting for it to suddenly appear, he asked, "Where is it?"

This was too much and I answered hotly, "It's bolted down under the back seat with all of our luggage piled on top of it."

He was a little upset too, because he spat a stream of "backer juice" out the side of his mouth and said, "Hell, I can't change a flat with no jack."

At this point I said to him, "I can't believe that you are making a AAA service call to change a flat tire on a GC pickup, and you ask me if I've got a jack."

"They didn't tell me it was no flat. Shit, I'll just tell them to send somebody else." With that he pulled himself mightily into the van and sped away.

Returning to the front desk, I explained what had happened. We had a good laugh and she placed another call to AAA central. After I explained this bizarre experience to the agent in Knoxville, she apologized profusely and said she would contact a representative in Kingsport rather than Johnson City. Again all information was checked and double checked and the second wait seemed longer than the first, so I finally changed my post to the front of the motel to insure that I didn't miss whoever was sent to rescue me. It must have been along about noon when I saw a large truck with a roll back bed on it. On the cab door was an Exxon sign, so I thought this must be the man. As he pulled up in front, I approached him and asked if he was on a AAA service call. He replied in the affirmative and asked where my vehicle was and I told him it was around the motel in the back lot. He asked me to climb in, and I began to jokingly relate my experience with the locksmith who came to change a tire without a jack. We both laughed heartily, and I said, "I can't believe that a Triple A representative would send someone to change a flat on a pickup without a jack, especially after all the information they asked for." He did not respond to this last comment.

He stopped the truck with its long roll back in the middle of the back lot and we both got out. He asked where my vehicle was and I pointed toward the pickup while walking in that direction. It was then that I noticed that he, too, was large, no taller than the other guy but considerably bigger around, and he moved with deliberation because there was much of him to move. After looking the situation over he said to me, "Why don't you back your truck across the lot and put the rear wheels against the curb over there."

Not believing, I looked at him and said, "My truck has a flat tire."

He looked embarrassed and also a little bit angry. He said, "Hell, I ain't asking you to drive it thirty or forty miles." A feeling of hopelessness was beginning to claim me, so I climbed into the truck, cranked it and carefully backed across the parking lot until the rear wheels were against the curb. The picture was beginning to take shape.

He again looked the situation over and finally asked, "You got a spare?"

"Yes, it's under the bed," I replied.

Still he hesitated and asked, "You gonna put the spare on, or patch the flat?" Here we go again, I thought.

"Can you patch or plug a tire?" I asked. He shook his head, so I said. "Well, we'll have to use the spare." He waited some more, and then slowly waddled over to his truck. He searched around in the cab for a few moments and then finally pulled a toolbox from behind the seat. He placed the toolbox on the bed of the roll back and then slowly made his way back to my truck.

I could tell he was struggling with something, and he finally said; "You know that long handled crank that fits up though that hole in the bumper."

"Sure," I said.

"You got one?" he asked.

Half laughing and half sneering I said, "Yeah, its under the backseat with the jack, still covered with 200 pounds of luggage." He looked like he might cry, so I said no more, but began to remove item by item from the backseat. Finally I could lift the back seat and unscrew the cover holding down the jack, crank, and lug wrench. Removing the crank, I handed it to him and he cranked the spare to the ground and waited for me to move it. There was no way he could get his bulk under the bed of a pickup.

Next he got himself down on one knee, and removed the plastic nuts, which hold the decorative wheel cover in place. This done he began to get down to the business of loosening and unscrewing the eight lugs which hold the wheel on. First he tried a ratchet with a handle about a foot long, but he couldn't get enough leverage to break the nuts so he switched to a long-handled bar using the same socket. He simply couldn't develop enough leverage while kneeling, so he had developed a system that worked and was a joy to watch. He positioned himself near the wheel, placing his left hand on the fender for support, he would bend enough to place the socket on the lug with the long handle extending to the left and parallel with the surface and now with both hands on the fender, he would place his foot on the end of the handle and with a mighty push aided by his weight the lugs would pop loose with a mighty screech. As the handle hit the ground and without moving his hands, he would simply flip the handle 180 degrees with his foot, and then bending slightly, he would grasp the end of the handle with his right hand and further loosen the lug by pulling upward with his right hand still supported by his left hand and this process was repeated lug by lug, until all eight had been loosened. At this point, he walked to his truck and maneuvered it until the end of the roll back was just in front of my truck. Now, standing by the truck bed controls, he first lowered and then extended the roll back until the end of it was underneath my bumper. He placed a length of wooden 4 X 4 between the bumper and the bed to prevent scratching, and then with the flip of a lever gently lifted the pickup until both front wheels were off the ground. Now it was a simple matter of removing the wheel with the flat and replacing it with the spare. With the front of the truck still off the ground it was considerably easier to do initial tightening of the eight lugs with the ratchet. The roll back was lowered and moved forward and final tightening and replacing of the wheel cover could be accomplished. With full weight on the tires, I noticed that the spare just installed was about halfway down. Both the triple A service man and I were ready to conclude this encounter, so as he quickly suggested that a BP station a mile or two toward Jonesborough had air, I smiled and nodded remembering having seen this station earlier.

As we sat under the tent at the festival and listened to the last two or three storytellers wind up this glorious three day event, I realized that we had just finished living out a story as unexpected, as funny, and certainly as authentic as a story can be. When we took membership in the American Automobile Association, we could not have imagined that a flat tire could lead to a comedy of errors lasting a whole morning And all this took place outside the cost of a ticket to the storytelling festival

David Denton
1/3/01

304

Pretending

Yesterday was Mother's Day. It was as pretty a Sunday in May as one could expect, a nice enough day to take in a symphony. The United States Air Force Symphony Orchestra was performing at Mount St. Mary's College; the drive up to Emmitsburg was glorious, setting a standard for the rest of the afternoon that was not to be met, unless one is content with pretending. The greater part of the concert was excellent, especially Beethoven's Symphony No. 4. Other selections featured, in addition to strings, the oboe and the bassoon, favorite instruments of mine. The afternoon's performance ended with a salute to the different branches of America's Armed Forces. As each anthem was played, members of the audience who had served in that particular branch of the Armed Forces were asked to stand. The first recognized was the United States Army, and a number of young men in uniform stood intermingled with the old timers. And then we heard the United States Marines' anthem, and the relatively unknown song of the United States Coast Guard…one lone soul stood. When the United States Navy was recognized, a friend sitting alongside me had to be nudged before he rose. This was a good man, a deeply caring American, a concerned and hopeful citizen; but, I instinctively understood his reaction. Like me, he did not want to be a part of the marketing of our nation's soul (if it still has one) for the price of a ticket to a Mother's Day concert, which happened to be exactly nothing, including tax. And finally the United States Air Force…"Off we go into the wild blue yonder…" I stood self-consciously, uncomfortably, and was grateful to be able to sit down and become lost in the crowd, a crowd which was surprisingly large for a gorgeous spring day, Mother's Day when people could be out picnicking, or whatever.

The setting was nice, but I had the unsettled feeling that I was about to be used. I thought that the eighties were gone and we were now ready for the "new world order." And then I knew for certain that we were still stuck there in the interminable decade of plastic flowers, when the Air Force Symphony Orchestra started playing, and the lilting voice of soloist Master Sgt. Bobbie "America" (that must have been her name) launched a Mother's Day version of Lee Greenwood's vacuous, feel-good song of the eighties, "God Bless the U.S.A." Hooray for Grenada, hooray for the invasion of Panama City, down with Noriega, down with Saddam Hussein, (I thought these evil men were our target, but both are alive), and hooray for Desert Storm, and to hell with the Kurds, to hell with the homeless – they deserve to sleep on grates. They are too damn sorry to work. To hell with the people in Bangladesh. Don't bother me with reality because I'm *"proud to be an American where at least I know I'm free."* I guess that depends on who you are, doesn't it? Pretending.

God knows I would like to be proud. God knows I would like to be free, too; but right now neither is more than some remote wish. How many years, how many of my deepest sentiments, how many dreams, beliefs, and wishes have been invested in what appears now to be nothing short of the most profound experience of deceit imaginable. *"There is no doubt I love this land...,"* that's the problem; I love it so much and I have believed so long and so completely that I simply don't think I can bear the self-deceit being asked of me at this moment. I thought loving one's land meant trying to make it better. I thought it meant pushing toward that ideal whether or not it was ever quite reached. But that no longer seems to be considered, required, or expected. No, this is a time for pretending; but first let me escape from this milling, mindless herd, this arena full of Americans willing to trade souls for symbols. You don't have to have any quality or character as long as you have the right labels, as long as your thinking is "politically correct." Who cares about the soul of *"this land..."* it doesn't matter as long as we are singing the anthem of the eighties, "God Bless the U.S.A." I think I would have probably felt less corrupted if we had been singing and moving to the beat of Michael Jackson's, "I'm Bad." Take your pick, these are the theme songs of Reagan's "Morning in America."

"I'm proud to be an American where at least I know I'm free." Yeah, if you happen to live on Rockwell Terrace or Mountain Laurel Estates. I guess it all depends upon where you experience this freedom; like the lady who cries at night from her bedroom in the John Hanson Apartments as her senses are brutalized by the pounding of boom boxes and by the endless obscenities screamed into the night by those who now own the souls of both the neighborhood and the children.

I guess it's more important under contemporary values to look patriotic, to display the symbols of patriotism and concern for God and country, than it is to actually harbor those instincts in one's soul and mind. Yellow ribbons and flags, Desert Storm tee shirts, $100 sneakers, spandex biker shorts on the boys, spandex leotards, tights, or whatever they are called on the girls – some of them with lace on the bottom, camouflage fatigue jackets like the big boys wear, ill-fitting Bugle Boy's, Dockers, the labels are on the outside. If you have no value inside, all you've got to do is wear your label outside so the world will know what you are made of.

Just a few moments away from the concert arena, I drove past a home with two flags out front...America on Mother's Day. I guess it didn't occur to anyone that the flags were inappropriately displayed. The American flag was upstaged by the Maryland flag which was positioned on its right and the Maryland flag was upside down. This was the home of a former county official. Pretending.

Mother's Day is over and it's Monday again. Out the window things look the same: the houses across the street on Clarke Place, the trees on campus, the fountain, the mall, the students coming and going. The pictures are the same. The sounds are the same, but it might as well be some place in Antarctica. It could not feel colder nor more remote nor more desolate and barren if it were that far away and that devoid of the warmth of sunshine. Looking out the window across Clarke Place...not much has changed. Some of the neighbors have died and others moved. Some of the Victorian homes have been renovated. Some of the trees are marginally larger, but all in all it is pretty much the same perspective with the same feeling...a quiet, settled neighborhood,

Americana. In the other direction, the perspective is radically different. The Ely Building sits where the old Main used to sit. The trees on the mall are full grown, and I remember when they were just saplings. The mall has evolved out of what was once a patch of grass between the old Academic Building and the Old Gym. Several crops of children have moved across this abbreviated American landscape, and teachers, too. The kids come along, grow up, graduate, and are gone. They make the same sounds. They make the same signs. They dream the same dreams; life goes on. But this time I am not really sure. Do they dream the same dreams; is everything the same or is it just that I have been willing to play along with the illusion all of these years believing, trusting, knowing in my heart that there was a purpose, that there were reasons, that believing was having? Pretending.

Those old American values would carry us through. This was MSD; this was a microcosm of all that was good in our country. This was a miniature community of principle, human dignity, individual rights, and individual responsibilities. We, who jointly occupy this place, would stand together and defend it because we all represented the same beliefs. While some from the school family were willing to endure exhaustion, and more, though gasping for life and breath were still standing with clenched fists, resolved to continue the struggle to preserve those simple principles which gripped them, others, who paraded under the orange and black banner of MSD, however, were attracted like butterflies to the biggest and brightest flower, without having to think or feel and no longer held within the grasp of those principles which had sustained them. These were driven instead by the lure of whatever is considered "in," even if it meant walking over others to get it. Principles which grip us are passe, and now we are looking for a principle which we can grip, at our own option…something gaudy, a symbol, a label…quality doesn't matter. Character doesn't matter. It's the image that counts, and the cheaper the better. In a way, it reminds one of the stampede created by an announcement over the intercom of a two-hour sale at K-Mart on Legg's pantyhose…seconds and odd sizes. Total communication, and total means complete and free, unrestricted, equally shared, and inclusive. There would always be a place here for anyone and everyone who had a connection with our mission. A nice myth, but a remote reality, we have come to learn. Communication perceived as a human right secured by an investment of pain, a birthright, an entitlement...Oh, but that too can be bought and sold like other property. What happened to the dream? What happened to that bright promise filled with sunshine? Well, I guess it got displaced by the old certainty of nightfall and darkness, didn't it? Believing together sort of became like everything else in the feel-good decade...I got mine...screw you! Pretending.

Freedom of the press; freedom of speech; good, solid American values; they were all wrapped up in, or at least they were a part of, this total communication thing; or at least some of us thought so. At least we believed so, for a hell of a long time. Only now when pretending is no longer possible do we fully understand the price of freedom of the press or some other freedoms. Only now when our childishness and our naivete have come back to mock us, do we understand that in this era of "let's pretend" what is freedom for one of us, can imprison one of our brothers. Like a flag displayed upside down, as long as the symbol is there, like a cheap yellow ribbon or a designer label stretched across the cheek of someone's ass, that's all that matters. The symbol is the thing. We can invoke the constitutional protection of free speech and devastate the lives of a family. The simple faith, or perhaps it was the simplistic faith, that allowed us to hang onto the belief that the truth was what mattered, now mocks us. To hell with the truth. It's the image that matters, and no one notices the incongruity of Lee Greenwood swaying sensually in his Calvin Klein jeans as he sings, *"I'm proud to be an American."* As the deaf, dumb, blind, and numb audience cheers, oblivious to the fact that many, many Americans...millions even, are imprisoned...imprisoned spiritually, emotionally, and intellectually by the excesses and the greed of those who would condemn the burning of the flag, but who would stand and stare vacantly when its deepest meaning has been ripped out and it is hanging upside down. Pretending? No more.

David M. Denton
May 13, 1991

Feelings and Impressions

Almost every time I make a trip I am confronted by the feeling that I should sit down and try to capture some of the moods, feelings, and impressions that become so much a part of the total experience of being on the crest of a tide of change – and perhaps a tide of confusion and uncertainty. I am interested primarily in the broad spectrum of expressions and emotions related to traveling, being away from home and the reasons therefor. If one could describe the spectrum of emotions as ranging from bitter on one end to sweet on the other, then it becomes easier to appreciate the total impact upon one being, of having to, or being able to, sample all along the continuum – the sharp contrast of the extremes and the confusion of melding or conflicting emotion along the center of the continuum.

There is a certain sense of urgency about what I am doing. It is right, therefore I continue to respond – and besides, I feel that I not only inherited the obligation but the talent as well.

Always before I go I feel a hollowness in my stomach – almost like homesickness – usually I don't sleep well the night before. What do I think about? I want to be with Peggy, the closeness, the physical contact. If I awaken I like to reach over and touch her – it helps reduce the feeling of loneliness associated with having to be somewhere I really don't want to be – even before I go.

Usually at these times, I want to also have the children around me. It is good for the family to be in the den together for a little while and watch TV. David and Mary are growing up so rapidly that these moments together become even more important. These moments cannot be allowed to pass without capturing and holding onto every sweet and lasting experience.

I think about our life together. How good it is and how rapidly it is passing by? Sometimes I resent the demands that my professional life makes on my personal life. What could be more important than my family? Are they really getting a fair shake?

The farm, now that we have one, is ever present in my thoughts. That little place in the country is helping me recapture a fundamental part of myself which might have remained buried. I am so grateful for the farm and what it is doing, not just for me, but for us! The farm is beautiful because we are a part of it, or it is a part of us. By contrast the view from my window, even though without flaw, is somehow imperfect. It is beautiful, but not a part of me in a personal way. Looking out to sea, the water is aqua for about one mile then it abruptly changes to a deep, dark blue. This in the point where the land shelf drops off sharply.

I dislike airports because they tend to reinforce the impersonal nature of so much of our lives in this era. Airports seem to epitomize the dehumanizing influence of urban living. It is almost as if the people milling around in airports all had masks. They seem unable to relate one to another at a personal level. They function mechanically at a very superficial and untrusting level.

Airplanes are worse if possible. They finish the job of severing person-to-person relationships and reinforce the loneliness that is the hallmark of public transportation. The only saving grace is that one might be able to enjoy a few hours alone reflecting and thinking – if the stewardess would not feel so compelled to interrupt every fifteen minutes and in her "pre-recorded and canned" voice continues to say, "Would you like to purchase a cocktail, sir?" Airplane food is as "canned" as the practiced niceties coming from the stewardesses.

This conference is unbelievable – hundreds of delegates from our 50 states and territories caught up in absolute chaos – perhaps half a dozen hotels are involved, and nobody seems to know what is happening or where. The banquet tonight lasted from 7:30 until almost midnight and was boring besides. The flamenco guitarists and dancers saved the day. Also, "our group," the deaf people and two or three of us "hearies," enjoyed each other's company. Boyce was especially enjoyable. Boyce is a rare individual especially in this era where it is almost customary to take the government's money to attend conferences such as this and contribute nothing. The sad thing is so few of our peers seem to have any sense of conscience much less commitment. This afternoon I was supposed to give my paper in a section scheduled from 4:00 p.m. to 7:00 p.m. (evidence of very poor scheduling). It turned out pretty well though, with a good, free discussion of total communication.

To sum up the conference, I would have to say that it was a waste of time, energy, and money and an insult to people who really care....in spite of the few nice things that happened. I have seen some beautiful artwork in San Juan: mostly painting, hand-carved woodwork and hand-crafted jewelry. Peggy would enjoy the music here. The guitarists are excellent and the music has a mariachi quality with a bit more beat, also a hint of calypso. Last night we went to a place called the Wine Cellar, where we enjoyed three different guitarists. A special treat was a guest who apparently was a Puerto Rican opera star. She did about three numbers including *Granada*. Her voice was probably the best I have ever listened to in 40 years. The richness, the power and control was limitless. This was shortly before the banquet; a local guitar and vocal quartet did *La Poloma* for me by special request. I wished so much that Peggy was here – or me there.

San Juan is a lovely city cradled by the hills, which seem almost to encircle it, and the blue Atlantic. Since I arrived, there have been clouds moving above. The air is hot and very humid. Showers are frequent, abrupt and short lived. Two showers were encountered this morning in a 5-block walk, and the sun kept right on shining. The hotel is very pretty and comfortable. My room is on the tenth floor, and I can hear the surf rushing rather strongly on the beach below. It is now 1:15 a.m. and the surf sounds louder than last night – maybe there is a little more wind.

Not 50 yards from the front of the hotel last night, I was propositioned by a "lady of the evening." Funny, I thought, yet sad. Could she have seen herself as I saw her? I suppose my maleness was flattered a bit by that, but I felt good knowing that I was luckier than most of the souls who became her customers.

There are policemen everywhere – one or two in every block, young men 20 –25, standing, swinging a night stick, or talking to a passerby. Interestingly, there was a policemen not far from where the girl approached me. I wondered if he received a cut of her fee for protection. That sounds a bit to cynical for me.

The favorite drink seems to be the pina colada or something like that. Basic ingredients are rum, coconut and pineapple juice with a strip of fresh pineapple. Very mellow and refreshing. Rum is to Puerto Rico what beer is to Maryland. You can see the smokestacks of the Ron Bacardi distillery from my hotel.

Yesterday morning I had breakfast in the La Concha Hotel restaurant. I ordered a plain omelet. The waiter brought me just that: no toast, no butter, no jelly, no nothing. That piece of fluffed up egg and a cup of coffee cost me $2.11. This morning I fooled them. I went down the street and found a small restaurant which caters to people of more modest means and had a hearty breakfast for $1.50.

This is Wednesday and I've spent the entire morning alone and enjoyed it. It is good just to sit or walk or read and not have to do anything. Visiting the souvenir shops is fun, but its merchandise is mostly junk.

I've noticed that real tortoise shell jewelry is almost a tradition in Puerto Rico. Some of it is really exquisite. Another island tradition is the small tree frog. The people of Puerto Rico love this little animal almost to the point of making it the national symbol (territorial symbol I should say). There are little artificial tree frogs everywhere.

I've been thinking about Maryland and the life we are building there. The feeling is indescribable. It's sort of like being there adds that element of fulfillment or completeness that we have never quite had before.

David Denton

Pushed Beyond Reach

O' Time – the great healer
Where is thy balm?
Though you seem without form
I bend 'neath the heaviness
Of a gravity not measured by pounds
The awful weight of hours
Filled with minutes

O' Darkness – the promise of rest
Why do you agitate?
Thine absence of light
Hides the blinding heat
Of a night where fever is king
No refuge under your coverlets
Dampened by sweat

O' Distance – And room to breathe
Where is thy comfort?
Though you grant safe space
And a promise of liberty
I am chained by aloneness
Separated by your invisible, intangible force
Pushed beyond reach

Diverse Flowers in a Common Garden
Variations on a theme – 1992 – Breaking up the Family – The
Deaf Community

O' Union – diverse flowers in a common garden
Profuse in beauty,
Growing together – holding each other up
Enhanced and dignified by contrast
Tiny crocus, glorious tulip, side by side
With the common daffodil – each lovely
Now diminished – fighting for sunlight.

On Home and the Loss of Family – 1991
(The Central and the Peripheral)

O' Family – and all that is holy
Can't seem to find you
Even when I was tiny, I knew "Home" was not mine to keep
But family was eternal, indestructible
Until the rules got changed
Family followed home away.

On Hope – When it is almost gone – 1991

O' Hope – Nourisher of dreams
Thine absence distresses
Though you preached eternal optimism
Your robe was in shreds
"You've got to believe!" you stated
"I'm a believer!" said I
And then you died.

On Saying Nothing at All - 1991

O' Words - playthings of the poet
Where is thy beauty?
The wisdom of the ages
You have held and proclaimed
Yet you seem powerless to relate
The yearnings of one simple soul
In its shriveled state.

Is this All There Is? 1991

O' Tomorrow – something to look forward to
A Sears package in a country mailbox
A letter from Mom in a G.I.'s shirt pocket
Held to be savored when alone and quiet
Tomorrow always – but that was yesterday
Sometime, anytime, perhaps never
Tomorrow or manana – but not today.

On the Matter of Still Waiting – 1992

O' Heaven – figment of some far future
Why do you tease?
Like a bottle of Thunderbird
To the man without hope
You promise what you will not provide
Deliverance, and a night of dreams

But you send instead – delirium,
On exposing your tender underbelly– 1992
O' Trust – without condition and complete
Once it was easy
You've got to take risks – extend trust
To receive trust – Every man must
Now and then stand naked
Vulnerability does not invite attack
Every time

Scorpio – 1991

O' November 8th sign of the zodiac
The season of Scorpio
You arrive with the glory of October
But like those born under your sign
Indian summer transformed to winter
Sullenly and without pause – Like a
Jekyll and Hyde.

Why Can't I Hear You? – 1992

O' Communication – A word that speaks everything
Though hard of hearing
Sometimes you seem too glib
Other times you have a point to make
And then you may say nothing at all
Forgetting that there are two of us
In this process.

O' Mother – A portrait of Grace
After ninety winters
You are yet the same
As when I was small
Soft and eternal – still giving
Your final son and his sister
Still need you!

O' Mother – not mine of course
But that of my children
We celebrate your womanhood
Across its magic span
From the rush and the blush of youth to the vibrant fullness of now
Fulfillment flows from your breast

O' Purpose – fuel for the minds engine
Super premium unleaded
Mine for a season – three hundred months
Twenty–five years – one–quarter century
It was summer when I came
And now November – last years' model
Needs paint – brakes worn – hole in the gas tank

O' child – raison d' etre
Do I know you?
You seem much larger – older too
And who is the child with you?
You traveled quite far – you two
Must be homecoming – or graduation, or
The new superintendent

What a Long, Long Road
(song for Granddaddy John)

Verse I:

What a long, long road that he walked
From a small town in east Tennessee
A son of the south Land, he answered the call
To enlist in the proud infantry.

Chorus:

Oh Private John, Oh Private John
Your children will miss you
But a war is going on
What a long, long road…

Verse II:

What a long, long road that he walked
With the third of Old Tennessee
From a battle of Shiloh to Cumberland Gap
While the roar of the muskets rang free.

Chorus:

Oh Private John, Oh Private John
You're missing your woman
But the troops keep marching on
What a long, long road…

Verse III:

What a long, long road that he walked
To the banks of the Mississippi
Captured at Vicksburg, a prisoner of war
In July of 1863.

Chorus:

Oh Private John, Oh Private John
Vicksburg has fallen
But the war's still going on
What a long, long road...

Verse IV:

What a long, long road that he walked
From the bonds of his sworn enemy
On through the night with its promise of dawn
Till the hills of his homeland he sees.

Chorus:

Oh Private John, Oh Private John
Your family still needs you
But the fighting rages on
What a long, long road...

Verse V:

What a long, long road that he walked
Too crowded in east Tennessee
Over the mountains his family he moved
To the place of the great Cherokee.

Chorus:

Oh Daddy John, Grandaddy John
The mountains are calling
And your children have come home
What a long, long road…

Ending:

The hope of a man to return to his land
When each step takes him further away
What a long, long road
What a long, long road.

The Day Carroll Creek Tilted

The conversation was light as usual, but the laughter was hearty, almost boisterous at times, among this group of older, retired gentlemen who gather every morning at 10:00 at the Village Restaurant. Every morning except Sunday, that is, because some of the fellows attend church and a few attend two services on a regular basis, at different churches. The group has even included a couple of preachers as regulars. The presence of a man of the cloth does little to dampen the spirits of these men, however. There is no noticeable change in demeanor, language, or subject matter when a minister is present. These men are beyond the time or need or inclination to seem pretentious or unduly pious. However, they are all good men who have tasted life in its sweetness and its bitterness. And now this time of togetherness is lived and appreciated in a way that only those who have tasted sorrow can fully accept, embrace, and express. The fellowship is rich and unconditional. To have a place at the table is to belong in the deepest sense. And to belong to this gathering requires a sense of humor, a skin as thick as leather, and a self-effacing spirit because the ribbing can be as strong as the laughter which it evokes.

No topic is too sacred, too sensitive, nor too controversial for comment. No issue is too serious nor too frivolous for debate. The opinions are as varied as the backgrounds of the individuals who hold them, and wonderfully no one is thought right or wrong for disagreeing. As one member observed: "We express many different opinions on many issues and topics, but we make no decisions." These men are as serious about their community, their world, as they are light hearted in the way they approach each other and the particular topics of the day.

The life and history of this coffee group covers many years and more than a single generation. The passage of time witnesses the inevitable passing of individual members. Miraculously the group has a life and spirit of its own, and as the numbers dwindle through attrition, the lost brothers' places at the table are filled with new voices and faces who in time acquire the badges of familiarity, acceptance, and belonging. All of this occurs naturally, without plan or scheme, as if it were a part of a larger and grander experience – perhaps it is. One matter is beyond question, and that has to do with the concern and devotion these men have for each other.

What the topic of the morning will be is anybody's guess. No subject is too complex, and none is too simple. The conclusions reached, if that occurs, are not important; it is the dialogue that matters. There may be a heated but good-natured debate about the national elections, or the sharing of some humorous experience that took place at church on Sunday. Two of the members are ushers in the same church, and their combined years of service would total close to a century. Doubtless, the spiritual life of the community would suffer gravely without these two buddies in attendance. Sometimes even the church is the subject of a good story. It seems that in recent months a new person started gracing this particular congregation at the eleven o'clock service. There was much competition about which of these two ushers would seat this comely stranger who seemed quite taken with the quality of the religious experience at this particular church. We assume that it was because of spiritual motivation that she continued to attend. One morning former police chief Charlie Main was practically bursting in his eagerness to share with the group, especially with his dear friend and fellow usher, Bud Radcliffe, that he had finally found out who this charming and mysterious woman was who had the good souls in the large stone church on Second Street and Bentz all atwitter. Charlie's face beamed as he described how he had escorted this elegant lady to her pew and had introduced himself by saying, "I'm Charles Main," to which she replied, "Yes, I know!" And then she proceeded to tell him who she was. As Charlie unfolded the story and smiled, Bud Radcliffe asked eagerly, "Well, what was her name?" Dear Charlie looked bewildered at first, then dumbfounded – after a moment's pause he replied sheepishly, "I forgot."

One of the regulars came in a little later than the others one morning and informed us that he had been looking over the Carroll Creek project. Since this man was a former administrator with the Metropolitan Sanitary Commission, he not only had an interest in matters pertaining to water, but considerable expertise as well. He stated, as a matter of fact, that he had checked carefully and at one of the new bridges crossing the Linear Park, Carroll Creek was two and one-half inches higher on one side than on the other. This highly interesting observation caused quite a stir around the table that day. The subject was too unusual to be dropped and was resumed the day following when a well respected, retired building contractor offered confirming evidence that his measurements too showed a two and one-half inch disparity between the two ends of the bridge, and indeed, it appeared that Carroll Creek had tilted

Every gathering of the Village Restaurant Coffee Group is just a little bit beyond ordinary. The fun and fellowship are always good. There are frequent high moments and an occasional low moment. From time to time, however, there have been experiences, incidents, and issues that would qualify as classics. Keep in mind that incidents which do not occur at the Coffee Club meetings are unselfconsciously related by the members themselves in an atmosphere of trust and good will. Here are a few of them.

Among the group's traditions perhaps the one that is most treasured is the daily coin flip to determine the winner who will go home with a few extra quarters. The coin flip is based on the ageless practice of "matching" coins to determine a winner and a loser. With numbers of persons larger than two, a winner is ultimately decided through elimination. For example, on a typical morning the "Quartermaster" would call, "O.K., there are eight of us. Coins on the table. Now those with heads, raise your hands." On a typical day, a couple of quarters will roll off the table during the flipping process. Members search until they are retrieved. Finally, three, four, five hands will be raised, and the "Quartermaster" will yell, "One, two, three, four, five... five heads.

Heads are out; now there should be three tails." Those three members flip again and sooner or later one person will be declared winner. Though this practice has been going on for approximately forty years, some individuals still have difficulty with the process.

There are ethical considerations with the matter of "gambling" and every once in a while coin flipping is the cause of mild unease among some members. This is particularly true of those regulars who happen to be "men of the cloth." During my years with the group (the mid 1970s) there have been members who were ministers. Strangely all of them have been ministers in the United Methodist Church. I have not yet been able to determine why this is so. What does it mean? Is there some deep philosophical, or even theological question posed by this unusual fact?

During my early years with the group, the Rev. Ralph Sharpe was a regular. He always enjoyed the fellowship, including the good-natured kidding and even the jokes. The gambling seemed, however, to make him nervous. He, of course, would not flip a quarter and would look aside uneasily as if thinking, "Lord, don't let one of my good Deacons walk past and observe this."

The Rev. Raymond Rhoderick was the next preacher to become connected with the Coffee Club. Ray, of course, didn't flip either, but he seemed less passive than Rev. Sharpe. He would often hold forth with some story or lesson of his own, while the "money changing" took place. With his well-honed preacher voice, he was able to create substantial distraction, and this somehow seemed to ease his conscience. It was not felt that Rev. Rhoderick had particularly negative attitudes about money. It was assumed that it was the gambling activity that did not rest well with him.

In more recent years still, another preacher from the United Methodist Fellowship has enriched our meetings. The Rev. Cecil Pottieger seems quite comfortable with the quarter flipping activity. Actually, he is considerably more adept at winning, too, and the elevator fund to which his winnings are committed probably is large enough to purchase a good-sized step ladder in case the futility of ever winning enough for an elevator becomes a topic of discussion and debate.

At times, members of the law enforcement fraternity have been active members of the group. First among these is former Chief of Police Charlie Main. Although Charlie is able to attend only on rare occasions, he is, I believe, the only living member of the original Coffee Club. The club has never had rules, or officers, or any kind of formal organization. While active and able to attend regularly, Charlie was our "monarch" and whatever he decided was pretty much the order of the day. He loved to play the role of Monarch and especially enjoyed ruling by the strength of his voice. Beginning perhaps a dozen years ago or more Charlie loved to get the attention of the group and the waitresses by yelling, "Coffee!" as soon as he was seated. Everyone would laugh including the paying customers seated around the restaurant. As he grew older, and as his entry into the restaurant became more infrequent, his exuberance increased and his voice level jumped by 60 or more decibels. Not long ago the "Monarch" slowly entered the restaurant with the help of a couple of buddies. Every eye was on Charlie, and a huge smile covered his face. Just inside the door he paused and lustily called, "Coffee" at the top of his voice. A customer seated in a booth by the window was so startled that he poured half a glass of orange juice on his pancakes. Toward the back of the room, a small girl with eyes as big as saucers hid behind her mother's coat sleeve. Just another morning in the life of the Coffee Club!

Sheriff Bob Snyder was a longtime member of the group and often teased his buddies about the possible illegality of our gambling. A new sheriff was elected – a man who might not look with the same air of indifference at the exchange of quarters taking place daily practically on the Square Corner. For a while, at least, we were able to avoid arrest and possible conviction with the help of Lem Keller. Lem, a local builder/engineer, made from solid brass rod the diameter of a quarter, coins for all of us. One side was stamped "heads" and the other side "tails." We were able to continue in our sinning ways, each of us carrying a perfectly legal quarter in our pocket. We were not, however, able to gamble with complete impunity. One morning officers of the law descended upon the Village Restaurant and "arrested" a sizable number of our group including Vernon Rippeon who was a resident of

Homewood who came to coffee on his motorized wheelchair. I believe Mr. Albert Powell, gentleman's gentleman of Frederick, then past ninety was inadvertently caught up in the mêlee. All of this took place before the eyes of the public and the flash bulbs of the press. This "Jail or Bail" incident turned out okay, and the gambling goes on as usual.

Lem Keller, the man who made our quarters, was creative in other ways, too. He loved music and played several instruments including organ and piano. Lem decided to build a pipe organ in the basement of his house and did the whole complex job himself, well almost. The pipes were arranged behind a wall, which extended the full length of the room. The boards comprising the wall were anchored in such a way that when particular keys were played on the organ the wall boards covering the corresponding pipes opened like louvers emitting glorious tones. As he sat at the keyboard and played, the wall boards opened and closed in perfect synchrony with the music, providing a visual accompaniment to heavenly sounds. Lem described to us how he accomplished the placement of wires through a very small crawl space above the ceiling extending from one end of the room to the other. He tied a string to the back leg of a cat, placed it in the small space at one end of the room and enticed it to the other end with food. Then he would attach a wire to the string and pull it through. He never said how many trips that cat had to make with a string tried to its leg, but it was a large organ with many, many pipes.

In Lem's last few years attending the Coffee Club he became a bit forgetful. Being forgetful is certainly not an unusual experience for many of the members, and knowing Lem's sense of humor, he might have been the one having the last and best laugh. From time to time Lem would pick up his quarter after the flip and return it to his pocket.

After Lem was no longer able to come to the restaurant, a few of us decided to visit him at home on the day we celebrated his birthday. The visit was arranged with his wife, and when we arrived at his home, Lem was groomed to perfection. He greeted us happily and immediately sat down and ate the birthday cake. We visited for a few minutes and Lem said, "When you first showed up, I thought it was that fellow who owes me five dollars." In his most disarming manner, Lem smiled at us as if to say, "Gotcha!"

Life and Death of a Family Farm

Right in the middle of Harwood Cove was a spring. A bubbling pool of clear cool water formed under the base of a huge poplar tree, literally flowing out of the base of the mountain. The land rose abruptly on all sides. To the right was a trail that meandered between several large rocks that had tumbled off the ridges at some time in the past. Just at the edge of the old fields was a grove of cherry trees, "black hearts" and "red hearts," planted years before by Granddaddy Harwood. Scattered throughout the fields and pastures were other fruit trees whose bounty was there for the taking. The wild creatures and folks alike beat a multitude of pathways to their favorite trees.

Up the ridge and to the left of the spring was a most unusual apple tree. Each year it bore heavily and its fruit was a rich gold hue tinted with a blush of pink, rose, or even red. This fruit looked almost too perfect to eat. The first one of these apples I tasted literally burst with juice when I bit down, but it was so sour I almost strangled. How could something that looked so delicious be so deceiving? Later, I asked Uncle Patton about these strange apples, and he smiled knowingly and said, "Oh, I call that apple 'the hypocrite!' "

In the thirties our first summer picnic was under the trees near the spring in the Harwood Cove. After church we would drive as far as the car would go and walk the rest of the way. The food would be spread on a large rock near the spring. Family members would sit here and there on logs or rocks and eat fried chicken and left over breakfast biscuits with country ham. We would also pick a native wild salad called "crow's foot." It was good, and the older folks liked it "killed" in hot bacon grease.

In the area below the spring, the cool water spread out among the rocks and small bushes. It became a favorite place to look for spring lizards and crawdads. This ever-flowing spring was the source of the stream that flowed by the house and then into Sweetwater Creek. We always referred to the stream as the branch. Dad called it "Pigpen Branch" and said that's what Granddaddy Harwood called it. That made sense to me because just where the branch turned and crossed the road "up the branch" was the pigpen. It was made of notched logs and had a wood shingle roof. It was there when I was born, and it was there when I left the county. Pigpen Branch, or the "Branch" was the lifeline flowing through this mountain farm.

How central it was to our lives came to be understood only years later. It is the wellspring of a thousand experiences and memories. The sound of moving water could be a lullaby. The old house was much closer to the branch than the new house we moved into in 1938. In the darkness the sounds of the moving water were a comfort to the members of our household, and the other creatures who shared these hills and hollows with us. They rested, too, under a blanket of soft and familiar noise. But at the climax of a summer storm those roaring, tumbling brown waters threatened all of us. The ancient bed of Pigpen Branch at sometime in the forgotten past lay where our vineyard used to be. That rocky swale at one time was a streambed.

On the other side of the branch is a familiar hillside now overgrown and hard to recognize. When the life of our farm was most active that hillside was covered with broom sage almost all the way to the tree line, which was near the top. Halfway up the hill was a large chestnut tree alive and strong except for the dead limbs at the top. That chestnut tree, as it was gradually destroyed by the blight, sort of forecasted the strangulation of that mountain farm, choked to death by the depression, a world war, and the next generation who never came home or moved away. But before the blight in all its forms took over, that hillside was a place bursting with life. In addition to the cows, horses, chickens, hogs and ducks were added sheep. Henry Crisp, David Holloway, and others dug a site in the side of the hill next to the chestnut tree for a sheep pen. The sheep pen was built into the hillside. It had an opening in the front, walls of rough oak lumber on the side and a wood shingle roof sloping back toward the hill. It was close enough to the chestnut tree that one could stand on the sheep pen roof and knock chestnut burrs off the tree with a stick. The pen was cozy inside and with a bed of straw and leaves made a warm and safe place for the small flock of Hampshire sheep that joined us on Sweetwater. Hampshire sheep have very distinctive black faces and are usually gentle. I loved them, except for one, and that was "Biller Knob," the ram. He would chase and butt us without provocation. Once we tried to break Biller Knob from butting by tying a tow sack with a large rock inside onto a swing and enticing him to butt the rock. He would attempt to butt anyone in the swing and had succeeded in knocking my sister out of the swing. As we swung the rock in the sack back and forth, Biller Knob watched intently. Finally rearing up on his hind legs and meeting the rock at mid-swing. The concussion was immense. He shook his head angrily and started looking for another target while we scattered.

A farm is not a place as much as it is a community of living things all tied together in a web of interdependence. But it is more still than that, a place of beginnings and endings, a place of life and death, a continuum of agonies and ecstasies. The life and death process going on in such a place breed and generate a quality almost spiritual, painful and raw, warm and tender. Changing but always holding promise. The past disappears into the now and the now moves into the future. The farm helps one grasp the significance of process. Nothing is ever quite finished but always becoming. Like the winter the sheep died. It was a hard winter like most winters are. Was it the last gasp of the depression or the sneak attack on Pearl Harbor? Was it another winter of Dad working away from home, or was it just the next chapter of a dying dream? I don't remember what year it was in reference to world events, which become time markers for all of us. It was just the winter the sheep died. There was too much snow, grazing was almost impossible, feed was scarce, and then they said the sheep ate ivy. I guess it was mountain laurel, which we called ivy. For a long time I felt like I should hate ivy, but it is so pretty when it blooms. It is even pretty when it snows. The leaves curl up like little green cigars. We never did have any more sheep after they died that winter. Was there a lesson in this for me? For us? Was this the end of innocence? No, it had to be more that that. The fact that the sheep died didn't take away the sweetness of holding and rubbing the calves when I fed them in the evening. When I carried a bucket of corn to the horses, they still neighed with the softness that speaks volumes. Still, and forever, I could sit on an upturned bucket with my head resting against the warm flank of a Jersey cow and know that I was a part of the ongoing life of the farm. In cold weather with my ear against the cow's flank, I could hear the gentle noises of life itself, the flow of vital fluids, digestion, respiration, milk production just on the other side of that hair covered tissue. There were smells, too, most of them pleasant: orchard grass and clover hay, dairy feed with cotton seed meal, and the aroma of warm, rich milk. Not a bad place to be on a winter morning. Can't help smiling as I remember that one of my favorite places on a rainy summer day was the barn.

The first horse I remember was George, who belonged to Granddad Denton. He was a bay horse, probably a Morgan, since that was the breed he raised. This must have been pretty early in my years because George was being stabled in the chicken house. It seemed strange even then, but it worked out all right. The chicken house was directly above the old house and had a log across the front opening, which had to be stepped over. I vividly remember the tale of my being kicked by George. I was proud of that even though I don't remember the incident.

At that time there was not a lot of stable space because Granddaddy Harwood's barn was already down, or was being torn down. That was a large log barn, which was located across Sweetwater Road from the rest of the farmstead. The crib had two stalls connected to it and they were used for cows. When we moved into the new house in 1938, the old house was immediately converted into a barn. Interior walls in the main part of the house were removed and four stalls built. Alongside the four stalls was a hallway with space on one end for feed and harness. The original log house portion was used for hay storage and the kitchen was converted into two cow stalls. Both the upper and lower porches had the floors removed and became storage for the farm wagon and various implements.

After George, the next horse to enter our lives was Bell, a grey Percheron. Bell was a good horse and would do almost anything she was asked to do. My fondest memories of Bell are associated with hauling wood on a sled up on the logging road. We would hitch Bell to the sled and haul wood from the logging road to the wood yard. Edwin was the teamster and he would make Bell run at full speed on this narrow road through the woods with Noell and me holding on to the sled for dear life while it bounced off trees, stumps, and rocks. When the fun and fear were over, we would load the sled with blocks of wood for the kitchen stove and fireplace and head home.

Bell's passing is obscure in my memory, but I clearly recall the day we acquired Alice and Pearl. Dad bought them from a horse trader named Fred Ledford. Some people thought Fred Ledford was crooked. Later on, I came to that conclusion myself. But Alice and Pearl were wonderful. They were both bay with black manes and tails. Pearl had a white strip or blaze, all the way down her face. Alice had a small white spot in her forehead. We loved to claim animals on the farm as our own. Though just a boy, I claimed Pearl as my own and Noell claimed Alice. This arrangement was okay with Edwin and Dad. All the animals belonged to all of us, but we were free to claim the ones we wanted. It was with Alice and Pearl that I learned to handle a team, first of all with the wagon and later with other implements like the mowing machine. Being able to plow was the mark of manhood.

One spring when it was about time for plowing, winter returned and claimed our spirits for a season and more. The team had been used pretty heavily snaking pulpwood, acid wood, and probably saw logs as well. They had been turned out on pasture for the weekend and by Sunday evening something terrible was wrong. Alice was down in her stall and in horrible pain. We were unable to get her on her feet and there was not a veterinarian within fifty miles. Besides we had neither phone nor electricity. We tried every remedy we knew, including "drenching" her with some preparation in a long necked bottle. It seems we were up all night working with Alice by the light of a kerosene lantern. Alice died. On Monday a grave was dug and Alice's body was pulled with a log chain by her teammate, Pearl. That hole which became Alice's grave seemed like the biggest cavity in the earth I had ever seen. While Alice was being covered up, Pearl was tied under the Ben Davis apple trees. The picture is stuck freeze frame in my consciousness of Pearl looking back alongside her body in the direction of her teammate's grave. Her head seemed to droop and to tilt to one side as if she was just too broken and weary to lift her gaze. The next day Pearl died. Another hole was dug and there they rest together as a team again.

What had killed Alice and Pearl was determined to be "sneezeweed." Sneezeweed is a wild plant which looks somewhat like Black-eyed Susan except the blossoms are a lighter shade of yellow. Also the stems have ribs extending along their length. Dad had bought about one hundred acres of property from Cleveland Cody and as it could be fenced and cleaned it was being turned into pasture. The horses had been turned out onto this new pasture the weekend they became sick, so the search for sneezeweed began. There was plenty of it growing at different locations on the new pasture and endless hours were spent in the months ahead searching for and digging sneezeweed. At times it seemed that sneezeweed had become a frightening obsession for all of us, especially Dad. Maybe it was partly because of the awful way the horses died, maybe it was in part something that Dad felt as a result of the whole painful experience – a brooding anxiety that it could happen again.

Plowing needed to be done, the first cutting of hay would soon be ready and the garden and potato patches lay fallow. There were no tractors in Graham County and every available team was busy. Fred Ledford enters our lives again. (Alice and Pearl had been bought a few years earlier from this dealer in horseflesh from over in Tennessee.) This time the horse trader arrived with a whole truckload of horses. It was a big truck with a stake body, and there must have been a dozen head of stock there. Many times I've looked back and wondered about the transaction that took place between Fred Ledford and Dad. Dad was under tremendous stress; I know that because the worry was heavy on his countenance. He was working and had very little time to handle a situation such as this. Money, of course, was a factor and Ledford, I'm sure, had no qualms about taking advantage of a man who was down. Dad bought a team of mares with the hope in mind that it might not yet be too late to have some sort of crop. Well, we were able to get through the growing and harvest seasons, but it was primarily with the saving help of Uncle Patton's mules, small "Jack rabbit" mules as Dad called them.

The new team was made up of a sorrel mare named Nell and a smaller bay mare Ledford called Della. Noell quickly changed Della's name to Cindy. The acquisition of this team turned out to be one of the major calamities in Dad's efforts to develop a successful dairy farm on Sweetwater. It was possible to get some of the plowing done but not without great effort. Noell was beginning to harrow the field below the road and had the team hooked to a disk harrow, a pretty heavy piece of machinery. He stopped the team across the road from the front yard and started toward the house for a drink of water. Gwendolyn walked into the yard with a quilt intent on sunbathing. She waved the quilt gently to spread it upon the ground, and the team spooked suddenly wheeling and running away. Out of the plowed ground they flew, through the meadow and into the tobacco patch, just plowed but not harrowed. As they galloped the disk harrow bounced and jerked creating great clouds of dust. Midway through the plowed field, where the tobacco patch was to be, the harrow turned completely over in the air only to land upside down with the long steel control levers driving deeply into the ground. With that the double tree splintered, the runaway horses seemed to gain speed, now free of the harrow. Trace chains and harness rattled and clanged and clods of fresh earth flew like popcorn through the air. Reaching the edge of the field the horses made no effort to turn or slow down. They crashed headlong into a rail fence, which had one strand of barbed wire on top. The team straddled a holly tree growing in the fencerow, destroying it and disappearing into Zim England's field, which was mostly a swamp filled with alder bushes. We found the horses a few minutes later, their sides heaving, covered with the froth of sweat and blood and their harness in tatters. The mare that had been on the left was now on the right!

We were discouraged, but not finished yet. A few days after the runaway with the disk harrow, Noell was preparing to harrow the garden. He had just hooked Cindy to one section of a steel drag harrow. They were not yet out of the barn lot when Cindy bolted, jerking Noell off his feet. With the harrow rattling and clanking behind her, Cindy circumnavigated the barnyard several times with the section harrow bouncing off trees and buildings until fatigue finally took over.

We had little choice but to try to make the best of what we had without giving up completely. Dad was home one weekend and was determined to see if he might be able to manage these horses himself. Hay was ready and Dad planned to take the mowing machine to Slaybacon and put some hay on the ground. The horses were harnessed and hooked to the Oliver mowing machine. Dad didn't dare ride the mower until he was certain the horses were under control. Dad was a big man and strong. He had the leather check lines over one shoulder, across his back with a rein in each hand. The gate from the barnyard was opened and Dad guided the team through and onto the lane through the orchard. It was obvious from the beginning the team intended to run and Dad leaned heavily backward, pulling the bits deep into the horses' mouths. Dad pulled with all his strength, digging his heels into the dirt. By the time they reached the point where the lane enters Sweetwater Road, Dad was being pulled at a trot as he struggled against the fury of these dangerous animals. As the team and mowing machine turned onto the road the horses literally exploded into action. Dad, all 230 pounds of him, was jerked headlong into a dead run. As the team's speed increased, Dad pitched forward sprawling face down into the dust, dirt and gravel. He held to the reins, breaking a finger, tearing his clothes and skinning his body until the reins broke, an inch and a half of horsehide leather. Free of the man who would tame them, they flew like the wind down the open highway, the mowing machine crossing from one side to the other. They disappeared as they passed the England house. Down the road we went following the tracks of two wild horses and a flying mowing machine. The tracks told us that the horses and machine rounded the England curve on the inside of the road, which would put them dead center in front of any approaching vehicles. Miracles do occur, it seems. We followed the tracks all the way to Charlie Garland's house without meeting a car, at least a mile.

From the tracks, the mowing machine had made the turn into the Garland driveway on one wheel, striking and splitting the gatepost. We found the team and machine under a walnut tree next to Garland's yard with a very upset Addie Garland holding one of the horses' bridles with her left hand and a four-foot long 2X2 in her right hand. It was as if the horses knew that "No one messes with Addie Garland!" They were content to catch their breath in the shade of her walnut tree. The horses were much more manageable on the way home. The steel wheels on the mower have rims probably five inches across and three quarters of an inch thick. The one that had struck the gatepost was cracked all the way across but continued to serve us for years to come. Oliver makes good machinery!

Only one other time do I remember that we tried to work these two horses as a team. We had a load of ammonium nitrate on the wagon that we wanted to store in the old house that stood near Marty Holder's house at the head of the pasture. The fertilizer would be scattered by hand on the pasture, which we were in the process of clearing and improving.

Dad was with me as we harnessed the team and hitched them to the wagon. The wagon was easy to pull and it would not have been a big load for the horses. We had gone only a couple hundred yards however, when the team quit. There was nothing we could do to get them to budge. In response to our efforts to get them to move, they kicked wildly, reared, and seesawed back and forth. They would also try to turn in their harness and try to climb over the tongue of the wagon. We struggled with them for at least two hours and moved not a foot. In what surely felt like total defeat, Dad at last said, "Son, while I unhook them, why don't you ease over to Uncle Patton's and see if you can borrow his little jack rabbit mules." As he spoke, I was sure I could see tears in Daddy's eyes. Whether from hurt, disappointment, sadness, or what, I could not be sure. But whatever it was, it felt sad. Uncle Patton was gracious, as always, and as those little jack rabbit mules hauled that load of fertilizer up the branch to the old Manuel Jones house, they required no more urging than a gentle "cluck, cluck, get up mule." Why do I remember this, I wonder, and why do I still feel sad about it?

It wasn't long before other horses entered our little community. I'm not sure where they came from. Dad had probably been searching for some time. From the beginning things seemed to go well and this pair of grey Percheron mares came to play an important role in my life for the next few years. Doll and Bell were most agreeable whether they were being worked as a team or singly. They were big horses and somewhat clumsy, but willing and determined. Tasks like plowing the garden or cultivating corn could be tedious. Pulling a four footed cultivator between two rows of corn and turning in a small enough radius at the end of the row to return to the next furrow without tramping down a half acre of corn was not easy, especially with Doll. Percherons have big hooves anyway and it doesn't take much of a misstep to create a mess. Cultivating corn was a pure joy when using Uncle Patton's mules. These dainty, small-footed creatures could plow all day and never knock down a stalk of corn. With Patton's mules cultivating corn or plowing gardens or small patches, they would turn at the end of the row without using the rein. With a cultivator we always used a cotton plow line and all we had to do was drape it over one shoulder and control the mule by voice. One of Patton's mules was so disciplined that she knew when 11:30 arrived and knew that at 11:30 it was time to go to the barn. At 11:30 she would invariably start skipping rows as a way of letting one know it was time for dinner.

Part of the new property that Dad acquired was the Walnut Cove. It was all woodland and was generally a couple of ridges to the northeast of the Harwood Cove. There was a considerable stand of good timber in Walnut Cove, including large walnut trees that would be priceless today. It was in Walnut Cove that I learned how to handle a team of horses logging.

Many of the local landowners would sell their standing timber to someone else who would do the logging. Dad wanted to do selective cutting and decided that we could do it ourselves. Cutting the timber part was fairly straight forward and, of course, I had been using an axe and saw all my life. If Dad was not home, he would get someone like Herbert Crisp to work with me. We would cut down what would equal several truckloads of saw logs and saw them into lengths of 16', 14',

12', 10', etc. The logs would then be snaked with the team to a landing yard where they could be loaded onto the truck.

After the trees had been cut, trimmed, and sawed into logs, we would bring the team and logging gear to the site and begin the process of logging. The ridges and hollows were steep and narrow and could be treacherous. In western North Carolina there is often water in the hollows and coves, so pulling logs down these steep, wet hollows requires some thought and skill. The tools of logging are fairly simple. In addition to stout harness, your team will require a strong double tree with necessary chains and hooks. A grab is driven into the log near the end. A grab is a steel hook, L-shaped with a piece of chain with hook or ring attached. More than one log can be pulled at one time by driving a double grab into the end of each log. A double grab is two L-shaped hooks connected by a piece of chain. The logs are connected end to end by grabs when snaking more than one.

Once the team is hooked to a log or logs, it usually requires a determined lunge by the team to break inertia and get the load moving. Once the logs are moving it is critical to keep them moving. So having the team gain momentum is very important. The teamster is, of course, moving with the team and logs. As can be imagined, it is necessary to keep control of the team, know what is in front of them, keep clear of the team, and keep clear of the logs. This may require moving at what is sometimes a full run. Sometimes logs will "ball hoot" or slide on their own, overtaking the horses. This is especially true when the logging road is wet and steep. For this reason, the use of Jay grabs and Jay holes is necessary. A Jay hole is in principle like an escape ramp for trucks on modern highways in the mountains. Loggers will often trim the bushes from a logging road at appropriate places to allow the team to be diverted into the Jay hole. Then the logs can slide past them without danger. This maneuver, of course, requires a Jay grab. A Jay grab allows the team to be hooked to the logs by a simple ring over a hook. As the horses move to the escape route the logs slide past and the team is disconnected as the rings slips off the hook. One can imagine what would happen to a team if the logs begin to "ball hoot" and there is no quick disconnect.

When a logger and his team reaches the landing yard, the grabs are removed from the logs with a grab skip which is a heavy hammer with a point on one side. The logger swings the skip like a heavy hammer driving the point under the grab, which forces it out of the log. Logs are then moved into position for loading with the use of a peavey or cant hook. Then it's time to return for more logs.

Dad and I had finished logging Walnut Cove. Summer would soon be coming to an end and I was thinking about early football practice. We were giving the horses a drink before unharnessing and feeding them. Dad turned to me and said, "Old man, you're about as good a teamster as I ever saw." That statement, totally unexpected, could not have meant more if it had been an announcement that I was a candidate for the Heisman Trophy. That is how much I loved football and how much my dad's recognition of my effort meant.

Nothing lasts forever, and really good things don't last very long at all, it seems. Bell died. The details of her illness and her death are gone. Was I too distracted by other forces in my adolescence to remember, or did the memories get buried with the carcass? What is remembered is what took place after she died. This time there was no one to help share the anxiety. No other soul to make decisions, to give directions. The digging of a grave was not to be a joint undertaking. It was like digging a cellar for a house with a pick and shovel through dirt, and then the rocks. Some of them I could lift out of the hole. One of them I had to put a log chain around and pull out with Doll. It was necessary to dig under the rock with a crowbar in order to get the chain around it. These rocks would come in handy though. They would be put on top of the carcass to keep the wild dogs from digging into the grave. That had happened before with my heifer, Margeurite. She died delivering her first calf. It was stillborn. Too big for a first time heifer! She died of a prolapsed uterus. We tried to put it back in. It was awful! How could an event so ugly swallow up all the wonder and sweetness that had started with a calf that I claimed? Then we buried her and the dogs dug into her grave. That was not going to happen this time with Bell. She made me a teamster! She even pulled my buggy. Yes! It was in Uncle Patton's carriage shed. So many times I had driven a wagon-load of hay past the old carriage shed and looked longingly at that buggy. He said I could have it for five dollars. Then he smiled and said, "You can work it out." I pulled it home by myself. Me, between the buggy shafts! After the buggy was restored, Bell, the big grey, sweet Percheron endured the indignity of allowing herself to be crammed between the shafts of that little buggy and pulling buggy, me, and two bushels of corn up the road to Fannie Roger's mill. She was allowing me and helping me live out a dream that spanned more than generations, maybe a century.

When that hole in the ground was finished, I harnessed Doll and with a log chain around her neck, Bell was pulled alongside the hole and the chain removed. It would not be right to do the rest of the job with Doll looking. So I took her back to the barn.

Over the next half hour I struggled to move the carcass enough to topple it into the hole. When it finally fell, it turned so that two of her legs were sticking up and lodged against the side of the grave. The hole was deep, but she was a tall horse. If I left everything as it was and covered her up, the two feet would be less than a yard underground. I realize now that would have been all right, but then I was haunted by the thought of dogs digging where this gentle animal was to rest. I did what I felt was necessary. I covered the carcass with dirt until nothing showed except the two legs. The rocks were thrown in to form an additional barrier and standing on the stones I broke the bones in Bell's legs with an axe and mattock. Emotionally and physically empty, I struggled through the remainder of this foul experience knowing that I couldn't walk away from what had to be done. Knowing too, that I owed it to myself and to this lead horse on the team that had led and pulled me behind a plow, on a hay wagon, and beside two tons of walnut logs "ball hooting" to hell down a steep and slippery ravine waiting for the teamster to utter a single word "Gee" and touch the leather check line, just enough to affirm what had already registered and prompted a response. As we stood breathing heavily, secure in that Jay hole, we shared a brief but splendid ecstasy. Feeling the ground move and hearing the thunder of undirected power and energy, yet safe and together, team and teamster.

Desert of Ice

Among the world's driest places is that vast island of ice called Antarctica. Antarctica, which includes the whole of the earth's southern polar region, could hardly be called a land mass because it is principally water, H_2O, permanently locked in a frozen state. Packed as hard as concrete and thousands of feet deep, this water for all its life giving qualities may just as well be buried under the blistering sands of the Sahara. Annual precipitation in Antarctica is a scant half a dozen inches, rivaling such waterless places as the high deserts of Mongolia. We recognize that the moisture which does fall on the deserts of the world quickly evaporates in the gale force winds of places like the Gobi or dissipates in the heat of the low deserts. Perhaps we fail to recognize that in the presence of so much water drought exists. In the calcified state, no medium exists which would act as a means of transmission of the very substance of water, though it is there, in abundance.

Perhaps in another realm we face an analogous situation, just as confounding and unexpected as the concept of a desert of ice. The analogy is that in the age of the Internet when our culture is literally buried under an avalanche of words, students across America are struggling to gain basic competence in language...stuck somewhere there on the "information superhighway." Most homes and most classrooms have computers and many among us spend an inordinate amount of time chasing the illusion of instantaneous knowledge or power so cleverly packaged and presented in e-mail or the cell phone. In this torrent of verbiage, which so characterizes the information era, we find the elements of language – some of them, but where is the medium by which the substance of language is transmitted? Perhaps that medium is the process itself, the manner in which the substance of language is transmitted.

Consider the deaf infant born to parents with normal hearing. By age three, this child has existed in a world of sound literally awash in a stream of spoken words not only from the lips of his parents, but also his siblings and all those others who make up his social cultural world. Typically this deaf child would have a vocabulary of zero, and worse still no concept of the world of language deafness drought in a deluge. What is missing is a medium by which the basic concepts of language can be received and expressed. Babies learn language by interacting with it by using it – receptively and expressively, present at birth, is a severe sensory handicap and precludes language reception. Though the deaf baby may be growing up in the midst of a literal shower of spoken words, he may remain without language, like a fertile seed not receiving enough nourishment to germinate. For this situation to change, the medium through which the living flow of language occurs must change first. We can see that deafness imposes a barrier to the normal acquisition of language – expressed through the spoken word and received through the ear – the auditory pathway to the brain. Of course, it is in the brain that language is processed, interpreted, understood and stored. With these matters in mind, it could be suggested that the most significant step made at the Maryland School for the Deaf during my twenty-five year tenure as superintendent was the establishment of a family education – early intervention program for deaf infants and their families. The services of this program extended right into the homes of deaf youngsters all over Maryland. Teams of professionals from the school traveled throughout the state providing instruction in the language of signs to parents and family members, and other vital support in helping the family understand the social, psychological, and educational implications of deafness. The services of this program were based upon the recognition that language acquisition and growth among infants, deaf or hearing, does not occur through instruction, but through spontaneous interaction with language through conversation. For babies who are deaf this meant that the first responsibility of the parents was to develop basic competence in sign language since the deaf member is unable to acquire language through an auditory symbol system. Family members must learn to communicate in a visual symbol system – sign language. Once the deaf member was able to express his own thoughts and feelings using a symbol system he could manipulate, and once he could grasp and comprehend the stumbling attempts of his parents to communicate with him using the same vivid and visual system of symbols that he was learning to use, that cocoon of isolation in which deafness had wrapped him began to unravel. Members of the family now had a common coin of exchange, and they could grow together in the richness of the communication experience. Hearing members of the family were encouraged to use sign language when conversing with each other providing opportunities for incidental learning by the deaf member. Once that three-year-old deaf child with a vocabulary of zero words was provided a set of language symbols he could manipulate for himself and an opportunity to interact with his mom and dad using these same language symbols, he would be expected to show not only a burst in language, but growth in other areas, too.

The beauty and power of language expressed through the spoken word cannot be denied, but for the child whose auditory pathway is blocked, the glory and richness of these sound-borne utterings will fall as quietly and as unnoticed as another trillion snowflakes settling on the glaciers of Antarctica. In the presence of another blizzard, drought still exists. The first necessary step in breaking the cycle of language deprivation for the deaf child is pretty straightforward. The system of language symbols must be changed from an auditory one to a visual one. The next necessary step is considerably less apparent than the first, but is no less important. This step has to do with altering the process by which we interact with language.

Here we are talking about a different medium through which language interaction occurs – a medium of language acquisition through conversation rather than through instruction. To illustrate, we have learned that it is quite difficult to teach English to a deaf child who has not yet communicated in English, or for that matter, any other language. We have learned, too, that children can and do develop language competence when immersed in the language conversationally over time.

Again we raise the question – why in the age of the Internet, when our culture is literally buried under an avalanche of words, are students across America struggling to gain basic competence in language? What has changed in American culture that would account for this increasing concern? Has information and communication technology altered the medium through which language interaction occurs? What is not happening in the age of the Internet? One who has visited long and thoughtfully in the realm of language and words has suggested that: "Conversation is the laboratory and workshop of the student." (Ralph Waldo Emerson American Poet and Essayist) Referencing again the deaf child, it is hard to imagine that there would be hours enough to teach him to read a language in which he must labor to converse. Once he has developed a familiarity and working knowledge of language through conversation, these emerging skills are more easily transferable into reading skills. The process will hardly occur when attempted in reverse sequence.

Elaborating on the process of interacting with language, Henry Ward Beecher speaks to us from another century offering insights, which almost seem to have been created for this moment. "Thinking cannot be clear until it has had expression. We must write, or speak, or act our thoughts, or they will remain in a half torpid form. Our feelings must have expression, or they will be as clouds, which, till they descend in rain, will never bring up fruit or flower. So it is with all the inward feelings. Expression gives them development. Thought is the blossom; language the opening bud; action the fruit behind it." (H. W. Beecher – American Clergyman)

In contemporary America the patterns by which we interact with each other and with the environment itself have changed dramatically. We hear of interactive television, interactive videos and games, and even interactive computers. However, many of these activities are passive rather than interactive and basically isolating in nature. The fact that we are such a mobile society compounds the problem of reduced interpersonal contact and increases isolation. The hours each week spent by Americans in such activities as those enumerated above are hours that cannot be spent in conversation or other forms of social/cultural interactions. Families spend less time together as families while the population in general is becoming more segmented by age and generation. The lack of ongoing contact and dialogue between generations lends to an increasing sense of isolation on the part of both groups.

It is understood and accepted that in many areas of human development, individuals grow when consistently confronted with the views, skills, knowledge, and understanding of individuals who are one or two steps beyond them on the developmental scale. This points up one of the benefits offered by cross-generational interaction.

Are we confusing the ever-increasing flow of data with an increase in knowledge? Are we interacting with each other primarily on the basis of e-mail? Are we losing the richness of our mother tongue? Are our conversations becoming cryptic, and our meaning and intentions obscure? Are we using language as a tool for organizing thought, or are we using language as cliche? In our culture the very cornerstone of educational achievement is basic competence in language. With respect to what we have learned about the acquisition of language and patterns of its usage, there is reason for pause as we ponder the cause and effect aspects of this matter.

Perhaps among all our social/cultural institutions the most altered is the American family. Some would suggest that it is not only the most altered but the most threatened, or even the most failed. The family and home are certainly antecedent to the school, and it is in this most basic of American institutions, the family, that reform must begin. It seems pointless to talk about educational reform without recognizing the implications of Ralph Waldo Emerson's statement for every family in our land. "Conversation is the laboratory and workshop of the student." It may be forever too late if we wait for the schools to teach English to children who are just learning to communicate. It's through a basic command of our national language that we are to understand and interpret our world and ourselves within it. Conversation is the medium through which the remarkable tool of language is acquired, sharpened, and exercised for self-understanding and self-expression not to mention the thoughts and expressions of others. Someone said: "Language is the amber in which a thousand precious thoughts have been safely imbedded and preserved. It has arrested ten thousand lightning flashes of genius, which unless thus fixed and arrested might have been as bright, but would have also been as quickly passing and perishing as the lightning." (Richard C. Trench, 1807–86, English Divine)

David M. Denton

Drought in a Deluge

Often, it seems, when an inordinate amount of time and emotional energy have been invested in a matter, when expectations are higher than usual, one may well be getting ripe for the picking in a harvest of grief. The summer of 1998 promised so much, and delivered so much more, but not of what was anticipated. It would be a time of family closeness, a visit with my sister, a few days in Florida with the grand kids, and then some time "at the head of the pasture," our family farm in Robbinsville. Talk about coming home! This would be the time of real "resettling" into what had been. Gwen's new log home was almost finished, and it had grown log by log it seemed from among the very stones which served as the foundation for the old house where we were both born.

Nothing that could have happened would have been nearly as spiritually significant as creating a new home where the family had been brooded. Finally, there could be a starting over for those of us who were left. Capturing and holding this dream, which was rapidly becoming a reality was so easy, so natural, and so self-evident. It did not occur to me, nor to Gwen, I am certain, that what was so obvious, so central to us last June was an esoteric last visit by us to a place and time that exists no more.

In looking back from the time we arrived in Charlotte a little more than a year ago, it is clear now, that we were caught in a passage. Change was the status quo, and by the first week in August, the transition would be complete. It would be a year, however, before the full knowledge of the reality and the finality of this transition was understood, if only murkily. Dreams are not easy to capture, but once held, they are even more difficult to let go. Sometimes it is less a matter of letting go than it is a matter of having something treasured ripped away. After holding determinably to the empty frame for a year, it was a double loss to leave it behind with the dream it once held, now withered, diminished, hardly recognizable. Lost not only is the treasured dream, but with it a measure of self in the knowledge that even if it could have been claimed, it could not have been shared. The map is the same. The names of places have not changed. The journey takes the same number of hours to complete. "Coming home" this time, however, lacked a destination. Yes, all the correct turns had been made. The landmarks were recognizable. There had been no confusing detours, but when we got there, Eden had vanished without so much as a leaf or a blade of grass or stone having been moved. No, this was not an aberration of geography, or even one of navigation; we had come to the right place, but could no longer know it in the mind that comprehends and believes what it is still able to feel. There was nothing wrong with the picture, but something vital was missing from the experience.

Parts of western North Carolina are like a temperate rain forest with frequent rains, low hanging clouds, soft earth and lush vegetation. The summer of 1999 was not only wet, but hot, too. Every day since we arrived on Sweetwater, it had rained. Most days it had rained several times, and there had been electric storms with wind, and once a severe hailstorm. The weather was gloomier than usual, and perhaps that was an omen. Even as nieces, nephews, cousins, and in-laws arrived for the first Sweetwater family gathering, even as activity increased and as music and laughter mixed with the sound of the branch and of rainwater pelting the metal roof of the new log home, it was not sufficient to fill the vacant space within.

Automobiles, pickups, sport utility vehicles, and one Harley arrived while tents of a variety of styles and shapes sprang up around the beautifully groomed lawn surrounding the new house and the homeplace so carefully and tenderly cared for by Matthew and Pat Williams. Children, from babes in arms to adolescents, were there in number. Cousins scarcely known to each other were laughing, playing, getting to know each other. The generation represented by the grandchildren of Bess and Gwynn was the dominant stratum in this layered assembly, their children represented the largest generational element.

When Gwen realized that she would never be privileged to come home and spend even one night in the log house, she stated carefully and powerfully her desire that the place be used and enjoyed by family. In all probability, Gwen knew when she signed the construction contract for the new house that she was building something she could not touch or even own except by giving it away. To her it was not a place, it was an experience. It symbolized all the forces and aspirations that had shaped and defined the lives of herself and her contemporaries. What she did not know in 1998, at the time her legacy was passed, was that sometimes as generations attempt to speak to each other, part of the essence of what is passed on is lost in translation. Sometimes the languages of generations separate those members as effectively as international boundaries would. Sadly, it is not always understood that even though people may be using the same words, they are yet facing emotional and cultural disconnect. Our sentiments reflect our life experiences, which are shaped by the values, practices, and traditions of our time and place. That log house on Sweetwater expressed for my sister a sentiment so precious, so treasured, so fleeting, that it had to be given physical substance to be transmitted. The log house, Gwen's gift, is sturdy and it is grand, though understated, like her, revealing less than it holds. There is a chamber within that may go unnoticed even by the frequent caller, but to have visited that place is to have walked the pathways of her mind and spirit. As you walk with her, you will see what she sees and feel what she feels, and know what she knows, because to know her world, to claim her legacy is, first, to seek it. To seek that particular inclination of her heart, that disposition of the spirit, which yearns to feel, as she felt; that is the key.

All weekend the rain continued. The tumble and roar of the branch increased as the waters rose. The ground was soaked, still children played and laughed. Boys were tossing a football and younger kids were playing in the creek, making a dam and splashing happily. Sunday morning came and the crowd began to disperse, slowly at first and then at a more determined pace. Tents came down, bags were packed and vehicles began to pull away in a number of different directions, one by one, and then they were gone. The rains continued in the Great Smoky Mountains while the gardens and cornfields boasted a healthy vitality and lushness uncommon even in this lovely place. Not far away no rains fall; the earth was baked and cracking like the dry skin on the back of an old man's hand. The leaves of corn were turned in upon themselves, twisted into a protective curl to preserve that last drop of life-giving moisture drought in a deluge.

Summer 1999

Lost Among Familiar Faces

The last oppressive dream was night before last. It seemed unusually long and was vivid in the extreme. Such dreams obviously represent something of basic importance to the dreamer, or they would not be so unsettling and lasting in their influence. Though the elements of a dream are symbolic, the emotions and situations they involve are as powerful and real as the actual experiences, possibly even more so. Dream experiences occur when the human organism is in a particularly vulnerable state, it would seem, thus the residual feelings, thoughts, questions, images, linger after the dream has passed. An awakened state may not bring relief.

Yesterday's dream ended abruptly with the jangling of the telephone. In the dream a climatic moment of desperation burst suddenly into a startled half reality with every nerve fiber jangling like the telephone. There was no transition from a dream state into a conscious state, there was an extension of that moment of high drama and agony into full daylight and stark consciousness. No opportunity for a sorting, a separation, a delineation of the elements and images of the dream from the elements of a state of wakefulness in which consciousness allows for reflection upon the aspects of the dream and interpretation of their meaning.

Dreams are thought to be both instructive and meaningless. Could they be both? That they reside within the realm of sleep is itself fraught with contradiction, for while one aspect of the dreamer slumbers another aspect awakens and drifts unhinged from restraints which rule in another state. Are there lessons in dreams, which need to be searched and probed and interpreted, carefully removed from the layers of mystery, which enshroud them? Or are dreams assertions revealing particular inclinations of the mind and soul already settled on and resolved? Are they questions or statements? Do our dreams represent endless dispute and ongoing litigation between sense and feeling, or do they suggest instead the liberty of reason?

Some dreams are difficult to ignore especially when pain filled, and especially when serial. A serial dream not only multiplies the experience given new life by the dream, but perpetuates over time the life experience, imagined or real, which spawns the dream in the first place. Surely, the dreamer is the author of his sleep fantasies and the writer of the script which gives them form and shadow, color and feeling. Can the principle of cause and effect be applied to the presence and the characters of our dreams? With these questions and thoughts providing a framework, let us examine the patterns and themes of some particularly powerful and recurrent dreams.

Why dreams about the military service have been so dominant is not understood, but among the serial-type dreams spanning perhaps fifteen years those about the military have been most numerous. Ranking second in numbers have been dreams, which transport me back to the Maryland School for the Deaf to revisit those parts of myself left there. The third category of repeat dreams deal with home and family. By home is meant the place where I grew up. Supposedly, everyone dreams and does so often and on a regular basis. Many people indicate that they seldom dream, or do not remember their dreams. It seems that dreams have been a common experience, all the way back to my childhood, and further that they have been dramatic and vivid. It has been only in more recent times that serial dreams have become experiences significant enough to arouse concern or to cause me to question their meaning.

In 1950 I enlisted in the U. S. Air Force and served as an aircraft mechanic and crew chief for a period of four years. Although military service during the Korean War and during the Vietnam War was not looked upon as favorably as during the World War II era, I felt reasonably satisfied with my time in uniform and, deep down, was proud of my service. Time passed and my life began to take more certain directions. Some goals began to be realized and before many years had gone by. I found myself in the midst of an exciting and satisfying career which continued for almost thirty-five years. During those years as a professional educator of the deaf, thoughts of the military slipped deeply into the recesses of my mind. It was a part of the past which was very seldom mentioned and seemed disconnected from matters and from people which were significant in my life as it had developed. It was unexpected when the dreams of being back in the Air Force began to visit my sleep about a dozen years ago.

At the time of my discharge in December 1954, re-enlistment had not at all been seriously considered. Re-enlistment bonuses were offered, and many were able to receive an upgrade in rank by signing up for another four-year term. My thoughts about the future and my expectations of returning to civilian status had become firmly fixed, and it was not until about a year after being discharged and dealing with unexpected and unsettling disappointments that the thought of re-enlisting was seriously considered. Once I had met Peggy and enrolled in college in Kentucky, the possibility of going back to the Air Force went underground for more than three decades. My first night visit to Luke Air Force Base as a subconscious experience was puzzling to say the least. After about the third or fourth episode of this dream, the need to understand its significance and meaning became imperative.

The common elements, which were present in all of these dreams about the military, were strikingly similar. Luke Field, though different than it was in actuality, was recognizable. I was able to achieve at least partial reconnection with my old outfits and able to continue the kind of work on aircraft I was familiar with. I felt fairly comfortable with the personnel populating the dreams, but from the moment of arrival felt a deep and growing uneasiness. I felt certain that I had actually re-enlisted, but I could put my hands on no paperwork and was uncertain about my rank. Knowing that I had served four years and held the rank of staff sergeant suggested that I should occupy a place of responsibility among the new men all around me. I could not find my orders and didn't know to which squadron I was assigned. I didn't know which barracks I was supposed to live in, and in each one of these dreams, I had to find an empty cot. The few personal belongings that I had, I would leave behind the cot I used, and in the next installment I would have to search for them. Each dream involved a long trip from home to the base or from the base back to wherever home was. Sometimes travel was by hitchhiking and sometimes my own car was used. In all the instances in which I had brought a car to the base, I was never able to find it when it was time for me to leave. This added to the feelings of anxiety, which already marked these dreams. Usually I would search out someone in a position of authority, a line chief or a squadron commander to try to determine my status. These efforts were never successful, and I was burdened with the thought that somehow I was in violation of my orders, perhaps had been absent without leave for months, or even guilty of desertion. What had happened to my orders? Had I been reduced in rank? Why didn't anyone seem to know were I belonged, and more basically what about my uniforms? In only one of these dream experiences did I wear a uniform, and that was simply a pair of fatigues like I wore in the fifties with staff sergeant stripes. There seemed to be no comfort in the knowledge that I was there where I was supposed to be trying to unravel the knots that bound me to this endless nightmare.

About five years ago, the dreams about Luke Field and the Air Force stopped abruptly. A month or perhaps six weeks had passed since the last Air Force encounter when I dreamed about returning to the military, but this time it was the Army. This difference registered very strongly in my conscious mind and I thought I had found at least a partial answer. The Army post was somewhere in the southeast, Georgia or maybe Alabama. That part is very distinctive because the travels to the base are places in the southeast. With respect to the major themes, these dreams, which take place on an Army post, are identical with the others. I have no orders yet I am supposed to be there. Why doesn't the Army know? They welcomed me when I stepped forward and signed up. The uniform situation is even more baffling, because of my lack of familiarity with that branch. Another soldier pointed out the supply depot, which contained a large store with a vast selection of uniforms. Interestingly, that building was there in every one of the

Army dreams. Money is an issue in these imaginings, and uniforms must be bought. In one segment I visit the uniform shop and buy a complete outfit, khakis and winter uniforms, caps and fatigues. The pervasive sense of uneasiness is there and sometimes more acute than in earlier dreams. The uniforms I bought were never delivered, so in recent times I am still out of uniform and with missing orders.

When my career in Education of the Deaf ended in 1992, it occurred in a manner, which I did not expect, and which left me searching for answers, reasons, causes – some workable explanation for the huge disparity between my perception of what was happening and the perceptions of others. My sense of self had been shaken. As the sense of loss and the sense of altered identity began to settle in about a year after I left the Maryland School For the Deaf, the second set of serial dreams began to provide unwelcome company in the darkness. For years the MSD community had been a central force in my life. I thought of this large community of people, who shared so much, as a family. The "school family" was more than a cliche, if not to all, then certainly to many who were a part of it. Retirement, as imagined, would provide a continuation of the warm and close associations that had been enjoyed for a quarter century. What had been imagined simply was not to be.

In my recurrent dreams about MSD there were again constant themes and patterns. My responsibilities at the school continued though I was no longer superintendent. I was aware of the same sense of obligation that I had always felt, still had a sense of mission. No longer did I have an office though I felt that I had to be there. Of course, I was aware in these dreams that there was a new superintendent, and that specifically did not cause concern. The most achingly, painful aspect involved my awareness that the staff, including people I knew, hated me and every encounter turned into something frightening. It was impossible to make them understand what I was trying to accomplish and I would find myself begging and pleading with them to listen, often crying in anguish and frustration. Sometimes they would taunt and mock me until I became angry, and this I dreaded and hated most of all. My mail was kept from me and when I would ask about it they would tell me there was none or my box had been changed. In the last one, I was told that my mailbox was # 81 and when I checked it, it had been covered over with tape and a "post-it" note.

Over time there have been dozens and dozens of these dreams. In instances where I drive my car to school, I am never able to find it and end up walking and searching for long spans of time. Frequently I dreamed of driving the state vehicle, which I did in actuality for years. Someone from the maintenance department always takes the car and locks it up. In these situations I go to the shop area only to find that the car has been moved elsewhere. There is never any sense of resolution in these dreams. On the one hand, the feeling that I have a duty to be there and to give to the institution and people whatever it is that I carry inside is as compelling as at any point in my career. On the other hand, the hatred that is expressed toward me, and the humiliation that I experience is beyond comprehension. Frightening it is and even maddening, this being provoked to anger and tears and a sense of utter desperation. In perhaps as many as 30% of these dreams which bring me back to the place that was home for 25 years, I must endure the shame of carrying on my responsibilities, among the people I loved while wearing no pants. It was not that I wanted to go about my work with no trousers. This state of ultimate vulnerability and nakedness allows no option; the dream rules and its prophecy of shame and pain is fulfilled there in the darkness where I seek repose. It is puzzling, even strange, that I do not learn from the bitter experiences of these dreams. With each episode, I go into the experiences full of hope and believing blindly that I can return to the institution that means so much and continue to lead and to teach as I was meant to do. Is this the expression of a need to go back and to complete something left unfinished? Am I fighting to reclaim something that was taken from me? Or, do these movies of the mind symbolize a faith that won't die in a dream lost and now owned by others, though still claimed by its author? Futility?

Sometimes it seems that dreams are prompted by specific experiences. This brings to mind the cause and effect question, and whether or not it applies in the realm of dreams. For example, the repeat dreams about the Maryland School for the Deaf, usually follow immediately upon some small experience with someone from the school: a telephone call, a letter, or other reminder. This, of course, cannot be avoided and as long as we continue to live in Frederick, it will be necessary to deal with the ghost of the former superintendent of MSD. At the time of my retirement, this matter was raised and the conscious and determined decision was made to continue our lives here. We reasoned that it would not be wise to attempt to leave something as significant as 25 years of personal and professional experiences behind with regard to either positive or negative memories. Whether or not this was the right decision, is a matter yet unresolved? If it had been possible to continue my relationship with the school after retirement in the manner I had imagined for so many years, would the serial dreams have been there to haunt me? The answer to that I can't know.

A partial answer to the Air Force dreams was stumbled upon, however, and it might offer limited insight. About five years ago in a deep and very personal discussion about my career the matter of wrestling with a sense of lost or severely altered identity was being examined. For all those years I had believed completely in the rightness of what we were undertaking in Education of the Deaf. I felt great contentment in what was being accomplished, and would have fought with all my soul to defend the school and its programs. Not being able to find rational and ethical explanations to the events surrounding the end of my career at MSD, I couldn't reconcile the disparity between my perception of what was happening and the possible perceptions of others. At times I began to feel that I must deserve what had happened and what was happening. I found no quick, nor easy, nor satisfying answers. It was suggested to me that my focus was centered more and more on the negatives that had occurred at the end of my career, and that to gain a more balanced and honest perspective it might be helpful to retrace, in writing, the span of my professional life from beginning to end and let the written record settle the dispute. This made sense, and I quickly agreed. Months later, I gave this person a draft of that document, and it was then that the Air Force dreams stopped. Some part of the knot had been loosened. Perhaps this paper is a work in progress that will lead some day to a thread that can be traced throughout the fabric of my dreams revealing a pattern that has logic and maybe even a touch of beauty – no longer a knot that strangles.

Last summer two separate reunions were celebrated by my family. One of them has been taking place for many years and includes members of all branches of the Dentons. At this gathering it is tradition to recognize the oldest male present, oldest female present, youngest member, etc. To my astonishment, I was the oldest male family member there. This came as something completely unexpected, a time warp. This little experience stirred me and brought me uncomfortably close to something I knew, but only superficially. The facts are clear, all five of my brothers and sisters are dead, and, of course, Mom and Dad. Ironically, Mom lived to the age of ninety-one and experienced the death of four of her six children. There is only one of a household of eight still alive, and that is me. Another irony is that I have lived longer than any of the other five siblings. All seven of this family of eight passed within a span of twenty years. The meaning and the extent of such loss is only beginning to be understood.

Down through time, there have been numerous dreams of family, but only a few have been centered in Robbinsville, the place we all thought of as home. Serial dreams of family are a phenomenon that is recent. Like the recurrent dreams about the military and those about Maryland School, these family dreams have common themes. Only two nights ago, I dreamed of returning home for a visit. Upon arriving, I went immediately upstairs to locate a place to sleep. Mom and Dad were not in the dream. First, I went to the bedroom at the end of the hall. When I opened the door, the room was occupied with perhaps eight or more beds, some of them stacked. Several of the beds had persons in them and the others had clothing, suitcases, and personal effects on them. Quietly, I closed the door and went to the first room on the right side of the hall, my room. Upon opening the door, I saw my brother Charles on one bed and Frankie, his wife, on the other. We greeted each other briefly, and I told Charles I needed to change clothes so I could go somewhere. The closet was full of someone else's clothing, and I looked around the room thinking that I had recently bought new clothes. On one wall, some clothing was hanging underneath a blanket. Thinking these were my clothes, I lifted the blanket only to find old clothes, nondescript, and dusty including my "Ike Jacket" from the Air Force. The scene changed and Charles and I were going up the branch to deal with a problem of undesirable and even violent people who are squatting on our property and refusing to leave. The elements of this dream that are common with the others about home are this: The bedrooms are full of people unknown to me, but they belong there. There is no place to sleep at home. In none of the dreams about home and family are all family members present, usually only one and maybe two. In almost every sequence, it is necessary to deal with the squatters. In some dreams, these intruders have shot at us and in others have rammed our vehicles. Some of them are living in houses that were on our land and others have built new buildings. The encounters with these dream persons are deeply upsetting, even frightening.

There are some other elements, which show up in some dreams but not in others. These include such matters as an ongoing rebuilding of the house I grew up in, but it remains unfinished even in recent dreams. Frequently the home dream deals with unplanted or unharvested crops, fields that have grown up, hay that is rotting on the ground, or pastures that need to be bush hogged. It is clear in these sequences that I am responsible for the farm though I don't live there. Occasionally there will be a dream in which the landscape has been changed until it is unrecognizable. The mountains behind the house have been obliterated by earth moving machines and huge homes cover what were once wooded ridges. In this altered environment I must search for something familiar. I know in my soul that the Harwood cove is "up there," but I can never reach it.

Believing that there is meaning even in the most obscure journey of the subconscious, I look for lessons in these unhappy night visits to a home and family that are no more. Perhaps the acknowledgment of a loss of this magnitude is too great to embrace as reality, all at once. Maybe the brief return visits to home and family members, one or two at a time, is a way of dealing incrementally with what can't be brought back. Maybe if I know why I dream as I do, it won't be necessary to dream any more. Maybe understanding that these serial visits home will finally bring us to the realm of spiritual reunion where none of us will again be lost among familiar faces.

David M Denton

Graham County – Elements of History

In the tiny settlement of Manteo, North Carolina, stands a sign which reads Murphy, North Carolina, 539 miles. Manteo is the easternmost town in North Carolina and is on Roanoke Island, one of the barrier islands that make up Carolina's Outer Banks. Murphy is the westernmost town in our state, thus the term "Manteo to Murphy" describes our state in its geographic extremes.

It was in 1585 that Sir Walter Raleigh established a colony of English men and women on Roanoke Island at Manteo. The settlers struggled mightily in this strange new world. Raleigh returned to England for more settlers and provisions only to find England at war with Spain. His return to North Carolina was delayed eighteen months or more and when he finally returned to Roanoke Island, the settlers had disappeared and had become the "Lost Colony."

Twenty-one years later in 1606, the first English-speaking Americans gained a permanent foothold at Jamestown, Virginia.

Three hundred years later and 539 miles west of Manteo in Murphy, county seat of Cherokee County, Graham County was established. When Robbinsville became a county seat in 1872, the United States had already experienced almost three centuries of growth and expansion all the way to the Pacific coast, and from Canada to Mexico. This left our piece of the world relatively unsettled and forgotten, both a no man's land and a veritable paradise encircled and hidden by the world's oldest mountains, which have continued to isolate us even into this new century. Connected and touched by the Internet and the information superhighway, we are still the only county in our state and possibly in all of eastern America without one mile of dual highway.

All of our lives it seems we have existed in two centuries and now it seems we are being propelled into a third.

Most of the counties east of us were settled as a result of gradual westward expansion and movement of people inward from the coast. The coastal plain and the Piedmont were settled in this manner. Except for a scattering of hardy souls, the heart of the Blue Ridge and the Smokies remained essentially unsettled until the latter half of the nineteenth century. Interestingly, most of the people who migrated into Graham County did not move here from somewhere further east down the state. Many of them came down the great valley of Virginia into east Tennessee and thus over the hills into the last unclaimed territory in eastern America. It was not the availability of rich level farmland that brought them. It was not the promise of gold. It was not iron, copper, or even coal. This place had vast timber resources, it is true but at the time when our families arrived, trees were obstacles to be removed, not resources to be harvested and sold. No, our folks came here for other reasons.

As early as the 1770s, the vast mountainous area making up western North Carolina and the "over hill" country, now east Tennessee was not wanted by the state of North Carolina. At that time, North Carolina extended to the Mississippi. In 1784 delegates from around the region met in Jonesborough (now Tennessee) to form the state of Franklin. John Sevier who had become a hero at Kings Mountain was to be the state of Franklin's governor. One member of the North Carolina. Legislature at that time said people across the mountains were the "off scourges of the earth, fugitives from justice, and we will be rid of them at any rate." North Carolina gave the "over hill" country to the federal government. The federal government would not accept it so for a time the state of Franklin was born, for a short life. In 1788, Sevier was elected to a second term, but he declined to serve and the state of Franklin was dissolved. Sevier was tried for treason at the state's westernmost courthouse in Morganton. Some of his friends and supporters sprang him and he escaped back into Tennessee.

The mountain people continued to endure the indifference and neglect of both the state government in Raleigh and the federal government as well. In the years following the civil war, the situation facing the mountain people only worsened. It was already divided country and the carpetbaggers, federal regulators, and others bent on punishing these southerners made life unbearable for thousands of families who had already suffered enough.

They trickled into these hills where only the Cherokee had been able to establish and maintain a viable culture. They came through the mountain passes and gaps, up the narrow river valleys fashioning homesteads and subsistence farms in a landscape that was essentially vertical. This was not the first time they had sought and found refuge in a strange land. They and their forebearers had felt the heavy weight of oppression before. Among those putting down their roots in the rocky soil of Graham County were Welsh, English, Irish, Scots, and Scott-Irish who had first fled Scotland to Ireland, and finally on to America. There was a small smattering of Germans, but most of those who came spoke the language of the British Isles. They brought with them their music, their traditions, their stories, and their songs. They carried their old guitars and fiddles along with their muskets and axes. They brought their religion and their commitment to the principles of law and justice. Most of all they brought an unyielding will to secure liberty and peace for themselves and their children. Maybe that could happen in the solitude of these wrinkled hills.

A cross section of the population would suggest that perhaps 60 – 70% of the citizens of this area would be Presbyterian based upon the beliefs and practices of those who came. Among the Irish immigrants to these hills, very few were catholic. Those who have studied the religious history of western North Carolina tell us the preponderance of Baptists and Methodists here result from the comparative ease with which these groups could establish new congregations as the population grew and spread. By contrast, decisions regarding the establishment of new churches among the Presbyterians required the consent and support of the church hierarchy often located in some distant city. By the time necessary actions had been considered and taken by the Presbytery, the Baptists had already organized two new congregations and were working on a third in the next valley. Today, scarcely more than five percent of the local population is Presbyterian, while a century ago probably fifty percent of county residents considered themselves Presbyterian.

By the 1880s the timber barons had discovered western North Carolina with its hundreds of thousands of acres of unspoiled woodland. With limitless financial resources backing them from cities in the industrial midwest and northeast, the lumber companies extended narrow gauge railroads into the Snowbird mountains and into places so remote that even today only a wagon road exists. They took the trees leaving gullied hillsides and brush behind. The heart of Graham County's beauty and its most precious natural resource was shipped out on company trains by the millions of board feet to build houses in places like Chicago. At best the big lumber companies provided brutally difficult jobs for some of the locals.

By the 1920s the forests were gone and the timber barons ripped up their railroad tracks and returned to the big cities leaving behind a scarred and desolate land and a population of citizens eminently poorer and wiser from this first major assault on their home. By the time the logging roads and railroad beds were being reclaimed by pokeweed, blackberry briars, locust bushes, and mountain laurel, the Asian blight had pretty well doomed the last of the American chestnuts. Dead chestnuts harvested for acid wood did provide some income for a few up until the time of World War II.

In the 1920s a new threat, which at the time looked like a promise, came up the gorges of the little Tennessee and the Cheoah River. Tallassee Power Company, the Aluminum Company of America, and finally the Tennessee Valley Authority. With new dams, the waters of these rivers could be harnessed and cheap hydroelectric power could be produced in vast amounts. Further, these improvements would provide flood control and fishing and recreational opportunities. Tallassee Power Company built Tapoco Dam on the Little Tennessee River creating Cheoah Lake. Tapoco was completed in the 1920s. Cheoah Lake is beautiful but almost inaccessible. Apparently, the power company owns the property surrounding Cheoah Lake because there is not a single private or commercial property anywhere adjacent to the lake. In 1928, Santeetlah dam was finished and the lake filled. There is no power generator at Santeetlah dam. Instead, the water is transported over land through a huge metal tube that creeps like a giant silver worm down the hollows and up the ridges from the dam all the way to the powerhouse at Rhymers Ferry. Rhymers Ferry is upriver from Tapoco Dam on the Cheoah Lake. The same water can be used for generating electricity twice; first at Rhymers Ferry and again at Tapoco powerhouse.

From the base of Santeetlah Dam all the way to its confluence with the Little Tennessee River at Tapoco, the Cheoah River, once a wild and pristine waterway, has been forever changed by a dramatic reduction in the water flow. What would be the overflow at Santeetlah is piped to the Rhymers Ferry powerhouse. The lovely Cheoah is now essentially a bed of naked stones and alder bushes with a mere trickle of water.

Fontana Dam was built at the headwaters of Cheoah Lake. The Tennessee Valley Authority undertook this massive project shortly after the beginning of World War II. Hydroelectric power was needed to further the war effect, particularly the Manhattan Project to develop an atomic bomb at Oak Ridge, Tennessee. Of course, none of us knew it at the time. The construction of Fontana Dam was a massive undertaking and involved the establishment of an entire community complete with school and hospital and other standard amenities. During the construction period, Fontana was a thriving community employing hundreds of people. Once the lake was full and the massive generators were producing electricity, the people left, the school and hospital closed, most of the buildings were dismantled, and Fontana died. Over time, it has become an attractive resort community, but what was there will never be again.

The valley of the Little Tennessee, upriver from Fontana, was wild and desolate country, but there were several small and thriving communities along its banks. Dozens of families had to be relocated and their homes and barns today lie buried under a couple hundred feet of cold water. As the old timers who lived there have died off even the names of these communities have disappeared. How many recall a place called Japan?

Even after World War II with three major dams in our county producing electricity, most of us did our homework or read comic books by the light of a kerosene lamp. It is ironic and a bit sad too that not one kilowatt has been produced for local consumption by the power companies which took our water and our land and in some cases, our homes. The little Nantahala Power and Light Co. did more to bring genuine illumination into the lives of local people than all the mega-companies put together.

In terms of what local people gave up as measured against what they gained from Tapoco, Santeetlah, and Fontana, the impact of their footprint on our small piece of the universe is no less than a second major assault on Graham County's soul. Who will be the next to take liberties with the generosity and basic graciousness of our people? Is it already happening to us? What of those who can afford to come for a season, build large homes on the best properties, take advantage of our tax structure and cost of living, escalate land and home values beyond the reach of many locals, and then conveniently slip away back to Florida when the matter of health care and nursing homes begins to enter the picture. The grand new homes being built lakeside or creek side or on the high ridges with lovely vistas are being built primarily by those most recently arrived. Many of the families who have struggled here a few generations find that the joys of a new home are reduced to what is offered by a double wide. Some are priced out completely.

Not a lot has changed since the ill-fated state of Franklin or those awful years of reconstruction following the civil war. Much of the state of North Carolina today sees Graham County as an isolated backwater where the people talk funny saying things like "you'ns" and "son." Political and economic influences are centered down east, and with so few people living in such a vast section of mountain land are woefully under-represented. The mountains are still a barrier between this place and the rest of the state, so in a way this is still "over hill" country. Recreating the state of Franklin is not an option now because much of Franklin is now Tennessee, and since North Carolina grudgingly reclaimed the Tar Heel part of Franklin, we are stuck with the realities of who we are and where we live.

Absent a hero like John Sevier to plead our case, we must find our own voices and state our own case, defining ourselves in terms of the rich and multi-layered history which shaped us, defining ourselves in terms of the principles we embrace and practice, defining ourselves in terms of the gracious and generous temperament of mountain people, defining ourselves in terms of our music, our religion, and our cultural heritage, and defining ourselves in terms of the will to survive generations of indifference and neglect by those who used us taking our forests and streams and befouling the landscape. In defining who we are and what we believe let our voices be heard speaking in the idiom of mountain people. But in the manner of our kind, let us do it in a gentle and understated manner with just a bit of tongue in cheek; stating without saying it that we understand a little bit more than we express.

Graham County

Being one of the thirteen original colonies of our nation, North Carolina is an old state. The English first attempted to establish a colony in North Carolina in 1585. Sir Walter Raleigh's small settlement on Roanoke Island literally disappeared and became known as the lost colony. It was several years after the disappearance of Raleigh's Roanoke Island community before the English gained a permanent foothold on Carolina's Atlantic coast. The British succeeded first at Jamestown, Virginia in 1606. Once started, however, development spread rapidly along the tidal rivers.

Graham County is a young county in an old state. It was carved out of Cherokee County in 1872 with Robbinsville being named the county seat. This was two hundred ninety two years after the first English-speaking settlers learned how to roast corn from the Indians on Roanoke Island. The United States had defeated England in two wars and the civil war had been over for seven years when Graham County was established. What forestalled the settlement of this small mountain area for almost three hundred years?

There are hundreds of definitions for history and I suppose the choice of a particular one depends upon specific circumstances. In thinking about Graham County's ultimate but delayed settlement, a definition by James A. Garfield seems particularly appropriate. Garfield said: "History is philosophy teaching by example, and also by warning; it's two eyes are geography and chronology." If the two eyes of history are the sequencing of events and the physical features of a land area it is understandable first of all that the mountains presented an almost impenetrable barrier to movement and commerce and secondly, that other events determined who would seek out these narrow and steep mountain valleys for settlement and determine from which direction the movement of settlers would come.

Thoughts of history often conjure up visions of conflict, forces determinably struggling against each other. Graham County's history is a literal study of competing forces: the Cherokee and early settlers, the timber barons and local citizens, the major electric power companies and local people. Alfred North Whitehead, American philosopher, suggests "History can only be understood by seeing it as the theater of diverse groups of idealists respectively urging ideals incompatible for conjoint realization." With the benefit of hindsight, we see with clarity the incompatibility of the ideals promoted and defended by the Cherokees and those who claimed a right to their lands. Similarly, the goals of the huge timber companies and those whose timber they wanted could never be reconciled. Each succeeding generation of Graham Countians becomes witness to the next inevitable struggle, witnesses to an unfolding history, which will shape to a large degree the direction and quality of their lives.

In some ways, I suppose, the elements of history chronicling the life of one county are much like those of another. Graham is not a large county and its population is small and scattered, but its life story, though short, contains elements of hope, struggle, and conflict equal in meaning, if not in scope to the tales of the world's great powers. The history of this region has been unfolding for eons before legislative action created the county named Graham out of the more newly settled and remote parts of Cherokee County in 1872. Communities existed at various places throughout the wooded valleys, and members of these communities were conducting their normal activities of agriculture and commerce, hunting and sometimes making war as they had been doing for centuries when the first Europeans arrived,

Those Who Were Here – The Cherokee

Any effort to capture and describe the beginnings of local history would recognize the central place the Cherokee people hold in the telling of such a tale. Of central importance is the fact that they were here at the beginning and are still here. Graham County is one of few places in the eastern U.S. where Native Americans were not driven out completely. This matter speaks volumes about the courage and character of the counties first citizens.

Sadly, Graham County played a significant role in what was called "the removal," the roundup and forced removal of the local Indians to Oklahoma was more poignantly recognized as "the Trail of Tears." Fort Hill was the location of one of General Winfield Scott's stockades where the Cherokee were held before the long march began.

The story of the Cherokee has been well documented by such historians as Nathaniel C. Browder in his book: The Cherokee Indians and Those Who Came After (Notes for a history of Cherokee County, North Carolina 1835–1860). An equally excellent resource is Carson Brewer's Valley So Wild. For many years, Carson Brewer wrote for the Knoxville news Sentinel. Valley So Wild is a folk history of the Little Tennessee River which comprises much of the northern and eastern borders of Graham County.

The Mountains and Rivers – Their Influence Then and Now

The barriers that the rugged mountains of western North Carolina posed in the movement of people, the conducting of agriculture and commerce are still significant factors in influencing the county's development and economic health as we enter the twenty first century. Not only did the presence of these ancient and imposing mountains delay settlement until late in the nineteenth century, they also helped determine from which direction early settlers would arrive. Further, the character of the landscape influenced to a significant degree who the early settlers would be. So many of those families who drifted down the great valley of Virginia and sought homesteads among the wrinkled hills of western North Carolina were from the highlands of Scotland, Ireland, Wales, and Northern England.

Natural Resources

At a glance it is evident that the most abundant of the areas natural resources are timber and water. The presence of these resources in such vast amounts figured centrally in two of the major economic struggles in the county's history. Between 1880 and 1925, the seemingly endless supply of timber was harvested by large companies from up east until there was scarcely enough marketable timber left to bother. Once the forests were gone the lumber companies left taking their machines with them, even including the rails from the spur tracks leading up the narrow valleys of Snowbird and Buffalo. The timber resources of the county were exploited and the wealth of those magnificent forest left the county never to return.

After the trees were gone, the county's second major resource, fresh water, caught the attention of investors and manufacturers who saw the potential for harnessing the streams with dams for the production of hydroelectric power. In succession, three major dams were constructed in the county. First was Cheoah Dam, built by Tallahassee Power Company on the Little Tennessee River at what is now Tapoco. Next was Santeetlah Dam, built on the Cheoah River by the Aluminum Company of America, and finally with the outbreak of World War II, the U.S. Government created the Tennessee Valley Authority which built Fontana Dam on the Little Tennessee River.

The impact upon the people of Graham County by the construction and operation of these major hydroelectric projects has been immense, and continues to be felt. The lakes resulting from the impoundment of rivers and creeks have become one of the leading attractions feeding tourism, which is becoming one of the major industries locally. The streams and lakes provide sport fishing, boating, swimming, and a growing number of new homes stream side or lakeside. The Cherohala Skyway along the backbone of the North Carolina– Tennessee border and adjacent to the Joyce Kilmer-Slickrock Wilderness offers the traveler the most spectacular views of the natural beauty of the mountains in the eastern U.S.

Early Settlers

Who were the people who chose to settle in such a beautiful but isolated place? Where did they come from and what were they seeking? The names of early families are still common among today's population. How did they live, and how did they make a living?

Perhaps it is easier to understand why the early arrivals to the county stayed, than it is to understand why they sought out this remote place to settle in the first place. Graham County is beautiful and it must have been spectacular in the middle of the nineteenth century when families were arriving regularly by cart, wagon, or on foot. The air was pure, the water was clear and plentiful, game was abundant, and the bottomland along the creeks and branches was fertile. There were trees everywhere.

The forces which pulled or pushed the first wave of Europeans to one of the most isolated corners of eastern America are harder to discern. That the preponderance of Graham County settlers could be traced to the British Isles may offer a clue. Clearly, these far away mountains offer something that our ancestors wanted very badly, wanted badly enough to endure generations of deprivation in order to keep. Was it privacy? Was it the freedom to be left alone? Was it the ultimate escape from the grasp of intrusive government? Was it the deep desire to live unmolested in the company of one's own kind? Maybe they came for all of these reasons and others. It will be remembered that the migration of settlers down the Great Valley of Virginia into the southern mountains occurred after the Revolutionary War as new federal lands were opened.

Many of the German immigrants settled and remained in Pennsylvania, Maryland, and the Shenandoah Valley of Virginia.

Those who reached our mountains became and remain one of the purest remnant populations of descendants of the British Isles to be found in eastern America. Early families were Irish, Scot-Irish, English, Scottish, and Welsh, with a smattering of German and French settlers.

At the time western North Carolina was settled, American society had not yet become mobile. Thus, family groups often relocated together, sometimes comprising several households of persons who were related. They brought with them the cultural beliefs, traditions, attitudes that gave them a strong sense of identity. This seems to have been a particularly strong practice among those whose ancestors came from the British Isles.

Agriculture

Farming has always been central to the way of life in the county. Essentially a form of subsistence farming was practiced enabling most families to remain self-sufficient. The mountain valleys were narrow and the hillsides were steep, so level cropland was at a premium. The soil, however, was productive and in most cases, families were able to grow enough for themselves and their livestock. Some of the families who did not own land had to rent patches from the more wealthy land owners on a shares basis. For example, the renter would give back to the land owner one third of the corn crop upon harvest.

Most mountain homesteads had a few fruit trees. Also walnuts, hickory nuts, and until the 1930s, chestnuts were abundant. It was a common practice to maintain several bee gums. Families grew their own meat or depended partially upon wild game. Meat was preserved before the days of refrigeration by curing or canning. Smoke houses were common.

Commercial agriculture was not a major factor in the early days because markets were distant and transportation extremely difficult. Further east and south, cotton growing was the backbone of the farm economy, but not in the mountains. The free ranging of cattle in the high mountain meadows and on the balds was commonplace in the late 1800s and into the twentieth century. Small gristmills were scattered along the creeks throughout the county, and there were a few larger mills that operated on a commercial basis.

From the very beginning it was often easier to convert a corn crop into usable income by distilling whiskey than it was to transport a crop of shelled corn to some distant market. The making of distilled spirits had been practiced for generations, even centuries by the ancestors of early county residents before they reached the shores of the new world. The making of whiskey was not seen in the narrow moralistic light that it came to be seen in during the early twentieth century right up to and beyond prohibition.

Tobacco became the most important example of commercial agriculture in Graham County. Eastern North Carolina has long been central to the production of tobacco and the manufacture of tobacco products. Tobacco farming in eastern North Carolina was big business with thousands and thousands of acres of flu-cured tobacco being grown by prosperous landowners. The story in the mountains was much different. First of all, burley tobacco was grown in the mountains. The production of burley tobacco is labor intensive and most of the farmers were able to grow only small, scattered patches. The preparation of next year's seedbed is taking place often at the same time that this year's crop is being air cured, graded, tied in hands, and packed into bales. Farmers often commented that it took thirteen months to produce a crop of burley. Tobacco, however, became the leading cash crop for many Graham County families.

Industry

Since timber has been the most abundant natural resource in the region, the harvesting of trees and the production of timber products have been mainstays in the local economy. The settlers used forest products in every conceivable way. Houses, barns, cribs, smokehouses, and other farm related structures were made of logs and later of rough sawn boards as small sawmills made their way into the county. Oak shingles were split with a mallet and froe to provide roofing for the buildings. Furniture was fashioned from oak and hickory and chair bottoms were woven from split cane or young hickory bark. Gunstocks were carved from walnut or curly maple, and the more skilled craftsmen did grand cabinetwork with cherry and other woods.

The large timber companies, which occupied our forests in the late 1800s and remained until most of the timber was gone in the 1920s and '30s, were focused singularly on profit. The profit, however, did not feed or fuel the local economy. The richness of Graham County forests flowed like quicksilver into the bank accounts of timber barons in far away cities. When the trees were gone, the timber companies were gone. During the heyday of the timber boom, local citizens did find jobs as teamsters, sawyers, cooks, and laborers in a variety of roles. Even those jobs were gone when the timber companies pulled out.

Fortunately there were companies such as Bemis Hardwood Lumber Co., which remained in the county providing economic support to the people right up until the 1960s or later. With the demise of Bemis, the Graham County railroad also died. Known as the "pea vine," the Graham County Railroad hauled millions of board feet of timber products from Robbinsville to connections with the southern railway outside the county. From these railway connections, the "pea vine" hauled carloads of goods to the markets and citizens of Graham County. National television covered the last run of the Graham County railroad and provided a moment of nostalgia to the American people. To the locals, however, it was more like a fist to the pit of the stomach.

As long as Bemis was in operation and the railroad was running, county people were still able to derive some income from the forests. When the chestnut blight destroyed the most populous tree species in the southern Appalachians, the bleached trunks of the dead trees stood like a million skeletons on the ridges. Chestnut wood is rich in tannin and during the depression years, many a subsistence farmer bought his kids a pair of shoes with money from a load of acid wood. In addition to acid wood considerable amounts of tan bark and pulpwood were harvested. By this time, however, most of the large trees were gone.

One of the first industries not related to timber came into the county when Lee Carpets opened a plant on property adjacent to Bemis

Lumber Company. There is a peculiar irony in this since the plant built by Lee Carpets is now occupied by Stanley Furniture Co., sort of a last gasp from the trees.

The production of hydroelectric power represents a huge industrial undertaking going back to the construction of Cheoah Dam at Tapoco and the Santeetlah Dam along with the power house at Rhymer's Ferry. Both of these dams were built in the 1920s, and their construction provided employment for scores of local people. These two dams built by Tallassee Power Company once in operation provided jobs for considerably fewer local people though their presence represents a huge footprint on the landscape. The electricity generated by Graham County water flowed with the profits it produced far outside the county.

World War II brought the construction of Fontana Dam, largest of the three. Like the others, the construction of Fontana provided countless jobs for county people. An entire small village sprang up adjacent to the construction site complete with a school and a hospital. When the construction period was over the jobs were gone, the school and hospital were closed, and Fontana Village became a tourist resort. Hidden under its dark waters are remnants of what were once small mountain communities, drowned forever along with a way of life.

Graham County Courthouse 1939

Graham County High School – old elementary school in background 1939

Printed in the United States
27960LVS00003B/1-39

9 781413 738728